Witness Protection 7
Bravo Foxtrot

Holly Copella

"The only easy day was yesterday!"
--U.S. Navy SEALS motto

ACKNOWLEDGMENTS

Copella Books: First Paperback Edition 2019
Cover Artist: Daniela Owergoor
Dani-owergoor.deviantart.com
Model by Grafvision
Stock Photography by NeoStock www.neo-stock.com
Printed by KDP, an Amazon.com Company

PUBLISHER'S NOTE

Chapter 1

Friday, June 13th. The abandoned meat packing plant was surrounded by woods in the middle of nowhere. The processing building had a long dirt driveway leading up to it, although it was mostly grown over. Despite its abandoned condition and that it was two in the morning, the old plant was dimly lit indicating there was unauthorized activity. Within one of the many dilapidated rooms inside the old structure, an attractive woman in her mid-twenties was tied to a rusted metal chair. The unfortunate woman wore only her sexy, white satin nightgown and matching white, satin slippers. Pinto Romano-Larue looked as if she'd been dragged out of bed in the middle of the night, which was, in fact, the case. Her long, copper-colored hair was mildly mussed and untamed. Although exhausted and slightly bedraggled, she appeared physically unharmed. Whereas most women in her situation would have been frantic, Pinto appeared more enraged than frightened.

"I so did not sign up for this," Pinto groaned then fought her bindings with disgust.

A taller, masked man with an impressive athletic build beneath his black combat uniform paced before her and then behind her as a form of intimidation. It was also possible he was undressing the rest of her with his eyes. She watched him suspiciously out of the corner of her eye while attempting to gauge his thoughts.

He leaned over her shoulder from behind and whispered seductively in her ear. "Just so you know; I'm considering this foreplay," he teased.

Pinto rolled her eyes at the comment. "Watch your mouth," she snarled. "My husband is a total badass, and he'll rip your throat out. *Literally*."

The masked man chuckled in his throat. "I'd like to see him try."

She sneered at the comment. "I should be home in bed," Pinto muttered.

§

In the far corners of the abandoned building, two men dressed entirely in black, Kirk and Monroe, crouched along a bland, concrete wall. They were members of the former Navy SEAL team, Whiskey Tango Foxtrot, sent to save Pinto. Kirk Mandel was a large, muscle-bound man who stood an imposing six-foot-four. He had broad shoulders, a large chest, and biceps the size of tree trunks that were barely hidden beneath his tight, black shirt. His buzz cut and thick facial stubble made him look moderately intimidating although undeniably handsome. His counterpart, Monroe Dallas, was a tall, lanky man in his mid-thirties with more of an athletic build. His light brown hair was neatly trimmed and his face mostly clean-shaven. Monroe seemed the type of man who took pride in his appearance.

Monroe fiddled with a state-of-the-art thermal imagining camera he held in his hand. Both men looked around while attempting to get a fix on their target. They heard a soft female giggle from nearby, hesitated, and looked alongside them. Jackie Falcone, an attractive woman in her mid-twenties, crouched on the stone floor with her back against the wall near where the two men stood. She had her finger to her ear transmitter and held a conversation with someone on the other end. Jackie wore a moderately formfitting, black stalking outfit that showed off her ample cleavage and athletic build. Her soft-soled, calf-high boots completed the ensemble. Her long, dark hair was pulled back in a ponytail indicating she was combat ready even though it appeared as if she were currently slacking off. Jackie joined the team a few years after her father, the team's former commander, had died. Jackie laughed at something that was said in her *private* conversation. Both men glared at her in stunned disbelief. Jackie caught their glares and grinned.

"Zack just told me the funniest joke," she announced and giggled.

"Do you mind?" Monroe demanded clearly irritated by her behavior. "We're in the middle of a rescue here. You shouldn't even be talking to him at a time like this. This is serious business. He's going to get all of us killed. Get ears on the proper frequency."

Jackie groaned then switched channels on her receiver and straightened. "Next time, we pair up like usual," she announced and cast her back against the wall.

Both men brushed off Jackie's lack of concern and returned to their *serious* business.

"She should be that way," Kirk announced and pointed down the hall.

Monroe tapped his ear transmitter. "Bogart," he announced. "We have a twenty on Pinto. She's about one hundred feet from your location."

They heard a slightly static-filled voice over their communication devices.

"I've got a damned spider on my face," Bogart proclaimed over their ear transmitters.

Monroe made a face then groaned. He took a moment to hold back his irritation before responding. "I don't care about the damned spiders crawling on your face," he snarled back. "Beck's wife is being held hostage."

"Daphne's always getting caught," Bogart responded over their ear transmitters.

Jackie snickered and received glares from Monroe and Kirk. She then hid her smile. "Sorry."

5

"Yeah, and you run a close second," Monroe announced with some irritation to Bogart over his ear transmitter. "What's your point?"

"Fine," Bogart groaned from the other end.

"It's like pulling teeth around here," Monroe huffed with annoyance.

"And you wondered why Ross opted out of this mission," Kirk muttered.

§

Their teammate and newest member, Bogart, headed through the dimly lit corridor of the abandoned building while periodically wiping imaginary spiders from his face. Bogart was a tall, well-built man in his late twenties. The charming country boy was 'hunky actor' handsome with flowing golden-brown hair now coated with thick cobwebs. Bogart didn't handle 'serious' situations as well as the rest of the team. As a retired conman, his talents were less physical in nature from his teammates. On this particular mission, he was tasked with sweeping the outer perimeter. Basically, they wanted him to guard the exit in order to keep him out of trouble and possibly out of their way. With all things considered equal, Bogart wasn't considered equal. At times like this, even Jackie, his own sister, didn't want to be responsible for keeping an eye on him.

Bogart was suddenly tackled against the nearby wall by a masked man dressed in black. Despite the hard hit that knocked his gun from his hand, Bogart managed to maneuver away from his attacker. With his gun now lost somewhere on the dark floor, Bogart's options were limited. As his attacker spun and lunged for him, Bogart attempted a sorely lacking karate kick at the man. Seemingly anticipating Bogart's move, his attacker easily caught his ankle and threw him off balance, sending him back into the wall with a thump. Despite that his attacker had a semiautomatic in a holster attached to his hip; he removed a large knife in his gloved hand. Gunfire would only bring unwanted company, and the man knew this. Taking out Bogart quietly seemed the better option.

Bogart saw the knife and managed to block the first strike. He caught the man's wrist to prevent him from stabbing him and countered with a left jab. His attacker dodged Bogart's fist and responded by grabbing him by the throat and slamming him against the wall. Bogart saw the knife in the man's hand as it coiled back.

§

Monroe and Kirk heard Bogart cry out over their ear transmitters, which was immediately followed by silence. Both men groaned their annoyance then glared at Jackie alongside them.

"So much for teaching your brother karate," Monroe announced with disgust. "Daphne number two has been caught now too."

Jackie frowned then shook her head and turned serious. "Let's go get them," she announced with a defeated sigh then extended her hand down the dimly lit corridor to the men. "After you."

"Now you're afraid of the dark?" Kirk snarled while glaring at her.

"Do you think I want spiders crawling on my face?" she demanded.

Monroe shook his head while glaring at his attractive, female partner. "You're right," he announced to Jackie. "Next time we go back to our usual partners. I don't know how Zack puts up with you."

They cautiously hurried down the corridor several yards, checking each darkened doorway. A masked man suddenly lunged out of the darkness behind Jackie and caught her around the waist while pinning her arms to her sides, forcing her to drop her weapon. Kirk and Monroe spun with their semiautomatics aimed. They didn't have a clear shot at the masked man, who now attempted to take her to the floor. Despite that he wasn't a large man; he had a lot of power behind him. Pinto was heard screaming in the near distance, possibly in physical danger from her captors. With her pinned arm, Jackie motioned for her team to go.

"I've got this bitch," she cried out to her teammates. "Go rescue Daphne one and two."

"We'd better go. It sounds like Pinto is in trouble," Monroe remarked while slapping Kirk on the shoulder and indicated Jackie with her attacker. "And *that* could take a while."

"Yeah, you're right," Kirk muttered.

Monroe and Kirk continued with their mission to save Pinto while Jackie broke the man's hold around her and went for her backup gun in her shoulder holster. The man easily kicked the gun from her hand, but it gave her enough time to plan her counterattack. She threw an aggressive roundhouse kick for his face. He ducked her booted foot, again caught her around the waist, and tackled her against the wall, harshly pinning her with his body. His mask face was only inches from hers. The manner in which he held her was a little too close and definitely sexual in nature. The devious grin revealed through the opening in his mask made her want to kick his ass even more. She easily broke his hold and attempted an aggressive groin shot, which he seemed to be anticipating and blocked.

Before she could even counterattack, he swept her legs out from beneath her, allowing her to crash to the floor. Her attacker seemed a little too pleased with his move and attempted to meet her on the ground. Jackie greeted him with a booted foot to his side and threw him to the floor not far from her. She sprang to her feet and removed her 'wuss sticks' from her back holster. She anticipated she had a few seconds for the man to recover in order to collect herself, but her attacker easily went with the roll and sprang to his feet only a second after her. Jackie flicked her wrists and her batons extended to two feet each. She aggressively attacked him with a baton in each hand, but he easily blocked her strikes.

Admittedly, Jackie wasn't as aggressive as she could have been, and she knew she should take him out quickly rather than give him time to strategize his next move. His quick reflexes allowed him to knock the batons from her hands before she could strike again. Despite that he had a semiautomatic in his shoulder holster, he didn't seem interested in shooting her, which was concerning in itself. He just wanted to play. As she spun into a fast, roundhouse kick, he ducked it and again attempted to take her to the floor. Now he was just pissing her off.

"I'm not in the mood," she snarled at the man and tossed him over her as she hit the floor.

Her attacker landed a little rougher than he'd probably anticipated but still managed to spring back to his feet just as quickly as she had. They were once again in a face-off. His unsettling grin seemed to mock her. She knew he was enjoying himself a little too much, and she needed to end his good time. It was time to get serious with this bitch. Jackie needed to reach his gun and finish this.

Chapter 2

Monroe and Kirk hurried through the building toward their destination to rescue their friend's wife. It was particularly unnerving that Pinto no longer made any sounds. Monroe again used his thermal imagining camera and got a fix on Pinto's location within the nearby room. They could see by the image of her heat signature that she was tied to a chair. The only other heat signature was that of someone motionless on the floor. Although the person on the floor radiated heat, they couldn't tell if it was a hostile or one of their own. They approached the closed door, paused a moment, and then burst into the room. They aimed their guns at the target on the floor, in case it was a setup. It was little surprise to either that it was Bogart on the floor, possibly out cold. He lay on his back while holding a wilted daisy in his hand. Pinto remained tied in the chair and now glared at them.

"It's about damned time," she snarled at the two men. "Get me the hell out of here." Her eyes then narrowed. "And remind me to kill my husband for thoughtfully involving me in this."

Kirk ran across the room to check on Bogart while Monroe hurried to Pinto's side. He was about to untie her when the masked man who had abducted Pinto entered the room with his partner. Kirk saw them enter and fired at them before they could open fire themselves. Monroe grabbed the chair with Pinto tied in it and pulled her several feet across the floor with him. He wanted to get her out of the crossfire while Kirk kept both men at bay just outside the open doorway. Monroe leaped behind the steel desk with Kirk. The sound of gunfire was deafening. Pinto screamed profanities that were barely audible within her secured location away from the crossfire. Monroe and Kirk continued to fire upon the men in the entrance of the room, who had successfully cut off their only escape route. Kirk's weapon clicked empty.

"Fuck! I'm out," Kirk shouted to Monroe alongside him behind the desk.

Monroe's gun then clicked empty as well. "I'm out too," he announced then groaned with defeat as both men hid behind the desk.

The two masked, armed men in the doorway ceased fire, realizing both men were out of ammo. They cautiously entered the room with their weapons aimed at the desk hiding the two men.

"Think Jackie's faring any better?" Kirk asked with a defeated groan.

Jackie was forced into the room by her masked attacker who was only a few inches taller than she was. He had his arm around her neck from behind, pinning her against him, and held his gun to her head.

Monroe shook his head and sighed. "No, I don't," he announced with defeat.

Both men groaned, raised their hands in the air, and straightened from behind the desk. It would seem they'd lost. Jackie rammed her elbow into her captor's side. When he loosened his grip around her neck just enough, she held the gun away from her head, turned, and kicked him in the groin. As he clutched himself and sank to his knees, she snatched the gun from his hand. His partners turned with their guns aimed when they heard the commotion, but it was too late. Jackie shot both men in the chest. They gasped and clutched the bright paint on their black shirts.

Pinto looked demandingly at them from where she was tied to the chair in the corner of the room. "Can I go back to bed now?" she huffed.

The two men who were supposedly shot removed their masks to reveal Jackie's fellow teammates, Gil Rafferty and Beck Larue. Beck, Pinto's husband, was a ruggedly handsome man in his mid-thirties. He stood over six feet tall and maintained an impressive athletic build beneath his black, paint-stained shirt. Beck vigorously ran his fingers through his short, light brown hair and appeared ashamed that he'd been beaten in their little espionage game. Gil, who had earlier ambushed Bogart, was on the upper end of thirty if not in his early forties. His short dark hair was peppered with gray, and the handsome man had a slightly distinguished look. Neither man appeared too happy about losing the battle.

Jackie lowered her weapon while grinning, pleased with herself. She then turned and extended her hand to the man on the floor by her feet. Zack Kinsley removed his mask while expressing some agony after Jackie's assault on his crotch and accepted her hand.

"Aren't you glad you wore a cup?" Jackie teased while helping him to his feet.

Zack was shorter than average but had a surprisingly athletic build, which would almost certainly go unnoticed beneath his black combat fatigues. He was easily brushed aside as harmless, which was far from the truth. His brown hair was kept short and neat, although moderately spiky on top, lending a look that was somewhere between intimidating and cuddly. Zack was Jackie's partner on most missions, since their martial arts fighting styles complimented each other. Zack didn't respond to her comment while enduring the agony within his most sensitive area.

As Beck approached his restrained wife to release her, Pinto eyed Zack with concern then glanced at Jackie. "Is he okay?" she asked.

Jackie waved her hand and didn't give it a second thought. "Ah, he likes when I assault his testicles," she remarked while grinning.

"A little rougher than usual," Zack muttered while gingerly touching his crotch.

"Then you'd better mind your manners next time," Jackie scolded.

Zack hid his devious grin at the comment. Bogart jumped up from the floor with disgust and tossed his wilted flower aside.

"Why am I always the first to die and push up daisies?" Bogart demanded.

"Because you're expendable," Beck teased while grinning as he cast Pinto's ropes aside then pulled his wife to her feet and into his arms.

Despite her irritation, Pinto let Beck kiss her but was quick to end his idea of a romantic moment. "You people are demented," she huffed and attempted to pull away from her husband. "Please don't include me in your little war games *ever* again."

"Come on," Beck teased while laughing. "You have to admit, that was hot." He held her against him and looked into her eyes. "I could still ravage you."

"Yeah, that mood has passed," she muttered and pushed him away.

As the others walked through the doorway to leave the room, Zack caught Jackie's arm, didn't say a word, and held her back. There was a small boom followed by smoke that engulfed them. The rest of the team coughed and waved the smoke away from their faces.

Zack released Jackie's arm and chuckled while grinning evilly. "I rigged an explosion," he announced. "You're all dead. I win."

The others waved the smoke away with their hands and frowned while continuing from the room. They muttered under their breath at the prospect of having lost their victory so quickly. Jackie eyed Zack and shook her head, although she couldn't hide her smile.

"Thanks for letting me live," she teased.

"Even in pretend combat, I'd never sacrifice you," he announced then shrugged while grinning. "Let's face it. When the world stops spinning, only you, me, and the cockroaches will survive."

"That's a pleasant thought," she muttered.

"We've got to eat something," Zack insisted with little emotion. "Cockroaches are surprisingly meaty and nutritious. Packed full of protein." He grinned. "And they taste like chicken."

Jackie grimaced and held her churning stomach. "I'll pass, thanks," she remarked as she passed through the doorway with Zack following.

"Lightly sautéed in olive oil with a little Cajun seasoning and garlic," he announced then groaned at the thought while grinning as he followed her. "Tasty eats. You really need to let me cook for you sometime. You don't know what you're missing."

"Not even if I were starving, Zack," she insisted without looking at him.

Chapter 3

It was a little after three in the morning. The old lodge was nestled in a massive clearing in the middle of nowhere Colorado as far as one could get from civilization. The lodge was located about an hour's drive from the abandoned slaughterhouse where the team played out their espionage war games. The recently renovated fifty-bedroom wilderness lodge had been restored to its original grandeur from decades past. It resembled a majestic log cabin only much bigger. The amazing wraparound porch was the showpiece of the secluded estate. Shrubs and hanging plants were obviously a woman's touch. Upscale gliding rocking chairs made of logs were sporadically positioned along the massive porch.

A new Bell helicopter sat out front among the few cars in the driveway. The commercial fourteen-passenger helicopter contained a spacious cabin with sliding side doors and adjustable seating. A new, black SUV and an older jeep drove past the helicopter and approached the lodge where they parked out front. All eight survivors from the slaughterhouse got out of the vehicles looking tired and worn as they headed for their getaway retreat. By the way Pinto and Beck cuddled on their way into the lodge, it would seem as if Pinto had forgiven her husband for including her in what he and his teammates considered a fun time.

Within the lodge, the massive lobby had been painstakingly renovated. The old-fashioned front desk was possibly antique and added class to the lobby. A large, walk-in stone fireplace took up the entire back wall, and an open staircase made of tree trunks led to the second floor guestrooms, which overlooked the lobby. Unfortunately, a satellite phone was the only real communication available in the middle of backwoods nowhere. After their survival game, everyone headed upstairs to their respective rooms. Surprisingly, Pinto allowed Beck into their bedroom and even mentioned something about a bubble bath for two. Monroe gave Kirk five dollars, having lost their wager on if Pinto would make Beck sleep on the sofa.

Jackie opened her bedroom door with as little sound as possible. She crept into her bedroom, quietly shut the door behind her, and removed her clothes before crawling into the occupied, king-sized bed. Her husband didn't stir as she collapsed with exhaustion beneath the covers. She hated to wake her husband, especially when she promised him a relaxing week at the lodge with the guys. Perhaps it was his own fault for believing anything involving her teammates would be relaxing.

"What was the emergency?" her husband muttered without turning over.

"Oh, the usual," Jackie replied as she turned on her side facing his back.

"War games again, huh?" Holden scoffed then rolled onto his back, cast a look at her, and sighed.

Jackie's husband, Holden Falcone, was a ruggedly handsome man in his mid-thirties. He wasn't built excessively muscular, but he had broad shoulders and a toned chest, which was now shirtless as he lay in bed. His neatly trimmed, nearly black hair was slightly mussed from whatever sleep he'd managed to get while his wife was off playing with the boys. He stared at her through excessively dark brown eyes and raised his brows with a curious look.

"Why can't you guys just play paintball like normal people?" he asked.

Jackie smiled sweetly through the dim lighting and lovingly caressed the light coating of hair on Holden's chest. "Zack's been banned for life from every single one in the entire state," she teased.

"I'm not surprised."

"You could join us, you know?" she informed him with a spark of hope in her eyes.

He snorted a laugh and managed a smile while watching her hand on his chest with more than a passing interest. "Thanks, but I'd rather sleep."

Jackie's hand lovingly ran along Holden's chest and across his abdomen while working its way lower.

"Are you sure you'd rather sleep?" she cooed seductively as her hand traveled his body.

Holden groaned with pleasure as her hand found its destination. He held back his grin and aggressively rolled on top of her pinning her to the bed with his body. She let out a tiny giggle. Jackie loved when Holden turned sexually aggressive. Too often, she felt she dominated him in bed, but he seemed to enjoy her enthusiasm in the bedroom and just about any other room.

"At least I get something out of the deal when we stay here the week," he teased while brushing his lips past hers, taunting her with his kiss.

She writhed beneath him desperately waiting for him to make the first move. Holden didn't disappoint. He kissed her passionately and with added aggression even though she was usually twice as aggressive with her response. His hands firmly traveled her body, which he kept pinned beneath him. Jackie groaned while enjoying a more submissive role for a change. Holden broke off the kiss, pulled back, and met her gaze with a strange look.

"Why do you smell like sulfur?"

"Zack set a booby trap and killed us all," she casually replied.

Holden shook his head and seemed to regret even asking. "Figures."

"Did you want me to take a quick shower first?" she asked while lovingly caressing his chest as she gently writhed beneath his body.

"No," he replied then grinned slyly. "I kind of like you dirty. It reminds me that I'm married to one hell of a dangerous woman."

Jackie chuckled in her throat as Holden eagerly returned to his original mission of ravishing her.

Chapter 4

Friday, June 20th. Early morning. The abandoned casino and hotel was located in a large clearing in the woods just north of Cripple Creek, Colorado. The building seemed structurally sound on the outside, although the old driveway was mostly grown over and the property lacked any sign of landscaping. When plans for the highly anticipated factory were scrapped, the highway was diverted away from the nearby town, and the owner's plans for the casino fell apart along with it. A small farm was oddly placed not far from the casino. Had the casino been finished, the farm would have been sitting on the edge of what should have been the massive parking lot.

An official-looking, black SUV pulled up to the main entrance of the casino alongside an expensive, black sedan. A man in his mid-forties leaned against the expensive car. The wealthy owner of the hotel awaiting the team's arrival was Pinto's father, Salvatore Romano. Sal was a robust man with a round cherub face and a youthful appearance. Even when dressed casual, he still had impressive taste in clothing. Although nothing was ever proven regarding his past dealings,

Sal remained everyone's favorite mob boss. Sal straightened as the SUV stopped a few feet from his car. Both front and back doors opened. Holden, Jackie, Gil, and Monroe got out of the government vehicle. Gil held open the back door, and a large, silver sable German shepherd jumped out of the back. Darth excitedly ran to greet Sal while happily wagging his tail. Sal affectionately petted the dog. Ironically, Darth had been part of Sal's mansion security team before Gil more or less stole the dog. After petting the dog, Sal then exchanged handshakes with the three men before greeting Jackie with an affectionate hug. Jackie's relationship with Sal had progressed over time, and he now treated her as if she were his own daughter.

Jackie pulled away from Sal, eyed the out-of-the-way casino, and cringed while gingerly rubbing her aching, right thigh. The last time she'd visited Sal's casino, she'd been shot, and the phantom pain in her leg was only now reminding her of that time.

"This feels familiar," she announced then cast a look at Sal. "One of my least favorite casino trips."

Sal chuckled warmly. "Yeah, you guys just about broke the house--literally," he remarked. "At least I recouped enough from the insurance company to have it knocked down."

"What happened here?" Holden asked. "When you called, I read the official report. Six men dead."

"Apparently, it was some sort of drug deal gone south," Sal informed Holden. "Honestly, it gives me a bad name. If I didn't have friends at the state police barracks, Johnny Local Law would have tried arresting me." He made a face and shook his head. "Then the lawyers get involved--" Sal waved them off. "Turns into a whole thing."

"They found drugs in the basement cash office," Holden reported. "Sounds pretty airtight to me."

"Oh, I'm not denying someone was playing fast and loose inside my abandoned building," Sal reported then shook his head. "It just doesn't have high stakes criminal written on it."

"How do you mean?" Gil asked while watching Darth sniff around the main entrance.

"Come on," Sal announced while waving them toward the casino. "Let's take a walk. The investigation was closed last night."

"When did this happen?" Monroe asked as the four followed Sal to the main entrance.

As they entered the once elegant casino lobby, Sal turned back to look at Monroe.

"They think late yesterday morning," Sal replied then paused before the first chalk outline indicating where a man was murdered.

There was a large amount of dried blood in the center with some blood spatters surrounding the area.

"The first body was found here," Sal informed them. "The man had a shoulder holster containing a semiautomatic. Still holstered and not fired." He then pointed to chalk circles indicating the bullet casings near the man. "He must have had an AK47. They found spent cartridges in relation to where they would have flown when they were ejected from his weapon. The weapon was missing."

"Nothing odd about that," Holden informed Sal. "Weapons are a big market. The shooter probably took it."

Sal raised his brows above his wire-rimmed glasses and indicated more chalk circles. "He was killed with a 9mm pistol."

He then led them across the elegant lobby to a hallway not far from the main casino floor and indicated another chalk outline.

"This man was also found without his weapon," Sal announced then eyed the four. "He was killed with a knife wound to his jugular."

"Now it's getting interesting," Jackie remarked as they continued to follow Sal to a third chalk outline.

"This man was presumably killed with the missing AK47. The casings found matched those fired from the first man's weapon," Sal informed them. "Our third victim's weapon is also missing." He led them to the casino floor and looked back as he walked. "This is where it gets interesting."

All five plus Darth entered the casino. The large, empty casino floor consisted of over thirty demolished table games that had once circled the center of the room. Above the large area where the table games were once located, a cathedral ceiling consisting of a large glass skylight allowed sunlight in during the day. There were rows and rows of slot machines on both sides of the casino floor. Most of the machines along the aisle were riddled with bullet holes. The bank of slot machines in the center was completely torn apart as if a bomb had gone off and ripped them to shreds. The sight was actually familiar to the team since they had been involved in the original destruction. A bulldozer, newly added to the casino floor, sat in the middle of what remained of the demolished table games and left a trail of destruction from where it came through the once boarded windows and rear door. In addition to the old, massive, dried bloodstains covering a large portion of the gaudy carpeting, there were newly added, fresh bloodstains.

"They found a man dead at the controls to the bulldozer," Sal announced then indicated two large, fresh bloodstains within two chalk outlines not far from the bulldozer. "And two more men were killed right there." Sal eyed the men and Jackie. "All three had their throats slashed by a yet unidentified weapon."

"An unidentified weapon?" Gil asked with a curious look on his face.

"They think possibly a samurai sword," Sal informed them.

All four exchanged curious looks.

"Not exactly the weapon of choice," Holden reported then eyed Jackie.

She caught his look and appeared surprised. "Don't look at me," Jackie announced. "I was with you yesterday."

"I know you're not much for swords," Holden replied and managed a tiny grin. "Any thoughts?"

"No," she replied. "I mean, apart from Zack."

"He has an alibi too," Gil remarked teasingly.

Jackie eyed the chalk outlines of the two men on the floor. They were directly side-by-side, which was interesting. "Both had their throats slashed?"

Sal nodded.

"I think it's safe to assume they were killed simultaneously," Jackie informed Holden while glancing at him. "*That* takes a lot of skill. One swipe is possible, but the second man should have seen it coming." She raised her brows and gave her husband a concerning look. "I think it was a man with two swords. Simultaneously slashing his victims." She then hesitated. "Or his attacker."

Monroe appeared deep in thought while holding his chin as he studied the two chalk outlines on the floor. Both men bled out at a fantastic rate, which meant it was a sharp blade and an incredible strike. He finally looked up at Sal.

"I'm curious," Monroe remarked while raising his brow. "Why did you call us out to look at this?" he asked then indicated Holden. "I get calling your friendly neighborhood fed, but why us?"

"I'm afraid it could be related to a phone call I received a few days ago," Sal informed Monroe then eyed the others. "Someone called me looking for information on the team." He fidgeted slightly. "The *old* team."

"You mean Ross, Zack, and my father?" Jackie asked with a curious look.

Sal nodded. "I didn't mention it to the police or the homicide detective," he insisted, "but around the same time, someone was poking around in county records and taking inventory on my real estate ventures. This place in particular."

Holden drew a deep breath and held it. "I'll start poking around and see if I can find out who was poking around," he announced.

"It certainly wouldn't be the first time," Gil reported and didn't seem nearly as interested as Jackie and Holden. "There's always the ever popular 'blast from our past' every now and again. It's usually nothing."

"Still," Holden announced. "I'd like to check into it."

"I thought you might," Sal replied then looked around and sighed. "This place is due to be demolished on Monday. I can't tell you how happy I'll be after it's destroyed."

§

As the five left the casino through the front entrance, Sal turned to face the others for their official goodbyes.

"Are you heading back to the lodge tonight?" Sal asked Gil and Monroe. "If Jackie and Holden haven't already invited you to their home, you're more than welcome at mine."

"I appreciate the invite, but I'm flying in to see Ellie," Gil informed Sal and attempted to hide his grin. "She has a three-day weekend and invited me to stay with her."

Monroe snickered at the comment and immediately received a smack on the arm from Jackie. He yelped in response then cast a look at her.

"Monroe is staying with us until Gil returns, and then he'll fly back to the lodge with Gil on Sunday," Holden informed Sal. "If you wanted to get together for dinner tonight--?"

"I'd love to," Sal announced a little too eagerly then smiled with some embarrassment. "I've been a bit bored lately. I need to find something to occupy my time. Idle hands and all."

"By all means," Holden announced, "let's find something for those idle hands. You and boredom are a bad chemical mixture."

Sal grinned and shook his head. "Oh, Holden," he announced and seemed prepared to deny the allegations once and for all. "If you only knew."

"Yeah, I don't want to know," Holden responded then headed for his SUV. "You can text us the time and place."

Chapter 5

Friday, June 20th. The twenty-acre Harris farm seemed unusually quiet considering it was late morning. The two-story farmhouse contained a large, wraparound porch, and it was surrounded by gorgeous flowerbeds along with a massive garden. Not far from the house was a small barn and a large horse pasture with wooden fencing. A newer, heavy-duty pickup truck towing a four-horse stock trailer drove down the long, dirt driveway toward the house. Two horses within the corral ran along the fence while snickering excitedly at the horse trailer and listened to the return whinny from inside. The first horse, Thunder, was a large black horse with a white stripe down his forehead to his nose and four white socks above his hooves. The second horse had large white spots on its otherwise dark brown coat that resembled clouds, aptly spawning his name, Storm Cloud.

Two fifteen-year-old girls ran from the house and hurried for the approaching truck. The girls, Monique and Colleen, were the ultimate tomboys in their blue jeans, cowboy boots, and plaid shirts. The only thing girly about either was their shoulder-length hair and even that they wore in ponytails beneath their cowboy hats. Colleen Cooper was a lean, dark-haired girl. Monique Harris, her counterpart shared the same build except she had blonde hair. As the truck parked near the barn, the girls slowed their approach. Bogart got out of the truck and grinned when he saw the teenagers. Both girls ran to him and practically jumped into his arms. He affectionately hugged them and lifted them off their feet at the same time.

"Hey, Squirt," he announced to Colleen then Monique. "Hey, Twinkie."

They squealed with delight then, once he released them, they excitedly bopped around him.

"I can't believe you brought Othello," Monique chirped and ran to the back of the horse trailer.

"Doesn't take much to excite the two of you," Bogart announced and joined them by the trailer door.

Monique was already opening the back door as Colleen untied the horse's lead rope from outside the stock trailer. Monique disappeared inside the trailer, caught the lead rope, and allowed the horse to turn around before making its journey down the step-off trailer. Both girls marveled at the impressive black Friesian stallion and shook their heads.

"I love Thunder," Colleen announced, "but that Othello is something else."

Bogart patted the large horse while grinning. "Yep, he's quite the half ton of dog chow."

Both girls groaned and booed him for his tasteless joke. The girls excitedly led the large horse to the paddock adjacent to the one containing their two horses. Monique unhooked the lead rope and let the horse run free in the paddock. Othello paraded around in front of the two male horses with his head arched as he snorted, attempting to assert his dominance. Monique and Colleen frowned their disapproval.

"He certainly has your ego," Colleen muttered to Bogart while watching the horse.

Bogart laughed at the comment. "If you're pretty and you know it--" he announced while cocking his head.

The girls' mothers approached from the house and greeted Bogart with motherly hugs. Marie Cooper was an attractive, dark-haired woman in her early thirties. Although a country girl much like her daughter, Marie attempted to cling to her feminine side with the way she dressed country casual. Monique's mother, Donna, was an attractive blonde woman also in her early thirties. Despite living in the deep country, Donna had a little city appeal to her style. The two women didn't seem the least bit bothered that their daughter's had a much older male friend. Bogart had saved their hides on a number of occasions and had earned their respect and trust.

"We'll have breakfast ready in about twenty minutes," Donna informed him. "That should give the three of you a few minutes to catch up."

"Appreciate it," Bogart politely announced while grinning charmingly.

As the two women walked away, Bogart couldn't help but admire their exit. He then seemed to realize the impressionable, teenage girls were watching him. Colleen seemed hopeful while Monique folded her arms across her chest and glared at him.

"I hope you weren't checking out my mother," Monique scolded. "My father will skin you."

"I hope you *were* checking out my mother," Colleen teased of her single mother.

Bogart hid his embarrassment and shook his head. "Habit," he announced timidly. "We discussed the whole 'why I won't date your mother' deal before."

Colleen frowned then nodded and waved him off. "It's okay," she replied. "I'm not really keen on you being my new daddy anyway."

Bogart frowned at the comment. "Ouch," he announced. "That hurt."

All three smiled and laughed, unable to maintain their seriousness.

"I can't wait to give you girls a good run for your money," Bogart announced then indicated his large horse. "With Othello, I finally have a chance of actually beating you in a race."

"You can try," Colleen teased.

Both girls then turned serious. Bogart read their expressions and appeared concerned.

"Something wrong?" he asked.

"We think that guy's back," Monique remarked.

His expression dropped at their words. "You mean that man who was spying on you the last time I was here?" he demanded. "He's back?"

"We think so," Colleen reported and shifted uncomfortably. "Kind of freaked us out. We haven't been back to the ghost town in days."

"He wasn't just spying," Monique insisted. "He was stalking. We thought he was going to chase us. We got out of there real fast."

Bogart frowned and cursed softly under his breath. He then managed a warm smile. "You don't need to worry about him," he announced. "I'll handle it. This time, he won't get away." He then nodded toward the house. "Go wash up. I'll be along in a minute. I need to call Jackie and tell her I made it here in one piece."

The girls nodded and hurried for the house. Bogart removed his cell phone and frowned.

"Son-of-a-bitch," he muttered then waited for the call to be answered. "Jackie, Martin's back."

Chapter 6

Saturday, June 21st. The following morning, the two girls and their mothers stood on the porch of the house and watched Jackie's helicopter land not far from the garage. Storm Cloud and Thunder were slightly excited about the landing aircraft, but Othello had seen enough of it in his time that it didn't even bother him anymore. Jackie, Holden, and Monroe got out of the helicopter and were greeted by Bogart. Once the helicopter had shut down, both girls ran from the porch to greet the three with excited hugs. Donna and Marie approached as well but not nearly as fast as their younger daughters had. After a brief greeting, it was on to unpleasant business. Donna and Marie were stunned to hear about the man stalking their daughters and immediately overreacted, which was why the girls hadn't told them.

Donna wrenched her fingers together while shooting looks between Holden and Monroe. "Blake should be here," she insisted. "Couldn't he come back early from his meeting? We should wait for him."

"I already discussed the situation with Blake," Holden informed Donna of her FBI husband, who was also Holden's boss at the Bureau. "He doesn't want us waiting for him. We're going to take this guy down quickly and quietly. No one will get hurt, I promise."

"How can you be so certain?" Marie gasped.

Holden tensed slightly. "He's already been identified from the last time he'd been seen in the area," he informed her while purposely leaving out that the man was Marie's supposedly dead husband and the part where Bogart chased him off the last time the girls reported being watched. "He's not considered violent."

"He's been stalking two teenage girls," Donna announced with astonishment. "Isn't that bad enough?"

Had they known the man was Colleen's father it would only make matters worse, especially since Colleen thought he was dead the last five years.

"We're going to handle it," Holden replied with confidence. "Bogart has already agreed to confront him. I assure you; if he were violent, we wouldn't let him go alone."

Bogart cast a sideways glare at Holden. "That sounded like a dig."

"It wasn't a dig," Holden assured him, although he was unable to make eye contact with his brother-in-law. "We'll leave in an hour."

"We'll saddle the horses," Colleen announced.

Donna and Marie gasped with alarm and stopped the girls before they could take off for the barn.

"You two aren't going anywhere," Marie launched with horror in her tone.

"We have to," Monique insisted. "If he doesn't see us, he won't come out."

"I have to agree with Marie," Donna remarked while insecurely rubbing her chilled arms. "I don't want you anywhere near that creep."

"They'll be safe," Holden reassured them. "I have a man on the interstate not far from the old ghost town who'll meet us there. Jackie, Monroe, and I will be in the helicopter overseeing everything." His look was serious. "They have to ride into the town, but they won't be anywhere near the guy, I promise."

"Is that what Blake said?" Donna asked while fidgeting.

"Yes, he agreed it'll be fine," Holden replied. "Bogart is all the protection your girls need against this guy. He's not going to hurt them."

Neither woman appeared convinced, but they seemed compelled to go along with it.

§

That afternoon, Jackie's helicopter had set down on a hillside not far from the old ghost town. It was far enough away that their teen stalker wouldn't notice them; yet close enough to swoop in for a rescue if necessary. Holden, Jackie, and Monroe stood on the hillside not far from the helicopter and watched the abandoned ghost town in the valley below. Without the use of binoculars, they could see the girls and Bogart riding toward the town, but the binoculars came in handy for a better view of details. Holden spotted someone lurking within the old sheriff's building on the edge of town near the large, sturdy livery stable. The horse and riders would enter from the opposite end of town, creating a buffer between them and their stalker.

"He's in the sheriff's office," Holden informed Monroe without taking his eyes from the ghost town below.

Monroe nodded and touched his ear transmitter. "Hey, Bogart, your bogey is in the old sheriff's office."

"His usual hangout," Bogart remarked back. "You'd think he'd learn some new tricks."

The three watched Bogart's horse break off from the group and head around the back of the decaying town.

"I know how to handle this," Bogart continued over their ear transmitters. "I've got this."

Monroe shook his head while frowning and sat on the nearby rock as he kept an eye on the girls approaching the town. "I don't get it," he announced. "Why would Colleen's Army deserter father come back again after Bogart threatened to expose him?"

"He probably tested the waters," Holden remarked while leaning against a nearby tree. "When he realized no one was

31

watching, he decided the coast was clear. It's his daughter. He probably just couldn't stay away."

"There's no way we can shield Colleen from this," Jackie announced with defeat. "Once he's captured, she's going to know he's alive." She shook her head. "That poor girl's world is going to crash around her. She thought the man died a hero, and now she's going to discover he was a deserter and a traitor."

"Maybe we should have told her before they went in," Monroe remarked.

"No," Holden announced without taking his eyes off the girls approaching the town on their horses. "There's no way of telling how she'd react. Even if she thought she could ride into town knowing it was her father, we don't know that she wouldn't get in the way. It's better we let her find out after he's in cuffs."

"That poor girl," Jackie whispered while holding back her emotions. "I can't imagine how betrayed she's going to feel." She then looked at her husband and Monroe. "By him and us. She may never forgive Bogart. He'll be devastated. He adores those girls."

"I threw you across the hood of a car and handcuffed you," Holden remarked to Jackie. "You forgave me and eventually married me. I think Colleen will forgive him."

Monroe drew a deep breath and shook his head. "I don't know," he remarked. "I never forgave Jackie for marrying you."

Holden lowered his binoculars and glared at Monroe lacking humor at the comment. Jackie held back her laugh.

Chapter 7

Monique and Colleen rode at a leisurely walk into the ghost town from the opposite end of the sheriff's office. They needed to give Bogart time to get into place. Since they'd already seen the interloper on their last ride out, both girls stared at the sheriff's office with some apprehension. Their stalker didn't seem to care that they knew he was there during their last visit, which meant he wasn't afraid of them. Was it possible he wanted to make contact? Neither girl wanted to find out and remained on their horses in case they needed to make another hasty retreat. As they sat and stared toward the back of town, nothing moved. Both girls had been equipped with their own ear transmitters so they could be fed information on a separate, secure channel. They somehow knew the mysterious stranger was in the sheriff's office even though they couldn't see him.

Monique and Colleen exchanged concerned looks and felt their horses tense beneath them. The horses knew their riders were anxious and became anxious themselves.

"I feel silly just sitting here," Monique remarked to her friend.

"Think Bogart got him already?" Colleen asked with some concern. "Last time; he was already heading into the street to greet us."

"If they had him already, they'd let us know," Monique reminded her and indicated her ear transmitter.

Despite being just fifteen-years-old, both girls were mature beyond their years. They'd had their share of encounters with bad men and the team of retired Navy SEALS. The girls knew how to handle themselves, and they had proven it many times. Monique had her rifle located in its sheath attached to her saddle, and Colleen had her bullwhip only inches from her fingertips. Still, their confidence in defending themselves aside, they often worried about Bogart putting himself in harm's way because of them.

§

Bogart tied his horse behind one of the nearby buildings and crept along the back until he finally reached the rear entrance of the sheriff's office. He noted the fresh, ATV tire tracks, which was Martin's vehicle of choice the last time he'd been caught spying on his daughter. Bogart slipped in through the back door while removing his semiautomatic from his hidden shoulder holster beneath his western blazer. Despite the ease of getting the slip on Martin during their last encounter, he wasn't taking any chances. Bogart checked his corners before proceeding across the back of the building. As he approached the back entrance to the office itself, he saw a shadow move past the front window, indicating the man he sought was just through the next doorway.

He paused before the doorway, collected his courage, and stepped into the sheriff's office with his gun aimed. To his surprise, two armed men already had their guns aimed at him. More alarmingly, neither man was Martin. A gun pressed against his neck from behind forcing him to tense with increased concern. The man behind Bogart removed the gun from his hand.

"Who the hell are you?" the armed man behind him announced then shoved him into the room toward the other men.

Bogart kept his hands in the air then turned to face the man behind him. To his surprise and horror, it wasn't Martin behind him either.

"I'm the girls' father," Bogart easily lied. "I want to know why you've been stalking my daughters."

Holden spoke through Bogart's ear transmitter having heard his conversation with the men. "Monique, Colleen, get out of town, now!"

"We're on our way, Bogart," Jackie's voice announced into Bogart's ear. "Don't do anything stupid."

"Those two kids?" the man demanded in anger. "I thought we scared them away the last time they showed up. You need to keep them on a shorter leash if you want them to live until they're full grown."

"It would seem we have ourselves a little misunderstanding here," Bogart remarked and eyed the three men, noting their positions within the room. "There are three of you and one of me." It was Bogart's subtle way of telling his teammates how many men to expect. "I'll just collect my daughters and leave you men to your little meeting. We respect your gang's claim to this area. I'll tell my daughters to ride elsewhere."

The first man laughed and exchanged looks with the others. "Gang? That's a good one," he announced then looked back at Bogart. "I realize you look stupid, but I know you're not dumb enough to believe we're part of a gang. We can't let you leave."

"Don't be stupid," the second man scoffed. "He's just a dad looking out for his girls. So what if he goes to the police? We'll be long gone before they get here. This stakeout is a dead end. We should move on anyway."

"You want to just let him go?" the first man launched with annoyance.

"He's just a dumb hick," the second man scoffed. "A concerned dad. You want to kill him for that?"

"He's seen our faces," the third man chimed in.

"So have his girls," the second man announced. "You want to kill them too? What's wrong with you?"

35

"He's right, you know," Bogart announced while glancing at the first man. "By the time we'd make it back to a populated area, you guys would be long gone. Honestly, I have a short memory. I'd probably forget what you look like before we'd reach the nearest town."

"You heard the man," the second man announced and replaced his gun to his shoulder holster. "Let him go." He nodded Bogart to the nearby, main door. "Go on. Collect your girls and go."

Bogart took two steps toward the man near the door who motioned him to leave. A gunshot rang out, and Bogart felt the chilling parting of air just before seeing blood explode out the back of the man's head. His partner had shot him between his eyes. Bogart watched in horror as the man who'd been only a few feet from him fell to the floor.

The first man then aimed his gun at Bogart. "Sorry," he announced with little emotion and raised his brows. "This ain't no democracy."

The loud crack of a bullwhip startled everyone. Before either man could react, the first man felt the sting as the bullwhip caught his right wrist. He attempted to turn, when the whip yanked his hand, knocking the gun from it. He involuntarily spun to face Colleen, who stood in the backroom doorway. The third man aimed his weapon at Colleen as she pulled her whip back. A rifle blast was heard from out front, shattering what was left of the broken window. The rifle bullet struck the third man in his shoulder. He clutched his bleeding shoulder and fell to his knees. The sounds of four-wheelers were now heard in the near distance.

Monique lowered her rifle from where she sat upon her spotted horse in front of the sheriff's office. She held the reins to Colleen and Bogart's horses as well, although it was unclear how she'd secured Bogart's horse so quickly from where it had been tied out back.

"We need to go, now," Monique yelled to them from where she nervously waited in the street. "There are more of them coming from the livery stable!"

Bogart motioned Colleen for the front door then bolted out after her. They ran for their excited horses. Both mounted without using their stirrups. Monique tossed them their reins as several four-wheelers raced toward them from the old stable. There were at least four men riding quads and approaching fast. The two girls and Bogart turned their horses and rode at a gallop for the opposite end of town with the four men on ATVs chasing them.

Chapter 8

As the three horse and riders raced from town, the four men on the quads easily caught up to them. One pulled ahead and swerved in front of them in order to cut them off. Another pulled alongside Colleen on her black horse and aimed his semiautomatic at her. Colleen cracked her whip, catching the man around the wrist, forcing him to drop the weapon. Before she could follow through with the second part of her plan, she saw the quad in front of her slide to a sideways halt, attempting to cut her off. Colleen jabbed Thunder in the sides with her heels to keep the horse from stopping. The black horse jumped over the man on the four-wheeler, striking him in the head with his underbelly as he leaped over him, and knocked the man to the ground.

As her horse landed, the bullwhip tightened around the wrist of the man who attempted to ride alongside her. When Thunder hit the ground running, the man was yanked from his four-wheeler by the bullwhip attached to his wrist, dragging him behind the running horse. Monique and Bogart still had men riding alongside them with their weapons aimed, attempting to fire at them while riding the bouncing vehicles. The two men from the sheriff's office were now racing behind them on their own quads and gaining fast. Without slowing their horses, Bogart removed a Bowie knife from his boot, flipped it in his hand, and caught it by the tip. He narrowly avoided a shot fired by the man racing alongside him. Bogart shirked from the close call, gritted his teeth, and threw the knife for the man. The knife struck the man in the eye. Bogart grimaced at the sight of his knife embedded in the man's eye. The man barely had time to gasp while slumping forward causing the four-wheeler to swerve to the right and crash.

The man driving alongside Monique fired several shots at her but missed due to his inability to keep the four-wheeler going straight at top speed with only one hand. Since he couldn't get a clean shot, he attempted to swerve his quad into the horse. Storm Cloud bolted sideways to avoid the vehicle and bumped into Bogart's horse. Monique was enraged at the attempt to harm her horse. With a flick of her wrist, she tied the reins around the saddle horn and removed her rifle from the holster. When the man saw her with the rifle cradled in both hands, he immediately slowed so he wouldn't be alongside her, taking away her clean shot.

Monique threw her leg over the horse's neck, spun around within the saddle, and now rode backward on the running horse. She aimed the rifle at the stunned man and fired, shooting him in the chest. The man flew off his quad and landed on top of his partner being dragged by the bullwhip behind Colleen on Thunder. The dragging man was dislodged from the bullwhip by the man striking him. Colleen now cracked her freed bullwhip and raced to catch up to her friends while the two men trailing behind them closed in on the horses. As the three horse and riders raced up the small hillside, Jackie's helicopter suddenly raised up sideways before them.

The horses raced past the helicopter, but the men on the four-wheelers slid to a halt. Monroe stood on the rung while tethered to the side opening and fired his automatic weapon at the two men. The rapid-fire bullets struck their four-wheelers, flattened their tires, and hit their engines. The men shielded themselves from the gunfire without a chance to fire back. Two open-top jeeps raced over the hill and surrounded the two men. Federal agents stood up in the open vehicles and aimed their weapons at the men. Both men dropped their weapons and placed their hands in the air.

§

As Holden helped his fellow feds collect the remaining men strewn along the area between the helicopter and the ghost town, Bogart tied the three horses to the disabled quad. Monique and Colleen hugged Jackie and Monroe for coming to their rescue.

Monique pulled back and suspiciously eyed them. "Be live bait, they said," she scoffed. "You're in no danger, they said." She shook her head. "Hey, if guys want to come after me, that's fine, but leave my poor horse out of this."

"You were supposed to fall back," Jackie insisted while glaring at both girls. "Which part of 'fall back' didn't you understand?"

Monique and Colleen exchanged looks and frowned at the question.

"She's got us there," Colleen muttered then looked back at Jackie. "How about you don't tell our mothers about any of this, and we call it even?"

Monroe rolled his eyes and groaned. "God, they're like little clones of you," he scoffed at Jackie.

Bogart hurried to join them. Monique and Colleen threw their arms around his waist and hugged him. He returned the embrace.

"Stupid kids," Bogart scoffed while attempting to hide his concern with irritation. "I hope your mothers give you one hell of a whooping."

Both girls pulled away and stared at him with concern for their friend.

"We were the only ones close enough to provide backup," Colleen protested.

"We weren't going to sit by and let them kill you," Monique added.

Two of Holden's co-workers led a handcuffed and slightly battered man to their off-road jeep. Holden approached another federal agent, who handed him a photo. Holden frowned and shook his head. Jackie didn't like the look on her husband's face and hurried to join him.

"What is it?" she asked.

Holden flashed the picture of Colleen's father, Martin Cooper. Jackie groaned.

"They were either meeting or looking to jump that guy," the agent announced while indicating the picture. "His name is Martin Cooper."

Colleen suddenly perked up and looked at the men. She headed toward them despite Bogart's attempt to stop her. Colleen ran to join Jackie and Holden. Holden returned the picture to the agent and sent him away before Colleen could see the photo.

"Martin Cooper?" Colleen demanded. "What about Martin Cooper?"

"This is an official investigation," Holden informed her and attempted to brush off her concerns despite his difficulties with the task.

"If what happened here today concerns my dead father--" Colleen began then hesitated. She stared at the look on Holden and Jackie's faces and became alarmed. "Oh, my God. He's not dead, is he?"

Monique hurried to join her friend with Bogart trailing behind her.

"What's going on?" Colleen demanded. "I have a right to know."

Chapter 9

The country mansion sat nestled on a large estate surrounded by woods. The old mansion had been painfully restored to its original grandeur including a gray stone exterior on both levels with marble accents. A magnificent stone fountain contained large, carved dragons spewing water into the cascading levels before reaching the bottom pool. The mansion's large, circular driveway contained several cars and a variety of catering vans were lined along the parking area just alongside the kitchen entrance. A fury of activity was located within the kitchen and back yard where men and women prepared outdoor tables and chairs beneath a massive tent just before the extensive garden.

Among several dozen caterers was a dashingly handsome, noble-looking man in his mid-forties. His dark, neatly trimmed hair was slicked back, giving his regal appeal a slightly intimidating look. He dressed in an expensive, black, hand-tailored suit. Although his home and wardrobe screamed wealth, Colonel Thomas Holloway was a military man. Rumor had it his wealth had been obtained by his late wife, although there seemed to be limited information on her. She'd tragically died while traveling abroad with her mother. Their deaths were supposedly the result of a mugging gone wrong, although there was speculation they were targeted because her husband was a colonel with the U.S. Army.

A large, brawny man in his mid-thirties hurried across the lawn and approached Colonel Holloway. The colonel sampled treats from a tray of hors d'oeuvres one of the attractive, female caterers presented to him. He charmingly smiled his approval to the young woman. The attractive caterer was pleased by his approval, possibly melting in his captivating blue eyes, and blushed before returning to her duties. Colonel Holloway took in a sweeping eyeful of the young woman as she crossed the lawn.

"Colonel," the brawny man announced with a sense of urgency and possible irritation.

Holloway rolled his eyes, his perfect afternoon being ruined by his second in command obviously having another crisis. He turned to face the large man.

"What is it, Major Dixon?" Holloway asked with a bored sigh.

Major Dixon stood almost six-foot-five and had a thick, muscular build that was easily noticed beyond his dress shirt. Despite not being excessively attractive, his build combined with his thick head of brown hair and his neatly trimmed beard was enough to ensure he was never lonely for female companionship. There was no shortage of beautiful women who'd accept a tall, muscular man no matter how deplorable his personality. Major Dixon was clearly irritated about something as usual.

"It's your pet project," Dixon reported.

A dark-haired beauty possibly in her early to mid-thirties was only a few steps behind Major Dixon. Katrina wore a simple yet elegant, formfitting white dress that revealed plenty of cleavage and a hemline that barely reached her knees. Her dark hair was neatly tied up in an elegant French twist. The raving beauty was party ready with perfectly applied makeup and ruby red lips. Despite her high heels, she was able to keep up with Major Dixon's long strides. She paused alongside Dixon, stood proudly, and raised an arrogant brow.

"There's no reason to cause a scene before the colonel's party," Katrina announced in the sweetest southern drawl, which somehow made her sexier.

Dixon cast a look at her. Despite ogling her cleavage and possibly being turned on by her accent, he managed to sneer at her.

"Save the innocent southern bell act for the bedroom," Dixon snarled then looked back at Holloway who rubbed his temples, obviously not wanting to witness the impending feud between the two.

"Will the two of you give it a rest?" Holloway groaned then eyed both. "This had better be important."

"It's not," Katrina insisted while just about seducing Colonel Holloway with her eyes.

"Put your bedroom eyes away," Dixon growled then glared at Holloway. "The *gift* she brought you didn't survive the trip."

Colonel Holloway tensed at the news, obviously disappointed then glanced at Katrina. "Is this true?" he asked her.

Katrina shrugged and hid her moderately devious smile. "It happens."

"That's the second time, Kat," Holloway insisted. "We discussed your method of handling fragile goods. Damaged is fine, but I need to be able to salvage some of it, or it's worthless to me."

"That's it?" Dixon demanded then shook his head while sneering. "You're going to let her off with yet another slap on the wrist?"

Holloway indicated Katrina with his extended hand. "You honestly expect harsh punishment dealing with a woman that beautiful."

Katrina grinned slyly and didn't bother looking at Dixon. It was obvious he was seething.

Colonel Holloway groaned and rolled his eyes. "Fine," he announced with defeat. "I'll put her over my knee later and give her one hell of a spanking."

"It's a date," Katrina announced and winked seductively at Holloway.

Dixon sneered and flexed his massive fists.

The colonel then looked at Dixon and inhaled deeply. "What about the gift you brought me?" he asked. "Is he ready to talk?"

"He's teetering on the edge," Dixon informed him. "Did you want a word with him?"

"I suppose I should have a look at him," Holloway remarked. "We need one viable package."

Colonel Holloway extended his arm to Katrina and grinned almost boyishly. She flashed a smile and seductively linked onto his arm.

§

Colonel Holloway and Katrina followed Dixon into the basement and past the guard, who was seated just inside the room alongside the door. The guard, looking more like an Italian mobster at a speakeasy, read the paper. He briefly looked up when he saw the three enter then returned to his newspaper without comment. The room contained a stone floor and walls. A drain was suspiciously located in the center of the floor and was stained with blood. The drain was chilling enough by itself, but the nearly medieval décor set the tone for the room. Not far from the drain was a sturdy wooden chair bolted to the floor. The torture device looked like an old-fashioned electrocution chair.

A severely beaten man sat slumped on the wooden seat with large leather straps tethering his wrists, ankles, and chest to the mammoth chair. He wore only a pair of boxer shorts, which allowed an unobstructed view of several burns and cuts along his torso and chest. The man had possibly been tortured to the point of unconsciousness many times in an attempt to extract whatever information he carried. Although his head hung down, he watched the three cross the room. They paused a few feet away from him despite that he wasn't any threat to them. His eyes lifted briefly when he saw Katrina, possibly enjoying the last time he'd ever have the opportunity to see such a beautiful woman. Katrina didn't even flinch as she met his gaze without emotion.

"You boys are like a cat playing with a mouse," Katrina scoffed while raising her brow. "Even after it's dead, you still continue to torture it."

"At least mine is still alive," Dixon scoffed.

Katrina spun on her high heels to face the large man and sneered at him appearing ready to spit venom. "I've gotten more information from men with my methods than you've ever gotten with yours," she snapped. "I have a highly proven track record. That's why I'm here."

"She's got you there," Holloway announced while smirking then laughed. "And her methods are more pleasant than yours."

Katrina indicated the suffering man while looking at Holloway and raising her brows. "May I?"

Dixon was about to protest when Holloway grinned and extended his hand to the securely bound man. "Knock yourself out," the colonel replied.

The scowl on Dixon's face was enough to convey his hostility toward the woman who easily swayed the colonel with her seductive nature. Katrina mocked Dixon with her smile, handed Holloway her white clutch bag, and approached the tied man. The badly beaten man managed to lift his head as she approached. She took in a long, sweeping glance of him as she walked past the chair and ran her hand along his bare shoulder. He attempted to watch her through mostly swollen eyes. She paused behind him, placed her hands on his shoulders and leaned close to his ear.

Katrina whispered something in his ear, although he didn't react. She straightened and continued around him until she once again stood directly in front of him. His eyes lifted from the clear view of her cleavage and met her gaze. She placed her knee on the chair alongside his bare leg and leaned closer to him, resting her left hand on the back of the chair behind his head. She was only inches from his face and stared into his eyes as he gazed almost helplessly back into hers. She placed her right hand gently on his face and whispered something to him. He said something back.

Katrina grinned, apparently pleased with the response, and affectionately caressed his face. Holloway and Dixon closely watched her with the prisoner, although they mostly had an unobstructed view of her sexy backside. Katrina placed her lips against the man's slightly swollen and bleeding mouth. She kissed him briefly but passionately, which he eagerly reciprocated. Dixon and Holloway uncomfortably shifted and had to look away from the erotic display. It was uncertain if they were repulsed or turned on by it. Katrina broke off the kiss, moved away from the severely beaten man, and turned to face Dixon and Holloway. She indicated the man tied to the chair and smiled.

"Do you have something to say to my boss and his trained monkey?" Katrina announced.

The emotionally and physically drained man managed to look across the room at Holloway and Dixon. "I'll tell her everything," he announced almost eagerly. "Only her, and then you can kill me."

Dixon's arms fell to his sides with shock and disbelief that she was able to get the man to agree to talk just because she flaunted her breasts in his face.

"No, he's not telling her anything," Dixon proclaimed while gesturing wildly. "He's playing her just as much as she's playing him."

Colonel Holloway chuckled while grinning. "He's all yours, Kat," he announced. "You get one hour with him after the party."

Dixon glared at his boss and conveyed his irritation. "You don't honestly believe he's going to tell her anything," he exploded. "She's just giving him a happy ending before he forces us to kill him."

"If she doesn't get anything from him," Holloway announced, "then he's all yours."

Katrina smirked at Dixon then looked back at the tied man and ran her fingers affectionately through his hair. "Until tonight, darling."

The tied man managed a smile with a strange glimmer of hope in his eyes. Katrina seductively walked across the room and joined Holloway and Dixon. She playfully ran her hands along Dixon's large bicep, successfully wiping the man's blood from her hands onto Dixon's shirt.

"Don't feel bad, sweetheart," she announced while mocking the brawny man. "For the job, I have better equipment at my disposal."

As they headed for the door and the guard, Katrina looked back at the exhausted prisoner and blew him a kiss then waved seductively. The man watched them leave and managed a weak smile.

Chapter 10

Colleen rode her horse at a gallop back to her friend's farm. She pulled Thunder to a sliding stop just before the house and dismounted before the horse had even come to a full stop. Colleen bolted for the house with Thunder staring after her, possibly dumbfounded. The black horse trotted after her to the house but stopped at the porch steps. Monique and Bogart rode up to the barn a moment later. Each dismounted but didn't follow the upset girl. Monique glared at Bogart, who appeared ashamed regarding the information he'd withheld from his young friends. The helicopter was heard in the near distance then finally came into view. When it landed, Jackie and Monroe were the only ones inside. Holden had returned to the Bureau to interrogate the prisoners. As Colleen approached the door, Donna and Marie greeted her on the porch. By their reactions, they had been contacted about what happened at the old ghost town after the attack.

"Are you okay, Colleen?" Marie asked.

Colleen stood before her mother with hostility the woman had possibly never seen before. "My father is alive," she lashed out in anger. "He didn't die a war hero. He wasn't any kind of hero. My father has been alive the entire time, and you knew it!"

Marie exhaled and appeared defeated. "I know you're upset," she announced. "But I only wanted to protect you from the truth."

"I had a right to know the truth!"

"That your father was an Army deserter and a traitor?" Marie snapped hotly while staring at her daughter. "Did you really want to know that?"

"Yes," Colleen fired back. "Because then I wouldn't have missed him so much!"

Colleen turned and ran off the porch for her awaiting horse. She sprang onto Thunder's back, spun him around, and galloped down the dirt driveway and away from the farm. Bogart and Monique watched the horse and rider race past them. Storm Cloud snickered after them as if asking why he was being left behind.

"Should we go after her?" Bogart asked.

Monique frowned and shook her head. "No, she needs time to cool down," she replied. "I'll give her an hour then go after her."

"Do you know where she's going?"

"I have a pretty good idea," Monique remarked with a defeated sigh.

§

Colleen sat on a ridge overlooking the valley for nearly an hour. She hugged her knees to her chest and fought her tears while her horse stood behind her and nudged her shoulder with his large lip. It almost seemed as if the horse were attempting to lighten her mood. She finally petted his nose. He placed his large head over her shoulder, which she affectionately stroked.

"At least you'd never betray me," Colleen remarked to the horse.

The familiar sound of metal horseshoes clunking against rock and the creak of saddle leather was enough to perk Thunder's ears. The horse turned its head toward the nearby trail, although Colleen didn't have to look. The familiar spotted horse appeared in the clearing with Monique upon his back and stopped a few feet away.

"What took you so long?" Colleen demanded without looking back at her friend.

Monique dismounted her horse and allowed him to roam free as she approached her friend. She sat alongside Colleen, held her knees to her chest in the same position, and stared off into the distance as well.

"Just thought you needed a little extra alone time," Monique informed her. "Everyone's worried. When are you coming back?"

"Everyone can go to hell," Colleen scoffed.

Monique didn't react nor look at her friend. "I know you don't mean that."

Colleen frowned then groaned. "No, I don't mean that," she muttered then finally eyed Monique as her anger returned. "They lied to me. My mother, Uncle Dave, and even Bogart. They knew my father was alive all this time and never told me."

Monique drew a deep breath and glanced at her friend. "It's a lot to process," she responded. "I think they were trying to spare your feelings."

"I missed him every day since the day they told me he died," Colleen insisted in a softer tone. "I told everyone about my father and how he'd died a hero. All of that was a lie. He wasn't a hero. He abandoned us, stole from the government, and betrayed his country. How could he do something like that? I don't know how to react to this news." Colleen once again stared at the valley in the distance. "How could he leave us like that?"

"I've heard some of the guys say war changes men," Monique gently informed her friend. "There was a time he was a good man, a good husband, and a good father. Just because he changed, that doesn't mean you can't love the man he was to you once upon a time."

"I'd rather not remember him at all," Colleen muttered then finally looked at her friend. "I have my Uncle Dave, despite all his faults. Then there's Bogart."

"And Whiskey Tango Foxtrot," Monique added. "Face it; we have one kick-ass extended family."

"I could use that kick-ass extended family right now," Colleen remarked under her breath.

Monique placed her hand on Colleen's shoulder and managed a tiny grin. "Then you're in luck," she announced. "During Holden's interrogation of one of the men from the ghost town, he must have learned something of great importance."

Colleen cast a look at her blonde friend and suddenly appeared interested.

Monique grinned with enthusiasm. "We're going to spend a few weeks at the lodge with the team until they feel the situation is safe."

"Really?" Colleen asked with some surprise. Her expression instantly dropped. "They know I'm not leaving Thunder behind."

"Already cleared," Monique announced cheerfully. "Bogart will trailer the horses to Ross's farm, so we'll be able to see them. Imagine. New countryside to ride."

"What about my mother?"

"They want her to come along," Monique informed her. "Uncle Dave intends to stay behind to keep an eye on your place."

"Is your mother coming too?"

"No, my mother has my father to look after her," Monique replied. "Besides, someone needs to take care of the rest of the horses. My father is convinced no one will bother with our place. Apart from you and your mother, apparently, I'm the only other real target."

Colleen frowned at the comment. "Just one more reason to hate my father," she muttered. "Now he's endangered our lives as well."

"More of a precaution really," Monique informed her friend then offered a tiny smile. "Jackie said she'll fly us to the lodge in the helicopter. A couple of weeks with Bogart and the rest of the team. New places to ride." She nudged her friend. "Could be a lot of fun."

Colleen managed a smile and nodded. "Yeah, it could be fun."

"Let's get back before Bogart sends out the troops to find us," Monique announced.

"I was kind of hard on him," Colleen muttered then frowned. "And on my mother."

"They understand," Monique replied. "It'll all work itself out, I promise."

Chapter 11

The outdoor garden party at Colonel Holloway's country estate was in full swing that afternoon. Nearly two hundred people attended, including several high-ranking officers who wore their finest Army dress uniforms. Colonel Holloway held his brandy in one hand while keeping Katrina securely against his side with the other as he talked with an Army colonel. Colonel Glenn Bamford was a distinguished looking man in his mid to late fifties with a thick head of silver hair. Despite the added years, the handsome man still maintained an impressive build and was more than intimidating even without the high-rank insignia proudly displayed on his uniform.

"I was surprised to hear of your retirement," Colonel Bamford announced and offered a sly smirk. "Guys like us don't retire."

Colonel Holloway chuckled and hid his smile. "I was sort of hoping to do some traveling, particularly someplace with sunshine, beaches, and fruity drinks," he announced. "*Without* worrying about having my head blown off."

"You'll be bored within a month," Bamford informed him while grinning. "After you travel the world, then what? What will you do with yourself once the novelty wears off? Golf? Racquetball?"

Holloway's grin broadened as he pulled Katrina closer to his side. "Oh, I don't know, Glenn," he announced. "I suppose I'll worry about that when Katrina becomes bored with my company. Until then, I think I'll manage just fine."

Colonel Bamford eyed the gorgeous woman clinging to Holloway's waist and chuckled with understanding. "Yes, I almost forgot."

"A distracting southern bell?" Holloway teased while chuckling lowly in his throat. "You need to have your eyes checked, Glenn."

Dixon approached them and politely smiled at Colonel Bamford. "Excuse me, Colonel," he announced. "May I borrow Colonel Holloway just a moment?"

Holloway eyed Dixon with disapproval. "Is it important, Major Dixon?"

"Yes, sir," he replied without hesitation.

Colonel Holloway smiled at Bamford as he removed his arm from around Katrina's waist and then took her hand. "I'm sorry," he announced to Bamford. "I'll catch up with you a little later."

Holloway led Katrina away from the colonel while following Dixon toward the house. As they paused on the porch, Holloway immediately turned serious.

"What happened?" Holloway demanded.

"Our men were ambushed at the ghost town," Dixon informed him. "The message came through Attorney Phelps from one of our men who was captured."

"Was it Cooper?" Holloway demanded with annoyance while squeezing Katrina's hand hard enough that she had to pull it free.

"No," Dixon replied. "An unknown party."

"Unknown party?" Holloway asked with some surprise. "How organized?"

"Only a few of our men survived," Dixon replied while glancing around to make sure no one was within earshot. "They had a helicopter with a sniper. A few minutes later, the FBI showed up and took our men into custody."

"The FBI?" Holloway announced with surprise. "Was it the FBI in the helicopter?"

"Our man says no," Dixon replied. "He said they reeked of special ops."

Holloway tensed as his mind appeared to reel from the information. "Someone from our payroll striking out on their own?"

"No, none of our guys," Dixon insisted.

"Who the hell is left that's not on our payroll?" Holloway demanded then collected himself. He drew a deep breath and straightened his jacket. "Tell our lawyer to get them out on bail. I don't care what it costs or who we have to pay off. I want firsthand accounts of what went down in that ghost town, and if anyone found our package."

One of his men stood in the kitchen doorway and motioned to get Colonel Holloway's attention. Holloway groaned, captured Katrina's hand, and pulled her with him toward the kitchen.

"What the hell is going on around here today?" Holloway grumbled.

Dixon hurried after them. They entered the kitchen, passed the flood of caterers, and followed the man to the dining room just off the kitchen.

"What is it?" Holloway demanded of his man while releasing Katrina's hand.

"It's our asset in the conference room," the man announced.

The conference room was the code name for the interrogation room in the basement.

"What about the asset?" Holloway demanded not having time to play games with his men. "Is he talking?"

"No," the man insisted with concern and fidgeted. "He's dead."

Holloway's eyes suddenly widened, and the vein in his temple instantly bulged. "What?" he just about cried out. "How?"

"I don't know what happened," the man insisted. "He asked for some water. I gave Gavin the okay. He took a swallow and almost immediately started convulsing. I hadn't even left the room yet. We thought he was playing us so we'd untie him. By the time we figured out he wasn't playing us, he was already dead."

"Poison?"

The man nodded.

Dixon spun to face Katrina and pointed an angry finger at her. "She did something to him," he launched.

"Me?" she snarled while glaring back at Dixon. "I wasn't anywhere near *your* asset." She folded her arms across her chest and turned to face Holloway. "He did this." Katrina cast a glare at Dixon. "He didn't want me getting information from him. I threatened his manhood. He probably killed him so he wouldn't look bad."

"If you weren't fucking the boss--" Dixon snarled while making a fist.

Holloway stepped in front of Katrina and attempted to keep them apart. Katrina stepped around Holloway and allowed her arms to fall to her sides.

"You'd what?" she snarled and kicked off her shoes. "I'll break you in two, you limp dicked Neanderthal."

Holloway immediately turned to face Katrina and placed his hands on her shoulders while meeting her eyes. "Okay, save the dirty talk for the bedroom, my dear," he gently replied and forced her to back a step away from Dixon and spoke softly to her. "I promise you Dixon didn't off the asset just to save face."

"He's a psychopath," Katrina informed him in a hushed whisper.

"We all are to some degree, Kat," Colonel Holloway reminded her then picked up her shoes and handed them to her. "Get yourself a drink and bring it down a notch. I'll deal with this."

"I'm going to kill him," she announced just loud enough for Holloway to hear while staring into his eyes. "You know I will."

"I know, but not today," he insisted then motioned her toward the kitchen door. "Please, get a drink. I'll handle this unpleasantness. Entertain my guests."

Katrina slipped into her shoes and frowned with annoyance. "You'd better keep an eye on him," she insisted. "He's screwing you more than I am."

"Let me worry about that," Holloway insisted then offered a tiny smile. "Please, get yourself a drink and control that inner beast. You can turn all snarly after the guests have gone home."

She frowned then nodded and left the dining room. Holloway drew a deep breath then turned to face Dixon with an unpredictable look in his eyes.

"You need to secure that shit around Katrina," Holloway lashed out at his man in anger. "She's not just another pretty face. She'll fuck you up, and when she does, I won't be able to stop her."

"You were there," Dixon shot out in anger while pointing demandingly at the kitchen door. "She slipped him something. She killed him."

"For what purpose?" Holloway demanded.

"To make me look bad," Dixon exploded.

Colonel Holloway held his head while shaking it. He vigorously raked his fingers through his hair while looking up at the brawny man. "I don't know why the two of you hate each other so much, but it ends now," he insisted. "Katrina didn't slip anything to the asset. We were there. We would have seen it."

"She kissed him," Dixon reminded him. "She slipped it to him then."

"Anything she could have had in her mouth would have killed her before she slipped it to him," Holloway reminded him.

"Poison lipstick then."

"I kissed her," Holloway remarked. "If she had poisonous lipstick, I'd be dead too."

"You'd better wake up, Colonel," Dixon sternly remarked. "She's going to turn on you. That woman is the devil in designer shoes."

"You let me worry about Katrina," Holloway insisted. "I know how to handle her. I trust her just as much as I trust you. He must have had the poison on him. Gavin probably missed something when he searched him. Central Intelligence Agents are crafty. Gavin never should have been in charge of watching an asset of that caliber."

Dixon frowned but didn't comment. "I'll arrange to move the asset after all the guests have gone home."

"No identifying markers," Holloway reminded him with a disgusted sigh. "Incinerate the head and fingers."

Dixon nodded then left the dining room with the man who had reported the incident to him. Colonel Holloway straightened his jacket, fixed his hair, and then headed for the kitchen door.

Chapter 12

Later that evening at the Harris farm, Jackie's helicopter remained grounded not far from the garage. With its rotors tied down, it was apparent it wasn't going anywhere anymore that night. Jackie, Monroe, and Bogart decided to spend the night and get a fresh start for the lodge in the morning. Their decision would allow the girls and Marie a chance to pack some things and for Monique to have dinner with her father when he got home from his business trip before she left for a few weeks or more. Despite the emotional roller coaster Colleen suffered that day, she was excited to have a sleepover with three-eighth of Whiskey Tango Foxtrot.

After dinner, the girls insisted they'd all sleep in sleeping bags on the living room floor. Colleen's mother would spend the night in the spare bedroom so they could leave first thing in the morning. Monique's mother and father turned in early that evening since neither cared for the gruesome movie the girls chose as the night's entertainment. The bloodier, the better was their motto. Marie stayed up for the first twenty minutes of the hack-and-slash film and called it quits after a zombie disemboweled its first victim.

Bogart was the only one who had shorts and a t-shirt to wear for the sleepover since he arrived with the intention of spending the weekend at the farm. Jackie and Monroe slept in their clothes, which they'd done too many times in the past. Monroe stretched out on the sofa while the other four sat on their sleeping bags lined along the floor for the sleepover. They feasted on their second bowl of popcorn while watching the gruesome film. Bogart and Jackie made faces at the gore content. Monroe was a little too comfortable on the sofa and would probably be asleep before the movie was halfway over. Occasionally, he'd poke Jackie in the back with his toe just to annoy her. At times, Monroe was more of an annoying brother than her actual brother was.

"Is this what you guys do when Bogart visits for the weekend?" Jackie asked while grimacing at the gory movie playing on the television.

"Pretty much," Colleen replied.

"We aren't allowed to sneak out for midnight rides anymore," Monique announced without taking her eyes from the television.

"There was that whole owl incident," Colleen added with little emotion.

Jackie eyed them. "Owl incident?"

Without looking away from the television, both girls pointed at Bogart.

Bogart groaned and rolled his eyes. "It wasn't a big deal," he insisted.

"Let me guess," Monroe announced without opening his eyes. "An owl flew into your face, you screamed like a little girl, and fell off your horse."

Bogart glared at Monroe, although he didn't see it. "I most certainly did not scream like a little girl," he huffed then hesitated and considered Monroe's comment. "How did you know what happened?"

Monroe opened one eye and peered at Bogart. "It's you," he casually announced. "Weird shit like that only happens to you."

Jackie, Monique, and Colleen all considered the assessment and nodded in agreement.

Bogart groaned and shook his head. "Whatever," he muttered.

Monique glanced slyly at Jackie several times during the movie then finally grinned. "Think I can fly the helicopter tomorrow?"

"No," Monroe responded for Jackie.

Jackie eyed Monroe's bare foot not far from her head. She grabbed his ankle and tickled the sole of his foot. He jumped while crying out.

"She *asked* me," Jackie snapped back.

Monique's eyes lit up. "Can I?"

"No," Jackie retorted just as firmly as Monroe had responded.

Monique silently pouted and resumed watching the movie. "You're no fun."

"I also want to live to see my next birthday," Jackie informed the teenager. There was a moment of silence. "Although I'm not opposed to letting you fly the plane sometime."

Monique became giddy. "Really?"

Jackie shrugged with little hesitation. "Why not? My father taught me to fly when I was much younger than you," Jackie informed her matter-of-factly. "I won't let you take off or land though."

"I'm fine with that," she announced excitedly.

"We're all going to die," Colleen muttered.

"Not me," Bogart announced while watching the movie. "Because I won't be there."

"Oh, come on," Monique pouted. "You have to be there. It wouldn't be right."

"It wouldn't be right all of us dying together either, Twinkie," Bogart informed her.

§

Monroe was asleep before the second movie started. Despite their best efforts to stay awake, Monique and Colleen fell asleep before the second movie had ended. Jackie turned off the television a little before midnight. When she returned from the bathroom, Bogart had abandoned his sleeping bag. Despite being a warm night, Jackie could feel a cool breeze. She entered the kitchen and saw the porch door was open. Since it had been closed earlier, Bogart must have stepped outside while she was in the bathroom. Jackie left the house and found Bogart sitting on the porch railing with his back against the support beam. He stared across the property at the horses grazing in the paddock. His expression suggested he was somewhere else. Jackie joined him on the railing, leaned against the opposite support, and faced him.

"Are you okay?" she asked her brother.

Bogart frowned and shut his eyes as he rested his head against the support beam. "No, not really," he replied. He then opened his eyes and looked at Jackie. "It's my fault, you know."

"How do you figure?" Jackie asked while giving her brother a puzzled look.

"I should have taken care of Martin the first time I ran into him," Bogart informed her while conveying his anger at himself. "I had him, but I let him go. If I had done things differently, Colleen never would have known her father was still alive. It could have been handled quietly. I had the opportunity, and I didn't take it."

"No, Bogart," Jackie announced while raising a demanding brow. "It was wrong for Marie to keep this secret from Colleen. You're just collateral damage."

"Doesn't feel that way," Bogart muttered.

"She's not mad at you," Jackie insisted. "Those girls adore you."

"I know she's not mad at me, but that doesn't mean I don't feel bad about how things went down," he replied while frowning. "I just--" He drew a deep breath and stared at his sister. "I just want to make things right."

"I'm not sure how you're going to do that," Jackie replied as she folded her arms across her chest. "It's not your fight."

"I disagree."

"Sometimes it's not about making things right," she informed him. "Sometimes you just need to be there when someone needs you." Jackie straightened, patted Bogart's shoulder, and headed inside.

Bogart drew a deep breath, raked his fingers through his hair, and shut his eyes.

Chapter 13

Colonel Holloway's lavish garden party broke up a little after midnight. The exhausted colonel entered his master bedroom and paused just inside the doorway. The bedroom was dimly lit by a fire burning in the gas fireplace giving the large chamber a romantic glow. Holloway grinned when he saw the romantic setting and looked toward the bed. To his surprise, it was empty. He appeared curious and approached the partially open bathroom door while nearly tripping over Katrina's discarded shoes. He then saw the white lacy panties tossed carelessly across the floor. Holloway grinned and just about ripped off his tie, casting it onto the floor, and then hurriedly pulled off his shoes. He was obviously hoping to make it in time to join the seductress in the shower or tub for a romantic interlude.

"You were absolutely amazing tonight," he called out while tossing his shoes aside, unconcerned how loudly they clunked on the carpeted floor. "Everyone loved you, Kat." His grin increased as he headed for the bathroom door and hastily removed his expensive jacket, carelessly throwing it to the floor alongside her white dress. "I was the envy of every man at the party."

Holloway suddenly hesitated and looked at Katrina's white dress lying on the floor. Even in the romantic lighting, he could see it was spattered with blood. His expression immediately turned to concern.

"Kat?" he called out and hurried for the partially open bathroom door as steam wafted out. "Kat?"

The colonel was about to charge through the bathroom door when it opened to reveal Katrina wearing a short, sexy, white satin robe that barely covered the tops of her thighs. Holloway abruptly stopped then appeared relieved to see her. He groaned while raking his fingers through his hair then chuckled nervously.

"I was concerned when you didn't answer me," he announced and hid his embarrassed smile.

She laughed in her throat, humored by his seemingly frayed nerves. "Did you think I slipped in the tub and drown?" she teased.

"No, not exactly," he replied then retrieved her dress and indicated the large amount of bright red blood on it. "What happened?"

She removed the dress from his hands, carelessly tossed it to the floor, and then ran her hands firmly along his chest while gazing lovingly into his eyes.

"I had some business to take care of before taking care of you," she teased and affectionately placed her arms around his neck.

Holloway stiffened while staring into her eyes with concern. "Please tell me Dixon didn't have an accident."

She grinned almost seductively while chuckling in her throat as her lips brushed past his. "Darling," Katrina cooed warmly. "I wouldn't do that without getting your permission first." She hesitated. "Or at the very least give you proper warning." Katrina offered a slight sneer. "He may be a disgusting bastard, but I know you still need him. Gavin, on the other hand, was expendable."

"What happened?"

"I ran into him after I left the party and asked him about the prisoner," she replied. "He denied seeing anything leading up until the time the prisoner died."

"Why did you kill him?" Holloway asked.

"He tried to blackmail me for sex," she replied with little emotion. "I wasn't amused." Her look then turned almost childlike. "Are you mad?"

Colonel Holloway snorted a laugh and shook his head. "No, he knows you're mine," he announced. "I would have killed him myself."

She gently ran the back of her fingers along his face while grinning. "I'm glad to hear that. I wouldn't want to do anything to displease you." Her hand caressed his chest then continued along his abdomen and for his crotch. "I only want to *please* you."

He groaned as her hand lovingly caressed the bulge in his pants then aggressively pulled her against him. "You always please me in every way," he announced while grinning. "I've been looking forward to this party for months, yet all I could think about was tearing off your dress and doing unspeakable things to you."

Katrina grinned and appeared pleased by his words while her hand firmly caressed him through his pants. "Well, I'm here now," she cooed seductively. "Do your worst, Colonel Holloway."

She took a step away from him, barely able to break free from his arms, and allowed her robe to fall to the floor. She wore a sexy, white lacy teddy leaving little to the imagination. Holloway groaned, took a quick step toward her, and aggressively pulled her against him. He sought her lips and passionately kissed her. She returned the kiss with added aggression and effortlessly leaped up his body, wrapping her legs around his waist. He caught her beneath the buttocks and carried her to the bed without breaking off the kiss. Holloway tackled her to the bed and pawed at her satin teddy. Katrina eagerly opened his pants, forcing him to react with increased aggression. She then flipped their position, tossing him onto his back and placing herself on top of him. She moved onto her knees while straddling his hips and tore his shirt open. He groaned, pleased with her aggressiveness, despite that she ruined his expensive shirt.

"Baby, you can interrogate me anytime," he announced with a pleased smile.

She grinned while running her hands firmly along his muscular chest. "Are we having one of *those* nights?"

Holloway caressed her backside then gently stroked her thong panties with his index finger. "No, not tonight," he replied. "I want to put my hands on you the way every man at the party wished he could."

She raised a sly brow while grinning. "You want to tie me up?"

He groaned and hid his smile. "I'd like that."

Katrina lowered her body against his and affectionately kissed his neck. "It's your night," she cooed between kisses. "You can do whatever you want with my body."

Holloway groaned, flipped her onto her back, and positioned himself on top of her. His hands firmly caressed her side and buttocks. "I'm going to take you up on that offer."

He kissed her quickly but passionately then moved off her with increased enthusiasm. She turned onto her side and seductively caressed the sheets while watching him leap for the nightstand drawer.

"One thing, Colonel," she announced catching his attention and stopping him in his tracks. Her seductive smile turned devious. "Don't be gentle."

Holloway groaned then fumbled through the drawer and removed a pair of handcuffs. "As you wish."

Chapter 14

Sunday, June 22nd. The following morning, Monroe placed three travel bags into the storage compartment of Jackie's helicopter while Bogart tossed the larger suitcases into his pickup truck. The girls easily loaded their horses onto the stock trailer with Bogart's horse. He would haul their horses to Ross's farm so the girls could visit and ride during their stay. The length of time they'd spend at the lodge was undetermined, so it was necessary to bring along their horses. Bogart had to take his horse back anyway so there was no reason they couldn't hitch a ride. Monique attempted to say a brief goodbye to her mother and father, but they seemed reluctant to let her go. Marie and the two girls secured their seats in the back of the helicopter. Ironically, Jackie's passengers were ready before she was. Jackie had to finish the call she'd just taken on her cell phone then rushed to climb inside the pilot's seat. Once she prepped the helicopter, they were on their way.

It was a short flight from the Harris farm to the Colorado Springs Airport. Jackie's helicopter set down on the tarmac in a more secluded area a short distance from the hustle and bustle of the busy main terminal. Monroe opened the back door for Marie, Monique, and Colleen, who all jumped out. He indicated the small building not far from the tarmac where Jackie had landed.

"There's a bathroom and vending machines in there," he informed them.

"So are we just waiting for Jackie to refuel?" Marie asked while nervously rubbing her arms as she looked around with deepening anxiety.

"Actually," Monroe announced. "Gil is almost finished refueling his plane on the other side of the building. The three of you will hop aboard with him. He'll take you to the private airfield closer to the lodge. Jackie and I will meet you there and fly all of you the rest of the way in the helicopter."

"Why don't we all just take the helicopter straight through to the lodge?" Monique asked then managed a grin. "I like flying in the helicopter."

"Jackie has to pick up some guests and part-time staff for one of Ross's neighboring ranchers," Monroe informed them. "The call just came in this morning. That's what she was doing when we were waiting to lift off. Since the job is on the way and Gil was already returning from his little side trip to visit his ex-wife, we thought we'd just switch it up a little. He can't land his plane at the lodge, and he was going to need a ride anyway."

Jackie approached them having heard the conversation. "And Mr. Hooper pays handsomely," she announced while grinning. "His youngest daughter is getting married in August, and I could be looking at several days' worth of air taxi services." She then glared at Monroe and raised a brow. "Too many *unpaid* trips lately." She then shifted her attention to the girls and smirked. "Holden's been a little grouchy about my fuel bills the last few months."

"Maybe someone shouldn't have bought a new helicopter with their share of the money from the last assignment," Monroe remarked while glaring at Jackie.

She folded her arms across her chest. "Maybe we need more *paid* assignments."

"That's not my fault," Monroe snapped back. "Talk to Ross and Beck. The honeymooners are more concerned with traveling the world with their wives than working. We haven't had a decent job since "Alpha Dogs"."

"Alpha Dogs?" Monique questioned.

"Our code name for our last mission," Jackie announced then glared back at Monroe. "After that fiasco, Ross put a temporary ban on any assignments from questionable clients."

"Questionable clients?" Marie then asked.

Monique leaned closer to Marie and muttered, "Mob bosses."

Marie eyed Monique and held back her startled gasp. She then glanced at Jackie and Monroe. "You take assignments from mob bosses?"

"That's classified information," Monroe remarked then glared at Jackie. "Next time you score a huge payday, you may want to consider saving some for a rainy day."

"I never know if I'll be alive to need money for that rainy day," Jackie huffed. Sadly, she sometimes felt that way. "We're not the only game in town. Ross can't afford to be quite so picky with assignments."

"Actually, he can," Monroe insisted and smiled deviously. "He's living comfortably because he saved his pennies for that rainy day."

The silver sable German shepherd ran across the tarmac for them and greeted Jackie. She crouched down and playfully scratched the excited dog.

"Hey, Darth," she announced cheerfully. "How was Virginia?"

Monroe snorted a laugh. "He wouldn't know," he muttered. "He probably spent most of his time locked outside the bedroom door."

"I heard that," Gil announced from several yards away.

Everyone looked across the tarmac at Gil as he approached them.

"I don't appreciate you turning my innocent visits with Ellie into some sorted affair."

"I would have used the term booty call," Monroe remarked then grinned. "But whatever term works for you."

Gil politely greeted Marie, who seemed mildly taken by his charm. Once Monique and Colleen finished playing with the dog, they excitedly hugged Gil.

"If you're ready," Gil announced and pointed across the tarmac. "My plane is fueled and ready to roll."

As the others left for Gil's private plane, Jackie returned to refueling her helicopter. Monroe moved closer to Jackie and appeared to have something on his mind. She cast several looks at him, knowing his moods too well, and groaned.

"You obviously wanted to get me alone the last two days," she finally announced. "What is it?"

"We never get time to talk in private without Zack nosing around," Monroe began.

Jackie groaned and shook her head since she already knew where the conversation was heading. "No, Monroe," she announced firmly. "We're not having this conversation again. We are not discussing Mac."

Monroe immediately tensed. "What happened at Beck's wedding has been bothering me," he insisted. "I'd like to talk about it."

"Nothing happened at Beck's wedding," Jackie scoffed with irritation. "Beck and Ross sent Mac packing. End of story. The team as a whole doesn't trust her. When the blood stops rushing from your brain to your nether regions, you'll realize it was the right thing to do."

"Stop acting as if I have a soft spot for Mac," Monroe huffed back. "I just feel differently about the way we ended things with her than the rest of you."

"No," Jackie snapped. "I voted to give her a chance too, but I was overruled. And it's not that soft spot you have for Mac that concerns me. It's the hard one."

Monroe sneered at her. "That's rude," he snapped while folding his arms across his chest. "Just because you and I dated once upon a time--"

Jackie groaned with annoyance and glared at Monroe. "We didn't date once upon a time," she launched back. "We had a brief, one-time thing before I went off to college. It wasn't even a one-night-stand. It was more of a training guide, and I wish you'd stop bringing it up."

"Training guide?" Monroe scoffed, clearly irritated. "That's all I was to you?"

She glared at him and attempted to keep from lashing out at him. "No, you were my friend," Jackie insisted. "*That's* all you were to me."

Monroe frowned and shook his head with irritation. "I'm going to grab something to drink," he snapped hotly then walked away.

Jackie cast a look at him as he left then frowned and shook her head. She hated being firm with Monroe, but it was sometimes the only thing that worked with him. Despite his insistence that he was over her, he continued to bring up their one-time indiscretion as if they had actually been in a relationship. She broke his heart because she didn't feel the same way about him, and she was going to make sure she never made that mistake again. That misunderstanding almost cost them their friendship once. She wasn't sure their friendship could survive another misunderstanding.

Chapter 15

Monroe entered the bland building not far from the main terminal. He was obviously upset with the conversation he'd just had with Jackie, and the stress was showing. He seemed ready to explode at the world. The building contained a waiting room, offices, and restrooms for travelers using private air services. The furniture within the waiting room, although comfortable, was old and worn. There was a counter near the front, where guests would check in for their private flights. Vending machines were located near the corridor that led to the restrooms at the back of the hall. A small group of five waited for Jackie to take them to Hooper's ranch. Apart from the attractive young woman who warranted a quick glance, Monroe showed little interest in the small group waiting on them.

The attractive woman and one of the men were possibly in their early twenties. Two of the other men were in their late twenties. One was a tall, muscular African-American man. His imposing frame caught Monroe's attention only because he tended to seek out the most dangerous man in any crowd. The last man looked like a businessman and didn't even warrant a second look from Monroe. Monroe headed for the vending machines and saw a woman he almost certainly recognized. The familiar woman headed down the long corridor toward the bathrooms and the back exit. It couldn't possibly be whom he thought. Monroe hurried into the corridor and dashed after the woman who was nearly to the exit door.

"Mac," he called after her.

The woman didn't seem to hear him and opened the back door.

"Mac," Monroe again called.

This time the woman turned. Macbeth was an attractive, dark-haired woman in her mid-thirties. She wore her long hair pulled back in a neat ponytail and usually had a stray lock falling across her face. Her athletic build suggested she worked out extensively. Although she could pass for a sophisticated woman, the truth was less flattering. Despite her casual attire and naturally rough beauty, she still gained plenty of male attention. Mac seemed genuinely surprised to see Monroe. Her mood then hardened. She frowned and demandingly folded her arms across her chest with her true nature shining through as she gave him a venomous look.

"I should have known I'd run into one of you here," she snarled with limited patience. "What are you doing here, Monroe?" Her eyes then narrowed. "You weren't following me, were you?"

"What?" Monroe asked with surprise then turned defensive. "No, Jackie needs to provide helicopter taxi service for one of the local ranchers. What are you doing here?"

"Not that it's any of your business," she huffed then shifted uncomfortably. "I was looking for work." Her eyes narrowed. "I was fired from my last bartending job for taking off an entire week without giving advance notice." She thoughtfully tapped her finger to her chin. "Hmm, now why was that?" Mac's glare then turned demanding. "Oh, that's right. I was hiking through alligator-infested swamps saving your ass from hired mercenaries."

"That's not fair," Monroe insisted while glaring at her. "As I remember, you insisted on coming along for the ride, and you were paid a substantial sum of money when the mission was over."

They heard the awaiting passengers moving around within the lobby. Mac tensed and ran her fingers through her dark hair.

"I really have to go," she announced. "I have another interview, and I can't afford to be late."

"Please, Mac," Monroe pleaded. "Just give me five minutes of your time."

One of the passengers appeared in the corridor and glanced around. Mac avoided being seen by the man while using Monroe as a wall.

"Fine," she scoffed then bolted through the doorway to her right.

Monroe followed her into the storage closet. Mac turned on the light that did a poor job at lighting the windowless room. Someone was heard in the corridor possibly approaching the restrooms. Mac flipped the lock on the door, catching Monroe's attention.

"Are you avoiding someone?" Monroe asked and appeared curious.

She frowned and again ran her fingers through her hair. "Yeah, but what else is new."

He stared at her as if awaiting an explanation.

Mac groaned and shifted uncomfortably. "The man who interviewed me was a bit of a jerk," she announced. "And you know I don't exactly play well with others--"

"And now you're avoiding a confrontation," Monroe remarked.

"More like I'd rather not be escorted out by airport security," she replied then leaned against the door while glaring at him. "What did you want?"

Monroe fumbled slightly over himself without taking his eyes off hers. "I'm sorry how things ended at Beck's wedding," he gently replied.

"Oh, you mean when you and your friends threw me under the bus?" she demanded while glaring at him. "And I was officially blacklisted from ever working for Sal or your little boys' club?"

"I don't remember it going down quite like that," Monroe insisted.

"I do," she snarled while harboring anger over it as she glared at him. "I was there."

Monroe tensed and held his breath while staring into her angry eyes. "I just wanted to tell you that I'm sorry for how things ended; that's all," he gently replied. "It wasn't my decision, and I hated the way things ended. I defended you. I wanted the guys to give you another chance."

Mac straightened while staring at him with genuine surprise. "You did?"

He nodded and shamefully lowered his head. "I regret not making a better case."

She shifted almost uncomfortably while staring at him. "After all our clashes, you were the last person I expected to hear that from," she remarked.

"If I held a grudge against every woman I've ever clashed with, I'd alienate half the female population," he teased and managed a smile.

Mac stared at him a moment in silence as if attempting to gauge his sincerity. She grabbed his face in her hands, startling him, and kissed him passionately. Despite being taken back by her sexually aggressive reaction, Monroe immediately returned the wild kiss, lost his balance, and knocked her against the door. It was unclear if she knew he'd lost his balance or if she took it as sexual aggression. Regardless, she pawed at his body and just about tore his shirt. Monroe attempted to keep up with her aggression, but Mac was already opening his belt with a sense of urgency. Before he could even open her pants, she already had her hand down his. Monroe groaned and sank against her despite her somewhat roughness toward his highly sensitive body parts.

Monroe was barely able to fondle her breasts over her tank top before she dropped to her knees in front of him. He braced his hand against the door in front of him for support, groaned loudly in response, and subconsciously placed his hand to the back of her head while clutching her ponytail. His ecstasy only lasted briefly when she pulled away much to his disappointment. As she straightened, her mouth eagerly sought his. Somehow, during the brief moment she was on her knees, she managed to slip out of her shorts. Mac threw her arms around his neck and leaped against him, wrapping her legs around his hips. Monroe again nearly lost his balance and knocked her into the door to help support her as she straddled him in an upright position. He groaned and thrust his body against her jolting the door with a loud clunk.

§

Jackie entered the small building and approached the five passengers waiting patiently in the lobby. Although she counted five, she thought there was supposed to be six. She offered as pleasant a smile as she could manage under the circumstances. She was actually a little irritated that Monroe seemed to have vanished on her. If he were in the bathroom, he was taking his good old time shaking it off.

"Good morning. I'm Jackie, your pilot. The helicopter is refueled and ready to go just as soon as I find my co-pilot," she informed the small group of five passengers. "Why don't you grab a seat anywhere in the back; and we'll be along in a minute?"

The others nodded and left the building for the awaiting helicopter. Jackie headed for the vending machines then looked down the corridor to the restrooms.

"Monroe?" she called out then heard a loud thumping coming from the door at the end of the corridor. It sounded as if someone were attempting to break down one of the doors. "Monroe?"

The pounding ceased. Jackie cautiously walked down the corridor and checked the men's restroom while keeping an eye on several closed doors. The men's room was empty. She approached the next closed door, which was the woman's restroom. If Monroe ran into someone with a grudge, he could be in trouble.

§

Monroe rushed to pull up his pants and close them then fumbled with his belt. He was flushed and out of breath as he cast peeks at Mac who dressed in less of a hurry. Oddly enough, she no longer seemed pressed for time and appeared almost indifferent to their quick but wild moment.

"That's Jackie," he announced out of breath. "She's waiting for me."

"Don't mention you saw me," Mac practically threatened while sounding annoyed.

Monroe was mildly surprised but then nodded in agreement. "You're right," he reluctantly replied. "We don't need this getting back to Zack." He finished dressing and moved closer to her while grinning almost boyishly. "How about we meet somewhere this weekend?"

She eyed him while she finished dressing then straightened. "I don't think so."

"Okay," Monroe replied with some disappointment but wasn't ready to give up just yet. "What about the following Friday?"

"Once and done, Monroe," she firmly insisted while locking eyes with him. "We both needed that, but it's not happening again."

Before he could protest or question her, Mac opened the closet door and shoved him into the hall, shutting the door behind him. Monroe stared at the closed door and attempted to open it, but she had locked it from the other side. When he glanced down the hall, Jackie was approaching with a look of irritation clearly on her face.

"Why didn't you answer?" Jackie demanded.

Chapter 16

The helicopter flew over the beautiful Colorado countryside heading toward the mountains. The scenery was void of homes, roads, and buildings leaving nothing but nature. The five passengers took in the visual beauty while talking among themselves. Jackie had her headset turned to a private channel, so she could have her own personal conversation with Monroe. Unfortunately, Monroe wasn't in a talkative mood. Jackie thought he was possibly still angry about their earlier conversation, but she knew the many moods of Monroe. He appeared to be sulking over something. She couldn't quite figure out what put him in that sort of mood so quickly. It couldn't have been their little discussion. He'd be over that by now. If one of the guys had called him on his cell phone, he would have shared that information.

Jackie's five passengers were being delivered to a ranch belonging to Ross's neighbor, which was actually a few miles from Ross's farm. Jackie knew little about Sig Hooper other than he was Ross's wealthy neighbor who owned a large cattle ranch. The rancher's youngest daughter was about to get married, and the quiet ranch was expected to become busy as the wedding grew closer. Jackie only knew as much as she did since Ross, his wife, and his extended family living with him had been invited to the wedding. The aerial view of Hooper's ranch was breathtaking. There was a large plantation style farmhouse with an impressive wraparound porch, large in-ground pool, a bunkhouse for the wranglers just across the paddock, and a massive horse barn near the bunkhouse. There was a large fenced pasture and smaller paddock for the many grazing horses. The cattle pastures seemed to extend forever. There were large herds of cattle in several areas, which were moved by the wranglers on a rotating basis to allow different pastures to grow. The helicopter was high enough that it didn't spook the horses or cattle.

"That's some piece of real estate," Monroe remarked, possibly speaking for the first time since they left the Colorado Springs Airport.

"Yeah, the guy's worth millions," Jackie remarked. "Flaunts it too."

"Any young, single daughters?" Monroe teased.

"Yeah, but she's spoiled," Jackie replied.

The helicopter lowered into a large clearing far enough away from any animals yet surprisingly close to the house. Jackie shut down the helicopter then got out and opened the back door for her passengers. Monroe opened the door on his side as well. The sole woman among the five passengers was polite, but she was engrossed in a conversation with the handsome yet nerdy businessman.

"I'll talk to Hooper," the young woman responded to the man before they headed off.

Jackie wasn't sure what their deal was, but she got the impression they were having some secret fling. Whatever was between them, there was some tension involving Mr. Hooper. The youngest of the three men climbed out on her side as well. Jackie was apprehensive about the handsome young man close to her in age. There was something about him that set her on edge, and she couldn't help wonder if their paths had crossed before. Something about him seemed familiar; a frightening familiar. He offered a charming smile and thanked her for the smooth flight.

Once their passengers were safely away from the helicopter, Jackie and Monroe were once again airborne. It would be a short trip to the private airfield where they would meet Gil with the girls and Marie. Despite the short flight, Jackie had grown tired of the silent treatment from Monroe, who was sulking about something.

"What's with the bug up your ass?" she demanded with hostility.

Monroe cast a look at her surprised by her demanding tone then frowned and looked back out the window, once again sulking.

"Nothing."

"Nothing my ass," she scoffed while casting looks at him. "Usually when you have that pitiful look on your face, some woman dumped you."

"Yeah, you would know all about that," Monroe snapped back.

She gave him several quick looks while debating whether she wanted to buzz cut the trees below to bring him out of his funk.

"Considering you haven't had a girlfriend in the last century, it can't have anything to do with sex," Jackie remarked while hiding her smirk.

If he wanted to take shots at her, she could play that game. Monroe tensed slightly, but it was enough for Jackie to take notice. She shot several quick looks at him with alarm on her face and horror in her eyes.

"No way," she gasped almost unable to look away while nearly flying the helicopter into a treetop. "What did you do? Bang the cleaning lady at the airport? It's not as if there were many women floating around--" Her eyes then widened. "Not our young passenger!"

"No, Jackie," he groaned with irritation. "Please, I'm not your oversexed brother. That's more Bogart's thing than mine. Give me some credit."

"Then who?"

Monroe frowned. "Promise you won't get mad and crash, killing us both?"

She glared at him with limited patience.

He drew a deep breath and nervously raked his fingers through his hair. "Mac was leaving as I entered the private lounge," Monroe reluctantly announced.

Jackie's expression dropped and so did the helicopter. Monroe screamed while clutching the seat and dash. She leveled the craft and glared at him while he panted from her bomb drop.

"How could you?" Jackie cried out.

Monroe panted a moment then caught his breath and looked at her. "I didn't, well, not exactly," he insisted. "We were arguing about the wedding reception, I apologized, and she, uh, well, jumped me. Literally."

"Literally," she scoffed while glaring at him.

Monroe suddenly became animated. "Yes, she *literally* jumped on me," he again insisted with more conviction then collected himself. "The woman is something of a predator. I was practically an innocent bystander."

"I call bullshit," she scoffed then glared at him. Whether it was true or not, she had to find a way to keep the peace. "Zack can't find out. I don't know what happened between them, but he's liable to kill you."

"Don't worry; he won't find out," Monroe huffed and sulked while looking out the side window. "She used me and tossed me aside. Said it was a one-time thing and nothing more."

"Good," Jackie announced with irritation at her friend. "Just forget about it and her. I finally have Zack just the way I like him, and I'm not going to let you ruin all the hard work I put into training him."

Monroe snorted a laugh and shot a look at her. "You trained him? Huh, that's a good one," he remarked while grinning then shook his head. "Sorry, Jacklyn, dear. Zack trained you. You're his little marionette dancing for his perverse amusement."

She glared at her friend. "I changed my mind," Jackie announced. "I'm crashing this bird."

§

The helicopter landed in the large clearing in front of the mountain lodge. As Jackie shut the helicopter down, Beck and another man appeared from the lodge and approached in time to open the back doors for their guests. The second man was Ross Madrid, a handsome, distinguished gentleman in his early fifties with a full head of moderately graying hair. Despite his age, he was in amazing physical shape with enough muscle mass behind him to put much younger men to shame. Ross offered a charming smile and assisted Marie from the back of the helicopter while Monique and Colleen sprang from the back, wasting little time with chivalry. Both girls gave Beck and Ross quick hugs then looked around.

"Where are Kirk and Zack?" Monique asked.

"Well, you know Zack," Beck announced with little emotion.

"So he's hiding from us," Monique continued while raising a cocky brow.

Beck nodded and chuckled. "Yeah, he's hiding from you," he agreed.

Monique and Colleen exchanged glares.

"I don't know about you," Monique announced to her friend, "but I'm offended."

"Yep, me too," Colleen replied. "I say we find him."

Both girls took off across the estate grounds. Darth barked excitedly and ran after them, thinking it was a game, which it actually was. Marie was about to yell to them then held her breath and shook her head. She cast a look at Ross as if silently asking him a question.

"They'll be fine," Ross insisted. "There's no one around for miles."

Jackie removed their bags from the back compartment of the helicopter and handed them to the guys. As the guys carried the three bags to the lodge, Kirk appeared on the porch eating a sandwich.

Monroe glared at him and shook his head. "Always conveniently absent when it comes time to do the heavy lifting," he remarked.

Kirk shrugged and casually ate his sandwich. "Probably because I'm not the bellhop." He then looked around. "Where are the teen terrors?"

"Playing hide-and-seek with Zack," Beck replied.

Kirk gave him a bewildered look. "Zack's not even here," he remarked. "He took your precious new SUV to town. You made such a big deal about him taking it. How could you have forgotten?"

"I didn't forget, but if the girls are busy looking for Zack, it'll keep them out of earshot long enough for us to discuss Martin with Marie," Beck replied.

Chapter 17

Monday, June 23rd. The digital clock on the coffeemaker indicated o-six-hundred. The unit turned itself on and began brewing its rich, dark liquid gold. Just before the last drop hit the carafe, Zack appeared on the back stairs looking freshly showered but weary. His excessively large mug depicted an assault rifle and the words, 'talk to me and die'. He headed straight for the coffeemaker on the main counter and filled his mug with black coffee. He lifted the mug to his lips and suddenly hesitated. Zack turned his head and looked behind him. Monique and Colleen leaned on the island counter on the opposite side while staring at him and smiling.

"Morning, Zack," both chirped in unison.

Zack groaned, turned back to the main counter, and sipped his coffee. "Yes, it is," he muttered in response.

The island counter chairs scraped the tile floor as they were pulled out. Zack groaned at the sound. The sound itself was annoying enough, but the fact that the two girls were making themselves comfortable only increased his agitation.

"Jackie said you're up every morning at six," Monique announced.

Zack sneered at the comment. "Wasn't that nice of her to mention," he snarled under his breath then turned to face the girls, who watched him with fascination. "Did she also mention I shoot people who talk to me before I've had my coffee?"

Both girls seemed to consider the question in all seriousness then shook their heads.

"Nope," they replied in unison.

Zack held up his mug and pointed to it. "Says so right here on my mug."

"Doesn't say anything about 'after coffee'," Monique informed him.

"The mug is wise," Zack replied.

"Jackie said we could hang out with you until everyone else is up," Monique announced with a little too much enthusiasm and practically bounced in her seat. "Could you teach us karate?"

"No," Zack replied curtly.

Both girls frowned.

"Why not?" Colleen pouted.

Zack eyed her and raised his brows. "Because I'm not supposed to hit girls." He took another sip from his coffee and saw the two girls were still eagerly staring at him. "Don't you have horses you can play with?"

"My mother said we aren't allowed to go to Ross's farm until after breakfast," Colleen informed him while frowning.

"Oh," Zack announced then turned to the main counter, set his mug down, and opened the bottom cupboard door. He turned and tossed two large, silver pouches onto the counter. "Eat up."

Monique and Colleen picked up the pouches and eyed them suspiciously.

"What's this?" Monique asked.

"MREs," Zack replied and reclaimed his mug. "Taste like shit, but they'll keep you alive."

Zack headed across the kitchen for the hallway entrance. Monique and Colleen jumped off their counter stools and hurried after him. Zack groaned when he saw them following. He entered the lobby without acknowledging the girls behind him.

"Ross's farm is an hour's drive from here," Monique reminded Zack. "We can't exactly walk."

Zack turned abruptly causing both girls to stop in their tracks. "Why not?" he demanded.

"That's like thirty miles," Colleen squawked. "We can't walk thirty miles. That would take hours."

"You could if you wanted to," he insisted then shook his head. "Kids nowadays are soft." Zack then pointed toward the lobby entrance. "If you go south through the woods, it's only about ten miles to Ross's farm. A nice, brisk jog and you can make it there in an hour."

Monique and Colleen exchanged looks and seemed to be communicating without words. Both shrugged then looked back at Zack.

"Tell my mom we went to Ross's farm," Colleen announced then followed Monique to the main entrance.

Zack frowned then cursed under his breath. "You're not walking to Ross's farm," he snapped with annoyance. "You'd probably be eaten by a bear, and then Jackie would somehow blame me."

"But you said--" Monique announced while giving him an innocent look.

"Why the hell would you listen to anything I say?" he suddenly demanded. "You shouldn't even be talking to me. I'm fucked in the head." He then hesitated and considered the last comment. "I guess I'm not supposed to curse in front of you either." Zack shook his head and groaned. "My entire morning routine has been compromised." He glanced at his watch and again eyed both girls. "How about watching cartoons instead? I won't get in trouble for that."

"Cartoons?" Monique asked with some surprise. "We're fifteen. We're too old for cartoons."

Zack shrugged and took another sip from his coffee mug. "Suit yourselves," he announced. "I'm watching cartoons."

As he headed back down the hall for the game room, Monique stared after him with a strange look. She folded her arms across her chest and shook her head.

"He's definitely not right," Monique remarked then eyed her friend.

Colleen held the open MRE bag and ate something resembling bread but flatter and dense.

Monique made a face at her friend. "Are you actually eating that stuff?"

"Yeah," Colleen replied and shrugged. "I'm hungry. It's not bad."

Monique appeared curious and broke off a piece. She made a face while placing it in her mouth. As she chewed it, she nodded.

"You're right," Monique remarked. "It's not half bad. Could use some jelly though."

Colleen removed a packet from the bag and handed it to her friend.

Monique eyed the packet and appeared intrigued. "Huh, grape jelly," she remarked then laughed. "I'll get my bag from the kitchen and meet you in the game room for cartoons."

Chapter 18

Tuesday, June 24th. The courthouse in Colorado Springs was bustling with activity that afternoon. Gil left the courthouse dressed in a stylish, black suit and looked dashingly handsome. As he walked down the steps toward the sidewalk, he removed his cell phone and placed it to his ear.

"Bail denied," Gil announced into the phone. "All four are being held for further questioning by the feds. I'm following their lawyer, an Attorney Phelps."

Gil kept a man in view a few yards in front of him. Attorney Phelps was a distinguished looking man in his mid-to-late forties wearing an expensive suit. He looked more like a mafia hitman than a lawyer. His dark hair was slicked back, he stood over six-foot tall, and had an impressive build suggesting he worked out extensively. The lawyer with the leather attaché case approached the curb. An expensive, black car pulled up to the curb as soon as he reached it. Attorney Phelps jumped into the back, and the car was on its way. Kirk sat on a motorcycle just a few cars away with his cell phone in his hand.

"I have visual on our man," Kirk announced then snapped a picture of the back of the car. "Sending the license plate to Monroe."

Kirk replaced his cell phone to his pocket and pulled into traffic to follow the expensive car carrying the lawyer representing the men from the ghost town. Gil approached the curb as a rental car pulled up. He opened the passenger side door and got in. He glanced briefly at Jackie behind the wheel. She concentrated on traffic and pulled away from the courthouse. Jackie wore a simple black dress and matched Gil's sophisticated look. Gil cast several looks at her and grinned while shaking his head. Jackie eyed him while watching the moderately crowded road outside the courthouse.

"Not a word," she snarled at the humored man.

"But you look like such a lovely, young lady," Gil teased and couldn't keep from snickering.

"It's in the middle of the afternoon," she remarked. "I shouldn't have to wear a dress for an afternoon assignment."

"Tailing a lawyer at lunchtime, Jackie," Gil insisted. "Our Attorney Phelps has a lunch date after the arraignment of the guys from the ghost town. If we want to get into that restaurant, we need to look the part."

"Yeah?" she practically demanded then glared at Gil. "Who's paying for this expensive lunch?"

Gil eyed her and grinned. "I vote Monroe."

Jackie cast a look at Gil then laughed. Gil's cell phone rang from his jacket pocket. He removed his phone and placed it to his ear.

"Yeah, Monroe," Gil announced. "Did you find something on the car?"

"Registered to a man named Craig Dixon," Monroe announced over the cell phone. "I'm running a check on him now. I'll report back with more details."

"The lovely Jackie and I are on our way to the restaurant now," Gil announced then smiled and winked at Jackie, who rolled her eyes at the comment. "We'll meet you at the restaurant."

Kirk followed the expensive car carrying Attorney Phelps a few blocks then veered off as a taxi pulled out in front of him and continued to tail the car. Zack drove the taxi and wore his usual, casual clothing while Monroe sat in the back seat working on his laptop computer. Monroe was dressed stylishly fashionable in a suit, minus the tie, and a flashy purple vest. He rocked the look. He had expensive taste in clothes, and it showed. Monroe shut his laptop and placed it inside his leather briefcase.

"We're almost to the restaurant," Zack informed Monroe then cut off a car to get into the proper lane.

The car he'd just cut off slammed on its horn. Zack stuck his hand out the window and flipped him off with his middle finger. Monroe glanced at the car Zack had just flipped off and shook his head.

"You just gave the finger to a little, old lady," Monroe informed him.

"She started it," Zack informed him with little emotion.

The expensive car pulled up to the restaurant valet. Zack pulled over to the curb. Both watched Attorney Phelps and a neatly dressed, brawny man, presumably Dixon, get out of the car. Dixon handed the valet the keys and headed for the main entrance with the lawyer.

"Okay, you place a tracker on the car once valet parks it," Monroe informed Zack and moved for the door.

Zack turned partway around in the front seat and glared at Monroe while indicating the meter. "That's twenty-four dollars," Zack announced in all seriousness. "Don't forget to tip."

Monroe glared at Zack. "I'm not paying you," he insisted with irritation. "You stole the taxi."

"And Ahmed Zafar should be compensated," Zack informed him while tapping the taxi driver's credentials on the dash. "The guy probably has a family. Now fork over the fare, or I'll have to shoot you."

Monroe seemed to consider his options then groaned and gave Zack two bills.

Zack eyed the twenty and the five-dollar bill. He glared back at Monroe. "You're tipping the poor guy a buck?" he demanded and shook his head. "Open up the purse strings, you cheap bastard."

Monroe sneered at Zack and handed him another five-dollar bill. He then slipped out of the cab before Zack could extort more money from him. Monroe no sooner left the cab when a man attempted to open the back door.

"I'm off duty," Zack called out and pulled away from the restaurant leaving the man stunned on the curb.

The taxi cut off Jackie in her rental car. She slammed on the horn and shook her head in disbelief. Zack stuck his hand out the driver's side window and gave her the middle finger while driving away.

Jackie glared at Gil with an astonished look. "Was that Zack?" she demanded. "Did he just give me the middle finger?"

"I'm pretty sure it was Zack," Gil informed her as she pulled up to the valet. He then eyed her and grinned. "He really gets into character when he drives cab. He makes a convincing New York City cab driver."

Chapter 19

Gil proudly escorted Jackie, who was linked onto his arm, into the restaurant. The power couple approached Monroe as he waited by the host's podium. Monroe eyed the couple, who could easily pass for a politician and his trophy wife, and shook his head.

"I thought we decided on three business associates having lunch together," Monroe remarked.

"We did," Gil responded with little reaction. "My associate and I are having an affair."

Jackie grinned and affectionately patted Gil's arm. "We plan on stealing your idea and pitching it to the boss as our own."

Monroe stared at them a moment in disbelief then shook his head. "This is why Ross doesn't allow us to develop backstories for our characters."

"Admit it;" Gil teased, "you're just upset that you didn't think of it first."

"A little," Monroe muttered then indicated the dining room. "Our lawyer and his driver are already seated at their table. They appear to be waiting for someone else. I slipped the host a tip to seat us closer to their table."

All three approached the podium, and they were immediately shown their table by the enthusiastic host. They were seated only two tables away from Attorney Phelps and Dixon. Monroe chose the seat with his back to the wall and removed his laptop from the bag. He worked on the laptop while Gil and Jackie took turns keeping their eyes on the two men. Monroe eyed his two teammates and offered a devious grin.

"We have ears on them," Monroe announced proudly.

All three subtly touched their hidden ear transmitters to listen to the conversation coming from the table not far from theirs. They could hear the men making small talk loud and clear.

"How did you manage that?" Jackie asked.

"Othello sent me a new program he'd been working on," Monroe informed them. "I'm able to pair with their cell phones."

"So we're actually listening to them through their own cell phones?" Gil asked with surprise.

"As long as they have their cell phones turned on, we can use them as microphones to spy on them," Monroe replied.

Gil and Jackie exchanged looks then simultaneously removed their cell phones and shut them off. Jackie casually cast several looks across the restaurant and saw a handsome man in his mid-forties cross the room. Colonel Holloway caught the attention of nearly half the women in the restaurant. In addition to his undeniably good looks, he oozed charm and self-confidence. His expensive suit didn't hurt his cause either. Gil and Monroe immediately noticed Jackie's distracted attention and zeroed in on the handsome man.

"What's this?" Gil announced with surprise. "Jackie's checking out another man?"

"I never thought I'd see the day," Monroe scoffed teasingly.

Jackie looked away and blushed. She then glared at her teammates. "He has a striking resemblance to Holden, don't you think?"

"Nice save," Gil teased.

"Not on Holden's best day," Monroe remarked and wasn't about to let her off that easily.

"In another ten or so years," Jackie insisted and cast another peek at the handsome, sophisticated man.

"Maybe," Gil offered and shrugged, "if Holden suddenly became ungodly wealthy in the next ten years."

As Jackie stole another peek, her expression dropped. She eyed Gil and Monroe. "Guess who he's lunching with."

Monroe and Gil shifted in their chairs and looked around the room. They saw the handsome, refined man sitting with Attorney Phelps and Dixon.

"I'm guessing we just found the big man behind the search for Martin," Gil reported in a soft tone.

The three men shared few pleasantries since they were all well acquainted. Holloway seemed interested in getting right down to business.

"Anything to worry about?" Holloway asked Attorney Phelps.

The lawyer shook his head in response. "No, but the judge wouldn't grant bail," Phelps informed him. "I'm afraid they're going to be sidelined the entire season."

"Did they have anything interesting to say?" Holloway pressed.

"Definitely not feds," Attorney Phelps replied and shifted in his chair. "The three in town were believed to be a father and his two daughters, but our men are convinced they knew the people in the helicopter."

"Fifteen-year-old girl, right?" Holloway questioned with a curious look.

"Yes," Attorney Phelps responded. "How did--?"

"It's Cooper's daughter," Holloway informed him while casually picking up the laminated wine list. "That means those in the helicopter were feds."

"Why would you assume--?"

Colonel Holloway groaned and glared at his lawyer. "Because the girl's friend is the daughter of one of the FBI's higher-ups. I've done my homework, Phelps. I wish you'd earn your salary and do yours."

"The men didn't get a look at the pilot, and they can't identify the man firing at them," Phelps insisted, "but they did get a good look at the weapon he used. Our man insists it was military and not something a federal agent would be issued. They weren't feds."

"I'll have some people look into it," Holloway announced and seemed bored with the conversation. "Anything on our friend?"

"No, nothing," Phelps informed him.

The colonel appeared disappointed and dropped the wine menu on the table as he stood. "I need to make a phone call," he announced. "Order a bottle of 2009 Tusk Estates Cabernet Sauvignon."

As the colonel left the table, Jackie, Gil, and Monroe exchanged looks.

"We need to hear that call," Monroe announced. "We won't be able to hear him through the app if he's more than twenty feet away."

Jackie gracefully stood and offered a polite smile to her teammates. "Excuse me," she announced. "I have to powder my nose."

Both men smirked at the comment they'd never heard come from Jackie's mouth before.

Chapter 20

Jackie headed across the restaurant in the direction of the bar and the bathrooms. As Jackie entered the bar area, she caught a glimpse of the handsome man in a secluded corner at the bar with his cell phone to his ear. Jackie approached the nearly empty bar and signaled for the bartender. She was far enough away from Holloway that he wouldn't suspect she was eavesdropping but close enough that she could hear his one-sided exchange. Jackie listened to the beginning of his conversation, but the bartender was a little quick to approach her.

"Yes, ma'am," the bartender announced cheerfully while taking in a sweeping eyeful of Jackie in the simple dress that allowed a generous view of her ample cleavage.

Jackie was starting to realize that borrowing a dress off Pinto was probably a mistake.

"Could I have a shot of Tequila and a glass of wine?" she asked hoping to end the dialog quickly so that she might hear Holloway's conversation.

"Any particular wine for the lady?" the bartender pressed and instantly annoyed Jackie.

She didn't drink wine, but in a fancy restaurant, it seemed appropriate and less suspicious. Unfortunately, her knowledge of wine was extremely limited to red, white, and blush. Jackie needed to get rid of the bartender and said the first thing that came to mind.

"Tusk Estates Cabernet Sauvignon," she announced.

The bartender grinned. "Excellent choice."

Jackie heaved herself onto the pub chair at the bar with some difficulty. She wasn't used to maneuvering in a dress, particularly one as form fitting as Pinto wore. Jackie realized she'd need to cross her legs in order to maintain her refined appearance, forcing her to turn the chair slightly in order to do so. To her surprise, Colonel Holloway was now standing next to the bar near her.

"Forgive me," he announced almost a little too suavely while offering an intoxicating smile. "I overheard your drink order and my curiosity was immediately piqued."

Jackie cursed herself for ordering the same wine she had heard him order moments earlier. Had she been busted? The cork could be heard popping on the bottle of wine. Holloway looked at the bartender and signaled him to bring two glasses without saying a word. He returned his attention back to Jackie with commanding blue eyes.

"What prompts a lovely young lady to order an expensive glass of wine with a shot of tequila?" he asked while attempting to hide his grin.

Jackie didn't know her wine, but she was great at winging a lie. "I'm here on a boring business meeting," she informed him and indicated the dining room. "Trust me; sneaking shots of tequila is the only way to survive."

Holloway's grin increased as he chuckled warmly in his throat then indicated the vacant seat. "May I?'

She raised her brows and indicated the seat next to hers. He sat on the stool about as straight and proper as humanly possible. Something about the man instantly struck a chord with Jackie, and she now realized what it was. He was a military officer! She'd stake her life on it. Now she understood why she had been so captivated by this man the moment she saw him. His mannerisms and the way he carried himself were almost identical to her father! As the bartender approached with an expensive glass of wine and a shot of tequila for each, Holloway exchanged looks with the man.

"Put it on my tab," Holloway announced.

"Yes, Colonel," the bartender replied.

Jackie felt her heart skip a beat. He was the same rank as her father but from a different branch of the military. Her father was a Navy SEAL Commander. Being a colonel meant this man was Army. It was too late to hide her intrigued look at the bartender's response.

"You're a colonel?" she asked while raising a curious brow.

"Retired," he replied with a humored smile. "Last Friday, as a matter-of-fact." Holloway suavely extended his hand while maintaining firm finger and hand position. "Colonel Thomas Holloway."

At least now, they knew the man's name. Jackie accepted his hand and anticipated a firm handshake but received something more sensual in nature. Between the handshake and the manner in which he gazed into her eyes, it was almost enough to make her uncomfortable. It felt as if he were ravishing her with his gaze.

"Jackie," she replied without offering her last name.

Once he released her hand, he lifted the shot glass of tequila and held it up in a toast. Jackie hesitated and picked up her shot glass as well.

"The liver is evil and must be punished," he announced then drank the shot of tequila.

Jackie chuckled in her throat while grinning and held up her glass. "To hell," she came back with her own toast, "may the stay there be as fun as the way there." She downed the shot and managed to keep from choking on the strong liquor.

Colonel Holloway laughed at her speech while maintaining eye contact as if attempting to hypnotize her with his blue eyes. "And here I thought this would be just another boring lunch meeting."

Jackie immediately tensed although maintaining her smile. "I appreciate the drink, Colonel," she informed him, "but you should know I'm happily married."

He barely let the comment sink in before responding. "I apologize for any misunderstandings," Holloway announced cheerfully. "I'm in a committed relationship myself." His smile broadened. "I'm just a terrible flirt. At my age; I'm pretty sure the term for it is 'dirty old man'."

Jackie couldn't help but stare at him after the comment. His brutal honesty was almost humorous. She managed a laugh even though she didn't believe his intentions were quite so innocent.

"Hey," Gil announced from nearby.

Jackie looked a few feet from the bar and saw Gil eyeing them with a stern look. He looked as if he were about to scold her, but she knew he was just concerned that she had been away longer than expected.

"I thought you were going to the lady's room?" Gil remarked and cast a suspicious and almost dirty look at Holloway.

Jackie just about jumped off the bar stool and took two quick steps to Gil. She placed her arms around his waist and offered Holloway a smile.

"This is my husband, Gil," she announced.

Although Gil must have been stunned to hear the news regarding his new and unexpected bride, he didn't react either way. The way he stared at Holloway was slightly concerning. Gil was considered mellow, but he often came across as stern and emotionless.

Holloway stood and extended his hand to Gil. "Colonel Holloway," he announced.

Gil reluctantly shook his hand and received the firm handshake Jackie had been expecting. Judging by the look Gil gave Colonel Holloway, Jackie was glad he wasn't actually her husband. Perhaps his somewhat jealous appearance was what caused so many rifts between him and his on-again-off-again ex-wife.

"I was just complimenting your wife on her excellent taste in wine," Holloway announced in an attempt to put Gil at ease of his intentions. "She's a lovely woman. You're a lucky man."

"I'd like to think so," Gil replied although his expression remained stern.

Colonel Holloway had no way of knowing Gil was just being Gil and possibly wanted to avoid another *misunderstanding* with a jealous husband.

"I should get back to my associates," Holloway announced and gave Jackie a polite nod. "It was nice meeting you."

Holloway collected his glass of wine and headed into the dining room while maintaining his commanding presence despite what must have been an awkward moment. Gil casually pulled Jackie into his arms, met her gaze, and suddenly grinned.

"Was I just promoted?" he teased.

Jackie patted his chest while staring into his eyes. "If I had to be married to one of the guys; you're the least likely to piss me off."

"I think that was a compliment," Gil remarked while chuckling. He kissed her quickly on the lips before releasing her then grinned. "I can't wait to tell Monroe."

Jackie snatched her glass of wine from the bar and glared at Gil as they headed back into the restaurant. "You'll do no such thing."

He eyed her and grinned as they walked together. "Can I at least tell Holden?"

She latched onto his arm and gave it a firm tug. "I want a divorce."

Chapter 21

Thursday, June 26th. Five o'clock in the morning. An abandoned factory was nestled in a field not far from a small town just outside Colorado Springs. The main factory floor was still moderately cluttered with machinery, conveyor belts, crates, and all types of junk. Open metal steps led to the second floor, which consisted of two offices containing interior glass walls to observe the manufacturing floor below. The main office was still furnished, although everything was decayed after years of abandonment. There was an old desk, a broken chair, and some rusted filing cabinets. A few of the interior windows looking down on the factory floor were broken as well. Beyond the desk, lying on the floor was a twin mattress that had seen better days. An old, tattered blanket covered a sleeping man.

The sleeping man, Martin Cooper, had a full head of thick, dark hair that was in need of a trim. His facial stubble suggested he hadn't shaved in nearly a week, and the dark circles beneath his eyes indicated the once handsome man hadn't slept much either. Although he was a tall, moderately muscular man, he was possibly malnourished, lacking food as well as sleep for quite some time. His clothes continued with the trending theme, suggesting he had been homeless for several weeks if not longer. A faint, metallic clatter sounded. Despite looking exhausted, Martin immediately woke, grabbed an assault rifle carefully hidden alongside the mattress, and sprang to his feet. He crouched down to avoid being seen through the office windows on the second floor, crept to the partially open door, and peered onto the factory floor below. Although he didn't see anyone, he could hear someone prowling around among the mess downstairs. By the sounds of it, there were several uninvited guests.

Two men appeared at the bottom of the stairs. They were dressed in identical black combat uniforms and carried automatic weapons. There was no doubt who they were and why they were there. Martin picked up a loose wire lying on the floor and attached it to a nail in the doorframe. He then crept back to his makeshift bed and hurriedly slipped into his black military boots. He pulled on his shirt and light jacket containing many pockets, which possibly held everything he owned. Martin grabbed a semiautomatic from beneath his pillow, placed it down the back of his pants, and hurried for a cardboard box in the corner of the room.

He quietly pulled the box away from the wall to reveal a large hole. Martin pushed the assault rifle through the opening then crawled in after it. He reached back into the room and pulled the box back into place, once again covering the hole. Two men appeared by the partially open office door. The first man pushed open the door, which struck the tripwire. By the time he heard the door scraping the thin wire; it was already too late. The taut wire pulled the trigger of a shotgun attached to a vice on the floor. The angled shotgun fired from only a few feet away, striking the man in the chest.

The second man jumped with surprise and watched his mangled, bloodied partner fall to the floor. The remaining man became enraged and aimed his weapon into the empty room. He carefully stepped over his dead teammate, checked behind the door, and then looked to the floor at the recently slept in bed. He returned to the doorway and peered out.

"He's not here," he called to the floor below.

Three men dressed in black combat gear appeared in various corners of the factory floor.

"We heard gunfire," the first man called up to him.

"Tripwire," the man from upstairs called back. "Desi is down."

The first man on ground level, apparently the man in charge, turned angry and waved his weapon. "Search the entire area," he cried out. "He has to be here somewhere. Find him!" The man then hesitated and reconsidered his comment. "Remember, we need him alive."

The three men on the factory floor quickly dispersed and started their hunt. The man within the second floor office was about to leave when he heard something behind him. He spun around and saw Martin standing only a foot away from him. He attempted to aim his weapon, but Martin was already lunging for him. Martin shoved the man against the wall while placing his hand over his mouth to prevent any noise and stabbed him in the neck with a Bowie knife. The man muffled a gasp beneath Martin's hand. Martin pulled the knife free, allowing the blood to pour from his neck wound. As the man swiftly bled out, Martin lowered him to the floor to keep the falling body from making any sound.

Martin wiped the blood from the knife blade onto the man's sleeve, replaced it to his boot, and reclaimed his assault rifle that he had slung over his shoulder. He silently approached the door and peered out. The three men had already moved on to continue their sweep of the factory. Martin slipped out the doorway and silently crept down the open, metal steps. Despite making some noise, the remaining men would assume it was their man joining them. Once he reached the bottom, he slipped behind some old, rusted machinery and took a lookout position for the remaining men.

He had two of the three men in his sight, but he could only get a clear shot at one. He'd need to stand up straight in order to get the second man. The first man was moving from his line of fire. Martin took the shot, striking the man in the chest. As the man went down, Martin immediately straightened and shot the second man in the shoulder. The third man made his presence known and fired back from the left. Martin ducked behind the machinery as the automatic weapon fire echoed throughout the abandoned factory. He darted along the back wall while keeping low to the floor as the two remaining men fired at the machinery where he once hid.

The injured man ran for the machinery under cover of his teammate's gunfire. He stepped around the machinery with his assault rifle aimed and discovered Martin was gone. As the armed man slipped behind the clutter against the wall, Martin crawled into a small opening. Martin set his rifle down and removed his semiautomatic since he had little room to maneuver. From his hidden position, he could see the leader across the factory making his way toward his partner's location. Martin remained still and silent, listening for either man now out of his view. He could hear the first man approaching from his right. He now had no idea of the second man's position, but he couldn't risk waiting to find out. He needed to make his move.

The first man came into view and looked directly into the small opening Martin occupied. Martin fired first, shooting the man in the head, and knocking him backward into the wall. Despite that the gunshot echoed and made it nearly impossible to tell where it originated, the clatter of the man and his weapon striking the metal wall was enough to give away his location. Without knowing where the second man had gone, Martin darted out of the opening with his semiautomatic aimed in the only logical direction. The second man wasn't there. He could hear him running along the back wall, where he must have seen his fallen partner.

Martin attempted to move as quickly as possible with little noise, but it was counterproductive. There was a loud clatter. Martin turned while crouching with his weapon aimed. The second man was on top of an old conveyer belt and fired at him. Martin fired back and rolled out of the way. As he took cover, he ejected his empty magazine and swiftly replaced it with a full one. He could hear the man jump off the conveyor belt followed by silence. The gunman was approaching despite that he heard nothing. He mentally counted the steps in his mind and knew the man was nearly upon him. As light entered the old factory from the dirty, elevated windows, Martin could now see the man's shadow.

The man was so close Martin could hear him breathe. Martin waited for one more step before springing into a forward roll and sat up with his gun aimed. He caught the man in his sights, since he had a good idea of his exact position, and fired two shots. The man fired his weapon at the same time and grazed Martin's leg. From his crouched position, the shot had narrowly missed his head that had been close to his knee. His first shot hit the man in the shoulder and the second got him in the chest. The man fell to the concrete floor and no longer moved.

Martin clutched his bleeding leg with one hand and removed his belt with his free hand. He tied his belt around his upper thigh above the bullet wound. Despite only being a graze, it bled freely. He could hear someone driving up the gravel driveway. Martin cursed under his breath, collected his semiautomatic, and hurried for the back entrance as fast as he could limp. Despite the pain shooting through his leg, he made it from the building and ran for the woods.

Chapter 22

Back at the Colorado lodge. It was just after breakfast that morning. Jackie lounged on one of the lobby sofas near the large window with her legs extended across the seat. The sun was shining upon her while she flipped through a tactical weapons magazine. She was actually alone for the first time in days and thought she would enjoy the peace and quiet. Unfortunately, her mind was wandering. Had she gotten so used to chaos and mayhem that she couldn't handle quiet time anymore? She heard the old building settle, being used to the creaks, but this one sounded different. Jackie looked around the lobby, but she was still alone. She again attempted to get into her magazine. She heard a frighteningly familiar metallic sound and tensed.

Jackie lowered her magazine and saw the tip of a samurai sword aimed at her face. Her eyes strayed up the glimmering metal blade to see Zack holding the sword looking like a homicidal ninja. Despite his serious look, she groaned and returned to her magazine.

"Not today, Zack," she announced with little reaction. "I have a headache."

Zack lowered the sword with a groan and frowned. "I'm bored."

"Go outside and play," she insisted.

"Only if you come out and play with me," he announced then grinned almost deviously.

She cast a look at him above her magazine. Jackie knew exactly what sort of play he had in mind, and she wasn't going to fall for it.

"Play with Monique and Colleen," she remarked.

"They don't like the way I play."

"No one likes the way you play," Jackie muttered. "At least they're willing participants."

Zack carelessly dropped the sword on the coffee table, which clattered loudly, and cast himself onto the sofa in the narrow space between the back of the sofa and her legs. He planted his booted feet on the coffee table with a thump rattling her teacup. Jackie attempted to move her legs out from beneath him, but he already had her partially trapped. He leaned closer, wedging himself alongside where she sat and eyed the open magazine in her hand. Zack indicated the picture of a belt buckle with a removable shiv.

"If you're Christmas shopping, I wouldn't mind one of those," he announced.

"Don't you have ten deadly belt buckles already?" she asked while casting a look at his face not far from hers.

"Fifteen," he replied. "But who's counting. Besides, that one would go well with dress pants."

Jackie again eyed him and raised her brows. "Since when do you wear dress pants?"

"I can name ten times in the last year," he replied sounding almost offended. "You people insist on dressing me up and forcing me to socialize."

"No one forces *you* to socialize, Zack," Jackie replied. "That was a failed experiment."

Zack groaned, pulled the magazine from her hand, and tossed it onto the coffee table. She glared at him while he stared back.

"Come outside and play with me," he again insisted. "If you don't, I'm taking a nap right here."

Jackie realized Zack was attempting to intimidate her with his gaze. She stared back and refused to look away first or give in. When he stared back without even blinking, she realized she wasn't ready for a stare-off contest with Zack.

"Fine," Jackie scoffed with annoyance and tore her eyes away from his gaze. "I'll play with you if you include Monique and Colleen."

Zack tossed his head back against the sofa and groaned. "Why are you pushing those two on me?" he demanded then glared at her. "Isn't that considered child abuse?"

"They adore you," Jackie insisted then considered the comment. "Although, I'm not sure why. They're hopelessly fascinated by you."

"Isn't everyone?" he muttered while sneering. "I'm a fucking lab experiment." Zack resumed his glare. "You're obsessed with pushing those kids on me. I'm not a babysitter, and I'm terrible with children."

"They're not children; they're teenagers," she reminded him.

"Even worse," Zack remarked then frowned. "They bruise easily."

Jackie shot a look at him. "I didn't say you should rough them up," she scoffed.

"Then what the hell am I supposed to do with them? Catch fireflies?" Zack gave her a stern look. "I'm not Monroe. I don't 'do' nice." He then frowned. "Girls scream a lot too. That shrill, ear-piercing scream."

Jackie gave him a cold stare. "I think I'm offended," she scoffed. "You didn't seem to mind me while I was growing up. I'm told I followed you around from the time I was able to walk."

"Yeah, you were annoying too," he groaned.

She rolled her eyes and again attempted to pull her legs out from under his. Zack applied zero effort to keep her from moving, but she couldn't move out from under his legs. He was obviously comfortable.

"Is that why you'd spent all that time with me?" she snapped back. "You certainly didn't mind being annoyed back then."

"That was different," he insisted.

"How was that different?"

He tensed and attempted to avoid the conversation. "I thought I'd be a father one day," Zack muttered. "You were a trial run. A failed experiment." He seemed a little too eager to quote her earlier comment.

Jackie glared at him and again attempted to move out from under him. "You think I'm a failed experiment?" she demanded. "I turned out pretty damned good, I'll have you know."

"Of course you did, but not because of me," he reminded her. "That was all Jackson."

"No," she insisted. "That was Whiskey Tango Foxtrot. All of you were my family growing up. Some of the faces may have changed over the years, but I have nothing but wonderful memories of my family."

He placed his hand on hers and affectionately patted it. "Oh, you poor, clueless little girl." Zack shook his head and sighed. "We ruined you." He hesitated then frowned. "I ruined you."

Jackie placed her hand over her eyes and groaned. "Don't start with that again."

He glared demandingly at her and raised his brows. "How long until I get you killed?" Zack frowned and shook his head. "I blame Holden."

"Now it's Holden's fault if you get me killed?" she demanded. "You're in rare form this morning. How is Holden to blame?"

"He should put his foot down," Zack boldly announced. "He should keep you away from all of us. We're like a basket of venomous snakes. If he loved you, he'd take you far away. Run back to Virginia where you both belong." He met her gaze with his own serious one. "Give it up, Jackie. Make some babies and live a happy life far from us. We're nothing but poison."

Jackie stared at Zack a long moment and knew his rantings were her own fault. She insisted on digging into his psyche and wanted him to open up to her. Now that he was opening up, she caught glimpses into his dark world of self-loathing. Zack carried his emotions deep inside him allowing them to fester and rot. No matter what he did or how cold he pretended to be, those emotions were still with him. Jackie placed her arms around him and pulled his head to her chest. Zack immediately clung to her and nuzzled her chest like a child with his mother. Although Zack often acted as if he didn't care about anyone or anything, most times he just needed to be coddled.

"My God," Monroe scoffed from across the lobby. "Get a room."

Zack sighed unnaturally against Jackie's chest. "I'm going to kill him."

Jackie sometimes wanted to kill Monroe too. He had amazing timing. Whenever she was making progress with giving Zack much needed emotional support, Monroe had a tendency to show up and make it into something depraved. Jackie understood why Monroe reacted the way he did. He was jealous of her relationship with Zack. Jealous and he didn't understand it. If Jackie dared even hug Monroe, in his mind, she was leaving Holden for him. Zack could practically hump Jackie while play fighting and break a man's neck two seconds later without conflict.

Zack attempted to pull away, but Jackie refused to release him. She wasn't just trying to keep him relaxed but also keep Monroe from a deserved beating. When Pinto entered the lobby with Marie, it was time to call an end to Zack's therapy session. Zack moved off Jackie's legs, sprang to his feet, and headed across the lobby where he could avoid people.

"Jackie," Pinto announced while offering an unusually pleasant smile. "I'm taking Marie and the girls on a little nature walk and maybe pick some blueberries."

Jackie cast a look at Pinto with great interest.

Pinto raised her brows as if secretly sending a message then offered a curious look. "Did you want to come along?" she asked.

"Uh, thanks, but no," Jackie replied and managed a smile. "When you decide to go target shooting or have paintball battles, I'm game."

Pinto laughed at the comment then motioned Marie toward the door. "The girls are already outside with Darth," she announced.

Monroe and Zack grew increasingly curious as they watched Pinto and Marie leave the lobby. Once the door closed, all three exchanged looks.

"Obviously something happened," Monroe announced with some concern.

"Yes, the ever popular blueberry picking nature walk," Jackie remarked. "I assume that's our cue to meet Ross in the conference room."

"The kitchen," Monroe corrected.

She eyed him. "That's what I said."

Chapter 23

The team gathered around the large kitchen table that comfortably seated all eight. Darth had skipped out on the meeting and had accompanied the ladies on their nature walk. The dog seemed more interested in playing the role of family pet rather than badass team member while they had teenage visitors. The six men and Jackie waited patiently to see why Ross had called a meeting. It undoubtedly wouldn't be anything good. It was usually bad news.

Ross leaned back in his chair and frowned. "Less than an hour ago, a sheriff's office in some off the map town picked up Martin Cooper," he announced while fiddling with his pen. "A couple of kids found him unconscious alongside a small stream with a gunshot wound to his leg. He was covered in blood." Ross shifted looks at the others and drew a deep breath. "Most of the blood wasn't his own."

Bogart seemed to take the news more personal than the others did and shifted uncomfortably in his chair.

"I radioed Holden twenty minutes ago," Ross continued, "and he told me they'd been called to a remote, abandoned factory two hours earlier by a local family who thought they heard gunshots. A lot of gunshots. They found the bodies of five men in the old factory."

"Let me guess," Kirk announced with little emotion and even less concern. "Martin Cooper was picked up a few miles from there."

Ross nodded. "After a quick patch job at the local clinic, he was moved to the sheriff's office in town. Holden was securing the necessary paperwork to pick up Martin from the sheriff's office when the United States Army declared it a military matter," he informed them. "They're sending some MPs tomorrow morning to fetch Martin and take him to Fort Hood for processing."

"Fort Hood?" Gil asked with some surprise. "Why Fort Hood? That's in Texas. Why not Fort Carson in Colorado Springs?"

"That's a good question," Ross replied.

"When I spoke with Martin, he told me he couldn't trust anyone," Bogart informed them. "He seemed to think his life was in danger from all sides."

"Did he tell you anything else?" Beck asked.

"Just that he was innocent, and he didn't do it," Bogart replied.

"Said every traitor ever," Kirk muttered while leaning back in his chair.

"Being I'm the nosy type," Ross announced as he eyed his team. "I contacted one of my old friends at Fort Carson. He doesn't seem to know anything about Martin Cooper. His file actually says he's MIA."

"We were told he was an Army deserter," Jackie announced.

"Colonel Bamford is going to poke around a little for me," Ross informed them. "In the meantime, he gave us permission to observe the situation and lend a hand."

"They contracted us to assist?" Monroe asked with some surprise.

"Not officially," Ross replied then smirked. "Sort of unofficially."

"Who's in charge of Martin's extradition?" Gil then asked with great interest while leaning on the table.

"Colonel Holloway," Ross replied. "He was Martin's C.O. prior to his, uh, disappearance."

"That's not the least bit suspicious," Monroe remarked with little emotion.

Gil and Jackie exchanged interested looks then returned their attention back to Ross.

"That's the guy we ran into at the restaurant," Jackie informed Ross. "He's the one who met with Attorney Phelps, the lawyer representing our friends from the ghost town."

"The same man who'd spent his entire lunch meeting ogling Jackie," Monroe reported. "That practically confirms he's the man behind the ghost town attack."

"If he has eyes for Jackie," Kirk announced and shifted looks around the table, "we could send her in--"

Everyone shot looks at Kirk almost threatening him from finishing that thought.

Kirk caught their stares and immediately frowned. "Why is it I'm the only one around here who gets volunteered to take one for the team?" he suddenly demanded.

Zack was about to speak when Ross held up his hand to silence him.

Ross casually glared at Kirk. "Ask Holden," he announced. "Then report back to me with his response." Ross looked around the table. "If Martin had been wrongly accused, and the colonel is in on it, it won't end well for anyone crossing him. Colonel Holloway has the Army on his side and access to every mercenary war ever created."

There was an odd silence within the room.

"Mercenaries? Sounds like fun," Zack announced and sprang up from his chair with a little too much enthusiasm. "I'm going to pack my fun bag and a toothbrush."

As Zack left the kitchen, Ross eyed the others. "We're only riding shotgun on this transport," he informed them. "Eagle One and Eagle Two will watch from the sky, and we'll have ground transport in the vicinity."

"If Martin is telling the truth," Bogart reminded them, "it's not the trip to Fort Hood that'll be the problem. Once he's inside that base, Colonel Holloway can make up any story he likes. If Martin is innocent as he claimed, he's as good as dead."

Ross nodded while frowning. "There's not much we can do about it," he replied and finally cast his pen aside. "Holden can't even touch this one, and he has more authority than we do."

"Colleen's father aside," Kirk announced and cocked his head. "Let's not forget the real possibility that Martin Cooper could be a deserter and a traitor." He shifted in his chair and thumped the table with his thick finger. "If that's the case, I say let them execute the bastard. Men like that get good men killed. Men we knew. Men that came home with a flag draped over their caskets."

Everyone squirmed in their chairs. Excluding Jackie and Bogart, they'd all lived similar nightmares involving their brothers in arms.

"We're not the tribunal here," Ross announced and eyed the others. "We're just the unauthorized escort. We bug out in twenty if we want to make that date. We'll keep eyes on the sheriff's office tonight and make sure nothing happens before the MPs arrive in the morning."

As everyone stood, Ross straightened and eyed his team before they could leave.

"Make no mistake, we're only doing this for that girl and her mother," Ross informed them. "If Martin Cooper is innocent, he deserves to come home. We're just going along for the ride to ensure he gets that trial." He then nodded them from the room.

The guys scattered to collect whatever gear they would need for the mission. Bogart and Jackie were about to leave when Ross stopped them.

"Someone needs to stay behind and keep an eye on Monique and Colleen," he informed Bogart.

Bogart's shoulders sagged with defeat. "I want to help," he announced. "I'm always being sidelined."

"And I'd think you'd be happy protecting those girls you love so much," Ross remarked with little regard to Bogart's feelings. "Out of everyone here, you're the only one who doesn't *speak* soldier. If we run into a situation, we can fall back on our rank and our affiliations. That makes you less useful out there and more useful here. Someone needs to keep an eye on those girls."

"Fine," Bogart huffed.

"Take them horseback riding," Ross announced a little more cheerfully and patted Bogart's shoulder. "They'll enjoy that. Pinto and Marie will be fine here by themselves. Pinto is familiar with the panic room."

"Beck locks her in it enough," Jackie muttered as she folded her arms across her chest.

"Beck needs to stop treating Pinto like china," Ross remarked with noted irritation. "Keep teaching her karate. Once she can kick his ass, he'll turn his overly protective attitude down a notch."

"Our schedules don't always line up," Jackie informed Ross. "Zack should give her some lessons now and again. He's here part-time."

Ross frowned and shook his head. "Zack has one mode; kill everything in sight," he remarked. "He's too aggressive for beginners."

"He helped my father teach me," she pointed out in Zack's defense.

"That was a different Zack," Ross informed her.

"I haven't noticed a difference," Jackie casually informed Ross and felt almost offended that he seemed to imply such a thing.

"No, you wouldn't," Ross remarked while seeming tense regarding the topic.

"What's that supposed to mean?" Jackie demanded while folding her arms across her chest.

It was one of the few times that Jackie took a defensive tone with Ross. Being he was like a second father to her, she seldom spoke that way to him, and he noticed. Bogart remained close by and waited to see what happened next.

"You're too close to him," Ross insisted to Jackie and seemed unusually tense. "He's on his best behavior around you."

Jackie wanted to comment on that since she hardly thought the way he acted around her could be considered 'good behavior', but she would then be confirming what Ross was attempting to convey.

"You don't see how he's changed since you were a little girl," Ross continued. "There's a reason he's been 'retired' so many times. After that last concussion, I'm wondering if it isn't time to retire him again."

"I don't think you can make that decision for him," Jackie remarked and felt her hostility toward Ross rising. She never felt anger toward Ross before, and it bothered her.

"Exactly," Ross announced. "He wouldn't go quietly." He then became tense. "And he wouldn't go anywhere without you."

"I'm not going anywhere either," Jackie remarked then tilted her head. "Are you suggesting I retire too?"

"No, of course not," Ross proclaimed. "We need your piloting skills." He drew a deep breath while staring into her eyes. "All I'm saying is, if Zack were to leave, he undoubtedly take you with him."

"I just told you I'm not going anywhere," she again repeated and wondered why Ross wasn't listening to her.

Ross held his breath while staring at her. "I'm suggesting he may not give you a choice."

"Wait," Bogart suddenly announced with concern. "Are you suggesting Zack is capable of abducting Jackie?"

"Zack is capable of just about anything," Ross continued in all seriousness.

Bogart sank into thought. Jackie frowned and shook her head. She wondered if she should tell Ross the things she and Zack had discussed. He'd then know what he was suggesting was completely off base. She held her breath. No, she couldn't betray his confidence. She promised to keep things he told her between them, and she couldn't go back on that promise.

"We're not having this conversation," Jackie finally insisted and left no room for debate. "Whatever you think Zack is going through, I'll deal with it."

Ross lightly threw his hands in the air and shook his head. "You're just as stubborn as he is," he announced with a defeated sigh. "You make a great team."

Chapter 24

Evening. The police station was a small, two-story building that appeared to have apartments for lease on the second floor. It was possibly one of the smallest police stations Ross and Kirk had seen in their time. The building was basic gray block stone with a few windows and some shrubs to give it a homey, small-town appeal. Ross and Kirk approached the main entrance. Ross held the door open for a beautiful woman with a sexy librarian appeal. She had her hands full while carrying several books and fumbling with her cell phone. The reserved yet sexy looking woman offered a thankful smile above her thick-rimmed glasses as she passed them. Ross attempted to sneak a peek without looking as if he were looking. Kirk's head turned so fast, he nearly gave himself whiplash. A lustful grin crossed the brawny man's face as he turned to follow the woman.

"I'll catch up with you," Kirk announced as he attempted to leave.

"Get back here," Ross growled.

Kirk frowned and entered the small building behind Ross. The building housed the mayor's office to the right and the sheriff's station to the left. They entered the sheriff's station and approached one of two desks in the main room. There was only one officer on duty that they could see. There was an office to the right, and the lockup was to the left. The door to the lockup area, which contained the cells, was solid steel and seemed sturdy enough. Kirk scanned the room and mentally took stock. He didn't seem impressed. The officer appeared bored and looked at the two intimidating men before his desk with little reaction. The deputy was a small, scrawny man with a slightly clueless look about him yet somehow he reeked of arrogance. Kirk managed a tiny laugh at what must have been crossing his mind and scratched his brow.

"Welcome to Mayberry," Kirk muttered to Ross, who easily ignored him.

"Can I help you gentlemen?" the officer asked while leaning back in his moderately old, rolling chair.

"I'm Ross, and that's Kirk," he announced. "Agent Falcone should have contacted you about our arrival."

The officer looked at him a moment and appeared curious. "Are you with the military?"

"No, we're your backup," Kirk announced with some irritation. His patience with the small town deputy was already dwindling.

"Oh, that," the officer remarked with little interest. "If you boys want to waste your time and hang out, that's fine with me, but I don't know what's the big deal. He's an Army deserter, not a criminal mastermind."

Kirk placed his fingers over his eyes and groaned at the deputy's ignorance.

"It's our time to waste," Ross informed him. "I'm not sure you grasp the importance of this particular soldier in your custody. If he's lying, you have nothing to worry about. If he's telling the truth, you could have some unsavory characters breaking down your door to get to him."

"If he's that important, why didn't the military send someone to get him right away?" the deputy asked while grinning slyly.

"Any number of reasons," Ross replied and seemed to consider the question. "Even an inside job requires collaboration from all those involved. That can be difficult in itself."

The deputy gave him a surprised look. "You think someone from the military may have reason to want him out of the picture?"

"It's one of many possibilities," Ross replied and nodded. "More than likely, nothing will happen here tonight. Even if it's an inside job, I doubt they'd try anything during transport. Not everyone would be involved. They'd wait until they reached their destination." He then stared at the officer with a serious look. "Or it'll happen before the escort arrives and reduce paperwork and red tape."

The officer stared at him with concern and straightened. "I hope you're just being paranoid."

"I'm not paranoid," Ross replied then grinned playfully. "I'm excessively prepared. Kirk and I will remain in the office with you until the transport arrives tomorrow morning. We also have some men scattered around outside. If something happens, we'll do our best to contain it." He then pointed to the holding cells. "Do you mind if I introduce myself to the prisoner?"

The deputy removed his keys from the desk and approached the door. "Knock yourself out."

§

Ross entered the holding area and approached the cell containing Martin, who sat on his cot with his back against the wall. He cast a disinterested look at Ross then appeared curious.

"You're not the deputy," Martin announced as his body involuntarily tensed.

"No, I'm Ross," he replied while pausing before the bars and leaned against them.

122

"Are you here to kill me?" Martin asked without taking his eyes off him.

Ross smirked and appeared almost humored by the question. "Well, you never know," he replied. "But for the moment, I'm tasked with keeping you alive."

"You're not with the Army," Martin remarked without moving from his cot.

"I thought about joining the Army once, but the recruiter told me my balls were too big," Ross replied without cracking a smile. "So I became a Navy SEAL instead."

Martin appeared interested and raised his brows. "I suppose I'd normally counter with a crack about the Navy, but I have enough people who want me dead already. Why the honor of your visit?" He offered a tiny grin. "The Navy want a piece of my ass as well?"

Ross eyed him. "I somehow think you meant that as a dig."

"No, just a happy coincidence," Martin replied and smiled for the first time. "Seriously though. Why would the Army send a Navy SEAL?"

"They didn't send me," he replied. "I answer to a higher calling."

"Oh?"

"A fifteen-year-old girl named Colleen Cooper," Ross replied and studied the man for a reaction.

Martin's expression instantly dropped at the remark. He jumped from his cot and lunged for the bars while staring at Ross.

"Colleen?" he gasped and looked toward the main lockup door. "She's not here, is she?"

"No, she's safe with some friends of mine," Ross informed him. "The poor girl just found out her father was alive. I don't want her going through the pain of losing him all over again."

Martin's shoulders sagged as he exhaled and shook his head with remorse. "Do you know how long it's been since I've seen my baby?"

"More than five years, I believe," Ross replied without giving it much thought.

"She must hate me," Martin muttered.

"Quite possibly," Ross remarked with little intention of making the man feel any better. "Maybe you'll have the opportunity to find out for yourself."

Martin shook his head and couldn't bear to look up. "I'm not sure I can face her or her mother." He then cast a look at Ross. "How do you know my daughter?" He hesitated and seemed to tense at the next question. "Are you a *friend* of Marie's?"

Ross grinned and chuckled. "No, I'm not your wife's boyfriend," he replied. "Lovely woman, though. We made her acquaintance through Donna's husband. My associate is married to one of his subordinates."

"Is that why you're here?"

"My team and I are here to give your military escort an escort," Ross informed him. "We can't protect you once you're taken onto the base at Fort Hood, but we can make certain you make it there in one piece."

"You're wasting your time," Martin muttered.

"Why does everyone keep telling me that?" Ross remarked and shook off the comment then grinned. "I'm retired. I have all the time in the world."

"Considering they're going to kill me sooner or later," Martin replied with defeat, "I guess it doesn't really matter which it is."

"Care to tell me about it?" Ross asked while raising a clever brow as he leaned against the bars. "One of my men said he had a run in with you at the old ghost town. You told him you were innocent."

He appeared surprised and stared at Ross. "That guy was one of yours?"

Ross shrugged. "I suppose I can't keep denying it," he remarked. "It looks bad, and Jackie gets mad at me when I insult him."

"I'm innocent," Martin announced but appeared defeated. "I'd rather not get into it. There's no point involving anyone else."

"I'm already involved," Ross countered.

"No, you're just here. It's best if we left it that way," Martin remarked then returned to his cot.

It was obvious Martin had been through a lot the last five years. Despite his time on the run, he seemed to have lost any spark that had been left. He was defeated and broken. Colleen's father aside, the man was possibly an Army deserter and a traitor. He wasn't about to get any sympathy from Ross or the team.

Chapter 25

Katrina walked along the basement corridor within Colonel Holloway's mansion. Her long hair was pulled up into a messy bun, allowing stray locks to add to her sexy librarian look. The stunning beauty wore a black, formfitting skirt with a revealing slit up the back. The white silk blouse she wore was nearly see-through and had enough buttons open to reveal plenty of cleavage. Katrina's black heels were daringly high, giving her legs an even sexier appeal. She entered the room at the end of the hall just in time to see a man being shot in the head only a few feet away from her. Tiny speckles of blood-spattered her white shirtsleeve. The man's lifeless body fell just short of her feet, his blood swiftly pooling around his head. Katrina casually stepped over the dead man and approached Holloway as he replaced his semiautomatic containing a silencer to his hidden shoulder holster.

Dixon and six equally brawny men stood around the conference table and now stared with little reaction or emotion at the dead man on the floor. Katrina hadn't been present for whatever had transpired before her arrival, and she didn't seem to care either. She paused before Holloway and extended a flash drive to him. His eyes swept across her body as did the eyes of the other men in the room.

"Any problems?" Colonel Holloway asked as he accepted the flash drive while allowing his fingers to graze her hand affectionately.

She offered a tiny, humored smile at the question. "Are you kidding?" Katrina remarked. "If I had undone one more button, the deputy probably would have turned Cooper over to me."

Holloway inserted the flash drive into the USB port of his laptop and pulled up the photos taken on Katrina's cell phone. He studied the layout of the sheriff's office and the building where it was located. He saw a picture of Martin in his cell taken from the detention room doorway.

Holloway cast a look at Katrina and appeared almost humored. "He let you look in the holding cells?" he asked with surprise.

Katrina removed a pair of thick-rimmed, sexy librarian glasses and slipped them on. She cast a suggestive look at him just above the glasses.

"Honey, he would have given me his badge and gun if I'd asked nicely," she teased.

Holloway groaned then laughed. "I'll bet he would have," he announced then turned his laptop toward Dixon. "Here's the sheriff's office and detention area." He then leaned closer to Katrina and whispered near her ear. "Don't change out of that, okay?"

She grinned her response to his request.

Holloway sat on the edge of the table and eyed Dixon. "What do you think?"

Dixon shrugged and straightened. "Like robbing a candy store," he replied. "A dozen or so men, four Humvees will converge on the town from the east and west. They'll never know what hit them."

"This isn't Fort Knox," Katrina scoffed while glaring at Dixon as she replaced the librarian glasses to her blouse pocket. "It's a little town the size of a zit. Give me a slingshot, and I could bust Cooper out of there."

"The FBI is involved," Dixon snarled back at her. "This is my mission, and I give the orders, princess."

Holloway groaned and covered his eyes. "Oh, boy," he muttered.

"Princess?" Katrina snarled in anger and folded her arms across her chest. "Call me princess again, and I'll shove my six-inch stiletto heel up your ass!"

"Why is this bitch even here?" one of the men suddenly demanded.

"Hey," Holloway shouted in anger. "That *bitch* will rip your throat out, so show a little respect."

"We're getting a little tired of you taking her side on everything," the man announced. "We didn't have any problems until she showed up. She's not even a part of this team."

"I'm in charge here," Holloway snapped back. "And she's a part of *my* team. I don't like having my authority threatened."

"And I don't like taking orders from some whore," the man lashed out in response.

There was some grumbling among the men around the table. Dixon seemed to distance himself from the argument to see where the chips were going to fall before inserting himself into the situation.

"Do you have a problem with the way I'm running my operation?" Colonel Holloway demanded then pointed toward the door. "There's the door. Consider yourself relieved of duty."

The man sneered at Holloway and took a step toward the door. Without warning, the man drew his weapon and had it aimed at the colonel before anyone even realized what had happened. Katrina grabbed the man's wrist and twisted his arm, forcing him to drop the gun. She spun into a roundhouse kick and slashed him across the face with her six-inch heel. He stumbled back from the hit and clutched his face that now bled from her stiletto shoe. Katrina easily caught her balance despite the height of her heels. The man was momentarily stunned as were the rest of the men in the room. Katrina glanced at Holloway. He frowned and gave her a quick signal with his hand.

Katrina took a swift step toward the man, who attempted to punch her. She blocked his fist, caught his arm, and rammed her elbow into his abdomen. When he doubled over, she caught him around the neck and threw her entire body into her grip. His neck snapped from the force. She released his head and stepped aside as he fell to the floor. The remaining five men stared at the dead man and the sexy woman who'd killed him. She glared back at the men without emotion.

"Anyone else have a problem with the way I run things around here?" the colonel demanded.

The five men returned their attention to Holloway and remained silent.

"Good," he announced with a smirk then looked at Katrina. "It's nothing personal, Kat, but we'll let Dixon handle this operation his way."

She frowned her irritation. "You know I can do it with less mess and less drama," Katrina insisted.

"Perhaps," Holloway replied. "But we want this to look like Cooper pissed off the wrong people, which is precisely why we don't want to wait until we have him back at Fort Hood. Too much red tape when a man dies in the brig."

"I'd like to go along," she announced despite her disappointment in his decision.

Holloway frowned and seemed less than enthusiastic by her request. "If you feel you must," he replied.

Dixon rolled his eyes at Holloway's response then looked at the remaining four men. "We leave in a few hours," he announced. "Get some rest."

"And someone clean up this mess," Holloway announced while indicating the two dead men on the floor. He then turned toward Katrina and gave her a stern look. "We need to discuss the way you always undermine my authority. In my office."

Holloway nodded to the hallway door. Katrina showed no emotion as she headed for the door and stepped over the dead man. As she stepped into the hallway, she removed the librarian glasses from her shirt pocket and placed them on her face. Holloway hid his smile as he followed her from the room. The moment the door closed, Dixon frowned and shook his head.

"She'd better watch her own ass out there," Dixon snarled while folding his arms across his broad chest. "I'm not protecting Holloway's little playmate."

"Maybe she'll have an accident," another man remarked then eyed Dixon.

There was an unusual silence as Dixon eyed the other man. A tiny grin crossed his face. "You never know," Dixon replied then snickered.

A round of low chuckles followed.

Chapter 26

Friday, June 27th. It was a little after four in the morning. Despite the small town element, Jackie was able to land her helicopter on the upper level of a small parking garage a couple of blocks from the police station. Even though the garage was only four stories, the elevated position was enough to keep a bird's eye view on the police station. Monroe was stretched out on the bench seat in the back of the helicopter and napped after taking first watch. Jackie sat on a rolled up sleeping bag she'd removed from the helicopter's cargo compartment and kept watch over the sheriff's station with her night vision binoculars. The building, as well as the town, was eerily silent. At least at the lodge, there were crickets and wild animals making some sound. She found the silence peacefully unsettling much like a morgue.

Since there was zero to watch on the streets at four in the morning, she scanned the area and located Gil's helicopter off in the distance. He landed on a secluded hillside, which offered a spectacular view of all roads leading in and out of town. She saw Gil looking through his night vision binoculars at her.

Jackie smiled and waved at him. He waved back. She then heard Gil over her ear transmitter.

"Welcome to o-dark-hundred, Jackie dear," Gil announced in her ear. "How's city life?"

Jackie touched her ear transmitter. "I somehow thought it would be more exciting," she replied. "How are things in your neck of the woods?"

"Mostly peaceful," he responded. "Do me a favor. I'm hearing unusual sounds behind me on my left flank. Do you see anything?"

Jackie scanned the area behind him to his left and zoomed in on what was almost certainly a man near the woods. She then realized it was Beck with his back to her while peeing in the bushes. Jackie sneered, disgusted with Gil, and shook her head despite that he couldn't see it.

"Whoever accused you of being the nice one lied," she snarled in response.

Gil laughed and blew her a kiss.

"Is Beck pissing again," Zack's voice announced over their ear transmitters. "He may want to see a pecker-checker for a firm groping."

Gil coughed into their ear transmitters then laughed. Zack chuckled with him.

"Okay, boys," Jackie groaned in response. "Lady present. Show a little class. You can jerk each other off later."

Zack and Gil simultaneously hooted in response to the comment. Jackie grinned, pleased with herself.

"Jesus, Jackie," Ross's voice announced over their ear transmitters. "You're just as bad as they are. Stop encouraging them."

"Uh, oh, guys," Gil teased. "Dad's got ears on."

"I wouldn't worry about Ross. I can hear him smiling," Jackie reported then laughed.

"Hey, Jackie," Gil announced through her ear transmitter. "What's silent, deadly, and always right behind you?"

Jackie spun around into a backward kick and nailed Zack in the chest. He was thrown back a step before catching his balance and straightening.

"You kick like a girl," Zack teased while rubbing his chest where she'd kicked him.

"Behave," she announced while pointing a warning finger at him. "We're working."

"You have an excuse for every occasion," Zack muttered then mimicked her. "Not now, Zack, I'm working. I'm sleeping. I'm taking a shower."

Her eyes narrowed while glaring at him. "If that last one ever happens, I'm shooting you."

"Do us all a favor and shoot him now," Monroe muttered from the helicopter.

"Do you have any coffee left?" Zack asked, unaffected by either of their comments.

Jackie returned to her makeshift chair, picked up the thermos, and handed it to him. She collapsed onto the rolled sleeping bag and again scanned the area near the sheriff's department through her binoculars. Zack sat on the concrete near her legs and helped himself to coffee from the thermos. Once he finished his coffee, he turned his back to her, stretched his legs out in front of him crossed at the ankles, and leaned back resting his head on her lap. She lowered her binoculars and cast a look at him. His eyes were closed, and he was possibly already asleep. She should have figured he'd eventually be around in search of a catnap. He'd undoubtedly been awake close to twenty hours now. She honestly didn't know how he did it.

Having no other place to rest her arm, she placed it across his chest and set the binoculars aside. She could only look through them so long before her eyes started to hurt. Without them, she could still see enough of the area around the sheriff's office. Zack placed his hand over hers and affectionately clung to it. He rarely showed his warm, compassionate side to the teammates he considered his best friends. On occasion, they'd caught him using her as a pillow, but she doubted they ever saw his affectionate side.

Jackie had only recently learned of a woman from Zack's tragic past. Although he never went into great detail about her, Jackie knew he made the ultimate sacrifice to keep the woman he loved safe from those who wished him harm by letting her think he'd been killed. Ultimately, she died anyway, possibly at the hands of someone out to harm him. Now, Zack was a hard, cold shell masquerading as a man. She often wondered what his life would have been like if he hadn't lost the woman he loved. Would he have everything he'd always wanted? A house with a white picket fence, a loving wife, a dog, and a kid named Scorpio.

As selfish as it sounded, Jackie wondered how different her life would have been if Zack had children. Sure, she played with other kids around the military base, but if Zack had children, she may have grown up with them in her life. His shattered dream was also hers. Jackie knew she was Zack's world. She knew he was co-dependent upon her. He often talked of taking off and living a solitary life on the sea, although his urge to end it all seemed slightly stronger recently. Jackie couldn't bear the thought of either and did her best to hold him together. Although she hadn't betrayed what Zack had told her in confidence, Holden strongly suspected the things she *didn't* say. Her husband put up with Zack's oddities because he knew Zack was her father's best friend and an important part of her life growing up. She often wondered how Holden put up with her and her attachment to her father's team.

Jackie stared at the sleeping man on her lap. She smiled warmly, leaned down, and kissed him lightly on the forehead. Despite not opening his eyes, Zack smiled and affectionately clung to her hand.

"We haven't got time for hanky panky now," he teased without opening his eyes. "Maybe after this assignment if you ask nicely."

Jackie groaned while rolling her eyes, gave him a playful shove, and attempted to pull her hand away from him. He refused to release her hand and laughed.

"You're such a prick," she remarked.

Chapter 27

A little later, Gil stood and stretched his weary back after sitting on the ground for the last two hours. Beck remained asleep in the back of Gil's helicopter and lightly snored. Gil lifted his night vision binoculars and scanned the area, careful to check all the roads leading into town. It was a boring town. There hadn't been a single person on the streets of town since his shift started at three in the morning. The only thing moving around were some stray cats. He scanned the rooftop of the parking garage and checked out Jackie's helicopter. He could just about make out Monroe sleeping in the back. As he scanned the roof, he spotted Jackie still sitting on her rolled sleeping bag with Zack's head resting on her lap as he slept. Gil chuckled and shook his head.

"How the hell does she tolerate him?" Gil muttered more to himself.

He again scanned the area and saw two vehicles approaching from the back way into town. He didn't have to wait to confirm that they were trouble. Both black, modified Humvees had their headlights off so they wouldn't be spotted.

Gil tapped his ear transmitter. "Guys, we have company," he announced loud and firm. "Two Humvees due west heading into town."

"I see them," Jackie announced through Gil's ear transmitter. "Looks like two modified Army Humvees. That can't be good."

"Ross you copy," Gil announced while heading for the helicopter. He kicked Beck's booted foot waking him.

"Yeah, I read you," Ross replied. "Prepare the welcome wagon."

"Eagle Two prepping for takeoff," Gil announced as he jumped into the pilot's seat.

Beck slipped into his bulletproof harness vest and attached it to the cable in the back of the helicopter. He left the side door open as the helicopter prepared for takeoff. Beck grabbed his rifle with night vision scope then whirled his finger in the air to Gil, signaling he was ready. The helicopter lifted off and headed for town. On the parking garage rooftop, Jackie prepped her helicopter. Zack sat in the back on the left while Monroe sat in the back on the right. Both collected their weapons and watched through their binoculars while waiting for takeoff. The helicopter lifted off from the parking garage roof.

"Two more Humvees entering town from the east," Gil announced.

"I count at least four men in each jeep," Beck remarked. "Could be more."

Zack tapped Jackie on the shoulder from behind and pointed to the sheriff's station roof. She nodded and flew over top of the building. Zack attached the cable to his harness and slid down from the helicopter as it hovered. He landed on the roof and slipped out of his harness attached to the cable, which Monroe electronically pulled back up into the helicopter. Zack ran across the roof to the front of the building with his night scope, sniper's rifle. The four Humvees converged on the sheriff's station at the same time, and half a dozen men leaped from each vehicle. Despite the noise from the helicopters overhead, the men weren't deterred. They ran for the building with automatic weapons cradled in their arms. Zack tossed two cans of tear gas over the side of the building, which erupted in a large cloud. Half the men ran back for their Humvees while the rest ran for the building and attempted to break down the door and complete their mission.

§

Katrina, dressed in black combat gear and a helmet, jumped into the jeep with four other men while holding a cloth over her nose and mouth as they attempted to escape the tear gas. Two of the other men were coughing and gagging from the toxin. Dixon sat rigid behind the wheel and watched the chaos through the thick gas outside the window.

"What the hell happened?" Katrina demanded while looking out the window at the two helicopters buzzing overhead through the slowly dissipating smoke. "Who are they?"

When Katrina looked back, the man in the middle seat alongside her had a Bowie knife in his hand and attempted to stab her. Katrina gasped with surprise and caught his wrist before he could plunge the knife into her chest. As they struggled over the knife, her surprise turned to anger. She removed a small knife from her cleavage and plunged the two-inch blade into the man's neck. The man gasped and seemingly froze while staring at her. As blood poured from his mouth, Katrina sneered and vigorously pulled her small knife free. She knocked the Bowie knife from his dying hand and drew her semiautomatic from her holster, aiming the weapon at the two men now staring at her.

Dixon shot looks through the rearview mirror with some surprise at the double-cross reversal. Katrina stared at the men with rage in her eyes and her finger firm on the trigger. It possibly took everything she had to keep from pulling the trigger and killing all of them.

"Anyone else want a piece of me?" she snarled. "I know all about friendly fire, and I'm not the only one who can have an *accident*."

§

Within the sheriff's station. Ross positioned himself just outside the cell area and removed his semiautomatic while Kirk took a lookout position at the entrance door. He kept his eyes on the main door beyond the corridor. The deputy fumbled with his keys attempting to open the rifle cabinet containing the shotguns.

"How many are out there?" the deputy cried out and finally managed to unlock the weapons.

"My team is telling me nearly two dozen," Ross informed him.

The deputy looked at the shotgun in his hand then tossed it to Ross. Ross caught the shotgun, replaced his semiautomatic, and pumped the weapon. The deputy tossed another to Kirk, who did the same. They hadn't brought their own assault weapons into the sheriff's office since there would have been too much explaining to do. The main door was finally broken down allowing more than six men to charge into the corridor. As they charged for the sheriff's office, Kirk shot the first man in the chest with the shotgun. Despite that the man wore a bulletproof vest; he was still thrown across the corridor. When a canister of tear gas was propelled into the corridor to deter the rampaging men, Kirk slammed the office door.

Just outside the building, Gil and Jackie's helicopters buzzed over the sleepy town, which rapidly came to life. Every light came on within each house after hearing the sounds of gunfire and the helicopters. When those in neighboring houses realized what was happening, every light in every house went out. The first modified jeep took off through town and raced off into the night. Several men on the ground fired at the helicopters while attempting to give their men time to break into the sheriff's office and retrieve Martin. Beck and Monroe returned fire from their vantage point in both helicopters. With gunshots raining down on them, the men on the street had little shelter from the attack. Half of them made a dash for their modified Army Humvees. They left a few men outside and those inside to fend for themselves.

Within the municipal building corridor, the five remaining men coughed and gagged from the tear gas filling the hallway.

Mass gunfire was heard outside. Some of it came from the helicopters while other shots came from ground level. After apparently receiving orders to abort their mission, the men in the corridor turned and ran for the main door. Zack appeared through the smoke wearing a gas mask and mowed the men down with rapid gunfire. As the smoke cleared, Zack kicked in the mayor's office door and took a lookout position opposite the sheriff's office. He removed his gas mask as Kirk opened the door across the corridor.

"The rest are scurrying like rats," Zack informed Kirk while nodding to the outer door. "Jackie and Gil have them on the run with the helicopters. I suggest we bug out before they regroup for round two."

Kirk looked back inside the office. The deputy fumbled with his cell keys while approaching Ross in the detention block doorway.

"He's yours," the deputy announced and handed Ross the cell door key. "Just take him. Get him out of my town. The sooner, the better."

Ross took the key and hurried into the holding area. Martin was already on high alert from all the commotion outside and raced Ross to the cell door.

"They're here, aren't they?" Martin announced.

"Actually, they're gone," Ross replied. "The deputy just turned you over into our custody. If they want you dead that badly, there has to be some credence to your story." He unlocked the cell door and opened it. "You're safer with us, and this town doesn't need a war at its doorstep."

Ross motioned him from the cell. Although he kept an eye on Martin, he didn't seem too concerned that the man was loose without handcuffs. Kirk and Ross hurried Martin into the corridor and toward the main door. The deputy nervously followed them and looked at the six dead bodies strewn across the corridor. Jackie's helicopter lowered onto the street being careful to avoid overhead power lines. The helicopter's spinning rotors caused a mini tornado between the buildings and flung debris down the street. Zack crouched by the helicopter offering armed protection, although the danger seemed to have diminished. Kirk handed Ross the borrowed shotgun then hurried Martin to the open helicopter.

The deputy shielded his eyes and looked onto the street as the air swirled heavily. He saw several cars had been shot up and there were another six bodies bleeding in the street.

"The sheriff isn't going to like this," the deputy muttered more to himself while scratching his head with his trembling hand.

Ross handed the deputy the two shotguns they had borrowed. "Call Agent Falcone," Ross shouted above the pulsating helicopter rotors then grinned. "He loves cleaning up after us."

Once Ross was secure inside the chopper, it slowly lifted upward, carefully avoiding the many power lines, and joined Gil's helicopter. The deputy watched in near shock as both air crafts raced into the night then allowed his gaze again to fall upon the dead men in the street. The deputy suddenly came back to life.

"Agent Falcone," the deputy gasped then ran back inside the building.

Chapter 28

Colonel Holloway hurried along the mansion's first floor hallway and entered the four-car garage in time to see only two of the four Humvees had returned. The garage doors electronically shut behind them telling the colonel that they weren't anticipating the last two vehicles. Two injured men holding their bleeding arms were taken inside. Out of two dozen men, only twelve returned and it was clear one man was dead inside the back of the Humvee. Holloway scanned the men departing the vehicles. When he saw Katrina get out of the Humvee with Dixon, he appeared relieved and hurried to join them.

"What the hell happened?" the colonel shouted. "What's this I heard about helicopters and snipers?"

"They were waiting for us," Dixon announced. "We arrived, and they ambushed us."

"Who's they?" Holloway demanded. "I thought there was only one deputy guarding the jail? An incompetent one at best."

"There was," Katrina snapped then glared at Dixon. "It must have been the FBI. You said the FBI backed off when the military took charge of the situation."

"They did," Dixon protested in anger. "This wasn't my fault." He turned his attention to Holloway. "That wasn't the FBI. That was a coordinated attack."

"What about Martin Cooper?" Holloway demanded. "Is he still in police custody?"

"The men who made it into the sheriff's office never reported back," Dixon announced and shook his head. "They're dead. A dozen good men dead."

"There wouldn't have been a dozen men dead if you had let me handle this by myself," Katrina scoffed in anger then looked back at Holloway. "This mission failed because of arrogance. Storming the fort was a bad plan. They saw us coming a mile away." She again glared at Dixon and appeared ready to explode. "I could have slipped in under the radar, quietly taken out the deputy, and removed Cooper right under their noses, but we had to do it your way."

"We're all under some stress--" Holloway announced in an attempt to keep the peace.

Dixon didn't take his eyes off Katrina. "I don't take orders from you," he yelled back while pointing his thick finger at her. "You aren't part of this team. You shouldn't even have been out there!"

"Yeah, I sort of guessed that when your men tried to kill me," Katrina launched back.

"Whoa, wait a minute--" Holloway attempted to interrupt but was easily ignored.

"It's not my fault the men hate you," Dixon shouted back and aggressively poked his finger into her shoulder as if attempting to provoke her. "You invited that by sticking your nose where it didn't belong."

Katrina sneered at him and shoved his hand away in anger. He swung his massive fist for her face. She blocked his fist, rammed her knee into his side, then spun into a roundhouse kick, and struck him in the chest. He flew backward and struck the jeep with a loud thump. Holloway stepped in front of Katrina and placed his hands on her shoulders. She jerked out of reflex and threw her fist for his face. She pulled the punch to keep from striking Holloway and stared into his eyes a moment. Katrina released the breath she'd been holding and attempted to calm herself. Holloway firmly caressed her shoulders.

"Okay, it's over," he announced reassuringly and forced her to meet his gaze. "Now tell me what happened. Did one of my men try to kill you?"

"I took care of it," she growled without taking her eyes off him.

Holloway seemed tempted to pull her into his arms but resisted the action. Public displays in front of the men was unwise particularly if they were already jealous over the attention she received from him.

"Why don't you go inside, wash up, and fix yourself a drink?" he announced and casually unbuttoned his jacket. "I'll handle this."

Katrina exhaled deeply while attempting to relax, nodded, and headed inside. Once the door shut behind her, Holloway's expression immediately dropped as he turned toward Dixon with anger and hostility.

"What the fuck happened out there?" the colonel demanded while keeping his hand on the gun in his shoulder holster beneath his jacket. "One of your men tried to kill her? Did you know about this?"

"What?" Dixon gasped, eyed the colonel's hand on his gun, and shook his head. "No, of course not. There's no love lost between Katrina and me, but I certainly wouldn't condone someone harming your girlfriend."

"I better not find out you're lying to me," Holloway snarled and removed his hand from his gun. "I don't tolerate harming women." He then pointed toward the house door. "Particularly *that* woman."

"I'll make sure it never happens again," Dixon insisted while frowning.

Holloway nodded. "You do that," he scoffed then collected his emotions and buttoned his suit jacket. "I want a full report by noon."

"Yes, sir."

§

Colonel Holloway entered his bedroom fifteen minutes later and saw Katrina sitting on the bed in her satin robe that clung to her wet, naked body. She glanced up as he entered then looked away and finished brushing her wet hair. He shut and locked the door behind him then studied her a moment before approaching the bed.

"Are you okay?" he asked delicately while expressing his concern.

"I'm fine," she scoffed but didn't look at him. "It's not the first time someone in my own ranks tried to kill me, you know."

Holloway joined her on the bed, touched her chin, and forced her to meet his compassionate gaze. "Perhaps," he replied while staring into her eyes, "but not on my watch. I won't allow it." There was a moment of awkward silence as he stared at her with a slightly unpredictable look. "Was there anyone else?"

She stared into his eyes a moment, hesitated, and then raised her brows. "If there had been, he'd be dead too," she insisted.

"I know you can look out for yourself, Kat," Holloway remarked delicately. "I also know you're extremely proud and excessively stubborn, but just this once, let me take care of you."

As he pulled her into his arms, she resisted a moment then allowed him to hold her. He held her head to his chest and she reluctantly nestled against him. Holloway affectionately caressed her wet hair and kissed the top of her head.

"I'm sorry I didn't listen to you," he announced warmly then drew a deep breath. "I'm stubborn too. Can you forgive me?" He attempted to look at her without pulling away. He seemed reluctant to release her.

She lifted her head then met his gaze and gave him a curious look with a teasing grin. "What's in it for me?" Katrina asked.

Holloway smiled and chuckled. "The world's most erotic foot massage?" he suggested.

Katrina chuckled in her throat. "Fine," she huffed dramatically then grinned. "I forgive you."

Chapter 29

Friday, June 27th. That morning, four horse and riders rode away from the moderately large, two-story barn on Ross's ranch. Monique and Colleen rode their horses alongside Ross's niece, Selena. Selena was a slender, thirteen-year-old girl with sandy brown hair pulled back beneath her cowboy hat. The young girl riding the spirited, gray gelding fit in perfectly with her two new friends. Bogart trailed behind them on his large black horse and seemed preoccupied. He had no way of knowing what was happening with the prisoner transport job. When the girls spoke to him, he'd put on a false smile, and maintain his usual country boy charm. None of the three teenagers picked up on his increasing anxiety. He had them fooled. Bogart prided himself on being able to con grown men and women, so conning a few teenage girls was all too easy.

Monique leaned closer to Selena and spoke softly. "What's with Bogart?" she asked. "He seems tense."

Selena waved them off. "He gets that way when he's stressing over something," she replied. "I find it best not to question guys over their moods. Pretty soon they want to start talking about their feelings, and that's just too exhausting for me."

Monique and Colleen laughed.

"So where are we going?" Colleen asked while looking around.

"Our neighbor owns this big cattle ranch," Selena announced. "He lets us ride the trails and roads throughout the ranch. It's nice riding among the cattle. Depending on which wranglers we run into, they'll sometimes let us cut cows. It's fun."

"Colleen and I only did that once," Monique announced then smirked. "It was sort of an unauthorized cow herding, if you get my meaning."

"Anyone our age at this ranch?" Colleen asked.

"Nah," Selena replied with a frown. "Hooper's youngest daughter is old. She's like twenty-one or twenty-two."

"If I told my mother twenty-two was old, she'd probably ground me until my next birthday," Colleen remarked to the younger girl.

"My parents were older when they had me," Selena remarked. "You've met my Uncle Ross. He's older than dirt. I mean, he's over fifty."

"He can still kick some serious ass," Monique reminded the young girl.

"Have you met Zack?" Selena asked while offering a curious look.

"When he makes one of his rare appearances," Colleen replied.

"Can you believe he's almost as old as my uncle?" Selena remarked then shook her head. "I couldn't believe it. He can scale walls and trees like a cat, and I swear he can make himself invisible."

"I believe that. He's been doing an excellent job of avoiding us," Monique pouted.

"Yeah, he's weird," Selena reported.

As they reached the ranch, Bogart came back to life. He'd been to the ranch with Ross's niece before. The rancher's older daughter was a ranch foreman along with her brother. Seeing the attractive, young woman always lifted his spirits. Despite his lust for the sexy wrangler, he always managed to play it cool in front of Ross's niece. Since the woman was married, it wasn't as if he would act upon his lustful impulses anyway.

Selena eyed Monique and Colleen and held back her giggle. "You should see Bogart's eyes pop out of his head when he sees Jasmine," she informed her new friends while grinning. "She has a huge rack on her." Selena gestured large breasts with her hands. "He literally breaks out in a sweat when she bounces around on her horse."

Monique and Colleen giggled along with Selena at Bogart's expense.

"He stares at my mom's cleavage all the time," Colleen insisted. "I've tried to pawn her off on him, but he resists the temptation." She then frowned. "Maybe that's because he knew she wasn't technically widowed."

"How's that?" Selena asked.

"It's a long, exhausting story," Colleen replied. "The wounds are still too fresh."

Monique suddenly stopped Storm Cloud while looking at the large ranch house in the near distance. She stared at a handsome man in his early twenties with an almost steampunk sort of appeal. His brown hair was kept short although moderately spiky on top, and his neatly trimmed beard looked more like a five o'clock shadow. He was slightly shorter than average, being a tick over five-foot-eight. He wasn't built very muscular and his moderately worn clothes kept in theme with his whole steampunk look.

"My God, who is that?" Monique just about gasped. "He's possibly the most handsome guy I've ever seen."

Selena looked at the porch, appeared bewildered, and shook her head. "No idea," she replied. "He must be new. He's with Brandi. Let's go find out."

"You know he's about twenty," Colleen informed her blonde friend.

Monique sneered while giving Colleen a quick once-over. "Yeah? And Bogart is almost thirty," she remarked in an irritated tone. "You don't hear me telling you to stop drooling over him."

"Are you ladies talking about me?" Bogart asked from behind.

"No," Colleen quickly replied then glared at Monique to shut her up. She looked back at Bogart and smiled. "We were just going to stop and say hello to Brandi."

Bogart's eyes caught what he was seeking, and a grin crossed his face. "Yeah, sure," he replied. "I'm just going to talk with Jasmine."

All three girls watched Bogart ride toward the attractive woman on her horse near a small herd of cattle. Jasmine Hooper-Smith was a tall and slender woman in her late twenties with long, strawberry blonde hair hidden beneath her brown cowboy hat. She wore a tank top under her plaid button shirt. The tank top clung to her large breasts and revealed enough cleavage to attract plenty of male attention even though she was married. Despite her attention-grabbing figure, her big green eyes were what men noticed first. All three giggled at Bogart's expense then continued toward the elegant two-story home that looked more like a plantation mansion than a farmhouse. The white home was two stories with eight towering pillars along the backside. It contained a covered, wraparound porch on the first and second floor and massive floor to ceiling windows lining both floors. There was a large, in-ground pool, and an enormous pool house not far from it.

The girls stopped their horses before a young woman in her late teens to early twenties. Brandi Hooper was a beauty in her own rights, although it didn't come nearly as natural for her as it did her older sister. Brandi wore more makeup and spent more time on her hair and clothes. She was only a tick over five-foot, making her almost six inches shorter than Jasmine. She may have once shared the same hair color as her sister, but she had chosen to dye her shoulder-length hair blonde. Although more approachable than Jasmine, Brandi didn't have her sister's brain for business. Brandi was more interested in having a good time than worrying about tending to daily business at the ranch.

Now that they had stopped at the house, Monique gawked at the handsome man on the porch standing just a few feet away from the young woman.

"Hey, Brandi," Selena announced cheerfully.

"Selena, hey," she cried out excitedly. "Who are your friends?"

"This is Monique and Colleen," she announced. "They're visiting for a few weeks." Selena then grinned and indicated the handsome man on the porch with her. "Who's your new friend? Did you trade-in Boyd?"

"No," she announced. "Absolutely not." Brandi then eyed the handsome man and shrugged. "Not a bad trade though." She then giggled. "This is Kane. He works for Daddy."

There were some brief pleasantries. Monique was almost giddy around the handsome young man. Colleen gave her friend several strange looks since she'd never acted that way before.

"We were hoping to wrangle a few cows," Selena remarked. "Think your sister will mind?"

"Well, she's in one of her moods," Brandi replied then grinned. "But I'm sure she'll say yes if you ask nicely. She likes you more than she likes me."

Selena glanced across the farm at the woman on the horse talking with Bogart then looked back at Brandi and grinned. "I think we have that covered," she replied then laughed. "See you later."

Chapter 30

Later that afternoon, Jackie's helicopter set down in front of the lodge. Bogart, Pinto, Marie, and the girls stood on the porch and watched with anticipation as the helicopter landed. Colleen clung to her mother while unable to take her eyes off the aircraft, anxious about what it possibly contained. Once the craft shut down, everyone tensed. The mood was solemn and quiet. Bogart and Pinto appeared concerned by what would happen once the highly anticipated passenger disembarked. As the back door opened and the guys filed out, Colleen released her mother and both tensed. Martin climbed out of the helicopter and looked at the familiar women on the porch. He fidgeted, drew a deep breath, and walked toward the lodge with the team.

Colleen pulled away from her mother and ran across the yard for her father. Martin released the breath he'd been holding and smiled while fighting his tears. Colleen jumped into his open arms and clung to him while sobbing. He held her head to his chest and cried in response while resting his cheek on top of her head.

"I'm so sorry, honey," he sobbed. "I've missed you so much."

"I missed you too," she whispered in response.

After a long moment, they finally pulled apart and headed toward the lodge with their arms around each other. Martin nervously looked at the porch as they got closer, met Marie's gaze, and managed a weak smile. Marie glared back at him then turned without a word and entered the lodge. Pinto held her breath and hurried after her. Martin hid his disappointment and clung to his daughter.

§

Pinto and Marie had prepared a banquet that evening for the returning team, but when it came time for dinner, Marie bowed out gracefully, refusing to be anywhere near Martin for the first few hours. Colleen was torn between her mother and father, but she couldn't abandon her father as easily as she once thought she would. Martin told her a few stories of places he'd been and things he'd seen but left out the unpleasant details. After dinner, everyone gathered in the game room, and Pinto was finally able to convince Marie to join them. Marie sat at the bar with Pinto and had a couple of drinks to settle her frayed nerves. She would periodically cast looks at her estranged husband while he played a board game set up on the poker table with Colleen, Monique, and Bogart. Kirk sat at the poker table but didn't part-take in the game. He was assigned babysitting duty since Martin needed round-the-clock supervision.

Marie shook her head and sipped her drink then cast a look at Pinto. "I didn't think Colleen would be quite so forgiving," Marie insisted. "I wish I shared her innocence of youth."

"She was just given her father back," Pinto reminded her. "My father and I didn't speak for the longest time. You'd be surprised how easily the good outweighs the bad when it comes to parents."

"When I first heard what had happened, I refused to believe Martin was guilty," Marie informed the young woman then shook her head. "But he abandoned me with a ten-year-old girl. If it weren't for my brother, I don't know how we would have survived. I'm sure he could have gotten word to me somehow. Just to tell me he was innocent. Anything." She shifted uncomfortably at the bar. "Colleen was so depressed about losing her father; I just about sold my soul to buy that horse for her. Getting that horse as a yearling for her was what saved our family. Now Martin just strolls back into our lives--"

"He hardly strolled," Pinto reminded her. "I believe the term 'jailbreak' applies here."

"Whatever," Marie scoffed and finished her drink. She abruptly stood and seemed unable to control her hostility. "I have to get some air. I need to get out of this room."

Pinto watched Marie leave the room and shook her head. Beck, who had been hanging out near the pool table, approached his wife.

"Not handling her husband's return so well, huh?" Beck asked.

"She's frustrated on so many levels, she doesn't even know where to begin," Pinto remarked with a sigh then eyed her husband. "I recommend keeping her away from the weapon's room."

Martin saw Marie leave the room. Despite their board game, he stood from the table and hurried after his wife. Kirk rolled his eyes with a groan and followed since he needed to keep an eye on their guest slash prisoner. Bogart tensed as he watched Martin leave, pursuing his wife. Monique and Colleen eyed their friend with matching looks of concern.

"Should I be worried?" Colleen asked him.

Bogart frowned a moment then looked back at Colleen, attempted a smile, and shook his head. "No, they're just being irrational adults. Happens to all of us eventually. They just need to work it out."

Within a few minutes, Martin and Marie were heard within the lobby shouting at each other.

Bogart drew a deep breath and tensed slightly. "And sometimes working it out requires shouting at each other," he added.

Although their actual words couldn't be heard all that clearly, the arguing couple was enough to make everyone within the room uncomfortable. Colleen was particularly bothered by the arguing. Ross stood, approached the game room door, and shut it. The arguing was muffled by the shut door, but they could still hear the couple yelling. Ross cast a look at Bogart from across the room. Bogart easily read his eyes and turned to the girls while attempting a smile.

"Why don't we watch a movie?" Bogart suggested.

Both girls eagerly agreed. The added noise from the television would drown out the arguing couple. Once the movie started, Bogart turned up the volume to help drown out any unpleasant sounds. Only fifteen minutes into the movie, the arguing stopped, and they heard the front door slam. Bogart was then able to turn down the volume on the television, and the game room was once again peaceful.

§

Two hours later, Jackie and Pinto joined Bogart and the girls for their second movie, which was a romantic thriller. Darth abandoned the girls and chose to cuddle with Jackie on the sofa. Colleen had finally relaxed enough to enjoy the movie while cracking jokes with Monique and Bogart. Colleen's mother and father still hadn't returned to the game room, and Kirk remained MIA as well. Beck and Gil played a game of pool on the opposite side of the room while Monroe hung out and waited to play the winner. Despite attempting to watch the movie, Jackie could hear bits and pieces of Ross and Zack discussing past missions while drinking expensive brandy. She wished she could hear the entire conversation. Rather than join them, she decided to mind her own business. Whatever the discussion, neither man looked to be in a very good mood.

Zack cast a look at Ross alongside him. "Maybe I should take a leave of absence," he announced. "If what happened at Sal's casino is someone from my past creeping out of the woodwork--"

"Whoever it is, we'll deal with it," Ross informed him. "We've all pissed off the wrong people at some point. We need to cover each other's asses. We stick with the team."

"I have entire countries pissed at me, Ross," Zack informed him. "My past can't keep putting the entire team in danger. I'm willing to take responsibilities for the things I've done."

"No, Zack," Ross snapped with irritation. "We're all in this together."

Zack snorted an uneasy laugh and shook his head. He then glared at Ross. "Are you speaking for Lee?" he demanded. "How about Pinto? When my past comes after them, will you stand by the decisions you've made?"

"You're not the only one with skeletons in your closet," Ross insisted. "We're all walking around with targets on our backs. That includes Jackie, you know. The legacy Jackson left for Jackie certainly isn't all roses."

Zack shifted uncomfortably at the comment.

"If you go dark attempting to protect us from your past, we all lose another set of eyes on our backs as well," Ross informed him. "We look out for one another. We always have, and we always will. That botched Midnight Requisition mission taught us all a lesson."

Gil suddenly looked up from the pool table and eyed the men at the bar. He attempted to make his next shot and missed.

Zack tensed at Ross's words and again shifted in his chair. "Don't bring that up," he growled with deeply rooted anger. "I don't need to be reminded of that *ever*."

"I choose not to repeat the same mistakes," Ross informed him. "We stick together and protect our own. No man left behind."

Zack hesitated a moment then nodded. "No man left behind." He cast a look at Jackie where she sat on the sofa watching the movie with the others. "Or woman."

"I don't pretend to know what goes on inside your head," Ross announced while sipping his brandy without looking at Zack and stared at nothing in particular. "But if you even think about going dark and taking your favorite toy--" Ross cast a serious look at Zack. "--I'll hunt you down."

"Relax, Ross," Zack snarled without looking at him. "I wouldn't dream of abducting Jackie." He shook his head with annoyance. "If Holden is that paranoid, why would he give me my own room in their house? The man is an enigma."

"Holden isn't the one who's concerned about your behavior," Ross informed him.

Zack cast a look at Ross and appeared curious. "Bogart?"

"We're not pointing any fingers," Ross replied.

"Maybe you're not--"

Chapter 31

Halfway through the second movie, the arguing between Martin and Marie resumed within the lobby. The feud was loud enough to hear above the movie, although the actual content was slightly garbled. The argument continued for nearly twenty minutes without a break. Colleen sat on the sofa hugging her knees to her chest. Despite staring at the television, it was obvious she was listening to her parents fighting rather than watching the movie. Monique attempted to comfort her friend, but it didn't do much good. Bogart could no longer concentrate on the movie. Instead, he watched Colleen's anxiety rise, which only increased his anger with her parents. Everyone was now uncomfortable by the arguing and the effect it was having on the teenager. Zack was the only one who seemed indifferent to the ongoing feud. Colleen could no longer control her emotions after hearing her mother tell Martin that she wished he had died. Colleen fought her tears and wiped her eyes on her forearm.

"Son-of-a-bitch," Bogart scoffed under his breath although loud enough for the room to hear.

Zack finished his drink at the bar and finally left the game room, leaving the door open behind him. Only a moment passed before the arguing abruptly came to a halt. A strange silence fell over those within the game room as everyone stopped what they were doing. Beck and Gil straightened at the pool table and exchanged concerned looks.

"Oh, that's not good," Beck muttered.

A loud crash came from the lobby followed by Marie's shrill scream. Darth snarled and bolted from the room. Those remaining in the game room sprang to their feet and ran for the lobby except Ross, who just shook his head and poured himself another drink. Everyone entered the lobby in time to witness Zack kick Martin in the gut, hurling him across the room. As Martin attempted to catch his balance, Zack was already on top of him and punched him in the face. Despite his aggression, Jackie knew Zack was holding back his punches. She tensed while watching the assault on Martin and considered stopping Zack since she was the only one who could safely intervene. For some reason, she held off. Marie screamed again and tried to stop the unfounded assault on her estranged husband. Martin attempted to defend himself against the attack, but Zack easily kept him from striking back. Zack put him in a headlock and punched him repeatedly in the gut.

"Stop it!" Marie screamed with each punch.

Zack glared at her without releasing Martin. "This is what you want, isn't it?" he demanded and hit Martin again.

Marie continued to scream.

"I'll deal with him," Zack informed her. "You'll never have to see this parasite again."

"No, stop!" Marie cried out as tears streaked her face.

Zack again glared at Marie. "You want him out of your life, don't you?"

"No," she sobbed.

Zack released Martin, who dropped to the floor from the aggressive assault. He held his abdomen while panting heavily. As Zack walked across the lobby, Marie ran to Martin and fell to her knees alongside him. Her love for him showed as she held her battered husband. Zack approached Kirk, who leaned casually against the front desk seemingly unaffected by the entire incident.

"You missed your calling as a marriage counselor," Kirk remarked while hiding his grin.

"Crude but effective," Zack replied.

Marie and Colleen took Martin to the kitchen to get him some ice for his slightly bruised face. Monique attempted to follow, but Bogart stopped her.

"They need some time alone," Bogart informed her. "Let them work it out."

Monique nodded with understanding. Bogart turned Monique by her shoulders and pushed her back to the game room to finish the movie. Kirk lazily headed for the kitchen to resume his watch on Martin.

"On that note," Beck announced with a sigh. "I'm going to bed." He placed his arm around his wife then looked at Kirk as he passed them. "I'll relieve you at midnight."

Kirk gave him a thumbs up and continued down the hall for the kitchen.

"I thought I had midnight to four," Zack remarked from the front desk area.

Beck looked back at Zack, snorted a laugh, and shook his head. "You're on a timeout," he announced then headed up the open staircase with Pinto.

"No one appreciates when I fix their problems," Zack scoffed while shaking his head.

Gil nudged Monroe and pointed down the hall. "Beck forfeits," he announced. "You're up."

Both men returned to the game room leaving Jackie alone in the lobby with Zack. Jackie joined Zack by the front desk and hoisted herself on the marble top. Zack cast a look at her, noted her grin, and rolled his eyes.

"Don't--" he threatened.

"Don't what?" she teased.

"Don't go making this into something it's not," he launched back.

"I don't know what you're talking about," Jackie replied despite that her grin mocked him.

"I didn't intervene because of the kid," he insisted.

"Sure you didn't," Jackie teased.

"You need a new act," he scoffed. "This one is getting old."

"You and I both know you held back," she announced then laughed. "Hell, I think Martin even knew it."

"I wanted to shut them up," Zack scoffed. "They were disturbing my peace."

"You couldn't handle Colleen crying."

"I don't give a rat's ass about those girls," he informed her then raised an arrogant brow. "I just like hitting people."

Jackie maintained her grin, which only resulted in irritating Zack more. "Are you up for a few rounds on the mats tomorrow morning?"

Zack stared at her with surprise then suddenly grinned. "Absolutely."

"Six A.M.," Jackie announced then sprang off the desk and walked past him.

He stared after her a moment and seemed to consider her sudden desire to spar. "Don't think about standing me up," Zack boldly announced while watching her pass him. "This is a verbal contract. No takebacks."

She smiled and waved as she headed across the lobby for the stairs.

"O-six-hundred," he called out and pointed a warning finger at her. "You don't show; I reserve the right to hunt you down."

"I'll be there, Zack," she announced as she headed up the stairs.

Chapter 32

Colleen sat on the kitchen table and watched as her mother dabbed the blood from the corner of Martin's mouth while he held an ice pack to his cheek. Marie shook her head with disgust and anger.

"I can't believe he attacked you like that," she scoffed. "The man's a monster."

Colleen refrained from commenting almost as if she knew Zack's reasoning. Martin removed the ice pack from his cheek and managed a tiny, painful smile.

"Trust me," Martin announced. "He was making a point. If he wanted to put a serious hurting on me, I wouldn't be standing."

Marie eyed her husband with surprise. "So he attacked you to play on my sympathies?"

Martin was reluctant to respond. Perhaps he feared another round of fighting.

"He probably wanted to stop the fighting," Colleen finally interjected causing both to look at her where she sat on the table.

Marie looked back at her husband and tensed slightly. "I guess we should have talked like adults rather than screaming at each other."

"I know you're angry, confused, and feeling a bit betrayed," Martin insisted. "I don't blame you if you hate me. I hate me. I had to do what I did. If I hadn't taken off, they would have killed me." He then hesitated and drew a deep breath. "Possibly even came after you and Colleen. At least on the run, I didn't have to worry about anything happening to the two of you. Believe me; it was the hardest decision I ever had to make."

There was a long moment of silence as Marie stared at the bloodied cloth in her hand. She drew a deep, tense breath and finally met his gaze.

"After you went missing, the Army came looking for you," Marie informed him. "They told me you'd stolen classified information and a cache of weapons."

"That's not what happened," he insisted and shifted in his chair. "I witnessed my commander killing someone within my platoon and stealing a classified case. When I reported him, they tried to arrest me. I didn't realize how deep the conspiracy went. I didn't know who I could trust anymore, so I disappeared. I tried to clear my name for a while, but I ran out of options and friends."

"So you just left us?" Marie remarked while doing a poor job at attempting to control her temper. "You never intended to come back?"

"How could I?" he replied and leaned back in the chair while gingerly rubbing his abdomen. "The home phone was bugged, and there were men watching the house for over a year. The old ghost town seemed safe enough and far enough away that I thought I could at least see my daughter now and again."

"I can't believe Bogart knew it was you the whole time," Colleen muttered.

He looked at her and appeared ashamed. "Don't be mad at Bogart. He did what he thought was right. He didn't want to hurt you by having your father arrested. I'm glad you have someone in your life who's able to step in and be a father to you." Martin then eyed Marie and shifted uncomfortably. "If he makes you happy, I understand."

Marie appeared surprised by the comment. "What are you talking about?"

"I'm guessing he thinks you and Bogart are a couple, Mom," Colleen reported.

Her mother looked from Colleen then back to Martin. "Bogart?" She shook her head and managed a tiny laugh. "No, he's actually your daughter's friend. His team saved Colleen's life, and they're always welcome in our house. As for Bogart and I? No, there's nothing between us."

Martin appeared relieved although he remained tense. "Under the circumstances," he announced. "I understand if you've moved on."

"I have moved on," Marie chimed in almost startling him and surprising Colleen. "You were wanted by the Army. They called you a traitor and a deserter. You were gone a long time, Martin. So, naturally, I moved on."

"I understand," he replied timidly.

"I've gone out on plenty of dates and had several boyfriends over the years," Marie continued almost as if attempting to hurt him with her candor.

Colleen gave her mother a strange look at the false admission, but she didn't call her on it.

"I didn't have any reason to wait around for you," Marie continued. "You ran out on me; on us. I needed to get on with my life."

"As hard as it is to say," Martin announced. "I'm glad you did. Unless some miracle happens, if I'm lucky, I'll spend the rest of my life in military prison."

Marie suddenly fell silent and stared at him with some bewilderment. "The guys couldn't clear your name?" she asked with surprise.

"Clear my name?" he asked then managed an uneasy chuckle. "The men who want me dead are still looking for me. There's no scenario where this ends well for me. That's why it's important that you've moved on. There's no future for you with me in it. I just want you to be happy. You deserve to be happy."

Marie sprang up from her chair and glared at him. "You mean you're not coming home?"

"Marie, they'll never let me come home," Martin insisted. "If the bad guys don't kill me, the good guys will lock me away for life. My only other option is to remain on the run, and your new friends aren't letting that happen either." He studied her angered look and appeared surprised. "I thought you knew that."

"I thought this nightmare had ended," Marie launched in anger. "I thought you were begging me to take you back. I didn't know this was goodbye forever."

"Marie, I--"

Marie turned and stormed from the kitchen. Martin groaned with defeat and allowed his head to fall into his hands. Colleen slid off the table and placed her hand on her father's shoulder.

"Don't worry, Dad," she announced sympathetically. "The guys will fix everything, and Mom will take you back. I have faith in them."

Martin attempted a smile, although he didn't seem to share her faith, and affectionately patted her hand on his shoulder.

Chapter 33

Saturday, June 28th. Morning. Jackie entered the basement gym where Zack was already eagerly awaiting their sparring adventure. His enthusiasm to battle with her was borderline creepy, reminding her more of a man preparing for a romantic date. She honestly didn't understand his perverted enjoyment. His main goal seemed to be getting her on the floor in a submissive position, yet it usually ended with her bashing in his boys. What sort of man enjoyed something like that? Honestly, Jackie didn't enjoy either component when they sparred together, but she reluctantly gave in to his depraved fantasy to keep him happy. She hoped the team knew the sacrifices she made in order to make Zack tolerable for them. Zack saw her and immediately grinned.

"I was thinking we'd start off Japanese style," he announced and revealed a samurai sword.

Jackie knew the blades were dull, but that didn't matter much. She had to stop the madness before it got started. "Not happening," she announced.

"They're not sharpened," he protested.

"They're still weapons," she insisted. "I'm not ready to kill or be killed for your twisted pleasure."

"Oh, Jacklyn dear," Zack announced while grinning. "You haven't even seen that side of me yet."

"And I won't," she replied while casually kicking off her shoes.

Their fights were bare feet and soft kicks only. They didn't actually need to kill each other while pretending to kill each other.

"You're no fun," Zack playfully pouted.

"I thought we'd make this a little more interesting," Jackie informed him.

Zack appeared curious and grinned his approval. "I'm up for more interesting."

Monique and Colleen entered the basement gym while giggling and joking around with each other.

Zack's expression dropped as he groaned. "That's cheating," he scoffed.

"The girls want to learn some self-defense moves," Jackie informed him.

"And you couldn't teach them?" he demanded.

"They wanted you," she replied while grinning deviously. "Don't worry; I'll still spar with you."

Zack frowned. "It won't be the same."

"Yeah," she announced with humor and affectionately clung to his arm while staring into his eyes. "No dirty fighting for a change."

"You ruined my whole morning," Zack muttered and refused to look at her.

Jackie smiled sweetly, despite that he didn't look at her, and kissed him quickly on the cheek. "I promise; I'll make it up to you."

Zack turned his head and looked at her only a few inches from his face. He frowned, considered the comment, and then pointed to his lips. Jackie managed a tiny laugh and kissed him quickly on the lips. Zack groaned with disgust possibly at himself and pushed her away from him.

"Fine," he muttered. "If it makes you happy; I'll rough up the kids."

Monique and Colleen talked between themselves and giggled over something. Zack clapped his hands together loud enough that it startled both girls.

"New recruits," he bellowed in a commanding tone, "fall in!"

Jackie stood on an imaginary line and indicated the mat alongside her. Monique and Colleen stood in line with Jackie and gave Zack their full attention.

"Welcome to self-defense one-o-one," he announced while pacing in front of them with his hands clasped behind his back. "Here you will learn throat punches, ball-breaking kicks, and how to snap a man's neck with your bare hands."

Jackie groaned and covered her eyes. "I knew this was a mistake," she muttered.

Zack spun to face Jackie and attempted to intimidate her by staring her down. "Do you have a problem with my authority, princess?"

She stared into his eyes without blinking and wanted to punch him in the mouth for the 'princess' comment. He knew which buttons to push, and he was about to push them all. Jackie resisted the temptation, knowing he was hoping for a confrontation.

"No, no problem," Jackie replied while withholding her disapproving sneer.

"No problem *what*--?" he demanded and raised a cocky brow.

Jackie's eyes narrowed as she stared back at him. "No, *sir*," she hissed.

Zack offered an unnerving smile and continued his character assassination. "That's a good girl."

Jackie sneered in anger as Zack turned. She suddenly spun into a roundhouse kick for his chest. Zack barely even turned his head and was able to block the kick with his forearm. He countered by catching her wrist and attempted to twist her arm. Jackie broke his grip and rammed her knee into his ribs. He barely flinched from the somewhat aggressive kick and caught her around the neck. In one swift movement, he threw her to the mats. She rolled across the mat and sprang to her feet before he could join her on the floor. Jackie considered a counterattack but took a step back instead.

"You're supposed to be teaching the girls," Jackie snapped. "Focus."

Zack frowned in disappointment. "Fine," he scoffed then turned to face Monique and Colleen. "Lesson number one. Basic kicks and punches."

Chapter 34

It was early evening when Ross, his wife, and Beck drove to the closest town from the lodge, which wasn't all that close. Pinto was singing at the club where she worked most Saturday nights, and Beck always attended when they weren't on an assignment. Ross picked up his wife from their farm, enabling him to spend a little extra time with her. Ross's wife, Leeann, was an attractive woman in her mid-twenties with wild, dark hair giving her a country girl appeal. Lee was easily half Ross's age, and he considered himself lucky to have a woman he felt was clearly out of his league. Despite her husband's additional years over her, Lee thought she was the lucky one.

The small, out-of-the-way town was a two-hour drive from the lodge. Despite being a little town, it had a population of nearly five thousand. It also had its own nightclub, which was something more country and less modern, several restaurants, a movie theater, bowling alley, and at least four bars. There was also a small motel on the way into town. The town was busy on weekends when local ranchers and farmers made the trek for fun and relaxation. Despite still being daylight outside, the lounge where Pinto performed remained dimly lit with mood lighting on small, round tables. There were larger tables and booths off to the sides. A massive bar lined the back wall of the large room. The club was packed as it was most Saturday nights when Pinto was the star attraction.

Beck had his usual table up front but off to the side where he could gawk at his wife while she performed. Despite that they hadn't been together all that long, it didn't seem as if Beck's fascination for his wife would dwindle anytime soon. He still got lost in his wife's beauty and talent. Ross and Lee were just along for the ride. The couple secretly laughed at Beck's lost puppy affection toward his wife. When he was around his wife, it was difficult to believe he could kill a man with his bare hands. Once Ross was finished teasing his number two in command, he turned to Lee.

"Were you able to get a hold of Othello?" Ross asked his wife.

"Yes," she replied and smirked at him. "Your 'brief question' had me on the phone for two hours with Othello. Doesn't he have any other friends?"

"Not that I'm aware," Ross teased while hiding his mildly sympathetic grin.

Lee glared at him. "That's why you wanted me to call him, isn't it?" she demanded. "You didn't want to be stuck on the phone forever with him."

"Guilty as charged," Ross replied and chuckled. "Although in my defense, I couldn't make that call from the lodge on the satellite phone."

"Not an excuse," Lee muttered.

"What did he say?"

"Do you want the short answer or the two-hour long one?" she demanded.

"The short version, if you don't mind," Ross replied while grinning.

"You realize your first night home, you're sleeping on the couch," she huffed.

Ross grinned, placed his arm around her, and pulled her to his side. "If that's what you want," he replied.

Lee stared into his eyes then groaned with defeat. "Okay," she reluctantly gave in. "You'll sleep on the couch the second night."

Ross kissed her warmly and again turned serious. "About Othello--"

"He was able to track your man's whereabouts during the time in question," Lee replied. "According to what he was able to find, your colonel has been a busy boy." She handed him a flash drive. "I downloaded everything Othello sent, which includes a few persons of interest you may want to have a look at."

Ross accepted the flash drive and squeezed Lee's hand. "See," he announced. "Those two hours on the phone with Othello were totally worth it."

She smirked at him and shook her head. "You're lucky I love you."

"Yes, I'm very lucky," Ross replied and leaned in to kiss her.

She held him back, surprising him. "He also mentioned something else he felt you'd want to know."

"What's that?"

"Othello got word that someone or possibly multiple someones have been asking a lot of questions about the team," she remarked.

"Did he get a name?"

"No, it was all second-hand," she replied then shifted uncomfortably. "But he did mention something else that he'd heard. Something weird."

"Weird?"

"Your old commander's name was being shopped around," Lee informed him.

"Jackson?"

Lee nodded. "Sounds like someone from the deep past is coming back to haunt you," she replied. "That's as much as he knew. Whoever is looking for the old team hasn't made it to Othello's doorstep yet."

Ross frowned and nodded. "Until we get a name and the reason for his inquisitive nature, you'd better put the farm on alert."

"Already on it," she replied and flashed her clunky bracelet. "I thought I'd do a little digging myself--"

"No, whatever it is, absolutely not," Ross announced. "I don't want you drawing any unnecessary attention to you or the farm until we know who we're dealing with."

"Are you expecting trouble?" she asked with concern while studying her husband.

"No, not really." He then frowned and shook his head. "Sometimes Zack's past comes back to haunt us every so often, and we have to be ready."

"Ross, everyone thinks he's dead," she remarked. "I don't know why it's a problem."

"Since Zack came back to us full-time, he's been poking his head out into the sunlight more and more," Ross informed her. "Eventually, someone is going to identify him and try to shoot his head off."

Pinto was introduced for her first set for the evening. There was a huge applause from the audience as she walked onto stage wearing a formfitting evening dress that revealed plenty of leg and cleavage. Her hair and makeup were styled perfectly. She was a vision of beauty. Beck cheered and clapped excitedly, which she was forced to ignore. The room was virtually silent as Pinto sang her first two songs. She had just finished her second song when there was a woman's scream and a crash not far from the bar area across the room. Ross and Beck looked across the room and watched the fight in progress.

Beck and Ross stood and folded their arms across their chest looking like superheroes supervising a fight. The young man Monique and Colleen met at Hooper's ranch fought three rather large country boys using impressive karate kicks and punches. Ross and Beck exchanged curious looks as they noted the young man's fighting skills. The large bouncers were swiftly upon what was meant to be a fight, but the fight was actually three country boys taking a beating. The fight had technically ended before the bouncers arrived to break it up. The young man, Kane, was that good. He was good enough to catch Ross and Beck's attention. Everyone involved in the fight was escorted outside by the bouncers. Ross and Beck witnessed the six men and six women being removed from the club. They once again exchanged looks.

"That was Marlon Hooper with them, wasn't it?" Beck asked.

"Sig Hooper's youngest daughter and her boyfriend too," Lee responded as she stood alongside Ross. "I don't know who the others were though."

"Damned good fighter," Ross remarked then looked at Lee and raised his brows. "Planning a visit to Hooper's ranch anytime soon?"

"I could find an excuse," she replied and eyed him. "Did you want me to drop by the ranch and catch up on local gossip?"

Ross seemed pleased with the idea. "If you wouldn't mind."

Lee grinned. "I'd love to."

Chapter 35

Sunday, June 29th. The gray Jeep Wrangler drove up the long driveway to the Hooper ranch house. The plantation style home was even more impressive than it had been from above. The jeep parked near a brand new sports car, which was uncommon for the isolated ranch location. With the first snow, the vehicle would be rendered useless. Lee got out of the jeep and eyed the expensive, powder blue sports car. It undoubtedly belonged to Hooper's youngest daughter, Brandi. Out of Hooper's three children, his youngest daughter had zero interest in the ranch. Somehow, despite her upbringing, she was born a city girl. Lee carried a large, double-stacked container holding two fresh pies she'd baked that morning. She approached the front door of the massive home and had to take in an eyeful of the place.

Lee had seen bigger homes, considering she had worked for Sal Romano before she'd met Ross, but Hooper's house was the largest in their area. She rang the doorbell but didn't have to wait long before the door was answered by Hooper's youngest daughter. Brandi saw Lee and squealed with delight possibly happy to see a female neighbor.

"Lee," she cried out excitedly. "I'm so happy you stopped by." Brandi stepped away from the doorway and allowed her to enter the massive foyer.

Lee stepped inside and marveled at the grand hallway and the broad "Gone with the Wind" staircase. She'd been in the house before, but its grandeur was always breathtaking, especially since the house was always filled with many beautiful flowers from the cook's garden.

"What brings you here?" Brandi eagerly asked. "Daddy had to run to town, if you came to see him."

"No, I actually stopped by to see you," Lee announced then handed her the pies. "I brought you some homemade rhubarb pie."

Brandi accepted the tote container with the pies. "Oh, I love your rhubarb pie," she announced excitedly. "We'll have it after dinner tonight. Did you want some tea? I could make some."

"Tea would be lovely," Lee replied then followed Brandi to the kitchen.

As they entered the bright, white kitchen, Lee saw one of the maids scurry into the servant's wing.

"Was that Alma?" Lee asked.

"No, that's the new maid," Brandi informed her then rolled her eyes. "She's not working out. Daddy will probably fire her after the wedding."

Brandi filled the kettle and placed it on the burner. She turned to face Lee while grinning.

"What did you want to see me about?" Brandi asked.

Lee cheerfully handed her the small envelope. "Hand delivering my R.S.V.P. for your wedding," she announced.

"You're coming, right?" Brandi remarked. "It's here at the ranch, so you can't say no."

Lee laughed and nodded. "Yes, Ross and I will be attending."

"Selena and Liam?"

"Of course," Lee replied. "They wouldn't miss it for the world." They sat at the island counter. "I don't get many opportunities to dress up in these parts. I'm looking forward to it."

"I'm so happy," Brandi announced while giddy at the thought. "It'll be the only exciting thing happening around here this year." She groaned dramatically. "These backwoods are so boring."

The kettle whistled. Brandi sprang to her feet, hurried to the stove to shut it off, and poured hot water into two mugs. Lee cast a look at the doorway and saw the handsome young man standing within the kitchen. Lee jumped with surprise at how quietly he seemed to appear out of nowhere. He was the same man they'd witnessed fighting the men at the club in town. Something about the strikingly handsome man made Lee uneasy.

"Uh, hello," Lee announced.

Brandi looked up and saw the man in the doorway. "He sneaks around here like a cat," she informed Lee then eyed the man. "Kane, this is our neighbor, Lee."

Kane smiled charmingly and approached Lee with his hand extended. She was grateful he was friendly. His little show at the club raised some concerns.

"Kane is helping Daddy around the house," Brandi announced as Lee shook his hand.

"It's a pleasure to meet you, Lee," Kane announced.

"You look familiar," Lee remarked while studying the young man.

"It wasn't me," he announced while grinning. "I've never been there."

Lee stared at him a moment, realized he was joking, and laughed almost nervously. She then played up the angle and allowed her smile to fade.

"Oh, now I remember," Lee announced. "I saw you at the club in town last night." She gently cleared her throat. "You, uh, were shown the door."

Brandi suddenly laughed. "You were there?" She laughed again. "That was amazing, right?" Brandi set Lee's tea mug before her and became animated. "Some guys were giving us a hard time, and Kane whooped their asses."

"It wasn't nearly that dramatic," Kane insisted while hiding his smile. "If something happened to the boss's daughter on my watch, I'd be looking for a new job."

"I'm pretty sure I saw an ass-whooping myself," Lee teased while grinning.

"I got lucky," he replied and easily brushed off the incident. "I'm usually pretty passive."

Lee stared at him a moment then offered a knowing smile and nodded. Ross would have disagreed with that statement. He seemed convinced the man was highly trained, and it was obvious he was downplaying the event to hide the fact. Kane maintained his smile and his polite demeanor. The confrontation in the club aside, Lee still thought he looked familiar. There was something about his eyes and his smile, but she couldn't quite place it.

"I should get back to work," Kane announced and gave Lee a polite nod. "It was nice meeting you."

As Kane left the kitchen, Lee stared after him then turned back to Brandi, who now sat at the counter with her mug of tea.

"Nice looking man," Lee remarked.

Brandi snorted a laugh. "He's not without his charm," she remarked. "But he's a little strange."

"Oh?"

"Have you ever watched a cat play with a mouse?" Brandi asked.

Lee grimaced. "Yeah, it's a bit disturbing."

"Most of the wranglers around the ranch are pretty much what you see is what you get," she announced then indicated the doorway. "That one--?" Brandi made a face and shook her head. "It's like he's watching and waiting to pounce."

Lee smiled and patted Brandi's arm. "Welcome to my world, Brandi."

Chapter 36

Monday, June 30th. Jackie's helicopter landed in front of the lodge. Martin and Gil had been standing on the porch while watching the aircraft touchdown. The wanted man was on edge and eagerly awaited their return. Ross and Beck got out of the helicopter before Jackie had completely shut her down and approached the lodge. Martin met them halfway and appeared hopeful.

"What did they say?" Martin asked.

"We need to turn you in by Friday," Beck informed him.

"My colonel buddy agreed to personally oversee your arrest and imprisonment," Ross informed him. "You'll be guarded around the clock until the trial."

Martin frowned and appeared defeated. "I'm as good as dead," he announced. "We're not talking one man in a high ranking position; we're talking a powerful man with a company of mercenaries to back him up. They'll keep me alive long enough to get what they want, and then I'll conveniently commit suicide."

"Ross and I were discussing that," Beck remarked. "Maybe there's an alternative. One with less of a happy ending for your Colonel Holloway."

"What ending is that?" Martin asked.

"You have something they want, and they're willing to kill you to get their hands on it," Ross announced as Jackie approached from the helicopter and joined them. "If you no longer have it, it may take some of the incentive away to kill you."

"I'm pretty sure they'll kill me anyway," Martin reported then eyed them. "Are you suggesting I tell you where to find what they want?"

"We can't keep the Army from arresting you and putting you on trial," Ross informed him. "But if Colonel Holloway is busy chasing us, he won't have nearly as much time to worry about you."

"He still has to keep me quiet," Martin reminded him. "I'll never make it to trial. He can't let me expose him as a killer."

"My idea was better," Jackie announced proudly.

Ross rolled his eyes while the others looked at her with interest.

"Recover the Army's property, stage your accidental death, and you can live out the rest of your life as Rafael in Costa Rica," she announced while grinning.

"Not that I don't appreciate you 'bumping me off'," Martin remarked. "But do you have any plan that lets me see my daughter?"

"Just the one where you face a court-martial and testify against Colonel Holloway," Beck replied.

"I want to do what's right," Martin announced. "Unfortunately, I enjoy breathing."

"Until Colonel Holloway is out of the picture," Ross informed him, "there's no scenario where you go riding off into the sunset with your wife and daughter. Spend some time with your family. We need to have an answer for them by morning."

§

Martin entered the game room where Monique and Colleen were sitting on the floor before the large sofa with Bogart between them. They watched a horror movie, ate popcorn, and laughed at the fake gore.

"That is so fake," Bogart announced and shook his head while grinning. "Where do the two of you find these awful movies?"

"You don't have to go far," Colleen remarked as she tossed popcorn into the air and attempted to catch it in her mouth. It went all over the sofa instead.

"Next time I pick the movie," Bogart insisted while squirming as he watched the gruesome movie.

Creepy, dramatic music played. A woman in the movie suddenly screamed. Monique and Colleen jumped and screamed while making faces.

Bogart pointed at the television and appeared annoyed with the gruesome scene. "That's not even physically possible," he announced with a groan. "You can't pop a guy's head off that way."

Martin managed a smile then turned and left the room before they noticed him in the doorway behind them.

"Have you ever cut a guy's head off?" Monique asked while casting a sideways look at him.

Bogart stared at his young, blonde friend with possible shock. "What?" he gasped. "No, of course not. Why would you even ask such a thing?"

"Zack gave us a karate lesson on Saturday," Monique replied. "And he was telling us the best way to decapitate a man."

Colleen nodded in agreement.

Bogart stared at both girls with a loss for words. "First of all; he shouldn't be discussing decapitation with fifteen-year-old girls," he announced with some irritation. He then paused while staring at them. "Secondly--" His look then turned annoyed. "How on earth did you get him to give you a karate lesson? I've been bugging him to teach me, and he just flips me off."

"Jackie made him," Colleen proudly announced while tossing another kernel of popcorn into her mouth then grinned slyly.

"How many men have you killed?" Monique then asked while gazing at him with a curious look. "Is it, like, more than a baker's dozen?"

Bogart immediately returned his attention back to the movie. "I'm not answering that," he scoffed. "And you shouldn't be so interested in asking such things. Capital punishment should only be used as a last resort." He shook his head. "I don't know why you two ask so many morbid questions." He indicated the television. "Just watch the movie."

A woman in the movie screamed as the sound of something splattering echoed throughout the room. All three grimaced at the image on the screen. The girls again lost interest in the gory movie and turned on the floor to face Bogart from either side.

"How many girlfriends have you had?" Colleen asked while perking up.

"Do you have any illegitimate children?" Monique quickly added the follow-up question.

Bogart tensed and avoided looking at both girls. "I'm starting to remember why we don't watch movies together," he muttered.

"Why aren't you married yet?" Colleen then asked as she leaned forward.

"Do guys only care about sex?" Monique pressed. "Two girls in our school are pregnant."

"What?" Bogart gasped with surprise.

"Yeah, her boyfriend--"

Bogart waved his hands and successfully silenced both of them. He raked his fingers through his hair, fidgeted with discomfort, and then groaned.

"No more questions about murder and or sex," he announced then indicated both girls with a warning finger. "And neither of you are dating until you're twenty-one."

"Fine by me," Monique announced with little concern and returned to watching the movie.

"Maybe never," Colleen added while grimacing. "Boys are gross."

"Damned right," Bogart huffed and folded his arms across his chest while attempting to watch the movie.

Chapter 37

Ross hung out at the island counter in the kitchen with Gil and Monroe where the three men quietly discussed some secret plan. Martin entered the kitchen, appeared tense, and eyed the men at the counter. All three men looked at him and appeared curious.

"Something on your mind, Martin?" Ross asked.

"I want my family back," Martin replied with conviction. "What do I have to do?"

"Well," Ross announced while sitting back in his chair and folded his arms across his chest. "You can start by telling us why they're hunting you. Typically, the military doesn't send out two dozen heavily armed mercenaries to kill an Army deserter."

Gil pushed out the vacant island counter chair with his foot. Martin climbed onto the chair, drew a deep breath, and nervously raked his fingers through his hair.

"Holloway, my CO, had just received his promotion to Lieutenant Colonel, and he was being shipped out in a few days," Martin began. "We liked the guy. Most people liked Holloway. He seemed pretty straightforward. The guys wanted to throw a surprise farewell party for him, and I was in charge of keeping him from the mess hall until the guys were ready." Martin shifted in his chair. "Only I couldn't find him. Things were pretty quiet on base with everyone gathered in the mess hall for the party. I heard voices from the motor pool. They sounded heated, so I decided to check it out but kept out of sight. Guys would sometimes vent in isolated places, and I assumed it was just some of the boys duking it out."

"We called that shore leave," Gil muttered.

"I was surprised when I found Holloway arguing with Captain Wright," Martin continued. "They were arguing over a duffel bag, of all things. I didn't know what was in it, but the exchange was nasty. Captain Wright intended to turn him in and tried to take the bag. You can imagine my horror when I saw Holloway sucker punch Captain Wright and stab him in the neck with his Bowie knife. I should have run for the MPs right then, but I was paralyzed with shock. I actually watched the bastard wrap him in plastic and place him in a jeep. He stashed the duffel bag and then took the captain for a ride to dump his body."

"I'm guessing this was where you got yourself into deep shit," Monroe remarked.

Martin shifted uncomfortably and nodded. "I know I should have found the MPs first, but I was afraid Holloway would remove the bag before I returned, so I took it for safekeeping." He frowned and shook his head. "Holloway must have forgotten something and doubled back. He caught me with the bag and tried to kill me. I fought him off, grabbed the bag, stole a jeep, and got out of there. I feared he might shoot me, but he knew better than to discharge his weapon on base. Everyone would hear it and come to investigate."

"So he dumped the body instead," Ross added with a curious look. "He figured he'd catch you when you showed up to report the incident."

"Holloway was smart," Martin announced. "I knew he'd make it look bad for me, so I hid the evidence first and reported him by phone. Naturally, they wanted me to come in since I was already AWOL. I agreed to meet them in public. Instead of your usual MPs, I was greeted by two men who tried to kill me. That's when I realized Holloway had too many men willing to back him up and defend him from the murder charge. Every time I thought I found a way to get my story out, he found a way to stop me. He even sent MPs to my house. That's when I knew I had to stay hidden until I could figure out my next move."

"What was in the bag?" Monroe asked.

"Another bag," Martin replied. "A square, nylon one. Nothing I'd ever seen before. Inside that bag was a metal case with a state-of-the-art thumbprint lock on it. Since I couldn't figure out what it was that he was willing to kill a captain, I stashed it someplace a little more secure in hopes I'd eventually figure out a way to clear myself. Colonel Holloway is well liked and respected. He also has a long reach. The guys he'd sent after me were good. I'm only alive because I'm good at covering my tracks."

"With your only weakness being your family," Gil reported and shifted in his chair. "They figured if they kept an eye on your family, they'd eventually catch you."

"Living so far from town was a blessing in disguise for Marie and Colleen," Martin replied. "They couldn't just park at the nearest curb and spy on our farm. Once Colleen got that horse, she was even harder to keep tabs on. That's the only reason I felt comfortable getting closer to her. I learned her routine and waited in the ghost town for her and her friend. I knew no one was following them because they'd be spotted."

"Unfortunately for you, you were the one spotted by them," Monroe remarked.

"Yes, and after Bogart confronted me, I stayed away for a while," Martin replied.

"It might benefit you to tell us where you hid this bag," Ross announced while studying Martin. "We have friends in high places."

"And low places," Gil muttered.

"We could relay your story on your behalf," Ross continued. "If we could turn over that bag, it may just help your case."

"Colonel Holloway wants whatever is in that bag," Martin insisted. "He wants it badly enough that he hasn't had me killed despite that I witnessed him murdering Captain Wright. That tells me whatever is in there is incredibly important to him. That bag is the only thing keeping me alive. He won't kill me until he knows its location." He eyed the three men. "If I give up the bag to you, he'll have a sniper pick me off without thinking twice."

"The Army is insisting we turn you over," Ross informed him. "Whether we believe you or not doesn't matter. We can't go against the U.S. Army."

"I know," Martin replied.

"Our only hope right now is Holden and Blake Harris," Ross informed him. "They're pleading your case to remain in our protective custody after the incident in town. The military seems to think you're better off in their protective custody. We'll relay the information you gave us to Holden and see what they have to say, but we really need that bag if we're going to get anywhere with the Army."

"I understand," Martin replied almost timidly. "I'll take you to it."

Ross nodded. "We leave first thing tomorrow morning."

§

Martin left the kitchen after his confession to the men and nearly collided with Marie, who waited in the hallway. Her look was serious.

"You're going back out there?" she asked with some surprise.

"I have to," Martin replied and attempted a smile. "For my family."

"Isn't there another way?" Marie asked while fidgeting.

"There are many bad options including this one," he replied. "But this is the only one that comes with the possibility of seeing you and Colleen again."

Marie shifted uncomfortably and met his gaze. "I lied," she announced. "There haven't been any boyfriends. There hasn't been anyone else."

Martin smiled with relief and nodded. "I shouldn't be happy about that, because you deserve so much more, but I'd be lying if I said I wasn't."

She moved into his arms, touched his face, and warmly kissed his lips. Martin returned the quick, passionate kiss. Marie pulled away, stared into his eyes a moment, and then kissed him again with more aggression. Martin eagerly returned the kiss. She again pulled away, hid her smile, and took his hand.

"I'd like to speak to you in private," she announced and led him down the hall toward the stairs.

As they passed the game room, Monique and Colleen stepped into the doorway and watched them head for the stairs. Bogart appeared behind them and hid his smirk. Colleen looked back at Bogart.

"Does that mean she forgave him?" Colleen asked.

"I'm going to guess so," Bogart replied then placed a hand on each of the girls' heads, spun them around, and guided them back into the game room.

Chapter 38

Tuesday, July 1st.   Early that morning, Colonel Holloway walked through an underground corridor that led from the mansion basement to a bunker buried beneath the garage. He entered the secured bunker that resembled a 1950s gangster's meeting room.   The furniture was a gaudy gold print.   The room contained expensive framed artwork on the walls, tacky red carpeting, and a large bar just off the sitting area. Holloway was greeted by Dixon.   They approached another man with his own pair of bodyguards and two of Holloway's armed men. Colonel Holloway greeted the small, mousy looking man with a polite handshake and a broad, charming smile.

"What have you brought me today, Nathan?" Colonel Holloway asked with enthusiasm.

Nathan's associates opened two cases sitting on the table to reveal three weapons in each case.   The mousy man removed each weapon and handed it to the colonel for his inspection.

"Nice, very nice," Holloway announced while looking over the fully automatic weapon.   "Not nearly as heavy as the last shipment you tried pushing on me."

"You want grenade launchers," Nathan announced sternly, "you need to expect additional weight."

Holloway inspected the remaining weapons.

"If you like them, I can get you two hundred each by next week," Nathan informed him. "Our Russian contact is eager to move the merchandise as soon as his ship arrives on the east coast."

Colonel Holloway sharply eyed him. "I'm not keen on your dealings with Russians," he remarked. "I don't need any more trouble with the Russian government. They no longer have a sense of humor where I'm concerned."

"Yes, the unfortunate hit on your wife," Nathan remarked. "I'd heard about that."

"We've come to an understanding since then," Holloway reported.

"Abducting a high ranking officer's teenage son?" Nathan remarked while raising a brow. He then shook his head. "Not exactly a brilliant, military strategy."

"I made my point," Holloway insisted with little emotion. "My men returned the boy."

"Missing a finger," Nathan scoffed.

"Just his pinky finger," Holloway casually replied. "The bastard had my wife killed. He's lucky I didn't kill his son in retaliation."

"I'd rather not get into your affairs with other governments. I have enough of my own problems," Nathan insisted. "I promise my contact isn't aware of your identity. Trust me; my supplier doesn't want any trouble with his government either. I don't share any information between buyers and suppliers. As a middleman, that would be counterproductive. I have a wife too." He then considered his comment. "I'm also very attached to my fingers."

"Aren't we all," Holloway teased. "The usual fee?"

Nathan nodded. "Our usual drop-off location?"

"I'm comfortable with that," Holloway replied and returned the weapon to the strange man. "When will you meet with your Russian contact?"

"I'll see him tomorrow night," Nathan replied. "I'll make the arrangements and give you a call before the weekend with a date and time for the sale."

There was a faint thump above their heads. Everyone within the room looked up. Holloway eyed his men and nodded for them to check the garage above.

Dixon glared at Holloway. "It's her, I'm telling you," he snarled. "You can't trust that woman. I know she killed Gavin to throw you off her scent."

"She's still in bed," Holloway insisted. "I left her right before I came down here."

"I'll bet she's not in your room anymore," Dixon snapped and gave his boss an arrogant look.

Holloway glared his disapproval at his man then considered the comment. "I'll find out," he announced and hurried from the bunker.

§

Colonel Holloway made it from the bunker to the main house in record time using the underground corridor, which would be faster than anyone attempting to make it from the garage to the back kitchen stairs. His underground tunnel bypassed the entire kitchen, which took more time to pass through. Holloway hurried up a set of secret stairs that came out behind a panel within the kitchen not far from the back stairs. He bolted up the staircase and sprinted along the second floor hallway for his bedroom. Holloway threw open the bedroom door, now slightly out of breath, and looked at the empty, rumpled bed. Katrina was gone. Holloway vigorously raked his fingers through his hair and cursed under his breath. He was about to storm from the room when he heard water splashing from the bathroom.

"Darling, is that you?" the sweet southern bell called to him.

Holloway collected himself, shut the door behind him, and fixed his suit jacket as he crossed the bedroom for the bathroom. He gently pushed open the bathroom door while attempting to control his heavy breathing after his healthy sprint across the estate. Katrina lounged within the whirlpool tub with her hair pulled into a messy bun on top of her head. Her nightgown lay on the floor leading up to the tub. She leaned on the edge of the tub and smiled sweetly at him.

"Did you come to join me?" she cooed. "You were up early and left in a hurry this morning."

Colonel Holloway smiled while watching the naked woman seductively stretch out in the jetted tub displaying her body for him. Holloway removed his tie and jacket as he approached the tub.

"I had an early morning meeting," he informed her and eagerly stripped off his clothes. "I didn't mean to neglect you, my dear."

She ran her hands along her naked body while keeping her eyes locked on him as he undressed. Katrina writhed within the water increasing his arousal and his urgency to join her. He slipped into the large jetted tub with her. The exceedingly hot, churning water was comfortably offset by the cool air lingering through the open bathroom window. Holloway immediately pulled her into his arms. Her hands firmly caressed his body, barely waiting for him to settle within the water. She eagerly kissed his neck while writhing against his naked body beneath the water.

"You smell like lavender," he groaned softly while running his hands along her body and pulling her into position as she straddled him in the tub.

She let out a pleased gasp and continued to kiss his neck while gently moving against him. "Never mind how I smell," she cooed between kisses. "How do I taste?"

Holloway groaned and eagerly kissed her neck and throat while she continued to grind against him while on top of him.

"If you're finished with meetings, I'd like to keep you in bed the rest of the day," she whispered while clinging to his head as she held it to her neck.

"Anything you say, my dear," he announced then hesitated. "We have that party at four."

"We'll be fashionably late," she teased.

He groaned his response and clutched her buttocks below the water then sharply pulled her against him. Katrina gasped with pleasure as she clung to his neck.

Chapter 39

Late morning. South of the old ghost town, two open-top jeeps drove along the old, untraveled road while Jackie's helicopter circled the area. Jackie flew the helicopter with Gil riding shotgun and Darth panting over their shoulders. He appeared excited while watching the scenery whiz past. Zack sat in the back with the side door open and half leaned out. That he wasn't tethered to the craft had Jackie on edge. He always appeared ready to jump, and it made her nervous.

"I must be getting old," Gil announced then indicated the first jeep below as it swerved onto the uneven ground. "I can't ride in a car with Kirk driving anymore. I've survived too many plane crashes and gunshot wounds just to die because Kirk wanted to go off-road."

Zack leaned between their seats along with Darth and chuckled. "Remember that time he posed as a limo driver?"

Gil laughed. Jackie cast a look at them. She hadn't been around for that one.

"Kirk pulls up to the rendezvous in half a limo," Gil informed her. "The Russian dignitary was pissing his pants in the backward facing seat."

"Still holding his champagne glass," Zack added.

Gil laughed at the memory. "Man," he announced. "I miss formal parties."

The first jeep on the ground was driven by Kirk, while Monroe sat in the front passenger seat clinging to the seat and the suicide strap for dear life. Bogart rode in the back and attempted to remain in his seat but was having a difficult time with Kirk's erratic driving. Their jeep was nearly a quarter of a mile ahead of the second jeep and tackled the rough terrain with speed and high impact jumps. Kirk was in his glory as the jeep was nearly airborne several times.

"Next time, I'm driving," Monroe groaned.

"I second that," Bogart announced while bouncing around the back seat.

"You're a bunch of big babies," Kirk replied then cried out with enthusiasm as they tackled another large mound of ground that again sent them airborne.

The second jeep lagged behind and remained on the old road, which was a pleasantly smooth drive. Beck sat behind the wheel and watched the cloud of dirt being kicked up from the jeep ahead of them. He pointed at the jeep in front of them with disgust while eyeing Ross in the passenger seat alongside him.

"He's like a little kid," Beck remarked while gesturing wildly. "No matter what we're doing, he's like a kid at Christmas."

Ross shrugged. "Sometimes playing in the puddles, at any age, can be fun," he remarked then eyed Beck. "Driving with you is like driving with my grandmother."

Beck shot a look at Ross. "You're saying I drive like a little old lady?"

"I'm saying," Ross announced while pointing, "stop being such an old man and give chase!"

Martin leaned over their shoulders from the back seat and grinned. He was about to speak when Beck shifted the jeep into the next gear and hit the gas pedal. Martin was thrown back in his seat then jolted around as Beck went out of his way to drive on the uneven terrain just off the old road. Ross laughed despite having to cling to his seat and the roll cage. Martin attempted to sit up and looked around.

"You missed the turn," Martin announced then pointed to their right. "We need to go back that way, toward the hillside."

Ross placed his hand radio to his mouth to contact the first jeep with the change of course when Beck spun the jeep around, startling both men. The jeep burned out and headed back for the hillside.

Ross laughed while eyeing Beck. "Now that's living!" He then gave the new direction change to the first jeep that was now nearly half a mile ahead of them.

Kirk's jeep spun around in a cloud of dirt, burned out while kicking up rocks and debris, and rocketed for the hillside to catch up to the second jeep. Bogart was nearly falling out the open side. The helicopter lazily circled above them. Within the aircraft, all three watched the jeeps bounding over mounds and nearly flying through the air.

"I think they're drunk," Jackie remarked while shaking her head.

"Face it, Jackie," Gil announced with little reaction. "You and I are the only mature ones on this team."

"Are you saying I'm not mature?" Zack demanded and gave Gil's profile an offended glare.

"Do you even have a driver's license?" Gil casually asked while glancing back at his friend.

"Yes, I do," Zack replied matter-of-factly. "Six of them."

"I think I've made my point," Gil muttered. As the jeeps finally slowed, reaching their destination, Gil pointed a little further away. "You can set her down over there."

Zack was already in his harness when they heard the snap of the carabiner clip being attached to the helicopter floor. Jackie and Gil looked back as Zack placed one foot on the landing rung.

"Don't you--" Jackie threatened but was too late.

Zack was already jumping from the helicopter and sliding down the nylon rope to the ground. Jackie slowed the helicopter just as Zack pulled the release. He hit the ground, rolled several times, and sprang to his feet. Jackie cursed under her breath while Gil shook his head.

"I told you," he announced. "We're the only adults around here."

Jackie landed the helicopter in the clearing where Gil had indicated. Darth barely waited for them to touch ground before jumping out the side and running after Zack.

"Zack's a bad influence on Darth," Gil muttered with disappointment. "I may have to limit your visitation rights."

"So you're punishing me for Zack's bad influence on Darth?" Jackie demanded while removing her headset.

"Zack spends sixty percent of his time with you and Holden," Gil informed her while giving her a stern look. "Possession is nine-tenths of the law. That makes Zack one hundred percent your problem."

"Your math sucks," she huffed.

"You're responsible for Zack's social interaction," he continued.

"Says who?" she demanded.

"We took a vote," he informed her while maintaining his serious look. "We just didn't tell you."

Jackie glared at Gil, who easily ignored her. They walked nearly fifty yards to reach the others by the hillside and looked around with confusion.

"So is this like some secret bat cave entrance?" Bogart remarked.

Martin removed a bundle of old brush to reveal an aging mine entrance that had almost completely collapsed. Beck groaned when he saw the narrow, dark opening and removed a large flashlight. He shined the light into the opening then straightened.

"This is going to be fun," Beck muttered then looked around. "I hate tight spaces."

"We should have brought the kids along," Kirk remarked in all seriousness.

Martin shot a disapproving look at Kirk. Zack walked past them, dropped to his hands and knees with a small flashlight in his mouth, and crawled into the dark opening. Darth barked excitedly and ran into the opening after Zack. They could hear the dog's barking echoing from inside.

Gil stared after his dog with disappointment and shook his head. "Traitor," he scoffed.

"It's just the entrance that's collapsed," Martin informed them. "The rest of the mine is secure."

"That mine was built in the 1800s," Ross remarked while raising a cocky brow. "Secure isn't the term I'd use."

"It's fine," Martin again insisted. "I've been in there dozens of times."

Martin turned on his flashlight and crawled through the small opening after Zack and Darth.

Ross drew a deep breath then looked at the others. "I'm going to need someone--"

"I'll stay," Beck announced while shifting uncomfortably and received several looks. He smiled and laughed almost nervously and pointed at the narrow opening. "I'm not crawling in there. I'll be the lookout."

"Jackie will stay with you," Ross remarked.

Jackie raised a demanding brow. "I don't think so," she announced. "I want to explore the mine."

She turned on her flashlight and just about dove into the opening. Monroe gazed upon her backside as she crawled through. It was a beautiful sight to behold. Bogart jabbed Monroe with his elbow, gave him a disapproving look, and a firm gesture with his hand. He then followed his sister through the opening. Monroe measured Kirk's broad shoulders with his hands then moved closer to the opening with his measurements. He looked back at Ross and shook his head.

"Unless you brought the plunger, there's no way Kirk's fitting through that opening," Monroe insisted.

"Fine," Ross announced. "Kirk stays with Beck." He then motioned Monroe and Gil to the opening.

Gil and Monroe crawled through the opening on their hands and knees and entered the mine with Ross bringing up the rear.

Chapter 40

The team only had to crawl on their hands and knees a few feet through the entrance before they could stand within the eerily dark mine. The mine was in excellent condition as Martin had promised. He then led the way. Zack kept pace with Martin at the front and shined his light around the pitch-black tunnel. Despite the age of the support beams, they were in surprisingly good condition, and the walls contained few crumbles.

"Air's a little stale in here," Monroe remarked.

"Smells like a tomb," Gil added while shining his light around as well.

Jackie brought up the rear with Bogart, who was intrigued by the mine.

"There was a mine like this near where I grew up," Bogart informed Jackie. "We used to play in there as kids."

"That must have been fun," Jackie replied while looking around.

"Popular make-out spot," he continued matter-of-factly then grinned. "Scored for the first time in that mine."

Jackie cast a look at him and became uncomfortable. She didn't want to hear about her brother's first time. "A little too much information," she remarked.

"I wasn't going to give details," Bogart huffed and shook his head. "I know about your first time. Why shouldn't you know about mine?"

Jackie glared at Bogart and raised her brows. "Who told you about my first time?" she demanded then glared at the back of Monroe's head as they followed him. She honestly wanted to kill Monroe some days.

"Holden," Bogart replied.

She stared at her brother with surprise. "Holden told you that?" Jackie practically gasped. "What would possess him--?"

"It just came up," Bogart remarked and cast a surprised look at her. "Why is it a big deal?"

"Because you're my brother," she huffed. "Isn't that reason enough?"

"We were friends before we discovered we were related," he reminded her. "I don't think I should have to watch what I say around you now that we know we're related. That should make it easier to share."

Jackie sighed and nodded. "I suppose you're right," she reluctantly replied.

"Of course I'm right." He was silent a moment. "Although I have to ask," Bogart remarked and eyed her with a strange look. "Why Monroe?"

She groaned with annoyance. "And this conversation is over."

"It's right up here," Martin announced.

Martin led them through the mine for nearly a quarter mile, before reaching a green, Army duffel bag. He opened the bag to reveal a padded, black nylon bag. The men and Jackie stared at the bag and appeared curious. Martin opened the padded bag to reveal a metal box with a state-of-the-art, thumbprint lock on it. Everyone stared at the box in awe. The box obviously contained something important.

"Ain't that official looking," Bogart commented and tilted his head with a curious look. "What's in it?"

"I'm not entirely sure, but Colonel Holloway killed a man for it," Martin replied. He removed a flash drive from the bag, straightened, and held it up. "This was with it, but it's encrypted."

Gil took the flash drive and stuck it in his pocket. "I'll give it to Beck and let him have a look at it."

Zack crouched alongside the metal box and lovingly ran his hand along it. "You've had this for over five years?" Zack asked.

"Yeah," Martin replied. "That's when I took it off Colonel Holloway."

"It's obviously a weapon of some kind," Ross announced while casting looks at his men. "You don't come across boxes like that for mere papers."

"Unfortunately, there's no way to access it to find out," Martin remarked with a defeated sigh. "If I knew what I had, maybe--"

They heard a beep from the bag. Everyone turned and saw Zack straightening while holding a titanium weapon resembling a sawed-off shotgun from the future. Zack's eyes were sparkling as he lovingly caressed the weapon.

"Happy birthday to me," Zack announced and shifted it within his hands as if getting a feel for it.

"Jesus, Zack," Ross cried out. "Put that down. There's no telling what that thing does. You'll bring the entire cave down on us."

Zack frowned and returned the weapon to the case. As he closed the lid, he removed a small piece of duct tape from the locking pad and seamlessly slipped it over the interior lock to prevent it from locking. His fluid action went unnoticed by the rest of the team.

"How did you open that?" Martin asked with surprise.

Zack gave him an innocent look. "Thumbprint lock," he replied. "The thumbprint from the last time it was opened was still on the glass. All I had to do was put some tape over it and press it." He grinned deviously. "Our government technology at work. They moved away from thumbprints over the years. Retinal scans are the rage now. I'd need Colonel Holloway's eyeball, and he probably wouldn't give it willingly." Zack ran his hands over the metal case and grinned like a schoolboy. "Can we take it back to the lodge and see what it does?"

Ross eyed Monroe and gave him a quick nod. Monroe grabbed the duffel bag and pulled it away from Zack.

Zack frowned and straightened. "I would have taken 'no' for an answer," he pouted.

"Unlikely," Ross muttered.

Monroe shut the black nylon bag then the exterior duffel bag, securing their find. He picked up the bag and slung it over his shoulder.

"Time to call Jackie's favorite FBI boy toy," Ross announced and received a glare from Jackie and a snicker from the guys. "We'll turn it over to him and see what happens when the dust settles."

Ross's hand radio crackled, alerting everyone to a potential problem. Ross held the hand radio to his mouth.

"Yeah, Kirk," he announced.

There was more static.

"It must be interference from the mine," Monroe informed him.

"Whatever he wants," Ross announced, "I'm sure it's not good. We'd better bug out."

Chapter 41

Despite making it to the narrow entrance in record time, it took the team a few minutes to crawl out and push the duffel bag out as well. Zack was first out of the cave and hurried to join Kirk, who stood near the jeep while watching the ghost town through his binoculars.

Kirk eyed the others then nodded to the distant town. "About two dozen men in a fleet of open-top jeeps converged on the ghost town ten minutes ago," he announced. "They already spotted Jackie's helicopter. They'll be on top of us in five minutes."

"Jackie and Monroe need to get that bag and Martin out of here in the helicopter," Ross announced. "The rest of us will run interference in the jeeps." He twirled his finger in the air. "Go, go, go."

Jackie, Monroe, Martin, and Darth ran for the helicopter, which was a decent sprint from the mine entrance. Darth easily took the lead. Sounds from the approaching jeeps were getting louder. All three hurried after Darth for the helicopter. Martin ran for the back, side door while Jackie headed for the front pilot's door. Darth stared at the helicopter and snarled as

Martin pulled open the door for Monroe carrying the bag. A man with an assault rifle was perched in the opening and aimed his weapon at them. He grinned when he saw Martin.

"Hello, Martin," the man announced then eyed the duffel bag Monroe held. "I'm glad to see you brought what we want. It'll save us from having to torture you for it."

Two men with assault rifles appeared from the rear of the helicopter and looked around with some confusion.

"Wasn't there a woman and a dog with them?" the first man remarked.

Martin and Monroe shifted their eyes alongside them. Jackie and Darth were gone. Martin seemed slightly surprised while Monroe didn't even flinch. Darth's snarl had alerted her to danger within the helicopter, giving her time to execute her own contingency plan. The man within the helicopter seemed alarmed by a gentle breeze behind him. He hesitated then looked over his shoulder. Jackie smiled sweetly from where she crouched in the opposing rear door then kicked him in the face. The man flew out the opening, knocking Martin to the ground with him. The two men at the tail of the helicopter had their weapons aimed at Monroe, but their own man being thrown from the helicopter temporarily blocked their view. In the brief seconds their partner and Martin hit the ground; Monroe already had his semiautomatic in his hand and shot the first man in the chest.

Before the second man could react, he heard a snarl behind him and spun around. Darth leaped on top of him, rode him to the ground, and sank his teeth into the man's arm while aggressively slinging his head. Monroe ran for the dog attacking the man. The man Jackie kicked into Martin landed on top of him on the ground. Before Martin could react, the man gave Martin a swift elbow to the ribs from behind then sprang to his feet facing his female adversary within the helicopter. Jackie leaped from the opening feet first, caught the man around the neck with her legs, and took him to the ground with her. She hit the ground and immediately rolled away from the dazed man.

Had it been Zack, the man would have sustained a broken neck. Jackie could never get used to the sound, which always sent a chill down her spine. Monroe had retrieved the dead man's assault rifle and was already firing at the approaching jeep. Martin grabbed the discarded assault rifle belonging to Jackie's opponent and joined Monroe. Both men fired at the rapidly approaching jeep.

"Jackie," Monroe cried out. "We need to get this bird airborne, ASAP!"

"Working on it," Jackie snapped back.

As the man attempted to stand, Jackie kicked him in the head. He dropped to the ground out cold. Jackie leaped into the pilot's seat and started the helicopter. Darth jumped into the back then sprang into the front passenger seat. Jackie glared at the dog, who excitedly stared out the front windshield while panting and wagging his tail. She shook her head and decided to let him have his moment as acting co-pilot. Monroe indicated the bag to Martin. Martin tossed the assault rifle over his shoulder, grabbed the duffel bag, and jumped inside. He then fired out the side, giving Monroe time to join him in the helicopter.

Both men fired their ill-gotten assault rifles out the side of the helicopter as it lifted off the ground. The men in the jeep attempted to fire back, but they were taking on too much gunfire from the two men. The helicopter flew out of range and then out of sight beyond some trees. The man Jackie had knocked out slowly moved to his feet and looked in the direction the helicopter headed. He stumbled toward the men in the jeep while holding his head.

"They have the prototype," he announced and got into the jeep with the others. "We need at least one of their friends alive."

The man in the front passenger side nodded and removed his hand radio, relaying the message to their team.

§

Even though Kirk reported nearly two dozen men arriving at the ghost town, their numbers seemed greater with seven, open jeeps containing two or more men in each, leaving the team sorely outnumbered with their meager two jeeps.

There were three jeeps on Kirk's tail and four on Beck's tail. They had either been watching the ghost town, suspecting that's where the item they sought had been hidden, or they had been searching for it themselves and happened to notice the helicopter's arrival. Since their response time had been slow, they were probably watching the ghost town. They then organized when they realized someone was there.

With enough open terrain, the guys could circle the area once, give Jackie enough time to get the bag and Martin to safety, and then head for a populated area, which would undoubtedly result in an end to the chase. By the time they saw the helicopter evacuating the area, another jeep joined them, making it four on one in the wild chase. Kirk drove the first jeep at top speeds while Bogart and Gil were staked out in the back and returned fire on the men chasing them. The jeeps behind them were having a tough time hitting the swiftly moving vehicle in front that swerved erratically. It also made it difficult for the men in the back to hit the jeeps pursuing them.

The second jeep with Beck at the wheel had peeled off and went a different direction to split up the bad guys in a divide and conquer scenario. Despite the speed the jeep was traveling, Zack had little difficulty hitting his target from the bouncing back seat. Ross managed to keep himself steady, but he didn't fire nearly as many rounds as Zack, who could remain steady in just about any condition. Zack took a moment for a precision shot. One of the jeeps was struck in the front tire, which blew out and sent the jeep into a roll. Ross cast a look at Zack and grinned.

"Twenty bucks says you can't do that again," Ross teased.

Zack grinned, straightened into a more vulnerable position to steady his shot, and fired again. Another jeep blew a tire and flipped several times through the air. Ross chuckled and resumed firing on the jeeps chasing them. Zack removed something from one of his many pockets. Ross eyed the grenade then immediately spun forward in his seat and sank down. Zack pulled the pin with his teeth and threw the grenade into the path of the closer jeep.

"Fire in the hole," Zack cried out and ducked.

Beck subconsciously shirked in the front seat. The grenade exploded just as the vehicle drove over it. The tailing jeep was launched through the air and landed on top of the vehicle not far behind it. Zack grinned and chuckled as Ross turned his head and viewed Zack's handy work. Beck peered through the rearview mirror to have a look for himself.

"That's a two-for," Zack announced and grinned, pleased with himself.

"Let's check on the rest of our team," Ross announced while slapping Beck on the shoulder and motioning for him to circle back.

Chapter 42

Kirk drove the jeep at high speeds across the rough terrain with four jeeps on their tail. Gil and Bogart managed to take out one of the men shooting at them, although the fourth jeep remained in hot pursuit along with his teammates. One of the pursuing jeeps gained on them. A stray shot struck Gil in the chest and threw him from the back of the jeep. He bounced several times across the grassy terrain before rolling to a stop where he remained motionless. The fourth pursuing jeep, which had lost its man riding shotgun, turned back around to make certain Gil was dead.

"We lost Gil," Bogart yelled to Kirk, who was now having some trouble controlling the jeep.

"We're also out of gas," Kirk called back. "They must have hit the gas tank!"

"Ah, hell," Bogart scoffed under his breath and attempted to process the information.

As their jeep slowed, the pursuing jeeps gained on them. One vehicle passed them and circled in front as Kirk's jeep rolled to a stop. They were surrounded.

"What do we do?" Bogart asked Kirk while clutching his assault rifle.

"In this situation, I recommend we surrender," Kirk replied dryly and casually placed his hands in the air. "Hope for the best."

Bogart cursed under his breath, tossed his rifle from the jeep, and placed his hands in the air. The men held their weapons on them and approached the jeep.

"You've got a better plan, right?" Bogart asked while eyeing him.

Kirk didn't bother looking back at Bogart. He frowned and sighed with defeat. "Nope."

The armed men approached but didn't shoot. They motioned them out of the jeep. Bogart and Kirk got out of the jeep with their hands in the air and faced the men with the guns.

"Where did your friend in the helicopter take Martin?" the first man asked.

"Fort Carson," Kirk responded with little emotion and without hesitation.

The armed men didn't appear pleased. "Tie them up," he instructed his men. "We need them."

The man then looked across the field to the jeep that stopped where Gil had fallen after being shot. He signaled to his man. The man signaled back and approached the motionless man in the field. With his booted foot, he pushed Gil onto his back. Gil's limp right arm covered his chest with his hand beneath his left arm. The man poked him with the barrel of his assault rifle. Gil's eyes suddenly popped open. He grabbed the rifle barrel and pulled the man down on top of him. Gil revealed the Bowie knife hidden in his right hand and stabbed the man in the throat. The man muffled a gasp, but nothing came out.

Gil snatched the man's assault rifle and kept low to the ground as he ran for the nearby jeep and safety. He paused a moment to rub his chest and plucked the bullet from his bulletproof vest, flicking it aside. While hiding behind the jeep, he peered at the others in the distance, but none paid attention to their partner. Gil crept alongside the jeep, slipped into the driver's seat, threw the jeep into gear, and sped away. The men finally looked back, but the jeep was already speeding out of view. They'd never catch him.

"He left us," Bogart gasped under his breath while casting a look at Kirk.

Kirk didn't show any emotion. "Yep."

"Why?"

"No point in all of us dying," Kirk muttered.

§

Beck's jeep raced along the countryside with Zack standing up in the back while holding onto the roll cage. He scanned the area through binoculars. Something caught his eye. He tapped Beck on the top of the head and pointed in the distance.

"It's Gil," Zack announced.

"Just Gil?" Ross asked and took the binoculars from Zack. He looked for himself and frowned as the jeep got closer. "Son-of-a-bitch."

The two jeeps pulled alongside each other while facing opposite directions and stopped, putting Gil in line with Beck behind the wheel of his own vehicle.

"What happened?" Beck asked with concern.

"Bogart and Kirk were captured," Gil informed them while frowning. "They took them prisoner. I thought we'd better regroup rather than attempt a solo rescue."

"They're probably heading back for the ghost town," Beck announced. "They'd be heading back this way if they wanted to reach the main road."

"They must have something going on in that old town," Ross remarked.

"Didn't Bogart mention seeing guys coming from the barn that day they chased after the girls?" Gil questioned and eyed his teammates. "It's worth a look."

"It's possible they want information on Martin and that bag," Ross remarked while sinking into thought. He glanced at his men. "They'll probably attempt to extract information from

Kirk and Bogart. Maybe keep one hostage in exchange for the bag's return."

"Then we'd better get to them fast," Beck muttered. "Bogart will crack like an egg."

"You might be surprised," Ross commented. "I don't know that he'd willingly give up Jackie."

"Let's not take the chance," Zack remarked gruffly, grabbed his assault rifle, and jumped onto the hood of Gil's jeep. He climbed over the windshield and sank into the passenger seat alongside Gil. "Circle the ghost town and drop me off just west of it. I can make it to the back of the barn undetected."

Chapter 43

Bogart fought the duct tape binding his wrists to the arms of the metal chair then looked at Kirk sitting calmly tied to the chair alongside him. Bogart groaned and gave up. He glanced around the large, open barn, which contained several rotting stalls to the left and a hayloft covering half the ceiling toward the back of the barn. Despite being early afternoon, the rafters within the barn were mostly dark. An old door within the loft could be heard creaking above them, possibly moving from a breeze. Six men had collected in the corner near the main barn door leaving three still missing. The men appeared to be in conference.

Bogart looked back at Kirk, who still hadn't moved. "Well, this feels familiar," Bogart muttered.

"Why is it whenever I'm captured, it's always with you?" Kirk scoffed. "It's like you're cursed or something."

"Me?" Bogart whispered loudly. "You can't blame this on me. You were the one driving."

"No, it's definitely you," Kirk remarked without looking at him. "Just once, I'd like to be caught with someone remotely useful."

"Sorry I ain't Zack," Bogart huffed.

"Zack doesn't get caught," Kirk reminded him then considered the comment. "Correction. He's only ever caught when there's a hot woman involved. Although, I'm starting to think that's on purpose. I'd get my fingers broken, and he'd get laid."

Bogart gave Kirk a stunned look. "Really?"

"He exaggerates," Zack muttered while crouched behind them.

Bogart tensed with surprise and cast a brief look back where Zack hid behind their chairs. Zack sliced the duct tape near Kirk's left wrist then moved to his right.

"That only happened once," Zack replied then sliced the duct tape holding Bogart's left arm to the chair. He paused to reflect upon the incident. "If she's still alive, I should look her up." Zack then cut the duct tape binding their ankles together. "That was the most fun I ever had in Bosnia."

When Kirk didn't make a motion to get up, Bogart remained seated as well with the tape still convincingly stuck to the arm of the chair.

"That's taking bondage to the extreme," Bogart remarked then hesitated and glanced behind him.

Zack was gone.

Bogart shook his head. "Jackie has to teach me that Ninja shit," he remarked then eyed Kirk. "What's the plan?"

"You sit there and be quiet," Kirk announced while remaining in the same position with the same expression he had before Zack cut him free.

The man Jackie had assaulted by the helicopter entered the barn, eyed the tied men, and then joined the other six men. The two men he'd hitched a ride with must have been outside securing the town. Two more men then left the barn, leaving just the five inside.

"I wish you'd let me in on the plan just once," Bogart whispered with some irritation.

"Listen for it and count to four," Kirk announced.

"Listen for what?"

"*It*," Kirk snarled. "Shut up and listen."

Bogart sat quietly and listened for anything unusual. He then heard a faint cracking sound coming from outside. A few seconds later, he heard a faint moan. That was two. Toward the back of the barn, there was another moan. That was three. A few seconds later, there was another cracking sound. That was four. Zack was good at what he did. Bogart glanced at Kirk, who still didn't move. The man in charge finally approached them with two men following him. The other two men stood guard a little further back.

"I'm not an unreasonable man," their leader announced to them. "I don't want to kill either of you. Honestly, I don't need to kill either of you. All I want is Martin, and whatever it was he gave your friends."

"I'll tell you what I know," Kirk announced to the man with little emotion. "As I told your friend there--" He indicated the man standing to the leader's right. "The helicopter took your friend to Fort Carson to meet with Colonel Bamford."

"Colonel Bamford?"

"Bastard. Asshole. Mother. Fucker. Anal. Retentive. Dick," Kirk snarled, spelling it out for him.

Bogart gave Kirk a strange look. "You just spelled Bamfard."

Kirk casually shrugged. "I couldn't think of a derogatory word starting with 'O'," he replied.

"I don't believe they went to Fort Carson," the leader announced and raised his brows while glaring at Kirk. "Tell me something I will believe, or my friends are going to start carving up some of your favorite body parts."

"Fine," Kirk announced while glaring back at the man. "First I'm going to dislocate your knee." He then indicated the man to his right. "Then I'm going to bust your friend's jaw. While my so-called partner here clumsily takes down that dickless ass wipe to your left, I'm going to tear out your throat with my bare hands." Kirk raised his brows. "Is that more believable for you?"

The man stared at Kirk a moment as if unable to believe what he'd just heard. He grinned and laughed. "I'd like to see you try."

Kirk made a motion to move, but the duct tape held him in place. He groaned with irritation. Bogart stared at him with horror on his face.

"Seriously?" Bogart gasped. "Are you trying to get us killed?" He then looked at the man, smiled charmingly, and laughed. "You have to forgive the big guy. He just found out he's got one of those infections where fire shoots out when he pisses. Makes him a little cranky."

Kirk's expression dropped as he slowly turned his head and glared at Bogart. "What is wrong with you?" Kirk demanded. "Why would you even make up something like that? You're completely fucked up in the head."

"I don't see you doing anything to get us out of this," Bogart proclaimed. "Let's just give the guy what he wants, and he'll let us go home with all our body parts. Because, honestly, I don't want one of Zack's fifty shades of bondage sex in this barn."

The three men standing over the bickering men exchanged baffled looks. Once the leader's attention was off him, Kirk thrust his booted foot into the man's knee, snapping it and sending him to the ground. As the two men alongside him went for their weapons, Kirk and Bogart both leaped from their chairs for their respective assailants. The two men by the door were about to intervene when the main door was thrown open. Beck and Gil crouched in the doorway and fired several rounds into the two men closest to the door. Bogart punched the first man in the face and spun into a clumsy roundhouse kick, striking him in the chest. The jolt was enough to send his opponent back a step but not enough to knock him down. The man regained his balance and charged Bogart, tackling him to the ground not far from the chair. The man punched him in the face.

Bogart looked up and saw Zack casually sitting on one of the support beams across the ceiling. He watched the scene and shook his head with disappointment. Zack made a jabbing motion with his two fingers. Bogart looked back at the man on top of him, blocked the punch that followed, and poked the man in the eyes with his first two fingers. The man cried out, clutched his eyes, and fell off Bogart. At the same time, Kirk punched the second man in the jaw, easily dislocating it, and then spun back for the leader, who attempted to stand despite his busted knee. He looked at Kirk with some concern. Kirk offered an unsettling smile and rammed his fingers into the man's throat. The leader gurgled while spitting up blood as Kirk tore out his throat. As the man fell to the ground, Kirk tossed aside the bloody mess within his hand.

Ross, Beck, Gil, and Kirk impatiently waited for Bogart to take down his opponent. Bogart saw the looks he received and was distracted just enough to take a shot to his abdomen. He doubled over while groaning and clutching himself. Beck groaned and removed his semiautomatic.

Ross caught Beck's hand and lowered the gun. "Let him fight his own battles."

"Oh," Beck announced and tensed slightly. "Actually, I was just going to shoot Bogart."

The man hovered over Bogart and was about to punch him in the head when Bogart snap-kicked him under the chin and then spun into a nearly perfect roundhouse kick, nailing him in the face. The man dropped to the ground and didn't move. Zack applauded from the rafters. Ross, Beck, Gil, and Kirk laughed and started clapping as well. Bogart sneered at his teammates.

"Ah, fuck off," he muttered then raked his fingers through his mussed hair.

Chapter 44

Jackie's helicopter was seen outside an old, dilapidated hangar at an abandoned airfield where they were waiting for the rest of their team. Gil's private plane sat on the old runway not far from the hangar. Jackie, Monroe, and Martin paced before the helicopter while Darth explored the area, thoroughly marking every object he found. Jackie looked at her watch several times.

"Holden's going to be here soon," Jackie remarked while fidgeting. "Where are the guys? They should have been here by now."

"The guys are fine," Monroe insisted. "We sent the feds to the ghost town. If anything happened, they'll provide backup."

Jackie remained concerned and started pacing. "I should have waited to call Holden."

"You did what Ross told you to do," Monroe insisted while studying her as she became unusually tense. "It's just Holden meeting us here; not the entire Bureau. He'll wait for Ross to get here before he does anything. I'm sure once the rest of the Bureau shows up at the old ghost town; he's going to want some answers." Monroe gave her a strange look. "You trust Holden, right?"

Jackie cast a look at Monroe and frowned. "Of course I trust Holden," she informed him. "It's just--" She looked back at Martin then returned her gaze to Monroe. "I'm not thrilled about turning over Martin. Holden will have to turn him over to the Army."

"That's why we're turning over the weapon and the flash drive," Monroe reminded her. "There's less chance of Martin having an accident if they're not in his possession. Colonel Holloway will have other things to worry about. Like covering his own ass."

"That doesn't mean he won't have his men kill Martin," Jackie snapped back attempting to fight Martin's case. "Martin can still testify against him. He should be in witness protection; not military jail."

"That's not our call, Jackie."

"It wouldn't be the first time we made our own call." Jackie again looked at Martin and didn't take her eyes from him. "The highway is only half a mile from here," she announced to Monroe although more or less instructing Martin. "He could easily take off when we're busy doing other things. Surely he could hitch a ride with a trucker." She then looked back at Monroe. "He can take care of himself. He's been hiding for years. Once Colonel Holloway has been arrested, he can come out of hiding."

"This is the military we're talking about, Jackie," Monroe insisted. "These are the guys who can make our lives very uncomfortable. I may skirt around the law and even the feds, but I won't turn my back on the military. I took an oath. That didn't end with my discharge."

"He's right, Jackie," Martin announced as he leaned against the helicopter and managed a tiny smile at her concern for him and his family. "I need to face this thing and end it once and for all. I want to clear my name and my record so I can be with my family."

Darth suddenly became alert and barked while wagging his tail. Two jeeps drove down the long, dirt road to the abandoned airfield. Despite that one belonged to the bad guys, they could see their teammates in the open jeeps. Jackie sighed with relief. The jeeps stopped near them, and the rest of the team jumped out. Everyone was accounted for as well as a bound bad guy in the back of the first jeep. Ross approached Jackie while the guys busily removed their gear from the jeeps and headed for Gil's plane.

"Is Holden on his way?" Ross eagerly asked.

"Yeah, he should be here in less than twenty minutes," she replied. "About Martin--"

"We don't have much time," Ross announced as Beck hurried past him.

Beck removed his laptop from his bag, set it on the back floor of the helicopter, and feverishly worked on it. He inserted the flash drive into the port without missing a keystroke. Ross looked around the back of the helicopter then met Monroe's gaze.

"Where's the duffel bag?" Ross asked.

"In the cargo compartment," Monroe replied and indicated the helicopter. "I didn't want it in plain sight in case we ran into trouble."

As Kirk approached the helicopter, Ross nodded to the cargo compartment behind him. Kirk opened the compartment, removed the duffel bag, and set it on the ground. He stood in front of the bag to ensure it didn't go anywhere. Darth approached Kirk and sniffed around his leg then attempted to paw his way into the calf pocket on his pants. Kirk glared at the playful dog.

"What's with you?" Kirk demanded with limited patience. "I don't carry treats around for you."

The dog stood in front of Kirk and barked several times then sat patiently and wagged his tail across the dirt.

"I don't have any treats," Kirk again insisted. "Stupid dog. Go away."

Darth sat up and begged, barked, and licked his muzzle. Kirk frowned with annoyance then reached into his calf pocket and removed some beef jerky. He tossed it to the dog, who easily caught it and happily chewed on it.

"That's all you get," Kirk snarled and pointed. "Now go away."

Darth barked and took off on command. The remaining guys busily removed things from the jeeps and carried them to the awaiting plane. Darth joined Zack by the jeep, sat in front of him, and barked while wagging his tail. Zack tossed Darth a piece of beef jerky, which he gobbled up then handed the dog a backpack. Darth grabbed the handle of the backpack and half dragged it to the awaiting plane with Zack following behind carrying his own bag. There was no telling what Zack stole from the mercenaries at the ghost town. It was best not to ask either.

Jackie, Monroe, and Martin watched the guys buzz around between the jeep and Gil's plane.

"What's going on?" Monroe asked now curious. "Did something happen?"

"We got a little closer to Colonel Holloway's mercenaries than intended," Ross informed him then nodded to the nearby jeep containing their prisoner. "His man in the jeep gave up a ton of information and is willing to rat out Holloway. Holloway has VIP prisoners in the basement of his mansion ranging from CIA to British Intelligence." He then indicated the duffel bag with a nod. "That weapon is a prototype. Once Martin no longer has that weapon and flash drive, they'll kill him."

"I did tell you that," Martin remarked.

"The military can't protect him. We can't afford to let Martin out of our custody," Ross announced then nodded Martin to Gil's plane. "You need to get out of here before Holden arrives. We'll deal with him and the Army. The information Holden gets from Holloway's snitch will be enough to issue a search warrant and have him arrested until the FBI can sort out the rest of this mess."

Zack approached Martin and shooed him toward the awaiting plane that was already preparing for takeoff. Martin nodded and hurried with Zack for Gil's plane.

"How's it coming?" Ross asked Beck, who continued to feverishly work on his laptop.

"Almost there," Beck announced.

Bogart ran to join them while holding a pair of binoculars. "I see Holden's vehicle. He'll be turning on the road any minute."

"Got it," Beck announced then pulled the flash drive from his laptop and slammed the lid shut.

Beck passed the flash drive off to Ross, stuffed his computer in his bag, and ran with Bogart for the awaiting plane. The door to the plane no sooner closed when the plane taxied down the runway.

Chapter 45

Gil's plane was already airborne when Holden's black SUV started its journey down the long dirt road. Ross, Kirk, Jackie, and Monroe were all that remained from the team. Jackie was still clueless as to what was happening, but since it was her husband, she didn't need to worry about putting on a show. She removed her leather bomber jacket from the front seat of the helicopter and casually slipped into it as the vehicle approached.

The SUV stopped alongside the two jeeps. Holden got out, eyed the bound man in the back of the first jeep, and then headed toward the remaining team and the helicopter. He eagerly smiled when he saw his wife. Jackie met him halfway and greeted him with a warm yet passionate kiss. He pulled away just far enough to meet her gaze and grinned.

"Does this mean you're coming home?" Holden asked cheerfully.

"I'm not entirely sure," she remarked then smirked while pulling away from him. "Ross is being mysterious and secretive again."

Holden rolled his eyes and groaned. "That's not good," he muttered then approached the others waiting by the helicopter. Holden immediately looked around and frowned. "Where's Martin?"

"We're going to need your help with that one," Ross announced then looked at Kirk and nodded.

Kirk picked up the duffel bag and with little emotion handed it to Holden.

Holden accepted the bag and eyed Ross. "What's this?" he asked.

"That is a secret military weapon Colonel Holloway stole," Ross informed him. "Martin took it from him as evidence and stashed it when he was branded a traitor and a deserter. It's also the only thing keeping Martin alive."

Holden carried the bag to his SUV, placed it on the hood, and unzipped the outer and inner bag. He stared at the metal box with the fancy, thumbprint lock. Holden looked at the others as they gathered around him.

"You haven't been able to get inside?" Holden asked with a curious look.

"No," Ross easily lied. "It's a thumbprint lock. You need some top brass's thumb to get in there." Ross then handed him the flash drive. "We believe this has information on it that explains the weapon inside that case. Whatever information is on this thing must be highly classified, or something Colonel Holloway doesn't want anyone to see. I think it'll help put him away and possibly clear Martin."

"So where is Martin?" Holden asked while accepting the flash drive, which he placed in his inner jacket pocket. He again looked around.

"That's the part you'll need to help us with," Ross continued.

Holden rolled his eyes and groaned while shifting uncomfortably. "Come on, Ross," he bellowed. "Don't do this to me."

"Martin is willing to testify that he witnessed Colonel Holloway personally shooting a man to steal that weapon," Ross continued despite Holden's reluctance to listen. "What you have before you should be enough to arrest Holloway, but Martin isn't safe in military prison awaiting trial. Holloway has mercenaries and active military willing to kill anyone who gets in his way." Ross studied Holden's annoyed expression and continued despite the look he received. "We ran into some of his merry men while retrieving that device. We also brought you a gift. He's in the back of the jeep. A songbird. He'll provide enough information on his boss to warrant an arrest without waiting on the Army to open that case and flash drive for you." Ross gave him a serious look. "Even after you arrest Colonel Holloway, Martin won't last a day in prison without having an accident."

"And you want to keep Martin in your protective custody until the trial?" Holden surmised while appearing uncomfortable with the assumption.

"A lot of good men and women never came home, and their children were left without fathers and mothers," Ross informed him. "I aim to see Colleen isn't one of those children."

Holden nodded. "I'll do what I can," he replied. "But you realize I can only do so much. I don't supersede the military."

"Talk to my colonel friend," Ross informed him and handed him a card. "He'll help from their end."

Holden again nodded and zipped the duffel bag. "Have it your way, Ross," he replied. "I'll do what I can from my end."

"I'm sending Kirk to ride shotgun with you," Ross informed him.

Kirk took the duffel bag to the passenger side of Holden's SUV then removed the bound man from the back of the jeep. He placed the prisoner into the back of the official federal vehicle. Kirk then hopped into the passenger seat and waited for Holden.

Holden frowned while studying Ross. "I suppose you're keeping my wife a few more days," he muttered then eyed Jackie.

Ross grinned and chuckled. "It's as if you can read my mind," he teased then walked away.

Jackie approached her husband and attempted a tiny smile. "I guess I won't be home for dinner after all," she informed him.

"When this is over," Holden announced in a stern tone, "I'm taking you away somewhere just the two of us." He then indicated the men by the helicopter. "And you're not telling them where either."

Jackie smiled and laughed. "It's a date," she replied then kissed him warmly and with some aggression while firmly running her hands along his chest.

Holden returned the kiss then groaned when she pulled away a little too quickly. "I intend to ravish you the next time I see you," he insisted.

She grinned at the thought and eyed him seductively. "I look forward to that."

He pulled her against him and kissed her with a little more aggression. He broke off the kiss and cast a look at Monroe and Ross, who stood by the helicopter with their arms folded across their chests while watching the romantic moment as if they disapproved. Holden groaned and released Jackie.

"Do they realize how uncomfortable it is when they watch us together?" Holden remarked.

Jackie laughed and patted his chest. "I'm pretty sure they do." She then raised her brows lustfully. "There's a cure for that though."

"Oh?"

"Do something racy in front of them that'll make them uncomfortable enough to stop watching," she replied and grinned deviously.

Holden chuckled almost nervously. "Although I appreciate the image," he announced while hiding his grin. "I'm even less comfortable with that. In fact, I'm positive I'd have performance jitters, and then Monroe would torment me endlessly the rest of my life."

She affectionately caressed his chest. "Then I guess you'll have to find another way to deal with them."

"And take another cold shower tonight," he muttered with a frown.

"I'll make it up to you," she replied then grinned. "I always do."

Holden kissed her quickly but affectionately, offered a warm smile, and then reluctantly returned to his vehicle where Kirk waited and watched as well. Jackie could imagine the uncomfortable conversation on their drive back to the Bureau. Kirk would almost certainly say something dicky to piss off Holden.

Chapter 46

It was late afternoon. Colonel Holloway stormed through the mansion with his cell phone to his ear and a concerned look on his face. He rounded the broad banister and ran up the main staircase taking the steps two at a time.

"How many?" he demanded. The response was enough to send him into a mild panic. "Do they have the prototype?" Holloway reached the top of the stairs, paused only a moment to rake his fingers vigorously through his hair, and then continued along the second floor hallway. "How long?" When he heard the response, he picked up his pace. "Lose this number." Holloway disconnected the call then pressed another button as he hurried along the hallway. "This is a level one emergency. Prep the helicopter."

Holloway didn't wait for a response. He stopped before his master bedroom doorway, smashed the cell phone against the doorframe, and charged into the bedroom. Katrina jumped with surprise and spun to face Holloway. She was dressed only in her red, sexy matching thong underwear and bra. She had three dresses laid out on the bed while attempting to decide which one to wear. His energized entrance startled her. She grinned slyly.

"If you're here for a quickie, we don't have much time," she informed him. "We're already going to be fashionably late."

He grabbed a black duffel bag from the closet and tossed it onto the bed on top of the dresses, startling her. "Pack some things," he ordered. "We need to bug out--now."

Katrina didn't even question the order. She ran to the dresser, removed some clothes and stuffed them in the bag. As she slipped into a tank top and a pair of black yoga pants, she looked back at him. He pulled a painting away from the wall and opened the wall safe. He swept everything from the safe into a small black bag, shut it, and tossed the bag onto the bed. He grabbed another black duffel bag from the closet and threw some of his own clothes into it. Katrina hurried to the gun safe and pressed in the code. When it beeped, she opened the safe to reveal an assortment of guns. She slipped into a shoulder holster containing a semiautomatic and extra magazines.

Without a word, she tossed Holloway an assault rifle, which he easily caught without missing a beat. He slung the rifle over his shoulder then caught two extra magazines as she tossed them to him. He placed them in his jacket pockets. Katrina removed another semiautomatic in a clip holster and attached it to the back of her pants. She grabbed a leather jacket from the closet and slipped into it. Holloway tossed her the smaller bag containing the valuables as well as their passports then took the two duffel bags. An emergency light flashed. Holloway hurried to the bedroom window and looked out. He cursed under his breath and watched the fleet of black SUVs speeding up the driveway. Holloway turned and nodded her to the door.

"We're taking the helicopter," he informed her.

Katrina nodded and hurried out of the room without a word.

§

Ten official, black FBI vehicles with flashing lights pulled up to the house and formed a line across the front. The men disembarked the vehicles from the left side, keeping the SUVs between them and the house. Each man wore their standard-issued bulletproof vest with FBI boldly written across the front and back. One man from each vehicle passed out assault rifles to the rest of the men in their party. Holden joined the men as they regrouped behind two of the vehicles.

"According to the snitch we have in custody," Holden informed them, "Colonel Holloway has a detention cell in the basement. There's a secret passageway in the kitchen. We may be looking at VIP prisoners. We need those captive men alive. My team will storm the basement once we're inside." He placed his helmet with face shield over his head. "There are also a dozen or more house staff. Watch your targets. We don't want to shoot any unarmed workers."

The men nodded. They were about to leave the safety of their vehicles when men from the house opened fire on them. One fed took a shot to his leg, and his men pulled him back to safety behind the SUVs.

Holden sank behind the vehicle and spoke through his helmet to the other men. "We have at least two snipers on the second floor."

"I count three on the first floor," another agent informed him.

§

Colonel Holloway and Katrina appeared in the kitchen from the back stairs and passed several men running across the kitchen with assault weapons. The frightened staff bolted out of the way of the charging men. Dixon joined Holloway and Katrina by the back door.

"The helicopter is prepped and ready to go," Dixon announced and opened the door for his boss.

"Get the staff into their rooms and out of the crossfire," Holloway announced to his men. "Prepare to bug out in ten minutes."

The colonel forced Katrina out the door and hurried after her with Dixon following. They could hear gunfire coming from the front lawn as his men kept the FBI from making it into the house. All three ran across the yard to the clearing behind the garage where the helicopter was prepared for their departure. Holloway handed the bags to Dixon as Katrina climbed into the back of the helicopter. Holloway gave her an added shove with his hands on her rear, helping her into the chopper before jumping in after her. Dixon stowed their bags then hurried for the front passenger seat. The moment the doors were secured, the helicopter lifted off.

§

Holden and his entourage of feds fired back at the house while another man called for an armored car as additional backup, although, it would be a while before the vehicle showed up at the remote location. The sound of the helicopter could be heard above the gunfire. Holden cursed and looked at the mansion. He could just barely see the helicopter in the distance flying away.

"Colonel Holloway vacated the premises," Holden announced to the others then removed his helmet and pulled his cell phone from his pocket. "We need air assistance. Colonel Holloway left in a helicopter. I didn't get a look at the markings. We need additional men covering every private airfield within a fifty-mile radius of the mansion. He could have a private plane standing by."

Within a few minutes, the firing from the house stopped. The federal agents kept their weapons aimed at the mansion and waited, but they didn't hear anything. Holden pressed another button on his cell phone.

"Team two, be prepared," Holden announced into the phone. "You're about to have company."

No sooner did the words leave Holden's lips when three modified, Army Humvees raced from the mansion. The black vehicles crashed through two SUVs blocking the lane and raced down the long driveway. Gunfire came from the Humvees as the men attempted to make their escape.

"They're coming your way now," Holden announced into the phone, replaced it, and then put his helmet back on. "We're going in."

The feds hiding behind the SUVs made a run for the house, but there wasn't any gunfire. What remained of Holloway's men had taken off in the Humvees, which would be met with a second team of feds on the main road. The feds easily stormed the mansion. As they fanned out into the lower rooms, they only found frightened servants with their trembling hands in the air hiding in the staff wing. Holden and four men stormed the basement, but they had been too late. The three prisoners they found had been recently shot in the head. Holden shook his head with disgust.

"Anyone find anything?" he asked through his helmet communication.

"No, sir," several men reported.

Holden cursed and motioned the men from the basement detention area.

Chapter 47

Wednesday, July 2nd. Late afternoon. Jackie and Gil worked in the kitchen together preparing dinner for the team and their guests. Gil seasoned the marinating, boneless chicken breasts while Jackie scrubbed whole potatoes. Gil moved past her, collected some oven mitts, and checked on the apple pies he had in the oven. Jackie watched him remove the pies and inspect them. He put them back in the oven while she continued to watch.

Gil cast a look at her and laughed at the way she stared at him. "What's that look about?"

"Where did you learn to bake?" she asked.

He eyed her and appeared almost humored by the question. "Where I learned to do laundry, iron, and make my bed," he replied. "The Navy."

Jackie cast a look at him. "My father couldn't bake," she reminded him.

"His generation was a little rougher around the edges," Gil informed her. "Ross, Jackson, and Zack were old school. Military lifers. Beck, Monroe, and I wanted to serve, but we also wanted careers outside the military." He chuckled at the thought. "I have a master's degree in teaching. A lot of good that degree did me."

"Monroe wanted to be a doctor," Jackie remarked then frowned as she sank into her own thoughts. "I sometimes wonder if it's my fault he gave up on that dream."

"Why? Because you rejected him?" Gil asked while giving her a curious look.

Jackie groaned. It sounded worse coming from someone else.

"The courses were too much for him, Jackie," Gil informed her without hesitation. "He didn't have the discipline to become a doctor. His skills were put to better use as a con artist and a fixer." Gil then chuckled at whatever was going through his head. "His sour grapes over you are just that. Trust me; you didn't break him."

"I'm glad to hear," she replied, although she wasn't completely convinced. "Considering the way he chased after me, I should have known better than to turn to him before heading off to college. That's not something you think about when you're eighteen."

"No, it's definitely not," Gil remarked while hiding his grin. "You couldn't have known he was a lovesick puppy and not just another horny sailor." He chuckled at the comment. "Personally, I've known more of the latter."

"Yeah, me too," she replied while grinning.

Gil continued to work then cast a glance at her. "I prefer you with Holden anyway," he remarked then shook his head and made a face. "I can't imagine you in a relationship with Monroe."

"Really?" she asked with surprise while glancing at him. "Why's that?"

"You're obstinate aggressive as is Monroe," Gil remarked. "Holden is reserved rational. There's a harmonious balance between you and Holden. You and Monroe would constantly clash."

"Did you just call me pig-headed?" she asked while casting a sideways glance at him.

Gil turned and looked at her. "The fact that you focused on 'obstinate' sort of proves that you are."

Jackie considered the comment then frowned and reluctantly nodded. "Yeah, I guess you're right."

"Of course I am," he concluded then grinned. "Because I'm reserved and rational."

She cast a look at him and chuckled softly. "I'd go with standoffish and exasperating."

"Someone who's obstinate aggressive would naturally think that," he casually replied then cast a sly look at her while grinning.

Her eyes narrowed as she glared at his profile. "You're usually nicer than this after getting laid."

Gil didn't bother looking at her and chuckled. "Now you're being passive aggressive *and* a tiny bit rude." Before she could even respond to his comment, he continued. "Not getting enough?"

Jackie glared at him and raised her brows. "Now you sound like Kirk."

"Coming from the woman who sounds an awful lot like Zack," he remarked.

"Touché," she replied while laughing. "Should we call a truce?"

"That's probably best," he announced.

Monique and Colleen entered the kitchen, which dropped the current conversation entirely.

"Have you seen Bogart?" Monique asked.

"He said he'd drive us to the farm to visit our horses," Colleen added.

"Dinner will be ready in an hour," Jackie informed them and sounded like their scolding mother. "He's not taking you anywhere until after dinner."

"Good grief," Monique moaned. "You're starting to sound like my mother."

Jackie and Gil exchanged looks. Gil smirked finding the comment humorous.

"If that's the case," Jackie announced to the girls. "Why don't you wash your paws and help out?"

"Sure," Colleen announced with little resistance. "What can we do?"

"You can rip lettuce and cut tomatoes and cucumbers for the salad," Jackie informed them.

The girls washed their hands at the sink near Jackie then tended to the salad fixings.

"Seems like there's always someone different cooking around here," Monique remarked while cutting the tomatoes. "What's up with that?"

"We switch it up," Jackie informed them. "Everyone pitches in when we stay here."

"We're usually in charge of setting the table and washing the dishes afterward," Colleen announced. "For some reason, we're not allowed to cook."

"Probably because of that time we burned the kitchen curtains," Monique remarked with little emotion and easily dismissed it.

"Yeah, that may have had something to do with it," Colleen replied.

Chapter 48

A few minutes later, Monroe entered the kitchen from the patio and grinned when he saw the girls helping prepare dinner.

"Someone is on mess hall duty," he teased then approached Jackie and Gil. "What's the ETA on the chicken? The grill is fired up and ready to roll in five."

"Not for another twenty minutes," Gil informed him. "Jackie's taking forever with the baked potatoes."

Jackie glared at Gil with disapproval. "I thought we were doing scalloped potatoes," she remarked. "They don't take nearly as long."

"I never said we were doing scalloped potatoes," Gil sternly insisted.

"God, you two sound like an old married couple," Monroe scoffed. "Now what am I going to do for another twenty minutes?"

Colleen handed him a cucumber.

Monroe groaned, took the cucumber, and found a knife. "I wasn't on salad detail," he remarked and began cutting the cucumber into slices.

"Neither were we," Monique replied and grinned at him. "Consider yourself volunteered."

"Now who sounds like an old married couple," Jackie teased and indicated Monique to Monroe.

"Did you guys used to date?" Colleen asked Jackie while tearing the lettuce into smaller pieces in a bowl.

Jackie cast a glance over her shoulder with some surprise while Monroe tensed at the question. Monroe looked at the girls, who concentrated on their work.

"We did," he replied then cast a sly look back at Jackie and grinned. "Briefly. Right, Jackie?"

Jackie rolled her eyes and stabbed each potato vigorously with a fork, which could just as easily have been Monroe. "Where did you hear that?" she asked the girls.

"Bogart," both replied in unison.

"He said you two had a history," Monique remarked then shrugged. "Whatever that means."

"It means they had sex, Monique," Colleen informed her friend.

"No duh," Monique remarked while rolling her eyes. "I assumed that much."

Monroe set the knife down and fidgeted. "I think I'd better check on the grill." He made a dash for the patio door and disappeared.

Gil smirked and chuckled. "Funny," he announced. "He's never been shy about the topic of sex before."

"It's like you can't even ask questions around here," Monique remarked with annoyance then shook her head in disapproval. "Everyone jokes and teases, but the moment you ask a question, they get all weird."

"Yeah, you guys are always talking about stuff like that," Colleen announced.

"Since when?" Jackie asked with surprise.

"All the time," Colleen replied. "We heard you guys discussing things before we came into the kitchen."

Jackie tensed and eyed Gil, who didn't react either way. She was concerned at what part of their conversation the teenagers overheard and felt embarrassed.

"And then they clam up the moment we walk in," Monique announced to her friend. "I mean, we're fifteen. Where are we going to learn about this stuff if no one will talk to us about it?"

"On the streets, I suppose," Colleen replied with a dreary sigh.

Jackie turned to face the girls at the island counter while they prepared the salad. "I'm sure you could talk to your mothers about that sort of thing."

"What do they know?" Colleen replied without looking back at Jackie. "My mother's been a nun for the last five years."

"And I don't need those images in my head of my mother and father," Monique announced then shivered. "Ewe. That's nasty."

Jackie leaned against the counter while facing them, drew a deep breath, and reluctantly sighed. "What do you want to know?"

Both girls turned and looked at her, surprised that she seemed to be offering to discuss it.

"How many guys did you date before you finally met Holden?" Colleen asked with great interest. "Did you sleep with them all?"

"Do you have to sleep with guys?" Monique chimed in. "We heard you have to sleep with them on the third date. Is that true?"

Jackie immediately tensed and cast a look at Gil, who eyed her and smirked almost evilly. He appeared interested to hear her response.

"Yes, tell us, Jackie," Gil announced. "How many guys did you sleep with?"

Her eyes narrowed while she glared at Gil's devious smirk. Jackie looked back at Monique and Colleen, who eagerly awaited some answers.

"Maybe we could have this conversation later," Jackie replied. "After I've had a few drinks. I, uh, should probably check on Monroe with that grill."

Jackie hurried from the kitchen to avoid the topic. Monique and Colleen groaned and threw their hands in the air at Jackie's hasty exit.

"Why are adults so touchy about things?" Colleen demanded.

"Adults are strange," Monique remarked.

Gil leaned against the main counter behind him and clutched the edge on either side while eyeing the girls. "No, you don't have to sleep with anyone if you don't want to," he informed them. "It doesn't matter if it's your third date or your thirtieth date."

"This girl at school got pregnant," Monique informed him and appeared tense. "She said her boyfriend told her if she loved him, she'd sleep with him then he dumped her when he found out she was pregnant."

"Well, he's a fucking coward," Gil informed them. "If he loved her, he wouldn't put demands on her or their relationship. If anyone ever starts a conversation with 'if you love me', they don't love or respect you, and you need to shake them loose immediately."

"Have you ever been in love?" Monique asked with a hint of a sparkle in her eyes.

"Of course," Gil replied.

"Did you sleep with her?" Monique continued with her line of questioning.

"I married her," he announced proudly.

"Your ex-wife, Ellie?" Colleen pressed.

He nodded.

"Why did you two get divorced?" the girls questioned in unison.

"I'm not easy to live with," Gil responded.

"Do you still love her?" Monique asked.

"Unconditionally," he responded without hesitation. "I'll love her until I die."

"So why don't you try to work things out with her?" Colleen continued.

"Because I want her to be happy," he replied then drew a deep breath. "Sometimes that means I need to remove myself from her life."

"How many girlfriends have you had?" Colleen pressed for information.

Gil held up one finger.

"How many women have you slept with?" Monique then added to the question.

Gil smiled and held up the same finger.

"Really?"

"Yeah, really," Gil replied without hesitation. "Ellie and I have a complex relationship. We grow. We change. She comes back around my way, and we try again. I'm hopeful we'll have 'forever' one day, and I don't want to do anything that may deter her from taking me back."

"So it's okay to wait for the right person to come along?" Monique asked.

"Absolutely," Gil replied. "You're young." He eyed them with a curious look. "What's the hurry?"

"None," Monique replied. "It's just, well--"

"All the girls in our school are boy crazy, and we're not," Colleen informed him and then frowned at the comment. "We're not normal."

"You're fine the way you are," Gil informed them. "Don't let anyone dictate how you live your lives. What you do or don't do is none of anyone else's business."

Monique and Colleen both smiled in response and seemed relieved.

"Thanks for talking to us," Monique announced. "It's sometimes hard getting an honest answer out of adults about adult things."

Gil offered a warm smile. "Sometimes they're just uncomfortable offering personal information about themselves," he remarked. "If we're all a little more open and honest about relationships, perhaps you wouldn't have to ask so many questions."

"We thought Bogart would confide in us," Colleen informed Gil, "but he just keeps telling us we're too young to discuss that."

"He's our friend," Monique insisted. "What's the point of having older friends if they can't give you advice without getting all weird?"

"I think Bogart's afraid he might say something and lose your respect," Gil informed them.

"We know Bogart has been around," Colleen remarked. "That's why we want to ask him things. He has insider information and can warn us of bad situations."

"Try opening with 'can I ask your advice'," Gil informed them while offering a reassuring smile. "That's the easiest way to get someone to tell you personal things without making it seem like it's personal."

"I hadn't thought of that," Monique announced.

Chapter 49

Thursday, July 3rd. Before sunrise, a black sedan drove through the alley alongside the federal building in Colorado Springs. The headlights were off making it nearly invisible to anyone who might happen to be on the streets at that hour. Dixon got out of the passenger side dressed in a black suit with a black shirt, looking menacingly handsome. He approached the secured alley door and eyed the electronic keypad lock. Instead of attempting to open the door, he fixed his jacket and waited patiently. The door opened to reveal a man wearing a janitor's uniform. The older man shifted looks around the alley then let Dixon enter. He quietly shut the door behind Dixon then motioned him down the basement corridor.

"We have to hurry," the janitor announced. "The guard will be back from his rounds in fifteen minutes."

"He doesn't come down here?"

"No, never."

They approached the evidence room where a guard sat behind the window. The guard frowned when he saw them, stood, and unlocked the door. Dixon slipped inside while the janitor stood watch outside. The guard hurried Dixon down the first aisle.

Dixon glanced at the security cameras. "Are the cameras disabled?"

"I rewired them, so they're playing a loop of me reading a magazine," the guard replied.

The guard led him to the green duffel bag and handed it to him.

Dixon unzipped it, saw the black bag beneath, and closed it. He then looked at the guard. "The flash drive?"

The guard nodded and removed it from his pocket. "I pulled it ahead of time for you," he announced and handed it to him.

Dixon accepted the flash drive and stuck it in his pocket. "You'll be able to access the money in two to three days," Dixon informed the guard. "The secured account we discussed."

The guard nodded.

"You know I have to make it look convincing," Dixon informed him.

The guard nodded as Dixon pulled his semiautomatic containing a silencer. "Left shoulder, right?"

Dixon nodded then shot the guard in the chest. The guard gasped while clutching his chest. He only had a moment to reveal the horror of the double-cross before falling to the floor. Dixon picked up the bag and headed for the evidence room door. As he stepped into the hallway, the janitor eyed the gun in his hand.

"How long should I wait to call for an ambulance?" the janitor asked.

"Ten minutes should do," Dixon replied then shot the janitor in the chest.

As the stunned man fell to the floor, Dixon continued for the exit door.

§

T wo hours and a vehicle change later, a black Army Humvee drove along the old washed out road in the woods before finally reaching a timeworn hunting cabin. Beyond the cabin, the helicopter could barely be seen beneath camouflaged netting. The vehicle stopped in front of the small home. Dixon got out of the Humvee with the duffel bag and entered the old cabin. The one-room cabin was old but clean and contained some deteriorating furniture. Dixon approached the fireplace and opened a panel to reveal a staircase. He entered the opening and closed the panel behind him. Dixon tossed the duffel bag over his shoulder as he headed down the stone steps only lit by the small penlight he carried. He paused at the bottom before a steel door, pressed a code into the electronic lock panel, and then entered.

Colonel Holloway's remote, underground bunker was almost luxurious with a large living room, a big screen television, bar, and a pool table. A small kitchen could be seen on the opposite end of the room. Not far from the kitchen, there was a doorway leading to the men's barracks. Another doorway led to Colonel Holloway's private quarters. Katrina entered the living quarters from the back bedroom, saw Dixon, and raised her brows with skepticism.

"Did you get it?" she demanded.

"I don't take orders from you," Dixon snarled. "Where's the colonel?"

She indicated the room she'd just left. "He's in the bedroom," Katrina announced.

Dixon rolled his eyes with apparent disgust. "At least we know why he keeps you around," he snapped. "I suppose you're good for something."

Katrina glared at him through squinting eyes. "He's on the satellite phone," she scoffed and folded her arms across her chest. "And my ability to satisfy his sexual needs is just a happy side benefit to my *other* qualifications."

"Yeah, you give great head," Dixon snarled. "I caught your performance in his office last week."

Holloway stepped out of the bedroom and glared with disapproval at Dixon. "Don't talk like that to my girlfriend," he snapped and approached the large man. "Show her some respect."

Katrina smirked and gave Dixon the middle finger while Holloway's back was to her.

"You have no idea what that woman is capable of," Dixon scoffed.

"I'm pretty sure I do," Holloway corrected. "So she flips you the bird when my back is turned." He took the duffel bag from Dixon and set it on the pool table. "We have bigger concerns right now. Most importantly, we need to find a buyer for this prototype and the schematics on the flash drive before we flee the country."

Holloway held out his hand. Dixon handed him the flash drive, which he slipped into his pants pocket. The colonel opened the duffel bag and removed the black bag. Dixon tossed the duffel bag aside as Katrina moved closer to have a look at the black nylon bag.

"What is it?" Katrina asked with great interest.

Holloway grinned proudly at his treasured recovery. "It's a laser prototype," he informed her. "And it's worth millions to the right buyer." He removed the metal box from the black nylon bag.

Katrina placed her hand on Holloway's shoulder and affectionately caressed it while staring at the metal case with anticipation. Holloway placed his thumb to the plate, and the case unlocked. Colonel Holloway grinned and drew a deep breath at the sound.

"I've wanted to get my hands on this for five years now," Holloway announced and lovingly caressed the case. "I'm only sorry I couldn't pay back Martin for the trouble he'd caused me."

He opened the case and stared at the empty hole in the foam where the device had once rested. There was a folded piece of paper in its place. For a moment, all three stared at the empty case in silence. Katrina removed her hand from Holloway's shoulder and took a step away from him possibly anticipating an enraged outburst. Holloway took several deep breaths almost as if he were unable to move. He finally reached into the case, removed the piece of paper, and unfolded it. Scribbled on the paper were the words, 'Kilroy was here' along with a crudely drawn image of a long-nosed, bald man peeking over a wall.

Holloway stared at the paper seemingly without breathing or blinking. He finally crumpled the paper and dropped it on the table. Katrina picked up the crumpled paper and stared at it with a puzzled look. She obviously didn't get it. Dixon now took a step back as well. Holloway violently tossed the case from the pool table and across the room. Dixon and Katrina moved further away from the enraged man. Holloway frantically felt his pocket and removed the flash drive.

"I want to know who those men are," Holloway announced in a strangely calm tone while firmly gripping the small flash drive. Despite sounding as if he were in control, he was obviously ready to explode. "I want them found, and I want them brought to me *alive*."

"I'm on it," Dixon announced.

"I'll find them," Katrina announced and took a step closer to Holloway. She placed her hand on his lower arm and stared at his profile. "Let me go."

Holloway straightened and looked at Katrina. He stared into her eyes a moment then nodded. "Go. Find them. Report back to me."

Katrina bolted into the bedroom and returned a moment later with a shoulder holster, her leather jacket, and a small backpack. As she passed Holloway, she caught his concerned look beyond the hostility. Katrina stopped, turned back, and kissed him quickly but passionately on the lips before leaving. Colonel Holloway somehow managed a smile while watching her leave.

Dixon shook his head and folded his arms across his broad chest. "You're making a mistake trusting her," he remarked with irritation.

"I can handle Katrina," Holloway remarked then glared back while indicating the flash drive in his hand. "I need to find a buyer for this. I need a new cash cow. Most of what I have I won't be able to touch, and the overseas accounts will only last so long." He inhaled deeply and again raked his fingers through his hair. "Keep me posted. I'll be in my office." Holloway indicated the nearby bedroom.

Dixon nodded and watched his boss head into his quarters. Once he shut the door, Dixon frowned in disapproval.

Chapter 50

Friday, July 4th. That afternoon, Ross's wife, brother-in-law, and niece drove up from the farm to spend the holiday with the team and their guests. Jackie was busy playing air taxi in order to import some of their dearest friends to spend the holiday weekend with them as well. When she returned, she brought Holden, Sal, and another man. The other man was Othello, the human; not to be confused with the horse Bogart named after his friend. Othello was a heavyset man with wild, curly dark hair. At first glance, the man wearing a superhero novelty t-shirt didn't look like a computer genius or possibly a criminal mastermind. When, in fact, Othello was both. It just depended upon the day and the job.

The lodge kitchen was alive with activity as the team pulled together to prepare a picnic feast for the Fourth of July holiday. On this particular holiday, the guys placed themselves in charge of preparing the meal. Lee, Pinto, and Jackie were familiar with the routine and let the men do their thing. Monroe prepared his secret barbeque sauce for the steak that he would later grill. Monroe was the self-proclaimed grill master and didn't like anyone moving in on his grilling territory. Kirk made his ever-famous, five-alarm chili. It was guaranteed to put hair on your chest and burn the lining of your stomach. Gil was in charge of a six-layer taco salad, making enough to feed the entire Navy, which he'd done many times while actually in the Navy.

Ross concocted a punch aptly named 'hair of the rabid dog that bit my balls', although he politely replaced 'balls' with 'hand' in front of their company. He also made a non-alcoholic version, which he came up with the name 'hair of the dog that bit my virgin daughter'. Beck made stuffed baked potatoes that contained almost as much bacon and cheese as potato and topped it off with sliced jalapeño peppers. Bogart was in charge of condiments, chips, and pretzels, which annoyed him because he wasn't allowed to 'officially' help. Jackie enjoyed watching the well-oiled machine as it worked. She was joined by the other women, who also got a kick out of watching the men storm the kitchen.

Judging by the way Lee and Pinto watched their men handle themselves in the kitchen; Jackie was convinced they were silently turned on. She couldn't say she blamed them. Jackie often became aroused watching Holden vacuum the living room. She wasn't sure why, but she was particularly turned on when he used the crevasse attachment. Jackie considered asking him to vacuum without his shirt on, but she knew that would just be met with a counterproposal involving her dusting in a French maid outfit.

Marie stood alongside the women and fidgeted while looking for something to do. "Are you sure they don't need some help?" she asked.

All three women laughed in unison.

"Trust me; they've got this," Pinto announced while grinning.

"I've learned to just stay out of their way," Lee informed Marie.

"This is *their* holiday," Pinto added.

"I would think that would be Veteran's Day," Marie replied. "I know Martin always took pride in celebrating Veteran's Day."

"They celebrate Veteran's Day a little differently," Jackie informed her.

"How so?" Marie felt compelled to ask.

"They drink excessively on the back porch, solemnly toast their fallen comrades, and swap war stories until they pass out," Lee remarked.

"I get that," Marie replied. "So what do they do for the Fourth of July?"

"The same thing as Veteran's Day," Jackie replied then grinned. "But in a cheerful way."

"I'm guessing I should send Monique and Colleen to bed early," Marie remarked while eyeing the other women. "Sounds like it might get a little rowdy."

"They'll be fine," Jackie announced and waved her off. "The cursing and bad behavior doesn't start until well after midnight."

"What's Zack like when he's drunk?" Marie asked with some concern while possibly reliving the way he attacked Martin in the lobby. "Does he get out of hand?"

Jackie suddenly laughed. "Zack is surprisingly reserved when he drinks," she replied. "It's the quiet ones you need to worry about."

Pinto rolled her eyes in response. "Beck and Monroe," she groaned.

"Gil turns into James Bond," Jackie teased and held back her laugh. "He oozes charm when he's plastered." She then frowned and considered something else. "Unlike Kirk, who's the complete opposite."

"He lets the F-bombs fly," Pinto remarked.

"Usually directed at Bogart," Jackie added and shook her head. "Thankfully, Bogart is a happy-go-lucky drunk and doesn't take anything Kirk says personally. I think they're better friends than either leads on."

"And Ross is, well, Ross," Lee informed Marie with a deep sigh. "He's just a little more, uh, Ross."

"Like Captain Ahab hunting his white whale," Pinto teased causing Jackie to laugh.

Lee groaned while grinning deviously. "Tease all you want, but Captain Ahab is pretty wild in bed," she informed them and suggestively raised her brows.

There was another round of laughter before they realized the men suddenly became quiet. They looked at the men, who now stared across the kitchen at them.

"And our sweet, angelic women are already talking dirty," Beck announced then nudged Ross. "Wait until they get a few drinks in them."

"Enough to make a sailor blush," Monroe scoffed then shook his head and grinned.

"I don't know," Kirk remarked and shrugged. "I kind of like it when they talk that way."

"We do not talk dirty when we drink," Pinto protested while folding her arms across her chest.

The men laughed and muttered something under their breath while shaking their heads. Lee and Pinto suddenly tensed and exchanged bewildered looks. They then looked at Jackie for confirmation that what the men said could possibly be true.

Jackie hid her smile. "Don't look at me," she announced. "I'm the queen of dirty talk when I drink. They all love me when I'm drunk."

Marie then looked around and appeared curious. "Where is Zack?" she asked. "Doesn't he have a duty for this holiday affair?"

"As always, Zack is in charge of fireworks," Jackie informed Marie. "He's on the hillside preparing now."

Marie's eyes widened. "The girls said they were going to hang out with Zack," she remarked with concern. "Should I have let them go along?"

"No," Lee replied.

Pinto shook her head. "I don't know why those two are drawn to him," she remarked.

"Because he's mysterious and strange," Jackie replied with a humored laugh.

"I can attest to that," Lee muttered.

"Should I be worried for their safety?" Marie then asked and fidgeted slightly. "Zack seems, well, unstable."

"I wouldn't say he's unstable," Lee remarked then considered the response. "Just mildly demented and unpredictable."

Marie eyed the three women. "Isn't that the same thing as unstable?"

"He may not be the most approachable person," Lee admitted, "but in a life-and-death situation, you definitely want him standing in front of you."

Chapter 51

The Fourth of July picnic started that afternoon and would continue into the night. Monique and Colleen had fun playing with their new friend, Selena. Rather than play traditional hide-and-seek, they played seek-and-destroy with large, pump action water cannons and had fun attempting to soak one another. Darth chased them around outside, although he didn't seem to understand the rules and attempted to bite the heavy streams of water. Bogart joined in and became the target of all three teenagers. Their battle took them around the lodge to the front yard where the shrill screams of all three teenage girls could be heard.

Despite the good time being had by all, Othello sat at one of the picnic tables with Beck's laptop in front of him and his own laptop alongside it. Beck stood over Othello's shoulder and watched the plus-sized computer geek work his magic on two computers at once.

"This is super-encrypted," Othello remarked but refused to give up. He didn't bother looking at Beck. "Did you hack the Pentagon or something?"

"No, just the U.S. Army," Beck casually replied with little emotion.

Othello raised a brow and eyed Beck hanging over his shoulder. When Beck grinned, Othello chuckled then resumed working. He was finally able to open the file and excitedly clapped his hands.

"Access granted," Othello cried out proudly. "I am a genius!"

Zack walked past them with a large water cannon in each arm then paused and eyed the image on Beck's laptop with great interest.

Beck pointed to the blueprint on the screen of the weapon they'd found. "That's the one all right," he announced. "What does it say?"

Othello scrolled down and raised his brows. "It's a laser gun," he announced then eyed Beck behind him. "Real 'rebel alliance' type stuff." Othello looked back at the laptop screen. "Apparently, it has a switch that powers it on. Looks like unlimited laser rounds. Fires like a semiautomatic. One round per trigger pull." He shook his head and seemed mesmerized by the weapon. "Amazing."

"Frightening is more like it," Beck remarked while staring at the screen and shook his head. "That thing can shoot through a concrete wall."

"I'm in love," Zack commented with a soft groan.

Beck and Othello looked back at Zack, who chuckled then continued on his way in the direction of the screaming girls out front.

"What else is in that file?" Beck asked and again leaned over Othello's shoulder.

Othello opened another file marked 'classified'. His eyes suddenly widened. "Oh," he gasped.

Beck pointed at the screen. "That's a schismatic for the laser, but what would it be used for?"

"Drones," Othello replied without taking his eyes off the screen. He scrolled down and revealed blueprints for laser drones. "That's some scary stuff." He continued to read. "It seems as if they're working on a stealth model."

"Silent but deadly," Beck scoffed then made a face. "Limited range though."

"Yeah," Othello agreed. "There appears to be video feed on it, but it looks as if the operator can't be more than a few miles away."

"Zack 'borrowed' a military grade drone," Beck remarked and shook his head. "That one can go more than five miles from the controller."

Othello looked back at Beck and stared with surprise. "No shit?" he gasped then shook his head. "Zack has to show me some of his toys."

"Good luck with that," Beck muttered. "He keeps it locked in his gun safe. Good thing too. It's rigged with grenades. He calls it 'the Z-boom'."

Othello chuckled and returned to the laptop before him. He scanned the file. "It says here a prototype for their laser drone hasn't been made yet."

"No wonder the colonel wanted Martin so bad," Beck announced and indicated the blueprints on the screen. "Without these drawings, they can't finish their weapon. What's that last file?"

Othello opened the last file and stared at the list of names and numbers. "I could be wrong, but this looks like orders for the weapon."

"By the thousands," Beck remarked and shook his head. "To some pretty unfriendly countries."

"So this colonel guy stole the schismatic for this weapon and a list of potential buyers," Othello remarked and appeared uncomfortable. "It's a good thing Martin kept it out of his hands."

"Unfortunately, it still exists," Beck remarked with a defeated sigh.

"Actually, it says the military scrapped it," Othello pointed out.

"Yes, but what you see is just a downloaded copy on my computer," Beck informed him. "The original is sitting in an evidence locker at FBI headquarters." He straightened and shook his head. "I should have just destroyed it rather than turn it over." Beck then looked across the patio to where Holden and Jackie sat with Ross and Lee. He appeared deep in thought while rubbing his chin. "I have to somehow convince Holden to destroy it."

Othello let out an uneasy laugh. "Good luck with that," he scoffed. "Holden is pretty straight. If he's caught tampering with evidence, he'll lose his job and go to jail. He's not risking that."

"That flash drive can't fall into the wrong hands," Beck insisted while frowning with concern. "Particularly a man like Colonel Holloway."

Othello raised his brows and looked back at Beck. "Want me to pull up the blueprints for the Bureau?"

Beck eyed Othello and grinned while patting his shoulder. "You read my mind," he replied.

§

Monique, Colleen, and Selena hid behind some shrubs against the side of the large porch in front of the lodge. They remained low to the ground and watched Bogart patrolling the area with his water cannon. Darth crouched alongside the girls and silently watched as well. Despite the dog's serious look, his tail wagged.

"Colleen," Monique announced and nodded right. "You take our right flank." She then looked at Selena. "And you take the left. I'm on point. When he's close enough, we'll fire on my signal."

Both girls moved behind the bushes in the direction they were instructed to go and took lookout positions behind the shrubs. Darth remained with Monique. As Bogart scoured the area, he got closer to the house. Monique held her hand up to signal the other girls. When Bogart was close enough, she gave the signal. All three girls and Darth leaped out of the bushes and fired their water guns at Bogart, soaking him while he cried out unable to defend himself. The girls laughed while Darth barked excitedly and bounced in place.

"You little squirts are so going to pay for that," Bogart announced and prepared to shoot them with his own supercharged water gun.

All three girls screamed and were about to flee when Zack rolled across the ground near them. He sprang up and fired at all four with a water cannon cradled in each arm, successfully soaking all of them. The girls screamed while Darth barked excitedly at the fun being had. Zack then soaked Darth as well. All four aimed their water guns at Zack and fired. He avoided the streams of water and ran for the side of the building. They were about to run after him when Bogart stopped them and conveyed a serious look on his face.

"No, he wants you to follow him," Bogart announced. "It's a trap. We'll circle around back for a surprise assault." Bogart circled his hand in the air and indicated the direction they were to head.

The girls excitedly ran toward the opposite side of the lodge with Bogart bringing up the rear although seeming less enthusiastic. They reached the opposite corner of the lodge when they heard a distinct thump from the porch. They spun toward the porch with their water guns aimed, but there wasn't anyone there. Bogart suddenly tensed then lifted his eyes up to the porch roof. The girls did the same. Zack stood on the porch roof and showered them with both water guns. They screamed and attempted to aim their own weapons. By the time they could see, Zack was gone.

Bogart frowned and shook water from his soaked body. "I think we need to surrender," he informed them. "You're dealing with a psychopath here."

"No, we'll never give up," Monique cried out then gave the signal. "Let's get him!"

All three girls screamed while running around the front of the lodge with Darth chasing after them and barking excitedly. Before they reached the corner, all three were again soaked by Zack's water guns. They screamed and ran back the other way with Darth leading the pack.

§

Just after dark, everyone gathered on the back patio with the lights turned out and watched the tree line for the pending fireworks display. Colleen cuddled with her mother and father, while Monique and Selena sat on either side of Bogart and affectionately clung to him. Ross and Lee sat on top of one of the picnic tables, while Jackie and Pinto sat on their husbands' laps to watch the fireworks. They didn't have to wait long before a series of spectacular fireworks were displayed within the dark sky above the tree line. Zack's display came close to a professional show. The grand finale was nothing short of amazing and received applause and cheers.

Once Zack returned on his four-wheeler from the clearing on the hillside, it was time for him to start drinking and catch up to the others. He'd remained sober the entire afternoon so he could safely set off his fireworks display, and he was now making up for lost time starting with a few shots of tequila. Ross passed around the box of Cuban cigars for those who wanted, and the real show was about to begin. Sal sat back in his patio chair with his glass of brandy and puffed on the cigar looking a little too "Godfather" for comfort. For a man who claimed he wasn't a mobster, he certainly had the look down pat. Martin joined them in a cigar, despite that he didn't normally smoke.

Othello and Ross's brother-in-law, Liam, were the only men who chose not to smoke cigars. Liam, Selena's father, was a moderately attractive man in his early forties with a slightly receding hairline. He had been married to Ross's sister before a car accident claimed her life several years earlier. Ross had already retired from the military at that time and enjoyed helping raise his sister's daughter since he was convinced he'd never have a family of his own. After he married Lee, the team started wondering if a family was still in their acting commander's future. Lee was much younger than Ross was, and it was possible she wanted children. He was a lucky man in every sense of the word, and he knew it.

Jackie took a few puffs of Holden's cigar. She didn't care to smoke, but she always stole a few puffs of one of the guy's cigars when they had one of their little smoking sessions. She was one of the boys and liked to remind them of it as often as possible. For some reason, they seemed to get a kick out of her puffing on a cigar. She wasn't sure why and just assumed it was something perverted. Keeping with tradition, Pinto made an effort to steal a puff from Beck's cigar, and every time she'd gag for ten minutes afterward. It was humorous to witness, and the guys enjoyed tormenting her about it. Lee tried stealing a few puffs from Ross's cigar once on a dare, but she never really grasped the concept. It actually made her slightly ill.

Chapter 52

A little later, Jackie sat alongside Holden at the picnic table as he joined Beck and Monroe in a drunken round of character assassination. Othello, although obviously drunk himself, sat quietly and listened. Pinto had enough of the men verbally assaulting one another after only a few minutes and abandoned her husband to hang out with her father, Marie, and Martin. Jackie sipped her excessively strong punch and grew bored with the same old argument, which now somehow involved her husband. She couldn't even defend Holden's drunken ramblings because they made little to no sense. Although, that could have had something to do with her own drunken condition, which was evident by her hand caressing her husband's inner thigh. Since they sat at the picnic table, it wasn't as if anyone would notice.

Beck leaned back in his chair with his usual arrogant grin when he thought he was right about something. Despite his irritation, he shook his head and chuckled at Holden's last remark.

"As usual, you're talking out of your ass again, Holden," Beck announced then leaned forward and thumped the table with his index finger. "You've spent too much time in that cushy office of yours while the rest of us are out there crawling through the trenches."

Holden was instantly offended by the remark. "I deal with the dregs of society every single day," Holden informed him while locking eyes with Beck over the table. "I don't just flash my badge and immediately get respect. I flash my badge and anticipate dodging gunfire."

Monroe eyed Beck and attempted to cover his drunken condition. "I don't remember you ever crawling through any trenches," he casually announced to Beck while sipping his poisoned punch. "In fact, I'm pretty sure you gave those shit assignments to me."

Beck turned his head and glared drunkenly through squinting eyes at Monroe. "Will you shut the hell up," he lashed out and gestured with his hands. "Just once. Seriously. Zip it. You're like a damned broken record."

"I'm just saying," Monroe continued his drunken rant. "I think I should be in charge once in a while. It's not as if you outrank me."

"Oh, I most certainly do outrank you," Beck scoffed back and refused to look at him.

"In your own mind perhaps," Monroe snapped back with a cocky look on his face.

"You had your shot at being in charge," Beck launched and finally glared at him. "Correct me if I'm wrong, but I remember you parachuted from a commercial airliner just before Jackie crashed it."

She cast a glare at Beck. "Excuse me?" Jackie demanded but was overshadowed by her drunken teammates. She wasn't sure she appreciated Beck's last remark. It wasn't as if she crashed the airliner for fun. It was already going down; she just assisted it to the ground. She didn't understand how she always got dragged into their drunken pissing matches.

"And why?" Beck continued his dramatic rant while easily ignoring that Jackie took offense to his comment. "Because you listened to Mac."

"Oh, don't start that again," Monroe lashed out defensively. "It was the only logical thing to do, and don't drag Mac into this."

Beck's eyes widened considerably. "Don't you dare start defending that conniving, vengeful succubus."

"Dragging out the big words now, huh?" Monroe growled in response to the derogatory comment. "She's not as bad as you want to believe she is. She does have some redeeming qualities, you know."

"You guys need to stay far away from that one," Holden announced in his own drunken tone and shook his head. "She's bad news."

Beck indicated Holden and offered a smug smile. "See, even Holden agrees."

Monroe glared at Holden then smirked. "You just don't like her because she pulled one over on you when you had Lee in protective custody."

"She pulled one over on you too," Holden snapped back then raised a clever brow. "Or did you forget?"

"I'm a little more forgiving than the rest of you," Monroe snapped back.

Othello, who had been silent until that point, stared at Monroe a moment and finally spoke out while grinning. "You slept with her, didn't you?"

Monroe fidgeted despite his drunken state and glared at Othello. "No, absolutely not."

"Jesus, Monroe," Beck scoffed and slammed his palms on the table. "Mac? Seriously?" He shook his head while glaring at his teammate. "How could you even think of something so depraved? You know how Zack feels about her."

"I didn't sleep with her," Monroe again insisted.

"How does Zack feel about her?" Othello asked with moderately slurred speech now taking an interest in the conversation.

It was possible Othello only met Mac that one time at Beck's wedding, and considering how wasted he was after the ceremony, he probably didn't remember much from the reception.

"Something happened between them when she saved his life," Holden offered. "He's had daggers in his eyes for her ever since."

"Oh, yeah," Beck announced while nodding. "He hates her with a vengeance."

"I didn't sleep with her," Monroe again protested, unwilling to let it go.

Jackie rolled her eyes knowing he was lying. It was time to abandon ship and find better company before they dragged her into it. It would only be a matter of time before her one-time indiscretion with Monroe prior to college was brought up again. She stood with some unsteadiness and received looks from all four men.

Jackie smirked at them. "Have a nice fight, boys," she announced and left the table.

§

The evening quickly went south with each ounce of spiked punch consumed. When Kirk was heard loudly throwing f-bombs at random, Marie had a look of concern about the example being set for the teenage girls. It was almost as if Liam had read her mind. Liam turned to his daughter, nudged her, and gave her a knowing look.

"Adult time," he announced to Selena. "Why don't you take Monique and Colleen to the game room and watch a movie before bed?"

"Sure, Dad," Selena replied then motioned for the girls to follow her.

Monique and Colleen sprang up and hurried after Selena. Darth ran after them. Marie was grateful when her daughter left the escalating scene on the patio and thanked Liam with a smile.

"Not my first rodeo with Ross and his friends," Liam informed her with a humored smile on his face. "If you're easily offended, you may want to join the girls in the game room."

"No, I actually don't mind. It's been a while since I've had 'adult time', and I'm enjoying the punch," Marie replied then smiled at her husband while squeezing his hand. "I think I'd enjoy a little more."

Martin grinned and sprang from his seat to refill both their cups with the strong concoction. Sal studied Marie's expression as it slowly faded to concern while she kept her eyes on her husband.

"You know, we've all been there," Sal informed her in a matter-of-factly tone.

Marie snapped out of her trance and glanced at Sal with a bewildered look. "Excuse me?"

"Wondering if there will be a tomorrow," Sal replied and sipped his brandy. "For some of us, we've lived that nightmare more times than we care to admit." He then indicated the team spread out along the patio. "Somehow, they always seem to sort it out. I could relay the story of the wedding from hell involving several mob bosses. A wedding of beauty and bloodshed."

"Please don't, Dad," Pinto muttered and groaned at the thought. "The wounds are still too fresh."

Sal chuckled lowly in his throat while keeping his eyes on Marie. "My daughter doesn't share my morbid sense of humor."

Pinto rolled her eyes at the comment.

"My point is," Sal continued despite Pinto's protests. "Each of them brings a certain skill set to the table." He indicated Bogart. "Even the ones you disregard. They all have a purpose."

"I wish that made me feel better," Marie replied timidly. "I just got my family back together, but it seems too good to be true. You know how it is. You can't possibly have everything you want and expect it to last."

Sal smirked in a mildly unsettling manner. "That's why there are always contingency plans," he informed her in an overly confident manner. "That's why there are people like Othello." His grin then broadened. "People like me. We're the equalizers."

"Daddy," Pinto scolded while glaring at him. "I wish you wouldn't say things like that. People will get the wrong idea about you."

"What's the contingency plan?" Marie asked, ignoring Pinto's attempt to silence her father, and eagerly sat forward while watching the questionable man with great interest.

"Like witness protection but unsanctioned," Sal replied with a humored smile.

Marie studied him while leaning back in her chair and seemed to consider what he was saying.

Chapter 53

Jackie joined the group of rowdies consisting of Ross, Kirk, Gil, Bogart, and Lee. After her short trek across the patio from the picnic table, she decided to take a break from the potent punch. It was starting to hit her pretty hard, and she didn't need to get out of hand. The guys still brought up the time she accidentally sat on Gil's lap when she'd mistaken him for Holden. In her defense, the patio wasn't very well lit, and Gil was roughly the same height and build as her husband. Harder to defend was that it took more than twenty minutes for her to realize her mistake. Although Gil got a kick out of it, Jackie was embarrassed by her drunken mistake.

When she approached the group, she realized there were no available seats. Gil teasingly grinned and patted his vacant lap. Jackie smirked at him with a hint of irritation. The guys laughed at her reaction. Jackie sat on the arm of Bogart's chair and leaned on his shoulder. He smiled and affectionately patted her hand. Her brother was happily drunk and loving the world. Gil and Bogart got along famously while drunk. Their personalities weren't that dissimilar, and alcohol was the great equalizer. Kirk retold one of his favorite drinking stories with strategically placed f-bombs every third word. Lee, who only had one or two drinks, rolled her eyes with each expletive.

Zack mysteriously appeared with an extra patio chair for Jackie, which she gratefully accepted. He again disappeared. A few seconds later, he returned and handed her a large plastic cup of punch. She cast a look at the smirk on his face, groaned knowing she'd regret it, and accepted the drink. And so, it began. Zack's master plan to get Jackie plastered and coerce her to spar with him. Bogart cast a disapproving look at Zack and the devious smile on his face. With the patience of a cat stalking its prey, Zack remained casually seated nearby where he'd watch and wait.

Kirk finished his curse-ladled tangent with an irritated wave of his hand. "Ah, fuck all of you."

Ross groaned and shook his head. "Do you have to talk that way every single time you drink?" he demanded with annoyance. "Your vocabulary is limited to bitch, bastard, and fuck."

"What the fuck do you know?" Kirk scoffed.

"I know you're a fucktard when you drink," Ross boldly announced.

Lee groaned at the direction the conversation was now heading and left her chair to sit on Ross's lap. As predicted, his attention immediately left the guys and focused on his attractive wife. He placed his arms around her and grinned almost boyishly.

"Is it bedtime already?" he asked with added enthusiasm.

"Whenever you're ready," she cooed while clinging to his neck.

Ross finished the rest of his drink in one swallow and stood while dropping his wife to her feet without releasing her. He grinned at his team.

"Keep the noise down," Ross announced then clung to Lee as he guided her toward the house and seemed surprisingly steady on his feet.

"The same goes for you, Ross," Gil called after him then chuckled.

Ross exposed his middle finger to them behind his back and received a round of laughter.

"Now that the fucking commandant is gone," Kirk announced, "let's kick this motherfucker up a notch." He took a large swallow of his strong drink then looked at Jackie and gestured. "Amuse us, Jackie. Kick Zack's ass around the fucking yard."

Zack eagerly jumped from his chair in response.

Jackie didn't even bother looking and pointed a finger at him. "Sit back down," she firmly announced.

Zack frowned and returned to his seat.

"Smart move," Gil remarked to Jackie and smirked. "He's liable to break your neck by accident."

"More like fucking hump her leg like some fucking froo froo dog," Kirk teased while chuckling.

Zack scratched his face with his middle finger in a not so subtle gesture at Kirk's remark.

"Show some respect," Bogart snapped with drunken irritation. "That's my sister."

They heard the sound of chairs toppling from across the patio. Everyone's attention was now focused on the picnic table where Monroe and Beck were witnessed rolling around the patio while punching each other. Gil, Bogart, and Kirk jumped from their chairs and ran to assist Holden who attempted to break it up. Unfortunately, Kirk's idea of helping was to cheer them on. When Jackie looked alongside her, Zack was gone. She finished her drink and headed across the mostly dark yard toward the distant tree, spotting Zack as she suspected she would.

Zack flopped onto the ground and rested his back against the large tree. Near the large tree, there was a marble headstone with Zack's name engraved on it. The headstone was a reminder of one of the many times Zack had officially died. Jackie joined Zack on the ground by the tree and gently patted his arm.

"Are you okay?" she asked.

"I'd be better if I were drunk out of my mind," he replied then eyed her with a look resembling insecurity. "I'm not a froo froo dog, right?"

Jackie grinned and laughed. "No, of course not," she remarked. "You're definitely a wolf."

"Not funny."

"What has you so bothered lately?" she finally asked. "You're always somewhere else anymore."

"An idle mind is the devil's workshop," he replied then cast a look at her. "My life's mistakes play out in my mind on an endless loop."

"You've been, well, different since that last concussion," Jackie insisted. "Maybe we should see about getting you a cat scan."

"No, no more doctors," he snapped then groaned and rested his head against the tree. He was silent a moment then cast a look at her. "Did I tell you about my hallucinations after the concussion?"

"The drug-induced ones?" she asked then nodded. "You mentioned them. Is that what's bothering you?"

"Partly," he replied and shut his eyes. "Your father's words keep haunting me. Then there's that image of us together--"

"We're not discussing any of your hallucinations that involve me," she boldly announced. "They weren't real."

He groaned. "It just bothers me, that's all."

"It shouldn't," she insisted then gave him a curious look. "Is it because of what Kirk implied?"

"A little," he replied then finally looked at her. "It really only matters what you think."

She sighed, clung to his arm, and rested her head on his shoulder. "We're good no matter what," Jackie announced. "Anytime you need me, you always know where to find me. I'm always here to talk you off the bridge."

He snorted a soft laugh. "It's not the bridge that should concern you."

Jackie lifted her head and met his gaze with a serious look. "I know," she replied. "Voluntarily going out in a blaze of glory isn't permitted either."

"It's been my destiny from the day I joined the Navy," he insisted. "You can't deny me my destiny."

"And that could easily be my destiny as well," she replied while staring into his eyes.

"No, never," Zack insisted and patted her hand clinging to his arm. "If you ever die sacrificing yourself for me, I'll kill you."

"Maybe you should talk to the guys about some of this," Jackie announced. "Maybe they could help."

"They already know I have a death wish," he informed her. "That's enough. What I think and feel stays between us. You promised."

Jackie managed a smile and nodded. "Yes, I promised," she informed him. "I won't say anything to them without your consent."

"I just hate having all these things in my head," Zack remarked. "Ever since that last concussion, I have all these emotions. I'm not used to feeling things." He glanced at her. "How do women deal with so many damned emotions?"

"We're born with them," she replied. "You learn as you go. If you get it out, maybe it'll go away."

Zack drew a deep breath, considered her comment, and groaned with defeat. "I wouldn't even know where to begin. Everyone I've lost; everyone I've hurt. Betrayal committed against me; betrayal committed by me. It just consumes me. I liked it better when I didn't feel anything." He met her gaze with a serious look. "I sometimes wish you'd just end my suffering."

"Stop talking like that," she snarled and lightly smacked his arm. "That's not happening, and we're not having that discussion again." Jackie drew a deep breath. "How about a little trip?"

"A trip?"

Jackie grinned and patted his arm. "We could track down Katya," she announced then raised her brows seductively. "You can have a weekend between the sheets. That might improve your mood."

He gave her a serious look. "You do remember she's a black widow spider, right?" Zack commented.

Jackie's smile faded. "Yeah, I forgot," she muttered. "With the mood you're in, that may not end well."

Jackie's thoughts strayed to Monroe and his professed quickie with Mac at the airport. Mac was a viable partner for Zack. She wished she knew what occurred between them in the few weeks they were alone together after Zack's near death experience. A few rounds in the sack with Mac would possibly cure some of what was bothering him, but his newly found loathe for the woman made that a non-option.

"We could find you a Russian prostitute," Jackie counteroffered.

Zack grinned and chuckled. "You can stop trying to cheer me up with pity sex," he announced but remained cheerful at the thought. "I'm fine. Really."

§

It was a little after two in the morning when Jackie and Holden entered their bedroom at the lodge. Both were pleasantly drunk, although it was possible Holden was a little more inebriated than Jackie was for once. The second floor hallway was slightly noisy as the other drunks headed to bed as well. Holden shut the door then reconsidered and locked it for good measure. He approached the bed and removed his shoes. Holden then sat back against the headboard and grinned while watching Jackie as she undressed. She caught his attentive stare and smiled while remaining in her matching lacy bra and underwear. She'd purposely wore the thong underwear for her 'after party' with Holden.

"Something on your mind, Agent Falcone?" she teased and approached him where he sat reclined on the bed.

He maintained his grin. "In actual hand-to-hand combat, how many of the guys do you think you could beat?" Holden asked slyly.

Jackie's playful mood faded at the question. It wasn't what she had been anticipating. She shook her head and groaned. "I swear; you say odd things when you've had too much to drink," she scoffed while hiding her grin.

"I'd like to know," he teased as he undressed her with his smile. It was as if he were initiating some bizarre form of foreplay. "Is there anyone you *couldn't* hold your own against?"

She considered the question and grinned. "Hands down; Darth beats me 99.9% of the time," Jackie teased.

"Yeah, that dog's psycho," Holden remarked. His smile again returned. "I mean with the guys."

"Kirk would be tough," she admitted. "He's a skilled fighter with a lot of force behind his muscle mass. Gil might give me a good run for my money. He has a few tricks up his sleeve."

"What about Zack?" Holden asked. "Do you think you could beat him?"

"I like my chances. I give myself a fifty-fifty shot," she replied while grinning. "I'd play dirty, I could tell you that." Jackie then frowned. "Although, he's been mastering his game for decades." She shook her head and sighed. "Seventy-thirty Zack."

Holden stood with some unsteadiness, approached Jackie, and pulled her into his arms. He grinned in a slightly drunken manner.

"I get all hot and bothered watching you kick ass," he announced finally revealing just how drunk he was.

She ran her hands along his chest and unbuttoned his shirt while grinning. "I thought it freaked you out."

"In life-and-death situations, yes," he replied then resumed his playful grin. "When there's little chance of you being broken in two, I can get into it." Holden caressed her shoulders as she opened his shirt and ran her hands along his chest. "Maybe you and I could go a little one-on-one sometime."

Jackie grinned slyly and slipped him out of his shirt. "I thought that's what we were doing now," she teased.

"You know what I mean," he remarked teasingly. "It's been a while since we've thrown each other around. Of course, if I'd pin you, I'd want to have my way with you."

Jackie hid her devious smile and worked on his belt buckle while keeping her eyes locked on his. "Are you saying you'd like things a little more aggressive?"

"Oh, yeah," he replied as she let his pants fall to the floor. He stepped out of his pants, pulled her against him, and ran his hands aggressively along her backside. "I love your aggressive side."

"Okay then," she announced then stepped out of his arms and used a karate move to throw him roughly onto the bed.

She jumped on top of him, straddled his hips, and held his wrists to the bed while writhing against him. She grinned. "This seems familiar."

"It should," he teased while grinning. "Our second meeting and the first time you handcuffed me to a bed."

Jackie laughed at the comment then held him down and aggressively kissed his neck. Holden groaned and writhed beneath her.

"Oh, yeah," he announced. "I missed you."

Jackie pulled away just far enough to meet his gaze and grinned. "As a little added bonus," she cooed while rubbing her body against his. "Ross's room is to the right, and Monroe's room is to the left." She grinned deviously. "I think it's time we made them uncomfortable for a change, don't you?"

Holden groaned and smiled while wriggling beneath her. "I like the way you think, you naughty girl."

"You think I'm naughty now?" she teased. "You'd better brace yourself, Agent Falcone."

Chapter 54

Saturday, July 5th. Zack entered the kitchen early the next morning and stopped just within the doorway. The kitchen was still a disaster from the night before. There was a sink full of dirty dishes, garbage bags overflowing, and a not so pleasant odor coming from somewhere. Zack made a face then groaned and rolled up his sleeves to tackle cleanup. He stuffed more garbage into the already overflowing bag and stomped on it with his combat boots until he could close it. He then crouched before the sink to pick up a few plastic cups that had escaped the bag when a shadow passed over him.

"Do it and die," Zack muttered then straightened and turned to face Monique, who had the water cannon aimed at him from only a few feet away.

She smiled innocently and set the water gun down. "Do what?" Monique teased.

He rolled his eyes, ignored her, and retrieved a new garbage bag. Colleen entered the kitchen and approached Monique.

"Did you ask him?" Colleen whispered to her friend.

"Ask him what?" Zack asked without looking at them while tossing garbage into the bag.

"We're going to Ross's farm," Monique announced. "Selena, Bogart, Colleen, and I are going horseback riding. We, uh, were hoping you'd come along."

Zack cast a look at them in near disbelief. "Horseback riding?" he asked then chuckled with a humored grin. "You're kidding, right?"

"Told you," Colleen muttered. "He never does anything fun. You're wasting your time."

"I have fun," he informed Colleen. "I have plenty of fun. I enjoy blowing up cars, planes, ships, and a wide variety of buildings. I like parachuting out of airplanes, jumping into shark-infested waters from helicopters, and shooting people without discrimination of sex, nationality, or religion." He leaned against the counter. "Straddling a thousand-pound animal with a brain the size of a pea does not sound like fun. You need someone killed? Call me. We'll talk."

"Insulting horses?" Colleen demanded then looked at her friend. "Okay, I'm done with him."

"You win," Monique announced to Zack while frowning. "We'll leave you alone."

They turned to leave.

Zack groaned and shook his head. "Fine," he huffed. "I'll go with you on two conditions."

Monique and Colleen looked back at him and appeared enthusiastic.

"Name it," Monique announced.

"You clean up the kitchen," Zack informed them with little emotion.

Both girls looked at the state of the kitchen and grimaced. They wouldn't let that deter them though. They exchanged glances, shrugged, and then looked back at Zack.

"Deal," Monique replied while grinning. "What's the second condition?"

"I get to ride the big spotted horse," he remarked and raised his brows.

Monique's eyes suddenly widened in horror. Colleen held back her gasp then looked at her blonde friend with shocked disbelief.

Monique held up her hand while choking on her words. "We'll need a moment to discuss it," she informed him.

"You didn't hesitate on cleaning this mess, but the spotted horse is a potential deal breaker?" Zack remarked with some surprise then indicated both girls with a wave of his finger. "Both of you. Weird."

Monique held her breath a moment then reluctantly sighed. "Fine, you can ride Storm Cloud." She pointed a warning finger at him. "But you'd better do exactly what I say and treat him with respect."

"It's a horse," Zack remarked.

Both girls again groaned.

"Abort, abort," Colleen gasped under her breath to her friend.

"A battle of the wills, Colleen," Monique announced. "Zack won't win this one."

Zack grinned and chuckled. "That's the spirit," he announced. "I'll follow your horsey rules. Deal?"

"Deal," both reluctantly agreed.

Zack indicated the kitchen. "You'd better get started," he announced and approached the kitchen table. "You're burning daylight."

He flopped into the end chair, placed his booted feet on the table, and rested his eyes.

§

Later that morning, Zack walked around Storm Cloud where Monique had him tied to the hitching post outside Ross's barn. Zack's hands were clasped behind his back, and he looked over the horse like a drill sergeant inspecting the barracks. Monique came out of the barn with Storm Cloud's hackamore bridle. Bogart stepped into her path, cut her off, and met her gaze.

"Are you sure you want to do this?" Bogart asked in a hushed voice. "You know he's crazy, right?"

"Yes," Monique replied proudly. "I know he's crazy; that's why he's my horse."

Bogart gave her a stunned look.

Monique grinned. "A battle of the wills," she announced. "Zack versus Storm Cloud. I'm putting my money on the thousand-pound animal with the pea-sized brain."

She walked past Bogart and approached Zack and Storm Cloud. Bogart and Colleen exchanged concerned looks and resumed getting their horses ready. Selena was just about finished saddling her gray horse and one of the other horses for Monique. Monique removed Storm Cloud's halter and slipped the hackamore bridle over his nose and ears. She placed the reins over his neck, checked the girth, and then smiled at Zack. She indicated her horse.

"You're up," Monique announced while grinning. "Do you know how to--?"

Zack approached the horse and easily swung onto his back without use of the stirrups. Monique took a moment to marvel at how easy Zack made it look, particularly since it had taken her months of practice to do what Zack just did with his limited riding experience.

"Feet in the stirrups, Josey Wales," Monique firmly instructed.

Zack placed both feet in the stirrups. She handed him the reins.

"You've ridden before?" she asked.

"A few times," Zack replied while shifting in the saddle. "I know where the gas and the brakes are located."

"Well, Storm Cloud is a limited edition model," she informed him. "If you give him a hard time, he's going to toss you."

"He can try," Zack teased and offered a playful smirk. "I've got the balance of a cat and twice as many lives."

Monique frowned. "You're lucky I like you."

"Not sure why," he replied.

"Rule number one," she announced sternly. "Never, under any circumstances, kick him. He takes it personally."

He cast a look at her and raised his brows. "You're kidding, right?"

"No," she hissed and seemed to be losing patience with her pet project. "Use light pressure to slow, stop, and turn him. He responds to a light touch. If you manhandle him, he's going to toss you."

"Again with the tossing," Zack huffed and groaned. "It's a horse."

"You've been warned," Monique announced and reluctantly sighed.

Monique threw her hands in the air and approached Selena with her loaner horse. Everyone mounted and headed across the field at a leisurely walk. Storm Cloud resisted being in the middle of the pack. As a stallion, he wanted to lead. Each time Zack attempted to slow him, he managed to pull ahead until he was upfront with Colleen on Thunder. Storm Cloud's ears perked forward now that he was in the front. Colleen eyed Zack on her friend's horse and had to laugh.

"Looking good, Zack," Colleen announced.

"When do we get to run?" he asked.

"Learn to master the walk first," Colleen replied. "We don't need you getting hurt."

"It's okay," Zack informed her then opened the calf pocket on his pants and removed a roll of duct tape. "I brought the first aid kit."

"How is a roll of duct tape a first aid kit?" Colleen practically demanded.

"Kept my intestines from spilling out once," Zack informed her.

Colleen rolled her eyes then signaled 'wagons ho'. She sent her horse into a nice, gentle canter. Storm Cloud trotted to catch up. Zack was eager to go faster and kicked the horse. Storm Cloud suddenly lunged forward and kicked his back legs up in the air while pinning his ears. His back hooves no sooner touched the ground when he reared up high in the air and angrily thrashed his front hooves, pawing at the air. Zack clung to the saddle horn and managed to stay on the horse's back despite the incline. Storm Cloud landed, pinned his ears, and tossed his head in anger.

Zack grinned and laughed. "That was fun," he announced. "Let's do that again."

Storm Cloud bared his teeth, swung his head around, and bit Zack's leg. Zack cried out with surprise and looked at Monique who now stopped alongside him.

"He bit me," Zack proclaimed while indicating the irritated horse.

"You were warned," Monique casually replied then flashed a sly smile. "Be nice, or he'll bite you in the ass when you get off too. Face it, Zack. Storm Cloud outranks you."

Zack held his hands in the air. "Okay, I'll be nice," he announced then leaned down in the saddle and attempted to look at the horse's face. "Let's call a truce."

Chapter 55

The five continued their lengthy ride along a trail through never-ending fields and lush pastures. Zack seemed to have come to terms with Storm Cloud's dominating personality, and he was actually enjoying the ride. Although he didn't say much, he seemed to be taking it all in, much like the horse he rode. On more than one occasion, the girls and Bogart caught Zack stroking the horse's thick neck and talking to him. The bond was complete. Hooper's cattle ranch could be seen in the valley below. Zack stopped his horse on top of the hill and stared at the ranch in the distance. Wranglers kept herds of cattle together in the larger pasture closer to the plantation style house and massive barn. From his hawk eye vantage point, Zack took it all in.

His eyes swept across the valley and finally settled on the back of the house. A young woman, whose features he could barely make out, stood on the porch and leaned against the support beam. She seemed to be staring back at him. His focus remained on the woman and hers on him. Storm Cloud was becoming anxious now that the others had continued onward leaving them behind. Zack finally took his eyes from the woman and sent the large paint horse into a gallop to catch up to the others. The riders bypassed the house and headed for the wranglers keeping watch on their herd. They stopped their horses and watched Jasmine canter on her horse toward them. Bogart was grinning like a schoolboy, taking in a sweeping eyeful of the seductive woman. Her large breasts bounced beneath her shirt that had enough buttons open to showcase her ample cleavage. Jasmine stopped her horse and greeted them with a smile. She instantly noticed their new addition and seemed intrigued by Zack despite his indifference toward her.

"Who's your new friend?" Jasmine asked cheerfully.

"That's Zack," Bogart announced then offered a teasing grin. "He's not really a people person."

Zack actually grinned at the comment. He almost seemed pleased with the insult. It also avoided any misunderstandings that he might be interested in conversation. Since he didn't have to talk to people, it was a win-win. Jasmine laughed at the comment, although she kept her eyes on him a moment longer. She finally looked at the others.

"Did you want to herd cattle this afternoon?" Jasmine asked.

"If it's okay with you," Selena announced then indicated Zack. "Sunshine back there needs plenty of activity to keep him occupied."

Jasmine eyed Zack and giggled at the comment. "Well then, let's accommodate him," she announced and indicated the nearby herd.

As they rode toward the herd, Jasmine rode alongside Zack, leaving Bogart somewhat tense.

"I'll shadow you," Jasmine informed him while maintaining her pleasant smile. "It's not difficult once you get the hang of it. The horse does most of the work. Just be ready for a lot of sudden direction changes from the horse."

Despite the enchanting temptress riding alongside him, Zack didn't even give her a second glance. It was possible he hadn't even noticed. Zack was at times so disconnected; the team swore he had an 'off switch' for his emotions. They spent the next hour keeping the herd together and occasionally cutting one from the herd just for fun. Zack seemed to be enjoying himself and the connection he shared with the enthusiastic horse beneath him. Zack chased the steer back to the herd with the others then spun his horse and galloped back to Jasmine. His devious grin revealed his enjoyment. Bogart watched from further away and sneered his disapproval. Despite that Jasmine was married, Bogart still enjoyed when she flirted with him.

Zack indicated the rope hanging off Jasmine's saddle. "Do you do the whole roping thing?"

"Yes," she replied and eagerly grinned. "Would you like to see how it's done?"

"Are you kidding?" he remarked with enthusiasm. "I want to try it."

"Well, you have to learn first," Jasmine informed him. "Watch me."

Jasmine removed the rope, galloped toward the herd, and singled out one steer. She chased the steer away from the heard, slung the rope in the air, and lassoed it. As the rope became taut, the steer instantly stopped. The steer knew the routine and didn't fight it. Her horse immediately backed up to keep the rope tight. Jasmine leaped off the horse and approached the steer. She removed the rope from its head and rolled up the lasso as she returned to her horse. Zack watched with some disappointment as she mounted her horse.

"You didn't do the whole flipping thing and tying the legs," he remarked.

She laughed at the comment. "I'd need a calf for that," Jasmine replied. "And I only do that when necessary. It's not exactly fun for the calf."

Zack appeared disappointed.

She was humored by the look on his face then offered a warm smile. "Would you like me to show you some roping techniques?"

"Yeah, that could come in handy someday," Zack replied and held back his devious grin.

She nodded across the pasture toward the woods. "There's a busted tree just over there," Jasmine announced. "You can practice roping that. Once you get the hang of it, we'll graduate you to an actual steer." Jasmine looked back at the others. "I'm going to teach Zack to rope." She then nodded to the herd. "Selena, tell Teddy I said he should let you move the herd into the fence near the barn."

"Really?" Selena cried out with enthusiasm. "Awesome!"

As Zack rode toward the woods with Jasmine, Bogart stared after them and frowned. He reluctantly followed the girls to join the head wrangler.

"Jasmine said we could move the herd into the corral near the barn," Selena announced to the wrangler.

The wrangler chuckled and nodded. "They're all yours," he replied then eyed Colleen's bullwhip. "You know how to use that thing?"

Colleen removed her bullwhip and grinned. "I can extinguish a candle flame with it."

The wrangler stared at her and seemed impressed. "Well, I'd love to see that," he announced then indicated the herd. "Ride across the back of the herd and make some noise. That'll get their attention pretty fast. The rest of us will keep them moving in the direction of the corral."

Colleen grinned and galloped behind the herd of cattle. She cracked her bullwhip, catching their attention. The herd took off in the opposite direction and headed toward the farm. Monique, Selena, and Bogart helped keep them orderly and headed for the corral.

Chapter 56

Jasmine and Zack rode into a secluded clearing. The attractive woman dismounted her horse and tied it to a nearby tree, giving the horse some shade from the afternoon sun. Zack followed her lead and did the same with Storm Cloud. Jasmine removed her rope and guided Zack closer to the edge of the woods where a tree had snapped off, leaving a four-foot tall stump. She showed him how to hold the rope while standing behind him, keeping her hand on his, and mimicked the movement of his wrist for him. Zack didn't even seem to notice or care that her large breasts pressed against his back while she instructed him. She finally moved away and sat on a nearby rock to watch him practice swinging the rope above his head. He tangled himself in the rope a few times, but he was quickly getting the hang of it.

"You're a fast learner," she announced while studying him closely. "What do you do for a living?"

"Retired Navy SEAL," he informed her without looking back. "Now I'm a free-lance mercenary for hire."

She eyed him with some surprise.

Zack cast a look back at her and laughed. "I was kidding about the last part," he announced then continued practicing with the rope. "My sense of humor is a bit warped, or so I've been told."

"Navy SEAL, huh?" she remarked while grinning and seductively ran her finger along her cleavage despite that his focus remained on practicing with the rope. "I thought you looked like a tough customer. Does that mean you served with Ross then?"

"Yeah, we served together," he replied with little interest in the conversation or any conversation.

Once he mastered swinging the rope, she approached and showed him how to release it, which again required her to stand close to him. As her ample breasts brushed against his arm several times when they really didn't have to, he finally seemed to notice them. Zack was typically focused on the bigger picture, and his sharp mind was better at keeping watch for danger than flirtatious women. He didn't often notice attractive women even if they were openly flirting with him. His focus returned to the tree stump, surprising Jasmine, who had obviously pressed her breasts against his arm on purpose.

"You're quite focused, huh?" she remarked with some disappointment and stepped back as he practiced tossing the rope.

He came close to the stump several times. "It's all about focus," Zack informed her. "Keep one eye on your opponent at all times." He indicated the tree stump as his opponent. "And the other eye on everything else around you." He cast a look at her as if indicating he'd been keeping an eye on her as well. Zack threw the rope and caught the stump then grinned, pleased with himself.

"Nicely done," Jasmine announced and again approached him.

He obediently awaited further instructions, dedicating himself to learning things that interested him. She removed the rope from his hand and dropped it on the ground, catching his attention. Jasmine moved in front of him, ran her hands along his chest, and then circled her arms around his neck. Her eyes were close to his as she smiled seductively.

"I'll bet you're great at a lot of things," she cooed while placing her lips close to his. "Do you think you could make me scream?"

Zack considered the question and smirked. "I'm pretty good at making people scream," he casually replied.

Jasmine chuckled while staring into his eyes. "Why do I get the feeling we're not talking about the same thing?" she teased. "Let's try the direct approach." She allowed her hand to travel down his body and along his crotch.

Zack tensed and allowed a soft groan escape his throat. "Yeah, we were talking about the same thing," he replied then grabbed her around the waist and pulled her roughly against him.

She gasped with surprise then grinned her approval. She now wildly pawed at his body and whispered in his ear. "Make me scream."

Zack snatched the hat from her head, tossing it aside, then grabbed her by the back of the head and kissed her with wild aggression. Jasmine gasped with surprise to his wild passion and attempted to keep up with the aggressive kiss. She groaned loudly while writhing against him as his hands firmly traveled her body. Without warning, he effortlessly took her to the ground with him.

§

Monique, Colleen, Bogart, and Selena rode at a leisurely walk in the direction Jasmine and Zack had ridden nearly an hour earlier.

"I hope he's a better student for her than he was for me," Monique muttered.

"They've been gone a long time," Colleen interjected.

As they rode toward the top of the hill before the woods edge, they could see Zack and Jasmine riding toward them. Jasmine's hair looked less tamed than it had originally looked. She had a permanent grin on her face, and her cheeks were unnaturally pink. Zack showed little emotion either way, although he seemed a little more relaxed.

"It was nice meeting you, Zack," Jasmine announced unable to contain her cunning grin. "Feel free to stop by again some time."

Jasmine politely nodded to the other four and sent her horse into a gallop back for the farm.

All three girls eagerly eyed Zack while Bogart watched Jasmine ride away with a strangely distrustful look on his face.

"Were you able to do it?" Monique asked.

Zack eyed her then considered the question and nodded. "Yeah, it was fun," he replied. "Are we heading back? I could use a nap."

"Yeah, we're heading back," Bogart replied then eyed Zack suspiciously.

The girls turned and headed in the direction of Ross's farm. Bogart cut off Zack's horse with his and glared at him.

"Did you screw her?" Bogart demanded in a low, irritated whisper.

"Not an appropriate question, Bogart," Zack remarked without emotion.

"Are you insane?" Bogart scoffed in anger. "She's a married woman."

"She didn't mention she was married, and we didn't really do a lot of talking." He then glared at Bogart and raised his brows accusingly. "And when did you become the new standard for morality?"

"I don't actively pursue married women," Bogart insisted with increasing hostility. "I can't believe you had sex with her."

"No," Zack remarked with little emotion. "You can't believe *she* had sex with me and not you. Don't turn this into something. You weren't going to pursue her anyway. She's married so what does it matter? I suggest you drop it."

Zack rode past Bogart.

Bogart spun his horse around and stared after Zack. "Maybe I'm worried you won't stop there," he called after him. "We both know you want to fuck my sister."

Zack stopped the spotted horse abruptly, causing the horse to skid. He then whirled the horse around and cantered back to Bogart. The horse again slid to a stop and now pranced around excitedly. Zack's look was cold and hard.

"I would never *fuck* Jackie," Zack snarled in anger. "She's my commander's daughter, my partner, and my best friend. I've loved her longer than you've known her. You don't have to like my relationship with Jackie, but you better damned well respect it."

Zack again spun the horse around and sent it into a gallop from a standstill. Storm Cloud raced across the hillside to catch up to Thunder. Bogart attempted to control his excitable horse then cantered after him, in no particular hurry to catch up to Zack after their minor confrontation.

Chapter 57

Later that day, Jackie's helicopter landed in front of the lodge as Bogart pulled up in Beck's cherished, new SUV with Monique, Colleen, and Zack. Zack headed for the helicopter as its rotors slowed. Bogart frowned, put on a false front, and shooed the girls inside the lodge. Jackie sat sideways in the pilot's seat and wrote in her flight log as Zack approached. She looked up when she saw him and offered a sly grin.

"So," she announced cheerfully. "How was horseback riding?"

"I learned there's no such thing as 'just a horse', learned how to rope, cut cattle, and had sex with an aggressive woman." He offered a pleasant smile as he leaned against the side of the helicopter near where she sat. "How was your day?"

Jackie stared at him a moment and tried to understand what he had just told her. "Back up a moment," she remarked with confusion while eyeing him. "You went riding with Bogart and three teenage girls. How did you manage to squeeze sex into that scenario?"

"There was a female wrangler at the neighboring ranch," Zack replied and folded his arms across his chest. "Now Bogart's throwing a tantrum because she seduced me instead of him."

Jackie stared at him with surprise then groaned. "Oh, Zack," she retorted. "You make my head hurt. Did you know Bogart had his eye on her?"

"No, of course not," Zack replied almost defensively. "I don't pick up on things like that. I live in my own world; you know that. It's not as if he was going to make a move anyway. He said so much. She's married."

Jackie tossed her notebook onto the passenger seat and glared at him. "Zack," she scolded. "This is a small, tight-knit community. You can't go around sleeping with other men's wives."

"You missed the part about her being aggressive," he remarked with insistence as if that excused the fact that she was married. "She came on to me, and in my defense, she never said she was married." He then considered the comment. "Honestly, she didn't say much at all."

"Oh, really?" she remarked while glaring at him. "She just introduced herself and cried 'take me now'?"

Zack stared at her a moment and raised his brows along with a tiny grin. "It sounds better when you say it," he teased then turned serious. "Actually, it was more like 'make me scream'." He considered the comment then shook his head. "I was pretty sure she wasn't asking me to tie her up and torture her, but I was a little uncertain for a moment there. Thankfully, she clarified her meaning."

Jackie stared at him a moment and wondered what actually went on in his head. The usual answer was 'don't ask; you don't want to know'. "Well, all is fair in love and war," she replied with a sigh. "I can't fault you for jumping on that offer."

"Be sure to tell Bogart that when he bitches to you about me later," Zack muttered under his breath.

"Bogart is wrestling with his own demons right now," she informed him. "He's reached an age where he fears he'll never get married. I'm afraid Ross and Beck getting married planted that seed in his head." She drew a deep breath and sighed.

"Then there's Monique and Colleen. The more he hangs around them; the more he wants children. I guess he's fighting his urge to sleep around, and it makes him a little cranky."

"Been there," Zack muttered.

"You and me both," she remarked then grinned. "How do you think I ended up with Holden?"

"You handcuffed him to a bed and molested him," he casually replied. "I guess some things never change. I heard all about your drunken antics last night from Monroe first thing this morning."

She appeared curious although attempting to hide her sly grin. "Was he pissed?"

"About as expected," he replied. "Not sure how I slept through that episode of wild kingdom."

"You were still outside when we all went to bed," she remarked then offered a humored smile at the thought. "Holden wanted to get even with Monroe and Ross, and I obliged him."

"Feel free to skip the details," Zack muttered.

"Yet you'd freely give up details of your romp," Jackie remarked while cleverly raising her brows.

"That's different," Zack replied.

"How?" Jackie demanded.

"It just is," he replied firmly.

Jackie knew better than to press him for details. She could almost imagine what he'd say. She slid from the pilot's seat and didn't press the current topic. She had other things on her mind at the moment and getting into another pointless debate with Zack sounded all too exhausting. Zack straightened and shut the helicopter door for her. Jackie was unusually quiet as they walked together at a leisurely pace toward the lodge. Zack eyed her several times and appeared curious.

"Something bothering you?" he asked.

Jackie frowned and nervously ran her fingers through her hair. "Holden got a call on his cell phone when we reached the federal building this morning," she informed him. "The evidence room at the Bureau was broken into." Jackie raised her brows while frowning. "A guard and the janitor were shot at point-blank range. You won't believe what was stolen."

Zack frowned and shook his head. "I'll bet I would."

"I called Ross from the Bureau building," she announced then sighed. "He's already working on a contingency plan for Martin."

"Colonel Holloway is still wanted for murder after his shootout with the feds," Zack remarked. "I think he has other things to worry about right now."

"Yes, but with that weapon and the list, he can sell it to the highest bidder," she insisted while casting a look at him. "He'll be able to disappear and send more men to kill Martin, if he chooses."

"Never underestimate a man seeking revenge," Zack replied with a sigh and shook his head. "They're the worst."

She cast a look at him and wondered if he were secretly referring to himself. He met her gaze and smirked silently answering her question.

§

Colonel Holloway stood on the old porch to the small cabin in the woods early that evening and watched the black, modified Humvee pull up the overgrown driveway. It stopped in front of the cabin. As Katrina got out of the Humvee, Holloway sighed with relief and hurried off the porch to greet her. He pulled her into his arms and kissed her quickly but passionately. She eagerly returned the kiss then caressed his chest as he pulled back just far enough to meet her gaze.

"Did you miss me or is Dixon driving you nuts?" she teased.

"Both," he replied with a small chuckle then affectionately caressed her face and hair while gazing lovingly into her eyes. "You've been gone two days. I was worried that something happened to you." Holloway managed a tiny, insecure smile. "Or you had a change of heart and couldn't face coming back to *this* place."

She laughed at his insecurity then touched his face and kissed him warmly on the lips. Katrina met his gaze and smiled seductively.

"You're not getting rid of me that easily," she cooed while firmly running her hands along his chest. "The sex is too good."

Holloway grinned and laughed. "I love hearing you say that."

Katrina then frowned and patted his chest as she pulled away from him. "I hope that's enough," she announced while relaying her disappointment. "I was coming up empty on your helicopter pilot, so I tried a different route. You're not going to like it."

"What won't I like?" he asked with concern.

"The helicopter is the property of a federal agent," Katrina informed him as she scanned his eyes for a reaction. "Special Agent Holden Falcone. This guy has gained a lot of fame for bringing down mob bosses. He knows people, influential people, possibly even *connected* people."

"Are you concerned he may know more powerful people than I do?" he asked while raising his brow.

"I know you need that prototype," Katrina announced, "but I think it's a bad idea to go after whoever these people are that have it. Without the U.S. Army to fall back on, you can't expect to go up against the FBI and win."

Holloway stared at her a moment then smiled charmingly as he brushed a stray lock of hair from her face. "Are you worried about me?"

"You lost your security net," she reminded him. "You're no longer untouchable." Katrina moved closer to him while staring into his eyes. "There's still enough money that you and I can leave here." Her eyes pleaded with his. "Just the two of us."

He groaned, apparently pleased by the comment then pulled her into his arms and held her tightly against him. "I love that you're concerned for me," Holloway whispered in her ear then affectionately kissed her neck. He pulled away just far enough to meet her gaze and touched her face. "But I have to try. I'm doing this for you. For us."

"I don't want you to risk your life because you think money will make me happy," she insisted while caressing his chest. "I'm begging you. Give it up."

"Forty-eight hours," he announced and kissed her quickly but warmly on the lips. "If I can't acquire the prototype in forty-eight hours, we'll do it your way." He smiled compassionately. "Just the two of us."

"Forty-eight hours," she reluctantly responded. Her look then turned serious. "In forty-eight hours, I'm leaving the country with or without you. You'll have to decide which you want more."

"It's you," he informed her and affectionately kissed her lips. "I promise; it's you."

Katrina frowned as her hands continued to caress his chest. He held her in his arms and studied her expression.

"I've disappointed you," he announced timidly.

"A little," she replied then managed a smile. "But I'll let you make it up to me."

He grinned and chuckled. "How do I do that?" Holloway asked. "Tell me what you want."

"Is dickless in the bunker?" she asked while frowning.

Holloway groaned and rolled his eyes. "Yes, Dixon is in the bunker."

She pulled away from him and clasped his hand in hers. "A nature walk it is," Katrina teased and pulled him toward the woods.

Holloway grinned, clung to her hand, and eagerly followed her.

Chapter 58

Martin and Marie joined the team in the kitchen where they sat at the table looking mostly solemn. Bogart was somewhere with the girls and the only one from the team who was missing. Marie and Martin saw the defeated looks on the team's faces and appeared concerned by what must have happened. Sal and Othello sat at the island counter huddled over Othello's laptop and worked on something possibly unrelated.

"Did something happen?" Martin asked while fidgeting as he eyed the team.

"The FBI evidence room was broken into late Thursday night," Ross informed them. "The prototype weapon and the flash drive were stolen."

"But Colonel Holloway killed all those men," Martin reminded them. "He's wanted for murder. He has more pressing things to worry about now."

"Yes," Beck replied. "But now he has the drawings for a very dangerous weapon that he's going to sell for billions. Even hiding underground, he'll have more than enough money to buy anyone he wants. When he does, there's a good chance he'll send someone after you and your family."

Marie withheld her gasp and nervously sat at the table while staring at Ross and Beck. "What do we do?"

"There's the obvious solution," Monroe announced and held his breath. "We put you into our version of witness protection. No government involvement. The three of you can virtually disappear without a trace with Othello's help. I've helped dozens of people vanish forever."

Martin placed his hands on Marie's shoulders and tensed at the news. "Isn't there any other way?" he asked.

"Colonel Holloway is in hiding. Undoubtedly, he's someplace well-hidden and heavily guarded," Ross informed them. "We couldn't storm his fortress even if we knew where and had the manpower to do it."

Martin drew a deep breath and straightened proudly. "I did this," he announced. "I don't want my family to give up their lives because I chose to steal that prototype from Holloway." He crouched alongside Marie's chair, took her hands, and met her gaze. "You've done fine on your own without me. I don't want to put you and Colleen through anymore."

"I appreciate that, Martin," Marie announced and squeezed his hands while managing a smile. "But we're a family again. We stay together."

"Would you like some time alone to discuss it with your daughter?" Ross asked.

"We'll tell her now," Marie replied then glanced at Ross. "It'll be fine."

"Tell me what?" Colleen asked as she appeared in the kitchen doorway with Monique and Bogart.

All three approached the table with shared looks of concern. Marie and Martin pulled Colleen closer and held her between them.

"Your father is no longer safe," Marie informed her. "Monroe has offered to send us somewhere secure with new names and identities."

Colleen stared at them as horror immediately swept over her face. "What?"

"It'll be fine," Marie insisted while offering a tiny, reassuring smile. "We'll be together."

Bogart and Monique stared at the unfolding scene with horror equal to Colleen's.

"But I'll have to leave Monique?" Colleen choked on her words.

Marie and Martin exchanged looks as the reality of what they were proposing dawned on them. Colleen looked at Monique and Bogart, who remained motionless with their mouths hanging open.

Colleen then looked at Monroe with increasing concern. "And Thunder?"

Monroe suddenly tensed and fumbled over himself. "I, uh, well," he began. "I hadn't taken a horse into consideration. It would be more difficult for you to--"

Colleen pulled away from her parents, backed up several steps, and shook her head. "No," she announced boldly and fought her tears. "I'm not leaving my home, my horse, and my best friend." She raised her head proudly. "I'll stay with Monique."

"That would be too dangerous," Ross gently informed her. "It would put Monique at risk."

"Then she'll stay with me," Bogart announced as his eyes glossed with tears. "I'll take care of her."

Colleen ran from her parents and into Bogart's arms. She threw her arms around his waist and clung to him. He held her while she sobbed softly.

Bogart proudly raised his head despite the tears streaking his cheeks. "It's settled then," he announced and took both girls from the kitchen.

Zack stood and left the kitchen heading up the back stairs. Marie and Martin stared after their daughter, held each other, and sobbed.

Martin then looked at Monroe. "I'm going alone," he announced. "You said before it was possible to make me disappear. Kill me off. If they think I'm dead, they'll leave my family alone."

Marie sprang up from her chair and ran from the kitchen while sobbing. The tension in the room was thick. Jackie groaned and fidgeted nervously while running her fingers through her hair.

"I know it was wrong," Jackie announced in a soft tone while shamefully staring at the table. She lifted her head and looked at the rest of the team surrounding her. Jackie drew a deep breath, reached down the front of her shirt, and removed the flash drive. "I lifted it from Holden's pocket back at the abandoned airfield. I swapped it with an old one I had in the helicopter." Jackie tensed and handed it to Monroe. "I felt guilty about it and planned on switching it back today before Holden told me what happened. I thought about coming clean with him, but I'm sort of glad I didn't."

Monroe accepted the flash drive then handed it to Beck. "It'll help," Monroe informed her. "But Holloway still has the prototype."

The laser gun fell to the center of the table with a clatter startling everyone. Zack stood by the table, raised his brows, and shook his head.

"Did you actually think I was going to let you take that little toy away from me?" Zack demanded. "I'd think you people would know me better by now."

Jackie cast a look at Zack and raised her brows. "I assumed you'd steal it," she replied while staring at him. "But I didn't see how you had the opportunity."

"I make my own opportunities, Jacklyn dear," Zack casually remarked while glaring back at her. "Your lack of faith is disappointing."

Ross reached for the weapon. Zack snatched it from the table.

"I'm still not giving it up," Zack announced and held it with conviction. "The point is; I have it, and Holloway doesn't. That's what matters."

"Jackie," Ross announced with a sigh while scratching his temple. "Take Zack's toy from him."

She looked at Ross with wide, horrified eyes. "Me?" Jackie proclaimed. "What makes you think he'll give it up without a fight?"

"He won't, but while you distract him, we'll seize the weapon," Ross teased and raised his brows. "It'll almost make up for that bad thing you did."

Jackie cast a look at Zack.

He jumped back a step while holding the laser to his chest. "Nope," Zack announced firmly. "There's *nothing* you can do that'll make me give up my new toy."

Jackie sighed with defeat then looked at Ross and shrugged. "I did everything I could," she announced. "He's not giving it up."

"You disappoint me," Ross scoffed.

Jackie knew better than to come between Zack and anything that went 'boom'. She wasn't entirely convinced he wouldn't turn on her if she attempted to take the bone away from that particular dog. Zack's growl was bad enough. She didn't need him biting her.

"Does this change anything?" Martin finally asked and looked around the table.

"It changes everything," Ross announced while smirking as he leaned back in his chair. "Now, we just have to find the bastard and flush him out."

"And then my family will be safe?"

"Oh, your family *is* safe," Ross replied then grinned. "I just want to take the bastard down on principle."

Chapter 59

Sunday, July 6th. It was a beautiful, sunny morning and, as a working cattle ranch, Hooper's ranch was alive with activity. A black, luxury sedan pulled up to the ranch, catching the attention of one of the nearby wranglers on his horse. Colonel Holloway got out of the driver's side looking suave and handsome, although very much out of place in his expensive suit. He buttoned his suit jacket as he rounded the car to the passenger side and opened the door for Katrina. He extended his hand to her and helped her from the car. The stunning woman in her simple yet sexy dress was enough to catch the wrangler's attention.

The wrangler stopped what he was doing, pushed up the brim of his hat, and watched the couple approach the front door. They didn't get many unannounced visitors and rarely ever any dressed so fashionably. Holloway straightened his suit jacket and rang the bell. There was barely a pause before the door was opened by a young maid, who had obviously been watching the strangers through the window. The young, attractive woman was immediately captivated by the handsome, wealthy man.   Colonel Holloway had that effect on women. The young maid instinctively smiled.

"Can I help you?" she asked and attempted to take a sweeping look of the wealthy stranger without acting as if she were checking him out.

"Pardon the intrusion," Holloway announced with a little added extra charm, aware that he caught the young woman's attention.

His smooth words and sexy voice instantly hooked the young woman, and he knew it.   That she didn't giggle was actually surprising.

"I'm attending to some business around here," he continued and added a sophisticated smile for effect.   "I'd heard there was a local air taxi service in the area, but the only private airfield never has anyone around.   A local in the nearby town said the helicopter may operate from this ranch."

"Oh, no," the maid announced while maintaining her smile. "She doesn't live here.   I think she lives at the farm a few miles from here.   She seems to go there a lot."

"There's another farm nearby?" Holloway asked.

"Yes, his daughter rides around here a lot," the maid offered.

"A man and his daughter?" Holloway asked then grinned. "I think they're the ones I'm looking for.   What are their names?"

"Liam and Selena," the maid offered.

"No last name?" he asked.

"I haven't worked here that long," she insisted.   "I'm sure Miss Hooper knows her name.   Would you like to come inside? I could get her for you."

"No, we've taken up enough of your time," Holloway replied then pointed up the road with added charm.   "Just a few miles that way."

"You can't miss it," the maid replied.   "There's not much else on this road."

Holloway smiled suavely at the young woman, who instantly blushed.   "Thank you very much," he announced.   "You've been a tremendous help."

Holloway took Katrina's hand and led her back to the awaiting car.   The maid remained in the doorway and watched as the handsome gentleman opened the car door for the beautiful woman then shut the door for her. The maid smiled dreamily then shut the front door. Holloway rounded the car and slipped into the driver's side seat. He immediately picked up his hand radio, since cell phone service vanished the moment they left the small town.

"Gather the men," Holloway announced into the radio as his look turned hard and cold. His charm had instantly faded. "We have a location on the helicopter. A farm just a few miles north of the cattle ranch. A man and his daughter." He hesitated then added. "I need them taken *alive*. Meet us a mile beyond the ranch driveway."

"Yes, Colonel," Dixon announced through the radio.

Holloway put the car in gear and drove down the long driveway away from the ranch. Katrina cast a look at the colonel.

"Sounds like I should probably change," she remarked then climbed into the back of the car.

Holloway cast a glance at her backside as she wiggled her way into the back of the car. "Remember, Katrina darling," he announced while peering at her through the rearview mirror. "I need them alive."

She rolled her eyes while unzipping her dress. "I have met a few people I haven't killed," she insisted sarcastically. "I think I can handle an old farmer and his daughter with minimal bloodshed."

"With the way his daughter flies that helicopter, she's not just some hick farmer's daughter," Holloway insisted while stealing a few peeks as Katrina changed out of her dress in the back seat. "She has some form of military training, which means the old farmer is undoubtedly retired military and part of those who took down more than a dozen of my men. We're looking at automatic weapons and skilled fighters." His eyes didn't leave her cleavage contained within the black lacy bra until she slipped into her black tank top. "I want you and Dixon to scope out the place before we make our move just to be sure."

Katrina slipped into her black pants and black boots then hastily tied her hair up in a messy ponytail. "Are you anticipating a small militia at this farm?"

"Half a dozen heavily armed men would be my calculation," he informed her.

As they reached the end of Hooper's driveway, Katrina climbed back into the front seat and caressed Holloway's thigh while leaning on his shoulder. He stopped the car and took in a sweeping eyeful of her then grinned with pleasure.

"God, you're sexy when you're dressed to kill," Holloway moaned.

She flashed a smile then grabbed his face and kissed him aggressively. He barely had time to return the kiss when she pulled away disappointing him.

"We have work to do," she announced and allowed her hand to stray to his crotch without taking her eyes off his. "There will be plenty of time for *that* later."

Chapter 60

The four, saddled horses grazed in the lush pasture on the remote hillside just out of view of Ross's farm. None of the horses were tied since none would stray far from their riders. Bogart and Darth sat with Colleen on a large boulder and watched Selena teach Monique how to shoot cans with a rock and a slingshot. Monique laughed each time she hit the can. She was getting quite good at it. Darth watched with intrigue and appeared ready to leap into action and chase the flying rocks but somehow thought better of it. Bogart glanced at the teenager alongside him and noted Colleen's distant expression.

"I thought you'd be happy now that your father doesn't need to go into witness protection," Bogart remarked. "What's bugging you?"

"You know he's not safe until that Colonel Holloway is captured," she insisted.

"Well, yeah," Bogart announced then fidgeted slightly. "But that's just a minor nuisance. Maybe a couple of weeks. It's not so bad up here. You'll survive a couple of weeks until the guys find him."

Colleen turned on her hip to face Bogart and stared into his eyes with a serious look. "I never thanked you," she announced timidly.

"Thanked me for what?" he asked.

"For what?" she repeated and laughed. "You offered to take me in so I wouldn't have to leave Monique and Thunder. That's a big deal, Bogart."

He shrugged with little reaction. "Didn't seem like a big deal to me," Bogart remarked. "I assume that's what families do. I ain't never had a family before, but I'm getting the hang of it. Families take care of each other. Jackie and Holden took me in before I even knew she was my sister. The guys eventually accepted me into their family too. You and Twinkie are like my annoying little sisters. You're fun to torment, but I'd go to hell and back to protect you rug rats."

Colleen smiled and kept from laughing. "I love you too, Bogart," she announced then hugged him.

Bogart returned the warm embrace then pulled away and attempted to hide his emotions. "I hope you can forgive your mother and father," he remarked timidly. "They only wanted to do what was best for you and their family."

"I know," Colleen replied and timidly rubbed her chilled shoulders despite the warm air. "I get it. He just wants to be a good father." She then clung to Bogart's arm and rested her head on his shoulder. "Maybe you could give him a few pointers."

Bogart smiled and patted her hand attached to his arm. "Do you actually think I'd make a good father someday?" he asked. "I've had my doubts. I never had any positive role models growing up."

She pulled back and looked at him with some surprise. "Bogart, you *are* a good father," Colleen replied.

Bogart held back his emotions and kissed the top of Colleen's head. "Thank you, Squirt. I needed to hear that."

"Awe," Selena announced as she and Monique approached Colleen and Bogart. "They're having a moment. Isn't that special?"

Despite her words, the devious look on the younger teen's face told a different story.

"Yes," Monique announced while grinning. "Let's get in on that."

"Pile on Bogart!" Selena screamed.

Monique and Selena jumped on Bogart as Colleen joined in. Darth sprang to his feet and barked at the girls as they attacked Bogart. All three girls toppled him off the boulder and onto the ground. Bogart immediately put Monique into a headlock and rubbed his knuckles on the top of her head.

"I'm going to lay some serious noogies on you," he cried out while Monique screamed playfully.

He cast her aside then captured Selena around the neck and did the same to her while she screamed. Monique and Colleen again pounced on Bogart and attempted to do the same to him. While they held him down, Selena rubbed Bogart's head with her fist.

"No, not the hair," he cried out while laughing. "Not the hair!"

Darth jumped in and excitedly licked Bogart's face while he was held immobile by the girls.

§

Bogart stood perfectly still while holding a six-inch stick in his hand. His concerned expression revealed his discomfort in the situation.

"I don't want to do this," he announced nervously. "You're going to shoot my eye out."

Selena pulled the rock back within the slingshot while watching the target. "Trust me," she announced.

Bogart pinched his eyes shut. "Oh, this is going to hurt," he muttered.

Selena let the rock fly from the slingshot. It struck the stick, knocking it from Bogart's hand. He breathed a sigh of relief then laughed.

"I was a little nervous a minute there," he announced while grinning.

"Yeah, that's the first time I've been able to do that," Selena teased.

Bogart gave her a stern glare.

Colleen uncoiled her bullwhip and grinned. "Let me try with the bullwhip."

"No way," Bogart cried out and pointed at her. "You nearly killed me with that thing once!"

"I did not," Colleen scoffed with irritation.

"Yeah, that was me," Monique replied. "And I did warn you I wasn't very good."

"You should let me teach you," Colleen announced.

"You did once," Bogart reminded her. "I had bruises for a week."

"Zack got the hang of it in twenty minutes," Colleen teased.

"That's because Zack likes things that can kill or maim," Bogart muttered. "It's creepy and unsettling."

Colleen flicked the bullwhip and hit the tip of his cowboy boot. He jumped with surprise and glared at her. She grinned and did it again. Bogart jumped and became annoyed.

"Stop that," he snarled.

"We're not heading back until you pick a weapon," Monique announced. "Bullwhip or slingshot."

Bogart groaned. "Fine, give me the slingshot," he announced.

Selena handed him the slingshot while Monique set up the cans for him.

"You're like Zack's youth army or something," Bogart muttered.

Chapter 61

Liam stood on a stepstool on the porch outside the farmhouse and attempted to hang a decorative wind chime. Lee kept the stepstool stable as he stretched while attempting to hang the noisily clanging ornament. Liam cast a quick look at her.

"Why do you always want to hang these things when Ross is away?" Liam asked. "We must have a dozen by now."

"Oh," she announced and waved him off, "because Ross hates them."

Liam managed to attach the wind chime then straightened on the stepstool and eyed her. "So when he gets annoyed, I'm your accomplice?"

"You catch on fast," she teased.

Within the woods more than fifty yards from the house, Katrina lowered her binoculars and appeared baffled by what she saw.

Dixon lowered his binoculars as well, although he didn't take his eyes off the farmhouse. "They're definitely alone," he announced. "I don't see the helicopter anywhere."

"Something's not right," Katrina muttered.

Dixon rolled his eyes and glared at her with annoyance. "Now what's bugging you?" he demanded. "You make everything more complicated than it has to be."

She glared back at him and frowned her annoyance. "It's a wonder you lived this long in your profession," Katrina scoffed. "It's noticing the little things that'll keep you expelling air longer."

Dixon groaned and straightened. "I don't have time for you," he snarled and shook his head. "All you women talk too much."

Katrina straightened and pointed her binoculars at him demandingly. "And you don't think enough," she shot back. "Does that man look old enough to be her father? He has ten years on her; fifteen max. That means we're looking for another man on this farm."

"Even if you're right, it doesn't matter," Dixon snarled. "We're talking about a man around sixty. One old man doesn't change anything. If he shows up, we'll deal with him. Quit being such a nagging bitch and report back to the boss."

Dixon turned and headed back through the woods toward the road. Katrina sneered, grumbled under her breath while shaking her head, and followed him.

§

A little while later. Liam sat on the porch railing and appeared deep in thought while Lee folded the stepstool and set it aside. She cast a glance at her brother-in-law and noted his expression.

"Something on your mind?" she finally asked then sat on the railing a few feet away.

"I'm feeling a little guilty," he replied.

"About what?" she asked then grinned teasingly. "Ross doesn't hate wind chimes that much."

"Not the wind chimes," Liam huffed but managed a tiny laugh. "Selena has been so happy having Monique and Colleen around lately. Maybe living up here so far from kids her own age isn't what's best for her. When her mother died, she was just a little girl. The farm was great for her." He drew a deep breath. "Now, I'm not so sure."

"Maybe you should be talking to her instead of me," Lee remarked.

"It's not just her, you know," he announced while studying Lee. "I came here to hide from the world almost as much as Ross did. I didn't want to be around people. I cut myself off physically and emotionally. Ross and I were a couple of recluses together." He held his breath then released a groan. "Then he met you, and he's been, well, happy. Maybe there's still hope for me."

Lee laughed and smiled. "You talk as if you're at the end of life," she teased. "Of course you can be happy. You're an idiot. You should be out there dating. Selena certainly wouldn't mind."

"Really?" he asked with surprise and appeared curious. "She told you that?"

Lee groaned and rolled her eyes. "She keeps asking me why her father isn't married like her Uncle Ross." Lee laughed. "She thinks there needs to be another woman in the house to balance out the testosterone."

Liam hid his smile and laughed. "Yeah, you're right," he announced and stood. "I should talk to her."

"Did you want some iced tea?" she asked as she stood as well.

"Uh, yeah, sure," he replied. "I just need to finish a few things in the barn first."

Liam headed off the porch and for the barn while Lee entered the house. She approached the refrigerator and removed the pitcher of iced tea. She set the pitcher on the counter and was about to remove two glasses from the cupboard when she saw a shadow pass through the sun shining on the living room floor just beyond the archway. Lee hesitated a moment and listened, but she didn't hear anything. She opened the utility drawer and removed a snub-nosed revolver. She hid the gun alongside her leg as she approached the archway. Lee stepped into the archway and saw an uninvited yet well-dressed man sitting on the bench before the piano. Holloway cast a look at her then played some classical music.

"You don't need that gun," he informed her. "I'm not here to hurt you."

Lee aimed the gun at him. "I'll be the judge on whether or not I need the gun," she snapped and cocked the hammer. "I'll also decide whether or not to let you speak again before shooting you."

"Hmm, feisty," he announced.

The gun was easily snatched from her hand from behind. Lee whirled around and looked at the woman standing behind her.

Katrina smiled sweetly. "I may object to you shooting him," she announced.

Lee tensed and nervously looked back at Holloway, who continued to play the classical love ballad.

"Don't worry, my dear," Holloway casually announced. "I won't hold that gun incident against you. A woman should want to protect herself from people like me." He glanced up without missing a note. "I'm proud to admit that I've never harmed a woman." Holloway then cast a quick look at Katrina, who casually spun the cylinder on the revolver as if she were bored. "As for my lovely associate--" He shrugged. "I'm not sure she can say the same." Holloway stopped playing the piano, turned on the bench straddling it, and offered a playful smile. "Why don't we do this the easy way? You tell me where to find Martin and my prototype, and we'll leave you without as much as a hair out of place on your head."

"Martin who?" Lee asked and pulled off the perfect bewildered look. "What prototype?"

Holloway groaned and allowed his shoulders to sag. "I thought we were going to do this the easy way," he announced then sighed. "Please don't upset me." His eyes burned into hers from across the room as his look turned stern. "I may forget I'm a gentleman."

"I don't know who you are," Lee boldly announced and straightened proudly, "but whatever grudge you have against my father, you'll need to take up with him. You have nothing to gain by coming after me. We don't even speak anymore."

"Your father?" Holloway asked and appeared curious. He glanced at Katrina in silent question.

Katrina raised her brow and gave a slight shake of her head. Holloway looked back at Lee.

"Who's your father?" he asked.

"You know who my father is or you wouldn't be here asking about some snitch," Lee easily lied without even twitching as she attempted the perfect intimidation con. "I actively avoid my father and all his mafia friends and foes. You have a problem with Sal? You take it up with Sal."

"Your father is Sal Romano?" Holloway asked with great interest.

Lee folded her arms across her chest and glared at him. "Didn't we already cover this? I've been through one Valentine's Day massacre," Lee announced and masked her concern with pretend irritation. "I don't need to be present for another." She allowed her arms to fall to her sides as she sighed. "I'll give you his direct number. You can even use my phone. Talk to him yourself. Just go meet him somewhere that's not here. I don't want to see him."

Holloway removed his cell phone from his inner jacket pocket.

"There's no cell phone reception up here," she informed him. "You'll have to use the landline phone." Lee indicated the old rotary phone on the end table.

Colonel Holloway stood, approached the phone, and studied it a moment. Lee stared at him and raised a brow.

"It's called a rotary phone," Lee remarked. "The little dial spins."

He cast a look at her, apparently not humored by her sarcasm, although it was obvious he was wondering how clever she really was. Holloway picked up the phone and dialed the number Lee recited. He held the phone away from his ear while remaining suspicious. There was a strange beeping sound. He slammed the phone down and ripped the cord from the wall.

Katrina jumped with surprise and stared at him. "What is it?" she asked.

Holloway glared at Lee. "Was that some sort of encrypted message?" he demanded.

"It was probably a busy signal, but thanks for ruining my phone," Lee scoffed.

Holloway shook his head. "I didn't want it to come to this, but you've given me no choice." He straightened proudly. "Dixon."

Dixon entered from the kitchen and tossed Liam across the living room floor. His hands were duct taped behind his back, and he had tape across his mouth. Lee jumped with surprise and stared at Liam. Although he appeared unharmed for the moment, it frightened her all the same.

"I told you it's not in my nature to harm women, but there are ways around that. That being said; I'm going to ask you some questions," Colonel Holloway announced while straightening his jacket. "If I don't like your answer, Dixon here will take it out on that man's face. First question." His eyes narrowed in anger. "Who did I just call?"

Lee held her breath and lifted her head proudly. "Everyone," she announced while staring back at the frightening man and showed no fear. "That was a scatter S.O.S." She held up her hand to reveal her bracelet that now pulsated a red, glowing light. "I hope you have an army because you're going to need one."

Holloway casually walked closer to Lee and stared into her eyes from only inches away. She was quite possibly frightened out of her mind, but she stared back and held her ground. She needed to sell it. The colonel suddenly smiled.

"I do have an army, and it's a fight I wanted," he informed her. "Thank you for obliging."

Chapter 62

In a pasture not far from the house, the girls and Bogart rode their horses at a leisurely canter with Darth running in the field not far from them. Selena suddenly pulled her horse to a stop and looked at her bracelet that now pulsated red. She stared at the flashing light and appeared alarmed. Bogart, Monique, and Colleen stopped their horses, turned, and rode back to her.

"What is it?" Monique asked with concern.

"Why is your bracelet doing that?" Colleen asked.

Bogart's eyes widened in horror. "Something's happened at Ross's farm," he gasped then looked at the girls. "Go to the lodge! Now!"

"My dad and Lee," Selena gasped. "They're in trouble!"

"I said go to the lodge," Bogart yelled and pointed away from the farm. "Red means danger; don't come home. The guys probably already received the S.O.S. I'll scope out the farm and meet them there."

§

Within the lodge, Beck hurried Pinto and Marie across the lobby and to the area just near the broad staircase. He slammed his palm against a plate, which revealed the panic room beyond a fake panel.

"Don't come out and keep quiet," Beck informed them.

Pinto nodded and hurried Marie into the room. Beck quickly kissed Pinto just before she pressed a button on.her side of the wall. A steel door slid shut. Beck closed the false panel and hurried across the lobby to join the others, who were now passing around the ammo and assault rifles. Jackie ran down the stairs while slipping into her leather bomber jacket. Zack tossed her an assault rifle, which she caught then hurried for the door where Ross waited.

"They're at my fucking house," Ross snarled and slapped the magazine into his assault rifle then cocked it. "We're dealing with a bunch of desperate mercenaries. Once my family is safe; no prisoners."

§

One of Colonel Holloway's men hurried into Ross's farmhouse carrying an assault rifle. He appeared enthusiastic and nodded toward the door.

"We have a visual on the helicopter," the man announced. "Our men on the road spotted it about ten miles north from here. With the way the back road winds, it's probably a good thirty miles by car."

"Contact our men in the helicopters. The rest of the convoy can meet us there," Holloway announced then grinned slyly. "Let's take this little party to them now that we have their location." He eyed Liam, who remained bound on the floor. "Leave him. He's of no use to us." He then indicated Lee. "I think we're going to need her though. The man who loves her enough to give her such fashionable jewelry will undoubtedly kill himself attempting to save her." He nodded to Lee, signaling Katrina to take the prisoner.

Holloway and his men hurried from the house, leaving Katrina to collect Lee. Holloway stepped outside and watched two of his helicopters approach from the south. As the first helicopter lowered, there was a gunshot from the house. The colonel turned with surprise and looked around. Katrina and Lee weren't behind them. Holloway ran back for the house with two of his men following. He ran into the living room and saw Lee lying face down on the floor with blood on the side of her head. Katrina clutched her bleeding right arm while holding Lee's snub-nosed revolver.

"What happened?" Holloway cried out. "We needed her alive."

Katrina sneered at him in anger. "The bitch had a knife," she lashed back then looked at the slice on her upper arm, which bled freely. "Or would you have preferred she killed me instead?"

Holloway took the revolver from her, tossed it aside, and gazed sympathetically into her eyes. "I'm sorry, darling," he announced and handed her his handkerchief. "One of the men will patch you up in the jeep."

She pulled away from him and appeared angry. "No, I'm going with you in the helicopter," Katrina snarled. "You're not sidelining me over a papercut."

"We need to go then," he insisted and hurried her out of the house.

They ran across the yard and jumped into the awaiting helicopter.

§

Jackie flew her helicopter across the countryside at record speed with Ross in the front. Zack and Gil sat in the back with their assault rifles and binoculars while scanning the surrounding area. The three teenagers could be seen running their horses through a less traveled path in the woods.

"There," Gil cried out. "I see the girls on their horses. They're heading for the lodge."

"What about Bogart?" Jackie asked through her headset.

"No sign of him," Gil replied.

"If the farm has been compromised, he's probably checking on Lee and Liam," Ross announced and motioned for Jackie to continue toward the farm.

Another helicopter suddenly appeared out of nowhere and nearly collided with Jackie's helo. She jerked the stick to avoid colliding with the helicopter.

"Shit," she cried out and attempted to control the sharply veering bird.

"It's him," Ross announced in anger. "Colonel Holloway found us."

Jackie then saw the second helicopter approaching. "Yeah, and he's heading straight for us. Hold on!"

She sharply veered left to avoid the second helicopter coming at them.

"Want me to blow that fucker out of the sky?" Zack demanded.

"No, we need confirmation on Lee and Liam," Ross yelled back. "If he's taken them, they could be in one of the helicopters."

They could see four, black modified Humvees in the distance racing along the winding, back road toward the lodge. Ross cursed under his breath and raised his hand radio.

"Beck, do you copy?" Ross announced into his radio. "They're bringing the party to you. We have four Humvees, two helicopters, and countless men. The girls are safe, but we don't have confirmation on Lee or Liam's positions. Watch your targets."

"Copy that, Ross," Beck responded back over the hand radio.

"I see Bogart," Gil announced and pointed to a clearing.

Bogart could be seen on his horse in the clearing below. He saw the helicopter, stopped his horse, and urgently waved to them.

"Take her down," Ross instructed.

Jackie took the express elevator down, dropping fast into the clearing. Bogart's horse pranced around from the excessive wind the rotors produced. Jackie didn't bother shutting it down since they were pressed for time. It was uncertain if the other helicopters would circle back and ambush them, but either way, she needed to be ready for a speedy takeoff. Ross sprang from the helicopter and ran across the field where Bogart sat on his excitable horse.

"Holloway and his men are heading for the lodge," Bogart shouted above the loud sounds from the helicopter and motioned toward the lodge. "I counted two helicopters and at least one jeep."

"Four Humvees," Ross corrected. "We saw them from the sky. The girls are safe. What about Lee and Liam?"

Bogart seemed tense. "Back at the house," he announced. "Liam is with Lee. Holloway and his men were all heading for the lodge."

Ross stared at Bogart with a strange look. "Something happened," Ross remarked with concern.

Bogart again fidgeted. "Lee's been shot," he shouted a little less loudly. "Liam is with her. We need to stop those men." His look was concerned. "I sent the girls to the lodge. They're going to ride right into a warzone."

"Give me your horse," Ross ordered.

"Liam has the situation under control," Bogart insisted.

Ross shouted in anger, "Give me your horse!"

Bogart dismounted the excited horse and held it still while Ross mounted. Ross turned the horse toward the woods and raced back for the house. Bogart ran for the helicopter and climbed into the back with Gil and Zack. All three stared at Bogart as he put his headset on.

"What happened?" Jackie asked.

Bogart groaned and shut his eyes. "Just get to the lodge."

Chapter 63

Jackie flew the helicopter back for the lodge where they again saw the Humvees on the back road. Gil pointed to the four Humvees that hadn't yet reached the long driveway. Jackie nodded and was about to head for the Humvees when the first helicopter came at them. Jackie cursed and was forced to veer out of their path.

"Zack," Jackie shouted into the back of the helicopter. "Tell me you have something up your sleeve to get rid of them."

Zack removed the laser weapon from his bag, held it up, and grinned proudly. "Oh, I have something for them," he announced.

"Is that a good idea?" Bogart asked while staring at the mammoth weapon with horror in his eyes. "You have no idea what--"

"It's a weapon," Zack casually announced. "You have the boom boom end--" He indicated the opening in the barrel. "And then you have the dangerous end." Zack grinned and indicated himself.

They watched as Zack aimed the weapon out the open side door. Gil immediately moved from his seat not far from Zack and took cover. Bogart saw Gil's reaction, appeared concerned, and did the same.

"Fire in the hole!" Zack pulled the trigger. Nothing happened. He made a face and fiddled with the weapon. "What the hell?"

"Maybe it's one of those weapons that requires charging," Jackie announced while attempting to outmaneuver the helicopter chasing after them. "I need a little help here, boys. Spit at them or something."

Zack fiddled with the weapon. It suddenly fired a laser out the open door and tossed Zack across the helicopter and into the opposing open door. Gil grabbed Zack's jacket and kept him from plummeting to his death.

Zack straightened with confidence. "Okay, I figured it out," he announced and gave a confident thumbs up.

Gil stepped behind him and shut the opposing side door. Zack took a firm stance, aimed the weapon out the door at the helicopter, and pulled the trigger. The laser fired, lighting up the sky, and struck the helicopter across from them. The helicopter exploded and rained flaming debris to the ground below. Zack was jolted enough that he struck the front passenger seat, but he managed to keep his balance. Zack cried out excitedly while Gil cheered him on. Zack firmly patted Jackie's shoulder and motioned for the convoy of Humvees.

"Let's join the caravan," he announced while grinning deviously.

Jackie nodded and flew for the four, black Humvees that now turned on the long road heading for the lodge and the team.

§

Colonel Holloway's helicopter landed in a clearing in front of the lodge, and it was instantly greeted with gunfire from the men inside. Holloway, Katrina, and four armed men leaped from the helicopter on the opposite side with their weapons and ran for cover behind Beck's brand new SUV. They returned fire, although they appeared to be conserving their ammo while waiting for the arrival of the rest of his army. Within the lodge, Beck sneered as he looked out the strategically placed peek hold in the wall at the men taking cover behind *his* new car. Between the wooden interior and exterior walls of the lodge was a solid concrete barrier, which offered the men inside protection from gunfire. After a botched mission tore a hole in the old building, they made some modifications to secure the place better. They also had the ability to put the lodge on 'lockdown', which would drop steel plates over the windows and doors. Unfortunately, they had too many people still on the outside to implement it.

"They would have to take cover behind my car," Beck snarled then shook his head. "I've owned it for two months. Not a scratch on it."

Kirk fired a dozen rounds into Beck's SUV then looked at Beck, who stared at him with surprise and horror.

"Now it's scrap metal," Kirk announced then pointed at the bullet-riddled vehicle. "So quit your whining and shoot the bastards."

Monroe hurried into the lobby from the kitchen hallway. "I'm going to take a lookout from the second floor. Greet their fleet before they arrive."

"I thought you were guarding the back," Beck remarked while glancing at Monroe.

"Sal and Othello are covering the back," Monroe replied then tensed. "They, uh, raided Zack's toy box. Be very afraid."

§

Jackie's helicopter buzzed past the caravan of black, modified Army Humvees approaching the lodge. She had to get close enough for Zack to take them out, which also put the helicopter within firing range of those in the Humvees. The men in the Humvees took advantage of their situation and fired at the helo. Jackie shirked at the sound of bullets striking the side of her helicopter. Zack aimed the laser weapon at the first vehicle and squeezed the trigger. The laser fired, shooting a brilliant light across the countryside, and took out the first Humvee. The gas tank exploded tossing the vehicle off its back end and onto its nose. The second Humvee drove directly into it and burst into flames upon impact. Bogart and Gil cheered for Zack just before the alarm on the chopper's control panel wailed. All three looked at Jackie as she frantically checked the controls. The helicopter sputtered.

"Son-of-a-bitch," she cried out and veered away from the remaining Humvees that continued toward the lodge while firing at them.

"They hit the fuel tank, didn't they?" Gil announced with concern.

"Yeah," she replied with some irritation. "I have to set her down." She fought the controls. "I can make it to the lodge before the caravan reaches it, but we'll need to evacuate immediately if we don't want our asses shot."

"Can you make it to the back yard?" Gil asked.

"Not enough fuel," she informed Gil. "We're going down too fast. We'll end up inside the lodge."

Zack pointed at Colonel Holloway's helicopter. "Just on the other side of their bird," he announced, indicating the tight space. "It'll offer us some cover while we make a run for the side of the lodge."

Jackie nodded and made it to the other side of Holloway's helicopter where she was able to land. Two of the colonel's men ran to greet them, attempting to get the slip on them. Zack slung the laser gun and claimed his assault rifle in order to fire precision shots. Gil and Zack fired at the approaching men while evacuating the helicopter. Bogart and Jackie leaped out and ran for the side of the lodge while Gil and Zack provided cover for them. They reached the side of the building and returned fire, giving Zack and Gil time to reach them and safety. The two remaining Humvees arrived just in time to provide additional cover for Holloway's men behind the bullet-ridden SUV. Beck and Kirk fired several rounds at the Humvees, but the bullets were deflected from the bulletproof exterior. Monroe fired several shots from the second story since he had a better view, but he was also unable to hit the men seeking shelter behind the impenetrable Humvees.

§

Othello and Sal stood on the back patio while fumbling with Zack's modified, military grade drone, which contained six grenades dangling from the bottom. It was obvious both men were a little more than intimidated by the presence of the grenades and feared touching them.

"No," Othello announced. "You have to--" He groaned. "Just set it down. I'll figure it out."

Sal set the drone on the patio table and stepped away from it while Othello fiddled with the remote control. The drone took off straight up in the air like a rocket.

"Not so fast," Sal cried out. "You'll launch it into outer space."

"I can't help it. Mine doesn't require such a light touch," Othello insisted while both watched the screen on the remote control.

He brought the drone down above the lodge then flew it across the roof and over the action. They could see the men hiding behind two Humvees, although some were branching off to circle the lodge.

Othello hovered the drone over one of the Humvees and grinned. "Fire in the hole," he announced, mimicking Zack as he pressed one of the buttons.

A grenade dropped from the drone and exploded near the men. Two of the men were taken out. Sal and Othello cheered until they saw the remaining men through the camera aiming their weapons at the drone.

"Move, move," Sal cried out.

"I'm trying," Othello responded while messing with the controls.

Though the display screen, they saw one of the men firing his weapon at the drone.

"No, no," Othello cried out at the small screen on the remote control.

The video feed went dark. The drone was struck by several bullets and it fell from the sky. It hit the ground not far from the building and exploded upon impact, vibrating the entire area. Toward the rear of the lodge, Sal patted Othello on the back and sighed while shaking his head.

"You did your best," Sal announced. "Too bad Zack's going to kill you."

Chapter 64

Monique, Colleen, and Selena arrived at the lodge and stopped their horses within the woods. All three stared at the chaos directed at the front of the lodge and were at a loss for a plan. Darth bolted from the woods for the lodge.

"Darth," Monique cried out while attempting to keep her voice down.

The dog either didn't hear her or didn't respond. There was nothing they could do about the dog. If they tried to call him back, they would draw too much attention to themselves. The girls held their breath and prayed the dog wouldn't be shot by the men out front.

"We should turn around," Selena nervously informed them. "Ride back to Hooper's ranch."

"That's miles from here," Colleen insisted. "Further if we avoid your place."

"We can't just ride up to the front door and knock," Selena snapped back while indicating the lodge. "There's a war going on."

"We'll stick to the woods and ride around back," Monique announced. "Maybe the back is clear."

"That's a bad plan," Selena announced with increasing concern.

"Let's just check it out," Monique insisted to the less confident, younger girl. "If we can't get inside through the back, we'll ride to Hooper's ranch."

Selena reluctantly agreed. All three girls rode their horses through the woods while keeping out of sight, even though they could see what was happening through the trees in the distance as well as hear the intimidating gunfire. Toward the side of the lodge, they saw Jackie and Bogart taking cover while firing at the men in the front. Zack could be seen crouched on the porch roof waiting to strike while Gil hurried past him for the second story window. He was attempting to reach the window Monroe fired out of to gain access to the lodge. Once Gil was safely inside the lodge, Zack raised the laser gun to take out the remaining Humvees and end the war, but he seemed to be having trouble with the weapon. He finally slung it over his shoulder and gave up.

As the girls rode closer to the back of the building that was more than one hundred yards away, they saw Sal and Othello pacing the patio not far from the kitchen door. They were guarding the entrance, but the back seemed secure and quiet for the moment. The three girls stopped their horses and observed the distant back patio area.

"We can make it to Othello and Sal," Monique insisted while quickly eyeing her friends.

"What about the horses?" Colleen asked with concern.

"We'll have to set them free in the woods," Monique replied.

"And hope they don't follow us," Colleen muttered.

"I don't have a better plan," Monique insisted with some frustration.

"I'm scared," Selena announced while shifting uncomfortably in her saddle.

Monique and Colleen looked at their younger friend and seemed to reconsider their options.

"Why don't you wait here," Monique informed her. "We'll see if it's safe. If anything happens, you ride to Hooper's ranch."

Selena nervously nodded. Monique and Colleen dismounted their horses and securely tied the reins around the saddle horns. Monique removed her rifle from her saddle, although Colleen left her bullwhip behind since it wouldn't do any good in their current situation. Both girls hurried into the massive clearing more than one hundred yards from the back of the lodge. Two men with assault rifles stepped out from their hidden location in the woods and aimed their weapons at them.

"Drop the rifle," the first man announced while keeping his weapon on Monique.

Monique frowned and dropped her rifle then placed her hands in the air. Storm Cloud lazily walked across the clearing toward them. The men saw the riderless horse but didn't give it much thought.

"Radio the boss," the first man instructed while grinning. "We have the perfect bait to flush them out. These two must belong to someone in the house."

A rock suddenly struck the second man in the groin and sent him to his knees in agony. A second rock was propelled from the woods, and it clipped the first man on the side of the head, scratching his face. He jumped with surprise. Storm Cloud's ears suddenly flattened, and the horse lunged for the first man. He snapped at the man's face, startling him, and sending him onto his backside. He attempted to aim his rifle at the horse, but Storm Cloud was already rearing up and thrashing down with his front hooves in a manner only meant to stomp and kill whatever was beneath him. The man screamed as the horse's hooves repeatedly struck his body. Colleen whistled. Thunder ran from the woods toward her. She signaled a command for the horse to slow but continue past her. A cantering mount was a game the girls often played with their horses.

As the horse slowed to a canter while passing her, Colleen leaped onto his back. She snatched her bullwhip from the saddle and spun the large black horse around without using the reins. The horse easily responded to subtle leg pressure and her body language, allowing her a hands-free turn. She galloped Thunder back for the second man as he straightened with his weapon. Colleen cracked the bullwhip at the man, caught his arm, and galloped past him. The man was yanked off his feet, and the assault rifle flew from his hands as he was dragged behind her. Monique swung onto her horse's back and motioned for Selena within the woods. Selena charged from the woods and galloped after them toward the back of the house where Sal and Othello now spotted them. Colleen flicked her wrist halfway to the back of the lodge, freeing the man being dragged behind her. All three girls pulled their horses to a stop just short of the patio.

Sal kept guard while Othello ran to Selena and just about caught her as she dismounted. He took her arm while shielding her body with his massive frame and hurried her into the lodge through the back door. Monique and Colleen leaped off their horses. Sal eyed the girls while attempting to keep watch with his weapon raised.

"Leave the horses," he announced and nodded to the kitchen door. "Get to the panic room."

Both girls reluctantly nodded and sent their horses running across the back yard. As they turned toward Sal, they heard a gunshot. Sal was thrown from his feet. He hit the patio and didn't move. Monique and Colleen simultaneously screamed then looked to the corner of the lodge saw two men approaching with their weapons aimed.

"Drop it," the man snarled while indicating Colleen's bullwhip.

After seeing Sal shot, Colleen immediately did what she was told. Both girls were terrified that Sal was dead when he didn't move. The two men grabbed the girls and hurried them around the side of the lodge away from where Jackie and Bogart had earlier been standing guard. Martin ran onto the patio from the kitchen, saw Sal on the ground, and hurried for him. Sal groaned while holding his bleeding shoulder and let Martin help him into a sitting position. His head bled freely from where he'd hit the patio after falling, which had briefly knocked him out.

"Are you okay?" Martin asked then looked around. He saw Thunder and Storm Cloud prancing around the back yard while staring toward the side of the lodge. He looked back at Sal. "Where are the girls?"

Sal then seemed to remember what had happened. "Two men," he announced. "They must have taken them." Sal then pointed to the opposite end of the lodge. "They came from that direction."

Martin returned Sal's weapon to him. "Get inside," he insisted. "You've been injured. I have to find the girls." Martin then grabbed his own assault rifle and ran for the side of the lodge.

Sal slowly pulled himself to his feet and swayed with some unsteadiness. He caught his balance and held his assault rifle with more conviction.

"I'll die later," Sal muttered.

There was a slight gust of wind. Sal spun with his weapon aimed. Zack landed on the patio from where he dropped off the porch roof.

"Where are Monique and Colleen?" Zack asked while casting a quick look at the two horses that were now picking up the pace while heading toward the side of the lodge to follow their owners.

"They were taken," Sal announced while enduring the pain in his bleeding shoulder. He nodded to the side of the house. "Martin went after them."

Zack saw the discarded bullwhip and again looked at the horses that were eager to follow the girls, possibly sensing they were in trouble.

Chapter 65

Monique and Colleen exchanged looks as they were hurried along the side of the lodge by the men who clutched them by their arms. The men chose to sling their assault rifles and kept their semiautomatics pointed at the girls' heads. Neither girl felt confident enough to resist their captors. Their silent exchange spoke volumes. Either girl could have called for their horses, knowing they would come to their rescue, but neither was willing to risk having their beloved horses shot over something that probably wouldn't work out in their favor in the end.

"Hold it right there," Martin snarled from the side of the lodge.

Both men spun with their teenage shields to see Martin with his assault rifle aimed at them. The man with Monique pulled her around the lodge and out of sight. She screamed to Colleen just before disappearing with the man. Martin held his rifle on the man with a gun to his daughter's head.

"Let the girl go," he announced.

The man crouched down just enough to use Colleen as a shield. "I don't think you're going to shoot," the man announced while smirking. He then indicated the girl. "She's your daughter, isn't she? That's why you were spending so much time at that ghost town. It wasn't about keeping the prototype safe. You were spying on your daughter."

"I'm the one you want," Martin insisted without lowering his weapon. "Leave her and take me instead."

"Do you have the flash drive?"

"Yes, but it's not on me," Martin replied. "Let my daughter go, and I'll take you to it."

"Toss down the weapon," the man announced.

Martin hesitated, frowned, and lowered the assault rifle. Colleen's expression dropped to horror.

"No," Colleen gasped. "Don't do it."

Her father tossed his weapon aside and held his hands in the air.

"Now let her go," Martin insisted.

The man suddenly laughed. "Why would I do that?" he asked finding the request humorous. "As long as I have her, you won't do anything stupid."

"Then I will," Colleen snarled while clutching the man's arm around her neck. She drove the heel of her booted foot into his shin then flipped him over her hip.

As the man struck the ground, Colleen kicked him in the face with her booted foot and ran for her father. The man reached for his discarded weapon. Martin grabbed the hidden semiautomatic from the back of his pants, aimed, and squeezed the trigger. The man's head snapped back as the bullet struck him between the eyes. Colleen screamed but continued for her father. Martin gathered her into his arms and attempted to hold her, but she protested.

"Monique," she gasped. "They took Monique!"

"I'll get Monique," Martin announced firmly. "I want you to--"

A bullet splinted the side of the building near their heads. Colleen screamed. Martin grabbed his daughter and ran for the woods with two men in pursuit. Darth suddenly ran from the woods and tackled one of the men to the ground. The man cried out and attempted to toss the vicious dog off him. Colleen looked back as they entered the woods. The first man was still chasing after them. He fired again, striking a tree not far from them. Colleen again screamed and ran with her father deeper into the woods.

§

Jackie and Bogart ran around the side of the lodge and saw Sal clutching his bleeding shoulder while attempting to maintain his balance from his head injury. They ran for him. Jackie immediately checked his injuries.

"Get him to Monroe," Jackie informed Bogart.

"Never mind me," Sal announced and motioned to the side of the lodge. "Find the girls."

"The girls?" Bogart suddenly gasped and appeared alarmed. Selena's nervous gray horse attempted to graze in the back yard. Thunder and Storm Cloud were gone.

"Monique and Colleen were taken by some men," Sal informed them. "Martin and Zack went after them."

"I should--" Bogart began but was cut off.

"Take Sal to Monroe," Jackie insisted with more conviction. "I'll help Zack and Martin."

Bogart frowned and nodded.

Sal refused to move and looked at Jackie. "Zack left something for you," he announced and indicated the nearby patio chair.

Jackie saw the laser rifle propped against the chair then looked back at Sal and nodded. She eyed Bogart and motioned him for the kitchen door. As Bogart helped Sal inside, Jackie set her assault rifle aside and picked up the heavy laser rifle. She took a moment to figure out the mechanics of it since it seemed to involve more than just pulling the trigger. As she turned, she saw Colonel Holloway aiming his semiautomatic at her from only a few feet away.

Holloway smiled charmingly while keeping his gun aimed at her. "What a pleasant surprise," he announced almost suavely. "Imagine; running into the same random, beautiful woman from the restaurant."

"Yes," Jackie replied with little emotion. "What a small world, Colonel Holloway."

Although Holloway maintained his smile, his irritation could be seen as he indicated the weapon. "I'll take that if you don't mind."

She couldn't just hand over the weapon, but if she didn't, he'd just shoot her and take it. If she did hand it over, he'd probably shoot her anyway. Jackie stared back at him and swiftly weighed her options of which she had few. Holloway stood just far enough away that she couldn't make any sudden moves that would take him down faster than he could pull the trigger and end her life. She was certain he didn't know her or her reputation, but he wasn't naïve enough to assume she was harmless either.

"I was told I had the best pilots money could buy, but it would seem I don't," he informed her and appeared almost offended. "Why aren't you on my payroll?"

Jackie considered the question and cocked her head. "Probably because I don't work for traitors," she announced as her eyes narrowed. "My father scraped men like you off his boots."

"I look forward to meeting your father. He sounds like someone I would like," Holloway announced then grinned. "Don't let the suit fool you. I'm only a gentleman when I want to be."

She snorted a laugh, surprising him. "You, sir, are no type of gentleman except maybe in that overinflated ego of yours," Jackie remarked. "You're nothing more than a two-bit conman in an expensive suit. You surround yourself with hired mercenaries who'd turn on you the moment the money runs out because true loyalty can't be bought. You came into power by sacrificing the lives of real heroes and tragically equate that power as respect."

"When a man points a gun at you," Holloway announced with little reaction, "you may want to consider showing a little respect."

"I don't respect people who point guns at me," she informed him then raised her brow. "And I don't see a man present."

It was possibly at that moment Holloway realized Jackie wasn't as sweet as she looked and that his charm wasn't going to work on her.

"I have a firm policy about not killing women," Holloway announced while glaring at her. "I *am* asking nicely. Now quit stalling and give me my weapon. Don't make me shoot you and take it."

Jackie gave him a moment to ensure he felt as if he had the upper hand. She then smirked and reluctantly gave in. "Well, since you asked nicely--" she hissed.

She tossed the weapon to him; being certain she overshot the mark. Despite her effort to ensure he'd miss, he easily caught the weapon. The weight threw him off, which forced him to drop his semiautomatic in order to use both hands. Jackie's ulterior motive was now evident. His semiautomatic no sooner left his hand when Jackie took a quick step forward and spun into a high roundhouse kick, striking him in the face. Holloway and his heavy toy were thrown to the patio. Despite his surprise, he was quick to discard the laser rifle and spring to his feet, skillfully unbuttoning his jacket as he did so, preparing himself for her attack.

She immediately went for the return kick, thinking she'd catch him off guard, but he easily blocked it. She followed through with two fast punches, which he also blocked. Jackie realized she'd have to step up her game since it seemed as if the colonel had some formal martial arts training. She went for a high kick and just about caught him in the face. He pulled back just in time and narrowly avoided the second kick that followed.

"You're not half bad," he announced then grinned slyly. "I've seen better though."

Jackie collected herself and watched him as he anticipated her next move. His calmness was unsettling, and she suddenly wondered if, like her, he was holding back. That he could have gone for his discarded gun and didn't was enough to give her pause. She needed to take him down without revealing all her best moves. That left her with her least favorite move. The 'ego buster' combined with the 'damsel in distress'. Jackie came at him with a knee kick to the side that she was certain he could easily deflect. Rather than deflect the kick, he seemed proud at how easily he caught her leg just below the knee and kept her awkwardly close to him. He stared into her eyes and grinned mockingly at the position he held her in. Now he was just playing with her for his own perverse, sexual pleasure.

Holloway attempted to subdue her since his ego dictated he'd want to put her in a submissive position. As he made his move to restrain her while holding her leg against his side, she jabbed him in the groin with just enough force to loosen his grip on her leg, mildly stunning him. Jackie used his grip on her leg to hold her in place as she swung her free leg backward, flipping herself upside down, and caught him around the neck with her legs. Her forward momentum and his mild agony was enough to take him down to the patio. He struck the stone patio with some force. Jackie immediately rolled off him and sprang to her feet. Holloway was slow to recover from the surprise assault. He moved into a partially crouched position and looked up at her with a strange smile on his face.

"I need you on my team," he announced and chuckled while attempting to hide the discomfort she'd placed on his groin. "Name your price."

"I'm not for sale," she snapped and was about to punch him in his smiling face when she was tackled onto the lawn.

Despite the surprise attack, Jackie threw the unusually light person off her and sprang to her feet to face her attacker. To her surprise, she stared at a woman only an inch or two taller than she was, explaining why she was able to toss her off so easily. Holloway moved to his feet while holding his lower abdomen but maintained his smile.

"That's Katrina," Holloway proudly announced. "She'll probably take off your head. Care to change your mind about working for me?"

"Fuck you," Jackie snarled at him without taking her eyes off Katrina.

Holloway shrugged then collected his semiautomatic and the heavy laser rifle. "Suit yourself," he announced with a defeated sigh then looked at Katrina and smiled. "She's my gift to you, darling. Enjoy."

Two of Holloway's men came around the side of the lodge and spotted him.

"Martin took off into the woods with a kid," the first man announced and pointed.

Holloway smiled at the women in a standoff. "I was actually looking forward to watching this," he announced. "Katrina, meet us out front when you're finished." The colonel hurried toward his men and nodded at the second man. "Keep an eye on that for me."

Holloway and one of his men hurried around the side of the lodge. Jackie cast a look at the man Holloway had left behind. He was only a few yards away from them with his assault rifle held casually in his hands. Jackie then returned her attention to the smiling woman in front of her.

"Your boyfriend is a dick," Jackie informed her.

"Yeah, but he's my dick," Katrina replied and spun into a roundhouse kick for Jackie's head.

Jackie ducked her kick, rolled across the ground, and sprang up into her own kick. She narrowly missed Katrina's head by a toe.

Chapter 66

Monique screamed and fought against the man dragging her across the front yard for the helicopter that now started. She attempted to kick the man, but he had her around the waist and around the neck making it impossible to escape the much bigger man. Gunfire from the lodge ceased at the sight of Monique within the enemy's hands. The man passed the blonde teenager off to another man inside the helicopter.

"We have our hostage," the man announced then motioned to the pilot. "Get us airborne."

As the helicopter lifted off, Monique fought the man attempting to keep her from diving out the side of the aircraft before it was too late to jump. The sound of a bullwhip cracking was just about heard above the loud rotors. Monique looked out the side of the helicopter and appeared stunned. Zack rode Storm Cloud across the battlefield that was once the front yard and chased after the rising helicopter with the bullwhip in his hand. Holloway's men hiding behind the Humvees turned just in time to be nearly trampled by the horse, keeping them from shooting at Zack.

Once Zack was past them, they pulled themselves to their feet, and again aimed their weapons. Thunder then ran past the men, knocking them back to the ground behind the Humvees as he chased after his best friend being ridden by the psychotic man. Monique stared out the side of the helicopter as best she could while being restrained, praying her horse wouldn't be shot. As the helicopter lifted off, Zack and the horse could no longer be seen. The faint sound of the whip cracking was again heard. The helicopter rocked slightly, catching the attention of both men in the back with Monique. The first man looked out the side door with his assault rifle aimed. He saw the bullwhip tangled around the landing rung. As he leaned further out the side, he saw the bullwhip dangled free. Storm Cloud could be seen racing away from the aircraft with Thunder following.

The man in the open side doorway turned to face his partner and the frightened teenager. Zack suddenly flew through the open door on the opposite side and kicked the man standing in the doorway. The man cried out as he plummeted from the swiftly moving craft. The second man attempted to aim his assault rifle at Zack, but there wasn't enough room. Zack easily caught the barrel, pulled the man toward him, and punched him in the face. The assault rifle flew out the open side door. Zack grabbed Monique by the arm and slung her toward the pilot.

"Up front," he yelled. "Now!"

Monique jumped into the front with the pilot, who cast bewildered looks from her to Zack while attempting to fly the helicopter.

"Please don't crash," Monique begged the pilot.

Zack and the man in the back punched each other being there was limited room for any fancy moves. Zack glared at Monique and pointed a demanding finger.

"Buckle up!"

Monique did as she was told and then insecurely pulled her knees to her chest. When she saw the man in the back being thrown in her direction, she ducked as he hit her seat. She again looked at the pilot.

"Might be a good time to land," Monique informed him with a concerned look on her face. "This isn't going to end well for any of us."

The pilot seemed to share her concern, although, it wasn't *her* safety that had him worried. The helicopter continued to rock as Zack and the man wrestled around the back. Due to the limited space, Zack didn't have enough room to maneuver and use any of his most effective kicks. The pilot struggled to control the helicopter and quickly became annoyed with the men rocking it. He removed his semiautomatic from his holster and aimed it into the back at Zack, who fought with the second man. Monique saw the gun, screamed, and grabbed his wrist, attempting to keep him from shooting Zack. The pilot held the stick between his knees, grabbed Monique by the throat with his free hand to subdue her, and again aimed the gun at Zack in the back.

Monique fought his hand on her throat while writhing in the seat in an attempt to pull away from him. She was just about on her back in the seat facing the pilot. She managed to wiggle free from his hand on her throat and kicked both of her booted feet for his face. The pilot brought his hand with the gun back into the front in order to block her kick. She wasn't about to give up and kicked him again, striking the gun. The gun accidentally fired with a loud pop, startling the girl. The pilot twitched as blood exploded from his neck.

As he slumped forward in his seat, the seatbelt harness held him in place. Monique screamed at the sight of blood gushing from the dead pilot's neck. The helicopter jolted slightly but continued on course since the pilot's knees still clutched the stick.

"The pilot's dead, Zack," Monique screamed while looking into the back.

Zack punched the man in the face then looked at Monique and the dead pilot with surprise. "You shot the pilot?" Zack suddenly cried out. "What's wrong with you?"

"It was an accident!"

The stick slipped from between the pilot's knees as the man in the back jumped on Zack and punched him. The helicopter flew on a steady decline and was getting lower to the trees.

"We're going down," Monique screamed to Zack as he punched the man in the back.

"Take the stick," Zack yelled back.

"Me?" she screamed. "You take the stick!"

"I'm a little busy," he yelled back and punched the man in the face. "There's a button on your side of the console. Push it. It'll revert the controls to your side."

Monique squealed in panic and looked at the controls. She saw the button and pushed it. The helicopter immediately dived down. Monique screamed.

"Take the stick!"

Monique grabbed the stick and pulled back. The helicopter shot upward on a hard angle.

"Not so aggressive," Zack yelled at her while flopping around the back seat with the man who had also lost his balance. "Like a video game."

"A what?" Monique screamed back while attempting to level off the incline. As she looked down, she saw how high they were. "Oh, shit!"

"Neck rein; not direct rein," he called back.

"Finally you're speaking English," she snapped back and gently maneuvered the stick, managing to keep the helicopter steady. "Hey, there's Ross's farm. I see Ross on Bogart's horse heading for the barn." She glanced back as Zack punched the man again. "Should we land?"

"Do you know how?" Zack asked while struggling with the man in the back.

"No," she replied.

"Neither do I," he shouted back.

Monique appeared horrified while looking back at him. "What? I thought you flew before."

"Yeah, and I usually crash land," he yelled back and punched the man twice before snap kicking him, sending him out the open doorway.

The man screamed the entire way down. Ross stopped Bogart's horse before the barn and was about to dismount when a man hit the ground just a few feet from him. The man just about exploded on impact. The black horse jumped with alarm and snorted while spinning around wildly. Ross stared at the splattered man on the ground then looked up at the helicopter flying overhead. Within the helicopter, Zack opened the pilot's door, unbuckled the dead man, and tossed him out the door. Monique cried out with horror. Zack climbed into the pilot's seat, flopped down, and looked over the controls. He switched the controls to his side and took the stick. The helicopter dropped down. He corrected for his heavy hand, and the helicopter teetered.

"I think I was doing better," Monique scoffed.

Zack turned the helicopter around on a hard angle. Monique screamed and clung to the seat and the ceiling. Once he straightened, he gave it more throttle. Monique again screamed while staring out the windshield and the countryside buzzing past.

"Too fast! Too fast!"

"No back seat driving," Zack snarled.

Monique pointed out the windshield with horror on her face. "Tree, tree, tree!"

"I see the tree," he shouted back and grazed the top of it, jolting the helicopter. Several birds flew from the tree and smacked against the windshield. One must have hit the rotors and speckled the glass with blood and feathers.

Monique screamed hysterically. "You killed the birds!"

Zack turned his head and glared at her with surprise. "I'm trying not to kill us," he announced. "Don't worry about the damned birds."

Chapter 67

Ross ran across the driveway from the barn to his house and took the porch steps two at a time. He had his gun in his hand despite Bogart's assurance that the intruders had vacated the farm. He busted through the kitchen door and startled Liam, who stood at the kitchen sink with a blood-covered dishtowel.

"Where's Lee?" Ross demanded.

Liam stared at Ross with his mouth hanging open and a strange look on his face. "She's, uh, in the living room," he gently replied then became concerned. "Don't go in there, Ross."

Ross ignored him and bolted into the living room. He saw the blood on the floor then looked across the room. Lee cocked a shotgun and glared at Ross.

"Is she dead?" Lee demanded in anger. "If she's alive, I'm going to kill the bitch!"

Ross stared at her with surprise and confusion. "Who?" he demanded.

Her eyes widened in anger. "The fucking bitch who shot me in the head!" She then turned concerned. "The girls are okay, right?"

"They were riding to the lodge," Ross informed her. "What happened?" He attempted to pull her into his arms. "Are you okay?"

She wiggled out of his arms and turned angry. "No, I'm not okay. I'm pissed."

Liam stood in the doorway with a glass of whiskey. "Trust me; she's pissed."

"I thought you were dead," Ross cried out then turned demanding while glaring at both. "Will someone tell me what happened?"

"Colonel Holloway and his femme fatale are what happened," Lee cried out. "They were looking for Martin and that prototype. For some reason, they thought they were here. He wanted to take me as a hostage so you'd hand over what he wanted. Once the colonel and his goon walked out the door, that crazy bitch just turned and shot me."

"She missed," Ross insisted.

Lee pointed to the neatly applied, bloodied strips across the graze on her temple that finally seemed to stop bleeding. "Does this look like she missed?"

"Yes," Ross announced and indicated the graze. "She didn't want him taking you hostage."

"That's what I said," Liam announced while holding up his whiskey glass. "That's when your sweet, little wifey dear went psycho on me."

"So shooting me was the better option?" Lee demanded in anger.

"Did she tell you not to move?" Ross asked.

Lee hesitated and thought about the question. "Actually, she did when she kneeled over me on the floor."

"For whatever reason, she didn't want him taking you hostage," Ross insisted. "No matter what the reason, she probably saved your life." He studied her a moment longer. "Tell me exactly what happened."

Lee approached the piano and removed the picture that had been lying face down. "The crazy bitch went over to the piano, looked at this picture, and then she sliced her own arm with a knife," she informed him. "I couldn't believe she did that to herself. That's when she shot me in the head with my own damned gun."

Ross took the framed photo from Lee and stared at it. It was an old picture of him, Jackie as a teenager, Jackie's father, and Zack standing in front of an old airplane with the name 'Old Marge' painted on the side. Ross sank into thought then looked back at Lee.

"How old was this woman?" Ross asked.

"Mid-thirties," Lee replied.

"Attractive?"

"If you're into crazy, psycho bitches, yeah, sure," she scoffed with irritation.

Ross drew a deep breath and looked at Liam. "This could be bad," he announced. "Colonel Holloway may be the least of our worries."

§

Katrina threw kicks and punches at Jackie that she was easily able to deflect yet the woman managed to block some of Jackie's best moves. Jackie kept thinking that the woman was toying with her. It reminded her too much of sparring with Zack. Perhaps the woman just wanted to have a little fun with Jackie before destroying her. Jackie couldn't let her guard down, but she also feared using her best moves. If Katrina wasn't giving 110%, Jackie didn't want to waste precious energy on a mere play date. Holloway's man sat on the picnic table and looked at his watch with some impatience.

Katrina eyed the man and smirked while dodging Jackie's high kick. "I'm sorry, Greg," she announced in her sweet southern drawl. "Are we boring you?"

"A little," the man replied. "Can you stop playing with your new friend and just kill her already?"

"I'll take it under advisement," Katrina remarked then eyed Jackie while grinning. "What do you say we kick this up a notch?"

"Fine by me," Jackie scoffed and saw her opportunity to take the woman down.

Jackie scaled the nearby half wall, flipped backward, and caught Katrina around the neck with her legs. Jackie took the woman to the ground, landing roughly on top of her. Katrina let out a loud groan from the impact and Jackie's additional weight.

The man sitting on the picnic table applauded. "Now, see, that's entertaining."

Katrina sneered, but she wasn't given the opportunity to make a snide comment back at him. Jackie straddled her on the ground and punched her in the face twice before Katrina bucked her off. Both women rolled into crouching positions and once again faced each other.

"Impressive move," Katrina announced while dabbing the blood from the corner of her mouth. "Who taught you to fight?"

"My father and his best friend," Jackie replied and immediately spun into a roundhouse kick directed at Katrina's face.

Katrina ducked her foot and kicked Jackie in the side before she could recover from the kick. Jackie jumped back a step and stared at the woman with some surprise. The woman could have destroyed her at that moment. What was with the soft hits? Jackie threw a punch she knew the woman would easily block. Katrina blocked the punch, spun Jackie around, and grabbed her around the neck. Jackie feared what would come next and gave her an elbow to the ribs. Katrina gasped but didn't release her. She kept her arm around Jackie's neck from behind and held her partially immobile. Jackie thought of at least four ways to get out of her predicament, but it seemed as if the woman was anticipating her every move no matter what the move. She seemed to know Jackie's fighting style, and it was concerning.

Katrina leaned over Jackie's shoulder, smiled deviously, and spoke in her ear. "Was your father Jackson Remus?" she hissed softly.

Jackie rammed her elbow into Katrina's ribs and flipped her over her shoulder. The woman landed roughly but quickly sprang back to her feet to face Jackie. Jackie stared at the grin on the woman's face.

"How do you know my father?" Jackie demanded as her eyes narrowed.

Katrina maintained her mocking smile. "Jackie Remus," she announced with a slight hiss to her voice. "I have to admit; you're even more impressive in person."

Jackie tensed while staring at the woman before her. Her heart was now pounding. Who was this woman that knew her father? It was enough to throw Jackie off her game, which was hard to do.

"I've wanted to meet you for a few years now," Katrina remarked while grinning slyly. "I have to admit; I'm a little jealous."

Jackie felt her entire body twitch at the woman's words. She already discovered she had a brother she didn't know existed. Was it possible she had a sister too? She'd be the right age for some fling before her father had met her mother. On the other hand, was it possible her father met this woman shortly before he died? A female soldier from some military base down south? A lover he never mentioned?

"How do you know my father?" Jackie again demanded and kicked her in the abdomen.

Katrina stumbled back a step while partially doubled over and clinging to her stomach. She straightened but maintained her smile as she removed a small semiautomatic and aimed it at Jackie.

The woman's devious smile increased. "I didn't know your father," she announced as her charming southern drawl vanished. She cocked her head slightly to the side and spoke in a thick, Russian accent. "I'm Katya."

Jackie's expression immediately dropped, and her heart pounded as the words left the woman's lips. She stared at Katrina in near horror.

"Zack's Russian booty call?" Jackie gasped.

It just slipped out. Katrina grinned her response. She aimed the semiautomatic and pulled the trigger. As the gun fired, Jackie shirked. The bullet struck the man on the picnic table in the chest. He barely had time to gasp before falling to the ground. Katrina looked back at Jackie and smiled sweetly while casually lowering the gun.

"I can see why he loves you so much," Katrina announced in her thick Russian accent.

Jackie stared at the woman and couldn't even understand any of what just happened. "I don't understand," she gasped. "What are you doing here? What are you doing with someone like Colonel Holloway?"

"What do I do with any man?" Katrina muttered and replaced her gun to the hidden holster in the back of her pants. She removed a flash drive from her cleavage and held it up. "This will get Colonel Holloway off your back. I'll lure him away from the lodge. I'm sure your team can clean up the remaining stragglers." She then smiled almost seductively. "Give Zack a kiss for me."

Katrina turned to leave. Jackie was still struggling to put it all together.

"Katya, wait," Jackie heard herself gasp and stared after the beautiful but deadly woman from Zack's past.

Katrina looked back.

"Stay, please," Jackie practically begged. "Zack could really use you right about now."

Katrina smiled and laughed at the comment. "Sorry, Jackie," she replied. "It's all business with me. He's your problem now. Whatever's broken with Zack, I'm sure you can fix it." She blew Jackie a kiss, turned, and walked past the motionless man by the picnic table. "Sorry, Greg. It's nothing personal. I actually liked you."

He groaned and attempted to open his eyes. Katrina removed her gun and shot him in the head as she continued past. Jackie heard the helicopter approaching the lodge. As she looked up, the helicopter passed overhead and hovered. Jackie stared with horror when she saw Zack piloting the craft and Monique in the seat next to him. She then witnessed the world's worst helicopter landing while holding her breath the entire time. As the helicopter shut down, Jackie ran for them. Monique jumped out and hugged Jackie.

"Save me," she cried out and pointed at Zack. "He's crazy."

"You just found that out now?" Jackie asked with surprise. "Go inside. Find the guys. They'll put you in the panic room."

Monique nodded and ran into the lodge through the back kitchen door. Zack got out of the helicopter and reclaimed the bullwhip that was still tangled around the landing rung. He approached Jackie while coiling the bullwhip and grinned indicating the craft.

"Look," he announced proudly. "One piece. A first for me."

Jackie tensed while staring at Zack. She didn't know how to tell him what just happened.

As he stared at her, his expression dropped to concern. "Did something happen?"

"Sort of."

Chapter 68

Katrina hurried around the front of the lodge and joined Holloway not far from the Humvee in the back. When he saw her, he straightened and looked at his watch.

"That didn't take long," he announced. "I thought she'd put up more of a fight."

"They're never as tough as they seem. Besides, we were pressed for time," Katrina announced then grinned and removed the flash drive from her cleavage. She waved it proudly. "One of her friends exchanged this for her life."

Holloway stared at the flash drive with surprise. "Is it the real thing?"

Katrina smiled, removed her cell phone, and showed him a fuzzy picture of a blueprint.

He squinted at the picture then grinned. "We have what we came for," Holloway announced and removed his hand radio. "Dixon, commence clean sweep. We have what we need. Once you've finished, gather the men and meet us five miles down the road."

"Yes, sir," Dixon replied over the radio. "Clean sweep is a go."

"Marco," Holloway announced into his radio. "Did you find Martin and the kid?"

"No, but they're around the woods somewhere," one of the men reported.

"Find them and kill Martin," Holloway announced. "We no longer need him alive." He then hesitated. "Don't hurt the girl."

"Yes, sir," came the response.

Katrina eyed Holloway and raised her brow while grinning. "You realize the men will never make it inside the lodge alive," she informed him.

"If they make it to the rendezvous, good for them. If not, oh, well." He shrugged without care. "You never cared for Dixon anyway," he announced then smiled. "Consider it an early birthday present. We won't have to share the wealth, and I'd prefer if it were just the two of us anyway."

"I like how you think," she announced.

Katrina grinned at his comment then handed him the flash drive. While his men kept gunfire from the lodge directed at them, Holloway and Katrina headed for the Humvee. Holloway opened the passenger side door for Katrina then hurried to the driver's side. He jumped in and started the vehicle. The Humvee burned out and drove away from the lodge.

§

Martin hurried Colleen through the woods and further away from the lodge to evade the man hunting them. They had managed to put some distance between them and the man pursuing them when he'd lost his footing on the rough terrain. Martin and Colleen could hear him chasing after them by the loudly cracking sticks and underbrush. Once they reached the clearing, they would be in the open and exposed to the armed man. He'd have a clean shot. Martin forced Colleen behind a large tree and motioned for her to keep quiet. Her father used different trees to remain hidden while working his way across the woods in hopes of getting behind the man pursuing them.

Colleen shut her eyes a moment and held her breath. She heard the familiar creaking of saddle leather and the snorting of a horse. Colleen's eyes suddenly opened and her heart raced as horror filled her. She looked around the woods and saw her black horse meandering among the trees. When Thunder saw her, his ears perked up. The horse snickered loudly and excitedly trotted toward his human friend. The man in the woods saw the horse approaching the tree and must have concluded Colleen was there. He picked up his pace and headed for the same tree with his assault rifle raised. The horse saw the man nearly upon them, pinned his ears, and reared up to stop his approach. The man appeared surprised by the horse's reaction and aimed his weapon at the animal.

Colleen peeked around the tree and saw the man about to shoot her beloved horse. She screamed in horror at what she was about to witness. There was a vicious snarl from behind the man. He spun around and saw a silver sable blur. Darth leaped on top of the man while sinking his teeth into his forearm. The man was thrown to the ground with the dog on top of him. They hit the ground with added force and rolled several times together. Darth was tossed off the man by their momentum. The man managed to sit up and aimed his rifle at Darth as the dog scrambled to his feet. The man was about to pull the trigger when Martin suddenly appeared over him, grabbed the muzzle of the rifle, and kicked him sharply in the head. Martin attempted to aim his pistol at the man. Being the man's finger was on the trigger, the automatic weapon fired several rounds. Bullets were rapidly expelled into the air and across the woods causing Thunder to take off. Martin tossed his semiautomatic aside in order to keep both hands on the assault rifle as the men fought for control over the weapon.

The man released the rifle and knocked Martin's legs out from beneath him. Martin reached for the discarded semiautomatic as the man leaped on top of him. There was a gunshot. Colleen stared at the two motionless men and gasped with horror. The man on top of Martin slowly moved off him and onto his knees. Colleen stared at the scene and was unable to move. The man hesitated a moment then looked at his bleeding abdomen. He met Martin's gaze just before collapsing. As the man fell to the ground, Martin slowly sat up. Colleen exhaled the breath she'd been holding and joined her father on the ground, leaping into his arms. He held her and buried his face into her hair.

"Are you okay?" he gasped.

Colleen couldn't stop sobbing long enough to answer her father. Darth joined them, whimpered, and licked their faces.

§

Beck and Bogart took turns shooting at the three men outside where they hid behind the remaining Humvee. Kirk took the opposite side of the lobby and awaited a clean shot. Gil was located on the second floor with eyes outside waiting to pick off any men attempting to make it to the house. Their goal was to stop them from reaching the lodge, but four men had already managed to make it through the gunfire. They were now on the porch looking for a way inside. Three slipped around back while the other two attempted to break down the front door. Monroe was near the closed panic room door behind the stairs where he did a quick patch job on Sal's shoulder wound. Once Monroe had finished patching up Sal, Sal grabbed his assault rifle and scaled the stairs. He then took a sniper's location on the second floor overlooking the lobby. He had a clear view of the entire lobby and could pick off any intruders making it through the front door. Monroe returned to Beck's side.

Beck indicated the hallway to Bogart. "Join up with Jackie and Zack in the back," he announced, "in case any of the men make it to the back entrance."

Bogart nodded and took off down the hallway to reach the back of the building.

"There are only about seven or eight of them out there," Kirk called out from across the lobby. "There are two out front and at least two making their way toward the back entrance."

"I've got three pinned behind the Humvee," Beck announced in response. "Gil also has eyes on them from the second floor window."

"We could put the place on lockdown," Monroe suggested as the gunfire seemed to calm now that the men were on the front porch.

"They have an armored Humvee," Beck informed Monroe. "Even if we would implement lockdown, how long until they roll right through the front wall?"

"You're right," Monroe replied with defeat. "The reinforced walls won't survive that much force."

"They're conserving ammo," Beck responded while sinking into thought. "It's possible they don't want to accidentally hit their men on the porch."

"Or it could mean they're running low on ammo," Monroe added. He then raised his brows in suggestion. "They're already splitting up."

Beck glanced at him and appeared curious. "Are you suggesting we call a cease-fire?"

"Navy SEAL style," Monroe replied while grinning.

Beck seemed to consider the comment only a moment then tapped his ear transmitter. "Zack, you copy?"

"Yeah, I copy," Zack announced. "Just waiting for you to bring the party this way."

"You should have two or more coming your way any minute," Beck informed him. "We're implementing a Navy SEAL cease-fire."

"So you finally grew a pair," Zack commented back.

Beck frowned. "Fuck you too," he announced. "Gil, do you copy? Confirm implementation of a Navy SEAL ceasefire."

"Copy and confirm," Gil announced over their ear transmitters. "Standing down."

Beck drew a deep breath, raised his brows, and then looked at Monroe and Kirk. "Ready?"

Both men nodded.

§

$\mathcal{S}$poradic gunfire came from one of the lobby windows, indicating there was possibly only one man left to defend the bullet-riddled fort. Dixon looked at the lodge from his secured location behind the Humvee.

"On my signal, unload everything on that one spot," Dixon announced. "We need to take that man out."

Both men nodded. Dixon gave them the signal. All three aimed their weapons at the window and fired nearly fifty rounds into the building of the suspected last man. They immediately reloaded their weapons and waited. There was no sound from within the lodge. Dixon then signaled the two men on the porch. They went for the door and worked on breaking it down. It took a lot of effort since it had bolts that went into both the floor and ceiling. They finally busted down the front entrance, aimed their weapons inside, and looked around. The two men then entered the lodge. Dixon sent word with his hand radio to the men heading around back then motioned for the two men alongside him to storm the lodge lobby. All three ran for the lodge and entered behind the first two men.

The once beautiful rustic lobby was now riddled with bullet holes, broken windows, and various destroyed objects. All five men fanned out across the lobby and looked around. To their surprise, there weren't any bodies by the windows.

Dixon became concerned. "It's a trap," he called out to his men. "They're hiding around here somewhere. Use caution. Sweep the building."

Dixon ventured down the main hallway while another man brought up the rear. Two men headed for the stairs while the last man approached the massive, old-fashioned lobby desk. The man rounded the desk and jumped into the opening with his assault rifle aimed. To his surprise, there was no one behind the desk. He turned around to relay his findings when Kirk dropped down from the rafters and landed on top of the man. The man barely managed a startled gasp before he was just about crushed beneath the big man's weight. Kirk swiftly stabbed the man in the throat to prevent him from making any further sound. The first man was already heading up the stairs while the second paused at the bottom. The man at the base of the stairs hesitated and scanned the area.

He didn't see his man anywhere within the lobby, and nothing moved. Kirk pulled the dead man the rest of the way behind the front desk, undetected by the other men. The second man looked up the stairs beyond his teammate and saw Sal and Beck appear from behind the tree trunk railing on the second floor.

"There," the man cried out and aimed his weapon in response.

The man part way up the stairs looked to where he pointed with his weapon aimed, but it was too late. Gunfire from Sal and Beck took out the man on the stairs and came close to striking the man at the bottom. The man darted out of their line of sight and hid along the side of the stairs not far from the undetected panic room entrance. There was a faint clunk behind him. He spun around to see the open panic room doorway. He was about to step closer to it when Monroe appeared alongside him and stabbed him in the throat. The man clutched his bleeding throat, unable to scream as he sank to the floor. Monique peeked out from the panic room opening, but she was quickly pulled back inside by Othello, who then sealed the door.

Chapter 69

The sound of assault rifle fire alerted Dixon and his companion in the main hallway of something happening in the lobby. Dixon and the man following him exchanged looks. He motioned for him to continue for the back of the building, confident his men were victorious. They approached the kitchen and cautiously entered with their weapons raised. Nothing moved. The kitchen was empty. Both men then heard a door open and spun toward the outer kitchen door with their rifles aimed. The first of his three men who had headed around the back of the lodge now stood in the back doorway with his weapon aimed back at them. The men relaxed when they saw it was just their teammates.

Dixon motioned with his hand, signaling which way his men should go. The man in the kitchen doorway nodded and hurried up the back stairs. The man behind Dixon hurried across the kitchen and toward the nearby dining room door. Two more men entered the kitchen from the back patio. Dixon signaled to each of them. The first man went toward the staff wing entrance while the second headed for the basement doorway.

Dixon remained in the kitchen checking behind the island counter and beneath the table.

The first man crept up the back stairs toward the second floor with his assault rifle leading the way. As he reached the top of the stairs, he leaped into the corridor and aimed his weapon. The second floor hallway was empty and eerily silent. The man headed down the hallway and paused before the first open bedroom door. He aimed his weapon inside and looked around the empty bedroom. He heard a floorboard creak and spun to see Bogart standing directly behind him. Bogart had been unprepared for the creaking floorboard beneath his foot, and the surprise showed on his face.

Bogart squeezed the trigger of his semiautomatic, but the man was already lunging for him and knocked his arm against the doorframe, forcing Bogart to drop the gun before it fired. Bogart subconsciously kneed the man in the crotch. As the man clutched himself while doubling over, Bogart spun into a roundhouse kick, struck him in the chest, and tossed him to the hall floor not far from the back stairs. Bogart seemed stunned that it actually worked for a change. The man pulled a knife from his boot as he straightened and lunged for Bogart, who was now taken by surprise. Bogart spun into a sloppy kick and nailed the man in the thigh.

The knife sliced Bogart's pants and scratched his lower leg. Bogart punched the man in the face, throwing him off balance, and then kicked out high, striking the man in the chest. The man was thrown backward and into the stairway. Bogart watched with surprise as the man tumbled down the stairs, loudly thumping the entire way.

Bogart cringed and made a face. "Oh, that's gonna hurt," he muttered.

Within the kitchen, Dixon straightened when he heard someone loudly thumping down the back stairs. He saw his man land at the bottom with his head twisted unnaturally to the side. Dixon was about to run for the back stairs when the man at the basement entrance was thrown across the kitchen and into the heavy table. Dixon spun with his weapon aimed and stared at the basement doorway. His man slowly moved to his feet with some disorientation while breathing heavily. The cracking sound of the bullwhip startled both men. The bullwhip snagged the heavily breathing man around the ankles. He screamed as he was pulled off his feet and clawed at the floor while being pulled back into the dark basement.

Dixon fired nearly twenty rounds into the open basement doorway without bothering to aim. The sound of someone thumping down the basement steps seemed to satisfy him. He hurried for the basement door as one of the men joined him from the staff wing.

"What happened?" his man asked as he paused behind Dixon.

"I got one of the bastards," Dixon proudly announced. "In the basement."

The man behind him suddenly groaned. Dixon spun around to the unusual sound coming from his man. The man stood before him with blood pouring from his mouth. He collapsed into Dixon's arms revealing the butcher knife impaled in his neck. Dixon saw Jackie standing directly behind the man whom she had just killed. Dixon dropped his man and attempted to aim his assault rifle at her. Jackie spun into a roundhouse kick and knocked the weapon from his hand. As the man from the dining room appeared in the doorway with his weapon aimed, Zack ran from the basement and leaped onto the kitchen table while firing his semiautomatic at the man in the doorway. Zack slid across the table on his hip, taking Jackie to the floor with him.

The man in the dining room doorway only got off one shot, since he was too busy taking cover from Zack's weapon. Jackie and Zack rolled across the floor. Jackie then dove beneath the table while Zack leaped behind the island counter. Dixon removed the semiautomatic from his shoulder holster while looking beneath the kitchen table. Jackie kicked the chair out with force and struck Dixon in the face with the back of the heavy chair. As he stumbled backward, Jackie slipped out from under the table and kicked Dixon's legs out from beneath him, bringing him down to the floor with her. She couldn't risk standing and letting the armed man in the dining room get a clean shot at her since she'd lost her weapon somewhere along the way.

The man from the dining room ran into the kitchen and aimed his weapon behind the island counter in hopes of taking out Zack. To his surprise, Zack was gone. As he turned, Zack leaped over the island counter from the side and kicked him with both feet. The man was thrown backward, dropping his weapon, and landed roughly on the kitchen table. The man writhed a moment in agony and then sat up on the table. Zack was already spinning through the air and kicked him in the face, sending him across the kitchen table and crashing to the floor on the opposite side. The flying man narrowly missed Jackie and Dixon, who were struggling with each other on the floor.

Jackie was on top of Dixon and got in two good punches before the large man bucked her off him, tossing her across the floor like a ragdoll. Zack aimed his semiautomatic, but it was already empty. Instead, he rolled across the table and landed on his feet near where Jackie had been thrown. She slowly moved into a crouched position after her excessively hard landing. Zack held his hand out to her. She slapped his hand, essentially tagging him in. Zack leaped back onto the table, so he was taller than Dixon and kicked him in the face. Dixon flew backward, struck his man, who was just moving to his feet, and knocked him into the basement doorway. The man flew down the steps with a thunderous crash.

Dixon caught his balance just before the open basement doorway and lunged for Zack. Jackie kicked the chair into his path. He easily avoided running into it and saw the chair as more of a nuisance than a deterrent. Zack took his cue and kicked Dixon backward against the chair. Jackie ran for the chair, jumped onto the seat, and spun into a roundhouse kick. She nailed him in the chest sending him backward against the table. Despite that she hadn't actually disabled him, she leaped from the chair and bolted away from him. As Dixon straightened, Zack leaped from the table, caught him around the neck with his legs, and flipped him through the air before taking him to the floor.

Zack's momentum, the man's weight, and sheer force caused his neck to snap. When Dixon no longer moved, Zack used his legs to shove the large dead man off him. Zack sprang to his feet then gingerly rubbed his backside.

"That kind of hurt," he announced.

Zack extended his hand to Jackie, who was still sitting on the floor. She accepted his hand an allowed him to pull her to her feet. He pulled her up with a little too much vigor, forcing her to collide with him. Zack grinned and held her against him in his arms. They heard a low, disgusted groan from the back stairs. Jackie pulled away from Zack as both looked across the kitchen. Bogart folded his arms across his chest and shook his head in disapproval.

"Jesus, Zack," Bogart scoffed. "Give it a rest."

Zack showed little emotion as he took a quick step for Bogart. Jackie caught Zack's arm and stopped him.

"Behave," she announced sternly.

§

Colonel Holloway's Humvee pulled to the side of the road approximately five miles from the lodge and parked. Holloway leaned back in the driver's seat while lovingly looking at Katrina then took her hand in his and suavely kissed it.

"So where should we spend our retirement?" he asked while caressing her hand. "Somewhere tropical?"

"Bathing suits optional," she teased.

"I like the sound of that," he announced and grinned while gazing into her eyes. "How do you feel about a wedding on the beach?"

She stared at him a moment and appeared surprised. "You want to get married?"

"There's no reason not to," he insisted while grinning. "Once we're out of the country, just the two of us, we can have everything we've ever wanted." Holloway again kissed her hand without taking his eyes off hers. "You're everything I want."

Katrina smiled warmly at the comment. She removed her jacket to reveal her low-cut tank top then moved across the seat closer to him. Since there was no center console in the modified jeep, she could slide up alongside him. She affectionately caressed his chest while lovingly gazing into his eyes.

"Do we have ten minutes before the guys return?" she asked.

"You mean *if* the guys return," he teased then chuckled. "Yes, we have at least ten minutes." Holloway grinned slyly. "What did you have in mind?"

She lovingly caressed his thigh then ran her hand firmly along his crotch. "We'd better keep it brief," Katrina cooed. "In case someone shows up."

Holloway groaned with pleasure as her hand caressed him. He then met her gaze and grinned. "I love the way you think," he teased.

He reached down to the base of the seat and allowed the seat to slide back. Katrina climbed over top of him, straddling his thighs, as he lowered the head of the seat back partway. She placed her arms around his neck and held his head to her exposed cleavage, allowing him to kiss her chest while caressing her backside. She affectionately ran her fingers through his hair then pulled back just far enough to kiss him on the mouth. She kissed him eagerly and with aggression. Holloway returned the kiss while holding her against him. He suddenly gasped, pulled his mouth from hers, and spit into his hand. He stared at the small, broken glass capsule now containing his blood where it broke in his mouth then looked at her with surprise and possible horror.

"What did you do?" he cried out then attempted to catch his breath.

Holloway tried to push her off him and reached for his throat. She caught his hand, resisted moving off him, and held his head to her chest while he convulsed.

"Shh," she cooed softly in his ear. "It'll be over soon enough. Don't fight it."

Katrina buried his face into her exposed cleavage and held onto him as he thrashed from the poison.

"I'm sorry, darling," she announced sweetly while caressing his hair. "There was no other way. It's nothing personal. I enjoyed our time together, I really did, but now we must part ways."

Holloway gasped and wheezed into her chest while his entire body tightened. She continued to stroke his hair and spoke softly into his ear.

"It'll be over soon, I promise," she whispered. "You'll finally be at peace."

His body finally relaxed and became limp beneath her. Katrina continued to stroke his hair.

"I hope I provided some comfort in your final moments," she announced then pulled back far enough to see his eyes were open. She closed his eyes, kissed his forehead, and then climbed off him. "I'm sure we'll meet again in the bowels of hell."

Chapter 70

The guys and Darth patrolled the area outside the lodge and checked on the dead men while looking for any stragglers. Jackie had been nervously pacing while talking to someone on the satellite phone. She finally disconnected her call and returned the clunky phone to Beck. Jackie drew a deep, tense breath.

"That was fun," she muttered sarcastically. "Holden and Harris are on their way to 'handle' the situation. Your Colonel Bamford is tagging along as well."

"The cooperation of the military in this situation would be nice," Beck replied while scanning the disaster surrounding the lodge. "Ross is staying at his farm with Lee. He's still trying to get her to the doctor to have her head looked at." He stiffened. "She's not being very cooperative. Liam is on his way for Selena though."

Bogart approached them and shook his head with some irritation. "We couldn't convince the kids to stay in the panic room," he announced.

"They certainly can't come out here," Beck insisted with some irritation.

"They're having a hissy fit about their horses," Bogart informed him.

Beck groaned and rubbed his eyes. "This place looks like a battlefield, and they're worried about their horses."

Bogart shrugged. "They love those horses," he remarked simply. "Martin and I will go with them to find their horses and escort them back to Ross's farm."

"Fine, do that," Beck groaned. "Marie can ride with Liam and Selena back to Ross's farm. Martin, Marie, and the girls can wait there until Holden and the feds are finished sorting out this mess." He glared demandingly at Bogart. "You get your ass back here ASAP."

Bogart nodded and hurried back to the lodge. Darth suddenly snarled and stared down the long driveway. Jackie tensed when she saw the black Humvee approaching the lodge. Jackie, Beck, and Kirk grabbed their slung assault rifles and aimed them at the Humvee as it slowed then stopped just outside the battle zone. The driver's side door opened to reveal Katrina or better known as Katya. She smiled sweetly and raised her hands in the air.

"Don't shoot," she announced with a teasing smile. "I surrender."

Jackie held her breath and was the first to lower her weapon.

Beck stared at the woman then cast a quick look at Jackie. "Do we know her?"

"Sort of," Jackie muttered under her breath.

"Who is she?" Kirk asked and appeared uncertain why Jackie lowered her weapon.

When Beck lowered his weapon, Kirk uncertainly did the same. As Katya approached them, Zack suddenly appeared before Jackie and aimed his semiautomatic at the unarmed woman. Katya stopped, smiled sweetly at him, and raised her hands in the air.

"Unarmed, Zack," Katya announced while taunting him with her smile. "Stand down."

Beck's eyes suddenly widened when he heard the Russian accent. "Is that--?"

"It most certainly is," Jackie replied and eyed Beck. "You've never met her?"

"Are you kidding?" Beck announced while snorting a laugh and eyed Jackie. "We had money on whether or not she was actually real."

Zack kept his gun on Katya while glaring at her through squinting eyes. Whatever was going through his head, it was personal.

"Zack," Jackie scolded with surprise. "I told you she helped us, remember?"

"She only helps herself," Zack informed Jackie without looking at her. He kept his eyes and his gun locked on the woman before them. "Remove yourself, Jackie."

Jackie was surprised by the comment.

Katya rolled her eyes and huffed under her breath. "I'm not going to hurt your girlfriend," the Russian woman announced then offered a teasing smile. "We've already met and had a little talk."

"The last time I saw you, I specifically remember you threatening to kill Jackie," Zack growled without taking his eyes off her. "I don't want you anywhere near her."

"I was having a bad day," Katya announced in her defense as she raised a brow.

"Yeah, so was I," Zack snarled back. "You tried to cut off my dick."

"A misunderstanding," Katya replied and again smiled sweetly. "I could have killed Jackie, but I didn't. That was all talk. Heat of the moment bullshit."

Jackie touched Zack's arm from behind him. "She could have, Zack," she confirmed. "It's okay. I'm not exactly turning my back on her."

He frowned and lowered his gun. Katya lowered her hands although she didn't seem the least bit concerned or offended that Zack had aimed his weapon at her.

"I brought you a peace offering," she announced then indicated the Humvee.

Zack approached the side of the Humvee closest to Katya while Kirk rounded the opposite side with his weapon aimed and peered inside.

Kirk eyed the dead colonel slumped in the passenger seat. "What killed him?" Kirk asked.

"He took a poison pill," Katya casually replied.

"I'll bet," Zack scoffed while looking in the back of the Humvee. His expression changed as he eagerly removed the laser rifle. He held up the weapon and lovingly caressed it. "Oh, I've missed you."

"You're not keeping it," Beck snarled.

"Yeah, we'll see about that," Zack scoffed back then looked at Katya, who was only a few feet from him. "What was the mission?"

"Colonel Holloway had dealings with one of our people," she announced. "He was buying stolen weapons. I needed to find out who betrayed us. I learned of his contact the day the feds raided his compound. I had to get away from his underground bunker to notify my government of their traitor, so I volunteered to find out who had Martin and their prototype." She offered a humored smile. "Of course, I already knew who took it."

"How did you know that?" Beck asked with surprise. "We didn't even know he had it."

Katya chuckled in her throat then removed a crinkled, folded piece of paper from her pocket. She opened it to reveal the 'Kilroy was here' note and drawing.

"I've seen these many times before," Katya announced, "although it's usually 'Z was here'."

Zack fidgeted because he knew he'd been caught in that one.

"My mission was over, but I knew Holloway would eventually find your hidden compound," Katya announced then looked around and nodded her approval. "A little messy, but it's nice."

"Getting off subject," Zack muttered with limited patience.

"I know our last meeting got a little ugly," Katya informed Zack. "Consider this my apology to you for my, uh, bad behavior."

"Trying to kill me is one thing," Zack scoffed. "You tried to cut off my dick. I took that personally."

"I didn't have to return to Holloway," Katya insisted while cleverly eyeing him. "I did that to keep him off your scent. When he found you anyway, I did what needed to be done. I did that on my own dime. I did that to protect you and your team." She raised her brows while glaring at him. "And with the way he was sizing up Jackie, you should thank me. If I had abandoned him, he would have done everything in his power to make her my replacement." Katya considered the comment and eyed him. "He may have been a bastard, but he was a charming one. A few months as his prisoner, she'd eventually have given in."

"Doubtful," Jackie scoffed in response.

Zack cast a look at Jackie and revealed his uncertainty. "Psychological chess," he informed her. "The brain and emotions are reprogrammed into thinking and feeling differently than their original programming. Most often used as a weapon by wanton women to make men do things they normally wouldn't do."

Katya eyed Jackie and smiled. "Sort of how you trained Zack."

Zack cast a sharp glare at Katya. She laughed at his irritation then moved closer to him and affectionately ran her hands along his chest.

"You know you've missed me," Katya cooed and moved her mouth closer to his.

Zack pushed her away from him, although she wasn't too surprised. He slung the laser rifle over his shoulder and removed a penlight from his pocket.

"Don't act like I don't know what really killed the colonel," Zack scoffed then held up the penlight.

Katya groaned with annoyance and opened her mouth. Zack shined the light into her mouth and inspected it. He shut off the penlight, frowned his disapproval, and then pulled her roughly against him. He just about grabbed her by the back of the neck, sought her mouth, and kissed her passionately and with aggression. Katya returned the aggressive kiss while firmly running her hands along his chest. She then pulled away just far enough to meet his gaze while grinning slyly.

"Is there someplace private we can go to, uh, disarm?" Katya cooed seductively while affectionately running her hands along his chest in a manner meant to tease him.

Zack released her without hesitation, firmly took her hand, and practically pulled her toward the lodge without a word. Katya smiled sweetly at the guys as she passed them and gave a polite wave. Beck and Kirk folded their arms across their chests and watched Zack and Katya until they disappeared inside the lodge. Jackie joined the men. She stood alongside Beck and Kirk, mimicked their stance, and sighed.

"We're not getting any sleep tonight, are we?" Jackie muttered.

"Nope," Kirk remarked with little emotion.

"We're never going to see that laser again either," Beck groaned.

"Nope," Kirk again replied.

Chapter 71

Tuesday, July 8th. Two days later. Jackie headed down the back stairs to the lodge kitchen and already smelled something wonderful cooking for breakfast. Since Holden was still in bed, she knew it wasn't him cooking. Ross and Bogart were still at the farm. Bogart would be transporting the girls' horses back to the Harris farm so Martin, Maria, and the girls would ride along with him. Kirk was never up before noon if he didn't have a good reason to be, so it had to be Beck, Monroe, or Gil making breakfast. Jackie secretly hoped it was Gil. He was the better cook out of the three. Jackie entered the kitchen and paused when she saw Zack at the large stove making breakfast. She was sort of surprised because it actually smelled good.

Jackie had known Zack to make a variety of meats for dinner, but she'd never seen him make breakfast before today. Not surprising, he'd spent the last two days camped out in one of the guestrooms with Katya. Food had disappeared from the kitchen, but no one had actually seen either since before Holden and Harris showed up after the massacre. Those staying at the lodge were glad Zack chose one of the guestrooms over his own room. With the sounds they heard coming from the rarely used end room; it was for the best. Jackie suspected Zack chose a room other than his own to keep Katya from poking through his things. She may have been his favorite 'booty call', but he didn't trust her not to kill him or steal his toys.

Despite her surprise to see him preparing breakfast, Jackie was happy that Zack was finally out of his 'torture chamber'. At least she knew he survived whatever was happening in that room with his beautiful Russian spy.

"You're alive," Jackie announced.

She approached him and leaned against the island counter, watching Zack at the stove. Zack glanced back at her and grinned a little too deviously for her comfort.

"Barely," he teased. "I haven't been this sore since being shot and thrown from that helicopter on Giovanni's island."

Jackie turned her head and held up her hand in protest. "Please, no details."

Zack turned and gave her a disapproving glare. "What sort of kinky shit do you think I'm into?" he demanded then shook his head. "I promise; you and your fed boy toy are into more kinky shit than I am."

She stared at him with surprise and felt her cheeks redden slightly. "How the hell would you know what sort of kinky shit Holden and I are into?"

Zack rolled his eyes and picked up a fried ball of dough that had been cooling on a paper towel. "You've been handcuffing Holden to the bed from the day you'd met him."

She almost couldn't deny that. "That's not exactly true," Jackie remarked although the comment was enough to make her tense.

He held the fried dough ball up to her mouth. Without thinking, she let him pop it into her mouth. Despite being heavily fried, it was actually delicious. A jalapeno popper wasn't exactly breakfast food, but she didn't mind the extra zing of peppers and hot sauce in the morning. Zack grinned and leaned his back against the main counter.

"Let's not even discuss the nightstand drawer in your bedroom," he announced.

Jackie nearly gagged at his words. She finished the popper and glared at him. "You just stay the hell out of my nightstand drawer." She shook her head with irritation. "You've been banned from my bedroom, remember?"

"I remember," he replied. "I've been respecting Holden's boundaries at your house." He pointed to the ceiling. "I'm talking about your room here." Zack returned to the stove. "At least I know what to buy you for Christmas this year. An assortment of double and triple-A batteries."

Jackie stared at his back with a stunned look and could almost feel his smile. She resisted beating the daylights out of him. He'd probably enjoy that too much.

"I thought I'd like you better after you had a full weekend of binge sex," Jackie scoffed while folding her arms across her chest and glared at him with added irritation. "I'm not sure how it's possible, but you're worse."

Zack chuckled then hesitated and turned to face her. His look suddenly turned serious. "Take her home," he announced. Before Jackie could speak, he interrupted her. "Seriously, get her out of here."

Jackie was surprised to hear him say that. "That was a short honeymoon," she remarked with surprise.

He rubbed his eyes and groaned. "I'm exhausted," Zack admitted. "When she didn't try to kill me; I'll admit, I was like a kid in a candy store, but Christ--" He sighed and shook his head. "I now know how she intends to kill me, and it won't be pleasant. It's going to be a very slow and painful death."

Jackie wasn't sure if she felt sorry for him or not. She reluctantly chose feeling sorry for him. "I planned on flying Sal and Othello home this afternoon," she admitted. "If Katya wants--"

"After breakfast," Zack demanded.

"Fine," Jackie scoffed and shook her head. "You big baby."

Zack sighed with relief as his shoulders sagged. "Thank you."

They heard someone on the stairs. Zack resumed cooking before he burned breakfast. Katya entered the kitchen looking shower fresh yet exhausted.

"Something smells good," she announced then saw Jackie and smiled pleasantly. "Good morning, Jackie. Sorry I didn't get to meet your husband yesterday."

"That was two days ago," Jackie announced with a knowing grin.

Katya smiled and laughed. "Oh, yeah," she teased. "Right. I lose track of time when I'm having fun. Is your helicopter fixed yet?" She leaned over Zack's shoulder to see what he was making for breakfast.

"Yes, I plugged up the leak and gassed her up," Jackie announced cheerfully. "I planned on taking Sal and Othello home after breakfast. Did you want a ride somewhere?"

Katya picked up one of the poppers and looked back at Jackie. "Any major airport would be wonderful."

"Colorado Springs?"

"Perfect," Katya replied and popped the fried treat into her mouth. She savored the flavor and groaned her approval. "Oh, that's amazing." Katya kissed Zack on the cheek and grinned. "You make the best cockroach pepper poppers."

Jackie's expression immediately dropped. Zack cast a look at Jackie and grinned deviously. She looked back at Katya and managed a smile through gritted teeth.

"How about waiting until later this afternoon?" Jackie then asked and raised her brows. "You can have a late lunch with the whole team."

"Even better," Katya replied then caressed Zack's shoulders from behind. "That'll give Zack and me a little more time to reacquaint." She turned toward Jackie and grinned. "I'm going to take in some fresh air before breakfast."

As Katya left the kitchen, Zack turned his head and glared at Jackie.

Jackie sneered back at him. "It is so on," she snarled.

Chapter 72

Friday, July 11th. Night. The abandoned airfield in Virginia was home to a large aircraft boneyard. Considered an eyesore, the boneyard was located in a secluded area of mostly junk land far from anywhere. Barely considered an airfield and its seclusion made it the perfect rendezvous or an excellent place to kill a man and hide his body. A familiar man in his mid to late twenties, Blake Maverick, got out of the security of his car and scanned the dark, creepy boneyard.

"Perfect," the man muttered while frowning. "This isn't at all creepy."

Maverick had been one of the four men Jackie flew to Hooper's ranch almost three weeks earlier. The man was devilishly handsome with flowing dark brown hair in a short, businessman cut. He stood about six-foot and had a solid, athletic build. Maverick walked through the airplane graveyard until he reached an old, wrecked plane. The four-passenger prop plane had the name 'Old Marge' elegantly painted on the side. The wheels and one wing had been torn off possibly when it crashed. The underbelly was severely scraped, and burn marks were visible beyond the seams of the engine compartment. Maverick studied the wrecked plane a moment and squinted at the windshield.

Despite the moon dimly lighting the area, he could make out an old bloodstain resembling a handprint on the windshield on the passenger side of the craft. The open doorway, missing its door, was level with the ground. Maverick entered the dark plane with his baton flashlight brightening the way. The moment he stepped into the plane wreckage, a large light blinded him and prevented him from seeing the man he was supposed to meet.

"You realize we could have met at some nice, cozy coffee shop," Maverick announced while shielding his eyes from the blinding light. "I'm not a fan of all this cloak and dagger business."

"You want Zack Kinsley or not?" the low male voice snarled from the darkness beyond the light.

"Yeah, I want Zack Kinsley," Maverick replied while keeping his hand to his eyes. "Where do I find him?"

"Not so fast, pretty boy," the man in the darkness remarked. "I'd like to know why you want him. You have some sort of grudge against him?"

"Me?" Maverick shook his head and appeared almost disinterested. "Never met the guy. My boss is really interested in meeting him though."

"Who's your boss?"

"Midnight Requisition," Maverick replied.

There was a brief moment of silence.

The man in the darkness suddenly chuckled. "What sort of stupid ass name is that?"

"You ask too many questions," Maverick replied without appearing fazed. He cocked his head slightly while squinting at the light. "Where will I find him?"

"I'll arrange a little introduction," the voice in the darkness announced. "I know exactly how to lure him out of his comfort zone and into whatever kill box you want."

"I never mentioned killing him," Maverick remarked without flinching.

The man in the darkness chuckled in an almost sinister manner. "Yeah, but they all want to--" There was a pause. "Eventually."

"How do you intend to lure him onto our playfield?" Maverick asked.

"Now who's asking too many questions?" the voice in the darkness teased with a sinister chuckle. "I intend to lure him to you with the siren's call."

"Siren's call?"

"Yes," the man in the darkness continued. "See, I know his weakness. Every man's weakness, I suppose. Women. In his case, one woman. A *special* woman."

"You won't hurt this woman," Maverick demanded. "There won't be any innocent blood spilled. No *collateral* damage."

"No, I won't hurt her," the voice in the darkness continued. "But he'll show up if he thinks he's there to rescue her. He always does. She's his Achilles heel."

A booted foot appeared from the darkness and slid an envelope across the plane floor to Maverick.

"There's the time and place," the man announced. "Don't be late. You'll only get one chance at him. If he suspects a setup, you'll never get another shot." There was a brief pause. "And he'll probably kill you."

Maverick picked up the envelope, placed it in his inner jacket pocket, and again shielded his eyes from the bright light. "Why are you handing him over? What's he done to you to warrant such betrayal?"

"Zack Kinsley is a plague upon this earth and needs to be taken out," the voice in the darkness announced with a vengeful hiss in his tone. "He's poisoned the mind of someone I love and turned her against me." The light went out, and the plane was once again dark. "He claims he loves her, but I know he's not capable of loving anyone or anything. He'll eventually take her from me, and she'll wither and die like everything else he's ever touched."

"Hmm, yeah," Maverick announced and fidgeted. "That's not at all dark and sinister." He gave a half-hearted salute. "Thanks for the rendezvous."

Maverick turned and left the plane. A cell phone lit up the hidden man's face. Bogart placed the cell phone to his ear and waited for the call to be answered.

"Is it done?" a male voice from the other end eagerly asked.

"One down; one to go," Bogart replied into the phone with little emotion. "Operation 'Witness Protection: Midnight Requisition' is a go." Bogart disconnected the call, shut his eyes, and rested his head against the interior of the plane. "This is not going to end well."

The End

Coming Soon!
"Witness Protection 8: Midnight Requisition"

A brother and sister duo finds themselves on an explosive collision course with a team of retired Navy SEALS.

Other books by Holly Copella!
Reviews left on Amazon are appreciated!

"The Battle for Andrea Marie"

A cruise ship attack turns six survivors into overnight celebrities after they take credit for the heroic act of a stowaway who died saving them.

The cruise is just what Jess needed--a bit of harmless fun far from her daily grind. But what begins as a relaxing vacation turns into a desperate fight for her life when terrorists take over the ship and start piling up bodies. Teaming up with a mysterious stowaway, Jess attempts to send out a distress call but knows they cannot wait for help to come. If she or the few remaining passengers have any hope for survival, Jess must act now. The papers dub it "The Battle for *Andrea Marie*," but to Jess it is the moment she fought side-by-side with her enigmatic Romeo, saving the ship--and losing him. She thinks the story ends there, but really, the nightmare is just beginning...

"Insanely Deadly"

When the dead return to life, it's up to an admiral's daughter and a mildly insane, former war hero to save their small town.

Jetta Cross, a Navy Admiral's daughter, is tasked with keeping her father's comrade, a former war hero turned town crazy, grounded in the real world. Capt. John Hunter is still fighting the war in his head, where imaginary dead people are part of his world. When a viral outbreak brings about a zombie uprising, Hunter is left to his own devices. He must resume his role as a one-man commando unit in order to destroy the ravenous undead. With Hunter still fighting his own inner demons as well as the undead, the townspeople fear their zombie neighbors may not be the only threat. Stranded at the island's luxurious resort with a handful of workers, Jetta is forced to live up to her father's reputation and take charge of the deteriorating situation at the hotel. She must wage her own war against the infected before the government declares her hometown a total loss.

"Deadly Institution"

A town recluse suspected of killing his wife teams up with a young woman in order to stop a killer.

After being accused of murdering his wife, Konrad Churchill turns his back on the town that once adored him. Ten years later, he still holds his grudge and the title of the most feared man in town. With the reopening of the burned mental institution, where his wife had died, former employees are now murdered one-by-one, throwing suspicion back on Churchill. A young local reporter, Jacey, is forced to reveal her long-time friendship with the infamous recluse in order to clear his name not only in the recent murders but to exonerate him in the death of his wife as well. Will Jacey's relationship with Churchill invite the killer closer to her? Or is the killer already in her life?

"Death Displacement"

A grief-stricken man travels back in time to seek revenge on the woman who murdered his girlfriend but inadvertently falls in love with her.

Kane is about to marry the woman he loves. His life is perfect. A few weeks before the wedding, a vindictive woman from his girlfriend's past mysteriously arrives and kills her. He learns of a traumatic accident that happened five years earlier, which triggers Riley's hatred for his girlfriend. Distraught over his girlfriend's death, Kane uses an antique time machine to travel into the past in order to find and destroy the woman responsible. When he runs into Riley's younger self, he realizes she's not the monster she later becomes, and he can't bring himself to destroy her. With a little help from his oddball friend from the past, they formulate a plan to prevent the accident that sends Riley down her destructive path. Kane's plan backfires when he falls for the younger Riley. His new tortured existence is further complicated when future Riley, his girlfriend's killer, shows up with her own devious agenda that doesn't include him. Will he be able to stop the time ripple, which ultimately ends with his girlfriend's death? Or will future Riley take him out of the timeline forever--

"Dead Village"

After strange happenings isolate a small resort town from the rest of the world, nearly one hundred residents seek refuge at the closed hotel. Only eight survive the night. And that's just the beginning...

One day after the entire population of Fox Ridge Village disappears, a car wreck forces several unsuspecting crash victims to seek help at the closed summer hotel. Within the hotel, they discover the grisly aftermath of a brutal slaughter. Crash victims Vander and Devon, a reluctant clairvoyant, team up to solve the riddle of the "haunted hotel" and the mass hysteria plaguing the remaining survivors. By the time they discover the hotel's secret, they're already drawn into the hysteria. As the body count continues to climb, it's a race to isolate the source and bring everyone back to reality before they kill one another. Will Devon be able to communicate with the traumatized spirits before their fate becomes her own?

"Town Darling"

After surviving a brutal attack that claims the lives of those she loves, a young woman seeks revenge on a corrupt town.

Going back home is never easy, but for Casey, it means returning to her corrupt hometown where she barely survived a brutal attack. Accompanied by two family friends, she seeks justice for the night that destroyed her life. Her physical scars are nothing compared to her emotional ones, forcing the local sheriff to believe that the town darling is back for revenge. As the conspiracy for her revenge appears to be leading up to the coveted town fair, the sheriff is determined to stop her from fulfilling her vengeful scheme...but guilt over his role on that fateful night continues to haunt him. Will his desperate need for Casey's forgiveness be his undoing? Or will Casey's desire for revenge destroy them both?

"Basement Dwellers"

A viral outbreak at a hospital leaves a mortician, sheriff, and coroner fighting for their lives against a horde of undead and the CDC.

After a massive car wreck leaves several survivors in critical condition at the local hospital, a surgeon uses experimental drugs on his critical patients and accidentally causes a zombie outbreak. When local mortician, Lexx, receives an infected corpse as her client, she becomes stranded in the hospital basement during CDC quarantine along with the local sheriff and the coroner. The infamous surgeon struggles to find a cure for his infectious blunder by using the other survivors as test subjects. Meanwhile, Lexx and the sheriff attempt to locate his missing sister, who's stranded somewhere in the battle zone that once was the emergency room. It's a race against time and the ravenous undead. Can they survive the undead before CDC sanitizes the hospital of all infection?

"Misfits, Inc."

A seemingly ordinary, young woman meets four misfits who claim she has given them supernatural powers.

While on a business trip to a remote island paradise, a bored secretary, Hailey, has her world turned upside down when her path collides with a psychic freak, Skyler. He attempts to convince her that they had met in his dreams, and she had chosen him as one of her four mystic warriors. After Skyler foresees a woman's death, they discover an unidentified creature has killed one of the guests. They are joined by a lounge pianist and a rich playboy, who also claim they had met her in their dreams. If Skyler's prophecies are genuine, the evil entity controlling the ravenous creatures needs to destroy Hailey to ensure its survival. Reluctantly accepting her fate, Hailey has to locate the last and most powerful of her chosen warriors, The Guardian. Their fate is in doubt when The Guardian turns out to be a self-absorbed, former cat burglar with a bad attitude. Can Hailey turn her company of misfits into an elite team of mystic warriors? Or will The Guardian's secret agenda destroy them all?

"Deadly Institution 2"

When blackmail turns into murder, a young woman finds herself caught in the killer's crosshairs.

The small town of Stony Ridge is no stranger to scandal and persecution of the innocent. When a brutal killing shakes the town's prestigious country club, Jacey McMurray seeks help from a self-proclaimed vigilante, Konrad Churchill. As her professional and personal worlds collide, Jacey fears the stress of the country club killings have finally taken their toll on Churchill. Can a stressed out vigilante stop the killer before he strikes again?

"Witness Protection"
Also available in audiobook!

After witnessing an execution, a resourceful young woman attempts to disappear while being pursued by a hitman and a handsome federal agent.

A helicopter pilot, Jackie Remus, reluctantly agrees to go on a date with one of her clients, but her date is unexpectedly cut short when she witnesses a man being murdered. After narrowly escaping with her life, she is placed into protective custody. When the safe house is breached, Jackie makes a daring escape from both the hired killers and the handsome FBI agent, who wants to return her to protective custody. With a little help from her sly and crafty friend, Monroe, Jackie is convinced she can disappear until the trial. While on her journey to meet with her friend, she solicits help from a few shady but lovable characters along the way. Although she manages to stay one-step ahead of the hired killers, the federal agent remains in hot pursuit. Will Jackie reach Monroe before she's captured by the FBI and returned to protective custody? Or will the hired killers silence her first?

"Unconditional"

A young woman puts her life on hold to care for an unstable, highly skilled combat soldier, who believes someone is trying to kill him.

A botched military coup leaves a team of elite fighters injured with one clinging to life in a coma. When Harlan wakes from his coma, he's left with no memory of his past life. His commander's daughter, Indy, takes it upon herself to care for the fallen war hero. She's challenged with more than just his physical care as she combats with not only his memory loss but also his newly found desire for her. His infatuation with her becomes the least of her worries when he sinks back into his role of a combat soldier. Believing his life is in danger, his fighting skills surface, turning him into an unpredictable and dangerous man. Will his memory return to him before Indy is forced to commit him? Or will he finally find his nemesis, "the coyote", and possibly claim the life of an innocent person?

"The Pen Pal"

In order to save her friend, she must enter the mind of a serial killer.

When her best friend is abducted, no one believes Jolynn saw it in a psychic vision. With nowhere to turn, Jolynn reluctantly joins Agent Harris Slade and his team on their hunt for a sadistic serial killer known only as "The Pen Pal". Finally confronted with the killer, Jolynn realizes she must enter the mind of the psychopath in order to stop the brutal killings. But when her vision reveals a particularly disturbing death, can Jolynn sacrifice her lover for her friend?

"Witness Protection 2"
The Return of Whiskey Tango Foxtrot

Believing she holds the clue to millions in missing laundered money, a young woman is placed into the protective care of a former Navy SEAL team.

Feeling sorry for her recently separated co-worker, Leeann invites Wiley to join her and her friends on their night out. Little does she know that finding her co-worker murdered is just the beginning of her nightmare. Leeann unknowingly holds the key to fifty million dollars in potentially laundered mob money. With hired killers pursuing her, the FBI places her into a different kind of protective custody. Former Navy SEAL team Whiskey Tango Foxtrot reunites to keep Leeann alive at their secret hideaway. What should be an easy assignment takes an unscheduled turn when secrets, lies, and betrayal threaten to derail their mission. Is the team prepared for a war on their own doorstep? Will Leeann's misguided trust endanger the lives of those sent to protect her?

"Witness Protection 3"
Alpha Mike Foxtrot

A helicopter pilot risks her life to help a team of retired Navy SEALs rescue two girls from a killer.

When former Navy SEAL team Whiskey Tango Foxtrot asks for a simple favor, Jackie reluctantly offers her air taxi services. What could go wrong? What begins as a search and rescue for two girls turns into a fight for survival against a heavily armed drug cartel. Wanted by the law with the cartel in hot pursuit and their home base breached, the team is forced to call in a favor from a questionable ally. Unfortunately, their new safe house isn't what it seems. Without knowing who the real enemy is, can Jackie and the team save their young witnesses from the hands of a killer?

"Already Dead"
Supernatural Collection

From the already dead to the undead. Three supernatural tales of "things that go bump in the night".

"Bloodletting" - A vampire themed resort allows guests to *participate* in their Bloodletting Ritual to celebrate the island's legendary vampires.

"Reaper of Souls" - A young woman must outwit an evil sorcerer in order to save her brother or become one of his minions forever.

"Already Dead" - When Flight 220 crashes, ten passengers make it to an isolated island, but only one man lives to tell the lie.

"Witness Protection 4"
O-Dark-Hundred

A simple assignment turns deadly when a retired Navy SEAL team uncovers a plot to kill a notorious mob boss.

When Whiskey Tango Foxtrot embarks on a simple stalking case, they're not prepared for a trip to a private island paradise owned by an infamous mobster. With one of their own suffering from traumatic head injuries, the team is left scrambling to decide what is real or imagined. The situation escalates even further when they uncover an assassination plot where everyone is a suspect. Now targets themselves, can the team survive their trip to paradise?

"Witness Protection 5"
Outside the Wire

After suffering several casualties on their last assignment, a retired Navy SEAL team discovers their misery is just beginning.

When Whiskey Tango Foxtrot returns home after suffering a devastating loss, they're hit with even more bad news regarding the rest of their team. Their grief is cut short when they discover their names are all on the same hit list. Hunted by relentless assassins, the scattered team must decide whether to remain safely hidden or find the man who put the price on their heads. Against the wishes of her teammates, Jackie strikes out on her own in order to save a friend who wants her dead. In a kill or be killed situation, will Jackie's emotions finally betray her?

"The Murder of Emily Fisher"

After finding their favorite teacher murdered, the lives of two teenage girls are forever changed.

Everyone loved Emily Fisher. While walking home one afternoon, two teenage girls, Sidney and Trisha, stumble upon a gruesome murder scene. The brutal murder of Emily Fisher, a young, attractive schoolteacher, shocks the small town of **Marilina**. After graduation, Sidney moves far away from the memories of the small town while Trisha retreats deeper into denial. Eight years after the murder, Sidney receives a desperate call from her childhood friend, forcing her to return home. Trisha believes Emily's killer was falsely accused and she manages to turn the entire town against her while attempting to prove it. When Trisha receives a death threat, Sidney realizes there may be some credibility to her friend's wild accusations. Is Trisha's mental breakdown a result of childhood trauma? Or is the real killer actually attempting to silence her? In order to save her friend, Sidney must answer the eight-year-old question. Who murdered Emily Fisher?

"Once Upon a Disaster"

A young homicide detective finds herself at the mercy of a hitman in the aftermath of an earthquake

While investigating the murder of a hitman, Detective Jade Wesson pursues a lead connecting the dead man to a break-in at a computer programming company. She's drawn into the world of nightclub owner and front man for the mob, Cody Riley. Her investigation keeps pointing to Cody's right-hand man and possible hitman, Vahn Lott. Despite her efforts to keep her investigation on track, Vahn has plans of his own for the attractive detective. When an unprecedented earthquake rocks their east coast town, Jade must put her life in Vahn's hands if she wants to survive. Can she trust a man who might be the killer she's hunting?

"Awaken the Dead"

A grieving innkeeper struggles to keep her haunted hotel out of foreclosure.

After losing her parents in a suspicious boating accident, Harley Brandon is determined to keep the family hotel out of foreclosure. Unfortunately, the hotel ghosts have other plans. Built with tainted money, the century old Horizon Hotel thrives on a tradition of murder, scandal, and suicide. As the paranormal activity increases to alarming levels, Harley discovers the truth about the hotel and its residents. Can Harley save her friends from the hotel's frightening hidden secrets?

"Castle Bloodshed"
Murder Collection

From a deadly island paradise to haunted castles. Three novella length tales of murder, mystery, and malicious intent.

"Castle Bloodshed" – A tour of Wesley Castle turns into a fight for survival as six stranded tourists discover the haunting secrets within the castle walls. A mystery writer teams up with an uptight butler in order stop a killer who may already be dead. Novella length paranormal murder mystery.

"Fleshies" – Is Uncle Rutger crazy? Five years ago, four business partners died within their newly purchased, fixer-upper castle. Their bodies were never found. The surviving partner, Rutger, claims a demon keeps him as its slave. Rutger's nephew schemes to save his uncle by sacrificing the lives of a group of stranded motorists and a high-profile novelist. Novella length supernatural murder mystery.

"Demon Island" – A group of strangers are invited to a remote island for the reading of a will. The guests soon discover they were brought to the island to be executed one-by-one. It's up to a private detective and a tenacious young woman to solve the murders and find a way to escape paradise. Novella length murder mystery.

"Brighton Island"

When a psychic visits a haunted island mansion, he inadvertently awakens the ghosts' tortured souls.

Something's not right with Simon. When Jacklyn brings her eccentric friend to her uncle's island mansion, she didn't expect him to slip into psychic overload. As Simon attempts to solve a decade-old, double homicide, Jacklyn is confronted with the possibility that she could be next to join the mansion ghosts. When they find themselves stranded on the secluded island, her Uncle Hyland wages his own war to save them from a flesh and blood killer. Will her uncle's "shock and awe" military tactics save them or get them killed? Can Simon bring peace to the tortured souls or unexpectedly join them?

"A.L.F. Resort"

A fantasy vacation turns into a nightmare when the resort's artificial life forms are compromised.

Welcome to A.L.F. Resort where you can live out your fantasies with safe, state-of-the-art artificial life form robots! When a young journalist and a photographer are sent to A.L.F. Resort to do a story for their magazine, Shay and Becka believe they've hit the jackpot of all work-cations. The engineers pull out all the stops to make their fantasies memorable. Unfortunately, the newly designed A.L.F., the Gen X, is smarter than his programming and creates havoc within Shay's fantasy. A computer malfunction removes their safety inhibitors and the A.L.F.s play out their own hostile fantasies. Zombies, bikers, and mobsters run amuck, turning fantasies into nightmares. Shay gets more of a story than she anticipates, but will she survive long enough to write it?

"Jungle Princess"

While stranded on a prison island, a young woman discovers a creature of "unknown" origin.

After their cruise ship sinks, Alex and two of her shipmates are stranded on a deserted, tropical island. Unfortunately, the castaways soon realize they're not alone. They discover an abandoned prison with over two dozen inmates living on the island's south side. While avoiding the prison on the far side of the island, Alex discovers a strange but loveable creature of unknown origin. When one of her fellow castaways is in trouble, Alex reluctantly seeks help from the prisoners. After the brutal murder of several inmates, their questions surrounding the abandoned prison are about to be answered. What really killed over one hundred prisoners? And is it still out there?

"Murder in Wax"

A series of brutal murders plague a quiet farming community when beautiful women audition for the same acting job.

While all the young women in town are fighting over a once-in-a-lifetime acting opportunity, Devon Vincent is excited about her new job at the local wax museum. Although supportive of her friend's acting aspirations, Devon has a hard time understanding the rivalry among the women in town. When the aspiring actresses are brutally murdered one-by-one, Devon fears her friend may be the next victim. Devon finds herself in the middle of a murderous revenge plot that leads back to the wax museum's doorstep and possibly implicates her boss as the killer. Will Devon's newly found feelings for her boss bring a killer closer to her? Or is the killer already in her circle?

"Witness Protection 6"
Alpha Dogs

An easy rescue turns into a wild ride for retired Navy SEAL team Whiskey Tango Foxtrot when everyone wants to kill their client.

It was a simple task. Rescue a young woman from her mob boss father-in-law. Little did Jackie and company realize that rescuing the young woman was the easy part. Keeping her alive would be a massive undertaking, especially when everyone wants a piece of the mafia heiress. The team fights for survival against their toughest adversaries yet. How many innocent people must die in order to save one woman? Can the team survive the ultimate battle between mercenaries and assassins?

"Midnight Requisition"

A series of brutal murders leaves a traumatized young woman on a hunt to find a killer.

When they were just babies, Scorpio and her twin brother, Kane, tragically lost their parents under mysterious circumstances. Refusing to accept his father was dead, Kane set off on a mission to find a man he'd never met. A home invasion gone wrong leaves Scorpio grieving the loss of those she loves. Out of the tragedy of her loss, two fallen heroes are thrust upon her. Scorpio soon realizes someone wants her dead and the killer may already be in her circle. As her entire life unravels in a web of betrayal and lies, can Scorpio trust her new, slightly questionable friends?

"Until Death"

Liars, cheaters, blackmail and murder. It would be a wedding no one would forget.

Despite knowing he's making the biggest mistake of his life, Raina Steele reluctantly attends her father's third wedding. What should have been a boring reception turns into a web of lies, betrayal, and murder. With no one above suspicion, Raina must put aside her feud with the arrogant yet insanely handsome butler in order to catch the killer before he finds his next victim. With a murderer waiting to strike and lives hanging in the balance, the real question remains...the bride is wearing white? Seriously?

"Tainted"

What happens at the Dark Forest Hotel, stays at the Dark Forest Hotel...for all eternity.

What secrets surround Dark Forest Hotel? After her parents die under mysterious circumstances, sixteen-year-old Jeri escapes foster care and seeks refuge at a "closed for the season" hotel. Over the next six years, Jeri graduates from teenage runaway to the hotel's assistant general manager. When she learns a convention is secretly held every year in her absence, she demands answers from her boss, friends, and co-workers. After getting conflicting stories, Jeri sets out to discover the truth. She's suddenly thrown into a horrifying new world where vampires and vicious creatures are craving her virgin blood. After six years of everyone lying to her, is there anyone she can trust?

"Midnight Requisition 2"
Amateur Night

A brother and sister duo team up to catch a potential kidnapper.

After finally reuniting with her not-so-dead brother, Scorpio and her friends are taunted into helping him with his new case. A wealthy cattle rancher believes someone wants to abduct his daughter, but the team suspects her ex-boyfriend is pulling off an elaborate scheme to win her back. What appears to be a slice of paradise in the Colorado Mountains turns out to be a venomous snake pit filled with lies, lust, betrayal, and murder. Surviving the depraved family becomes the least of the team's worries when a botched kidnapping turns into murder.

Coming Soon!
"Witness Protection 8"
Midnight Requisition

ABOUT THE AUTHOR

Holly Copella has been writing since the age of twelve when her frustration at a book's poor plot drove her to author her own story. Over the last decade, she's written a number of screenplays, some of which she's now adapting into novels. Her fascination with zombies and other darker material lends an edge to her writing, which tends to lean toward horror. As a fan of Agatha Christie, she appreciates the craft of a good plot and the importance of creating significant characters.

Hailing from Pennsylvania, Copella lives in the Endless Mountains on a farm with her rescue horses and other animals. In addition to writing and reading fiction, she enjoys riding horses and traveling to Las Vegas and Disney World.

www.ingramcontent.com/pod-product-compliance
Lightning Source LLC
Chambersburg PA
CBHW070358260626
47161CB00001B/182